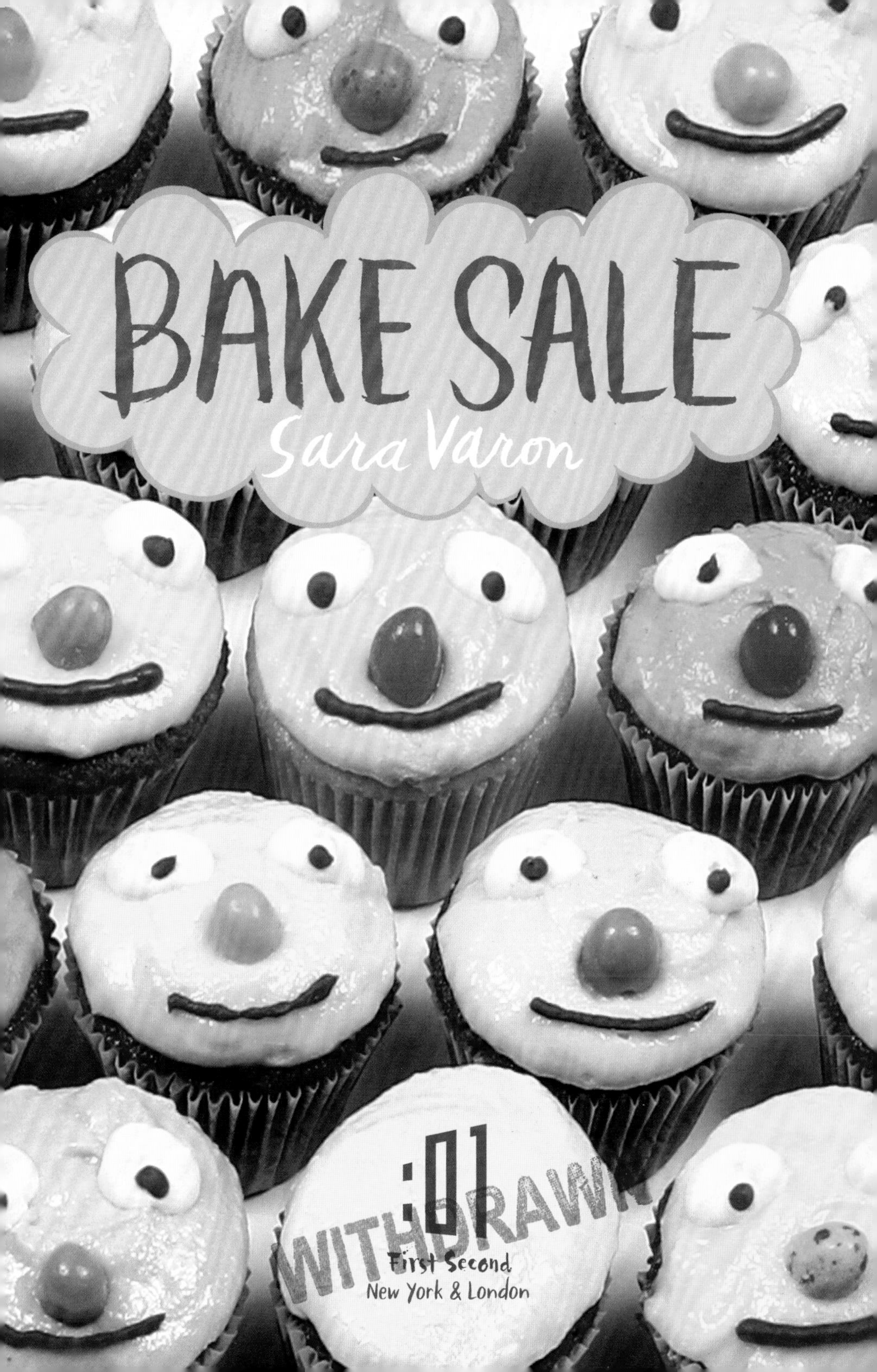

BAKE SALE

Sara Varon

:01
First Second
New York & London

:01

First Second
New York & London

Copyright © 2011 by Sara Varon

Published by First Second
First Second is an imprint of Roaring Brook Press,
a division of Holtzbrinck Publishing Holdings Limited Partnership
175 Fifth Avenue, New York, New York 10010

Distributed in the United Kingdom by Macmillan Children's Books,
a division of Pan Macmillan.

Book design by Sara Varon & Colleen AF Venable
Cupcake photo by Ken Goldfield/Cupcakes by Sara Varon

Cataloging-in-Publication Data is on file with the Library of Congress

Paperback ISBN 978-1-59643-419-6
Hardcover ISBN 978-1-59643-740-1

First Second books are available for special promotions and premiums.
For details, contact: Director of Special Markets, Holtzbrinck Publishers.

First edition 2011
Printed in China
by South China Printing Co. Ltd., Dongguan City, Guangdong Province

Paperback: 10 9 8 7 6 5
Hardcover: 10 9 8 7 6

chapter

one

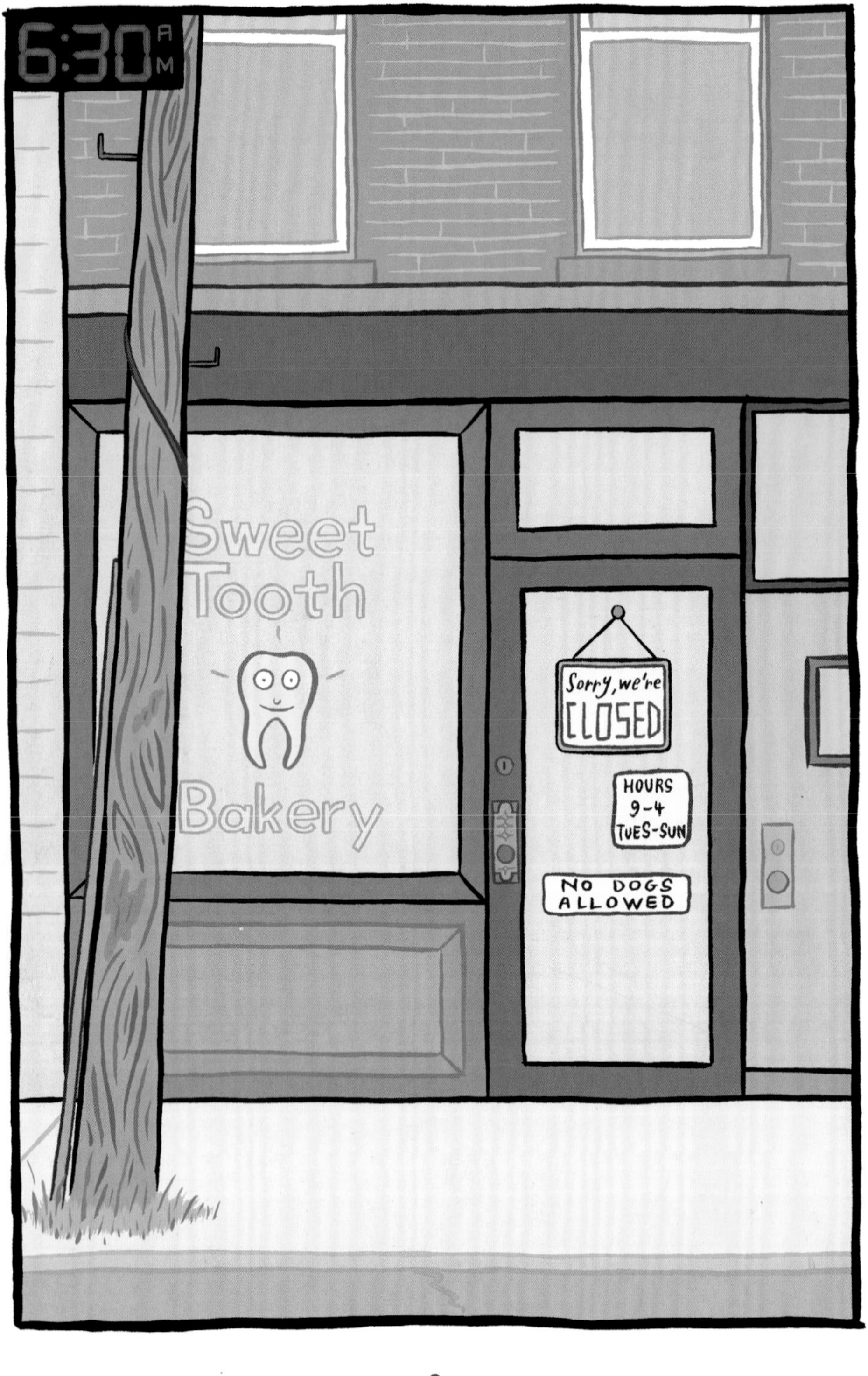
6:30 AM
Sweet Tooth Bakery
Sorry, we're CLOSED
HOURS 9-4 TUES-SUN
NO DOGS ALLOWED

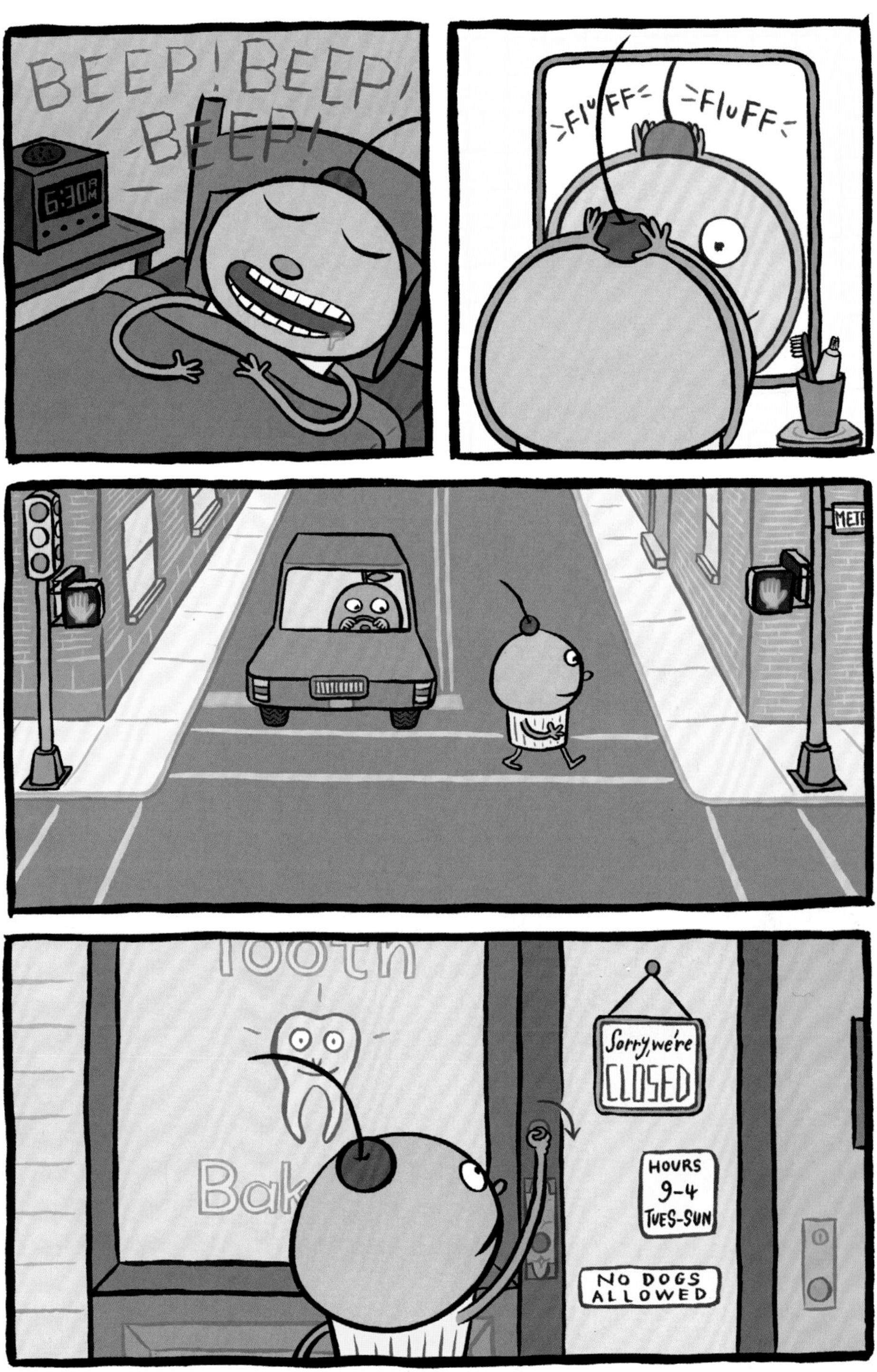
BEEP! BEEP! BEEP!
6:30 AM
FLUFF FLUFF
METR
Tooth
Bak
Sorry, we're CLOSED
HOURS 9-4 TUES-SUN
NO DOGS ALLOWED

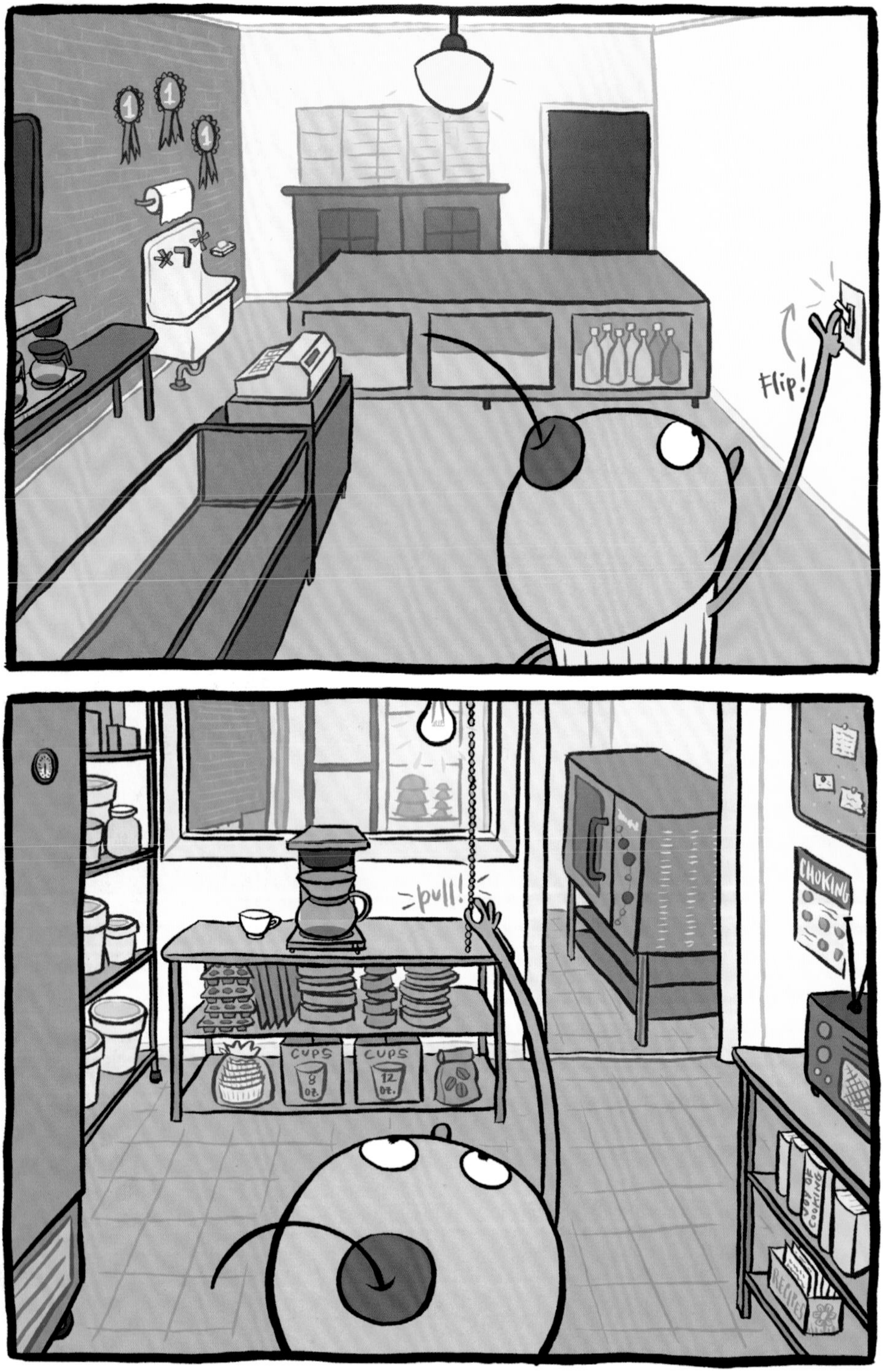
Flip!
pull!
CUPS 8 OZ.
CUPS 12 OZ.
CHOKING
JOY OF COOKING
RECIPES

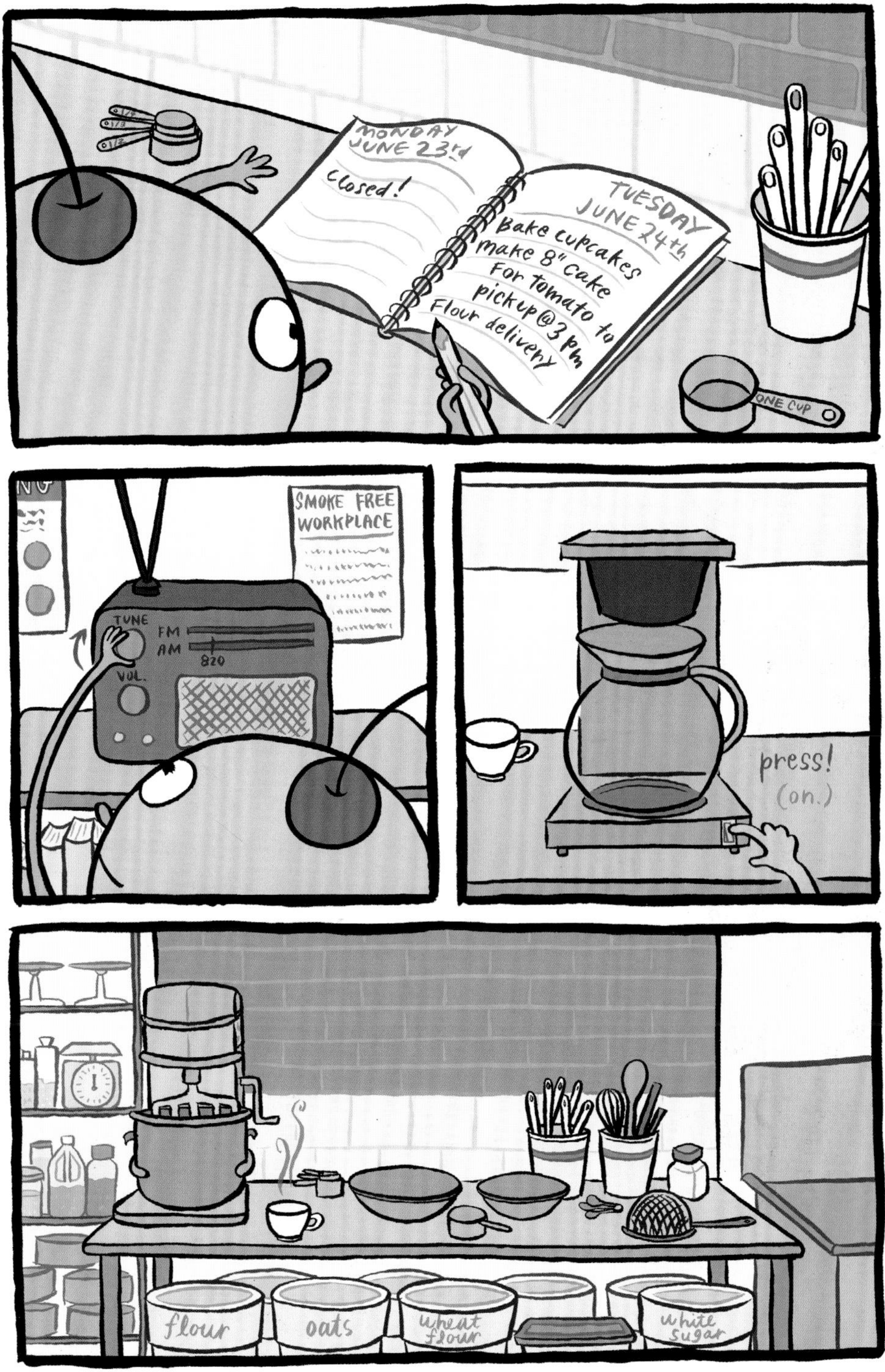
MONDAY
JUNE 23rd
closed!
TUESDAY
JUNE 24th
Bake cupcakes
make 8" cake
for tomato to
pickup @ 3 pm
Flour delivery
ONE CUP
SMOKE FREE
WORKPLACE
TUNE
FM
AM
820
VOL.
press!
(on.)
flour
oats
wheat
flour
white
sugar

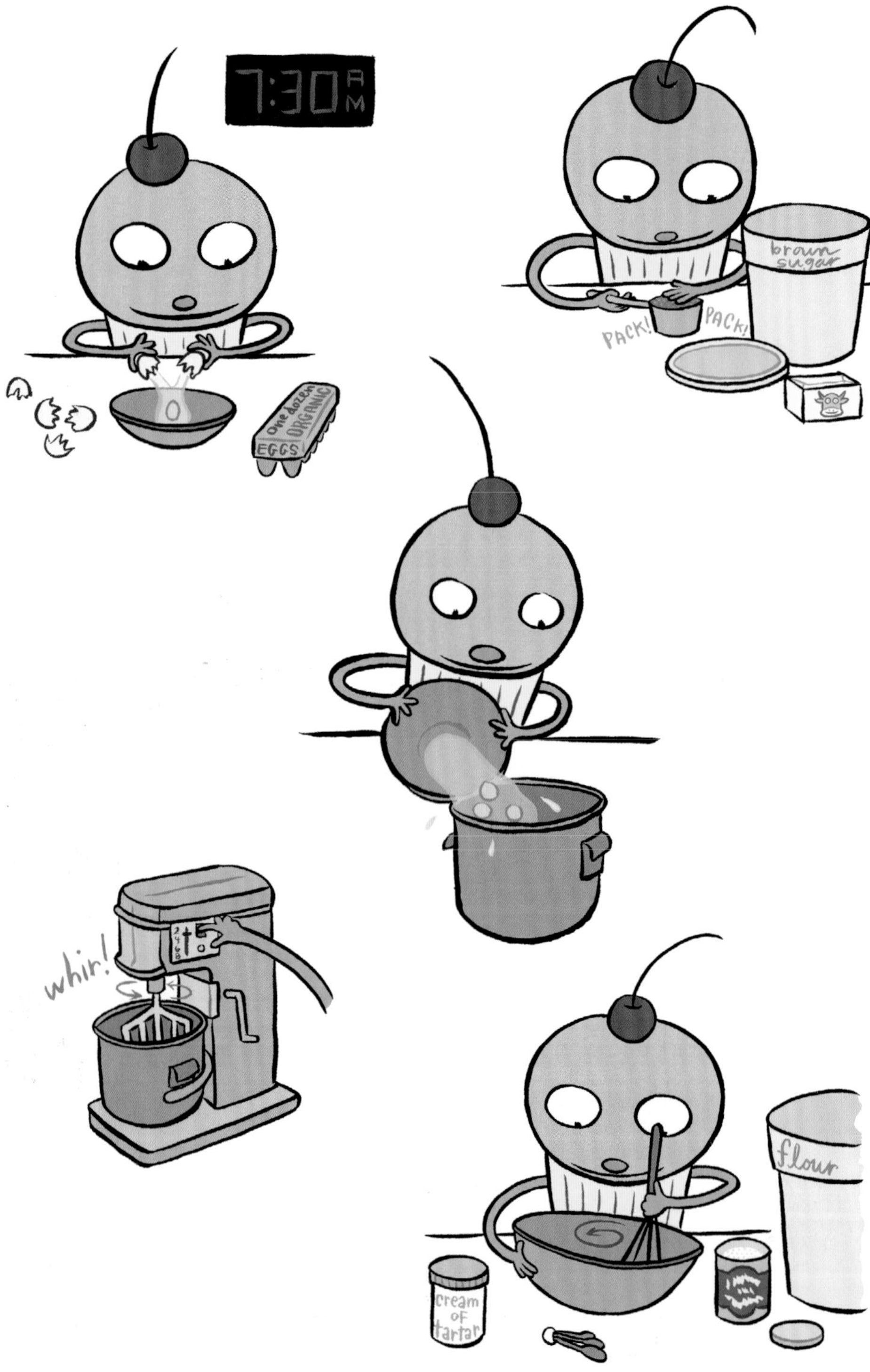
7:30 AM
One dozen ORGANIC EGGS
brown sugar
PACK! PACK!
whir!
flour
cream of tartar

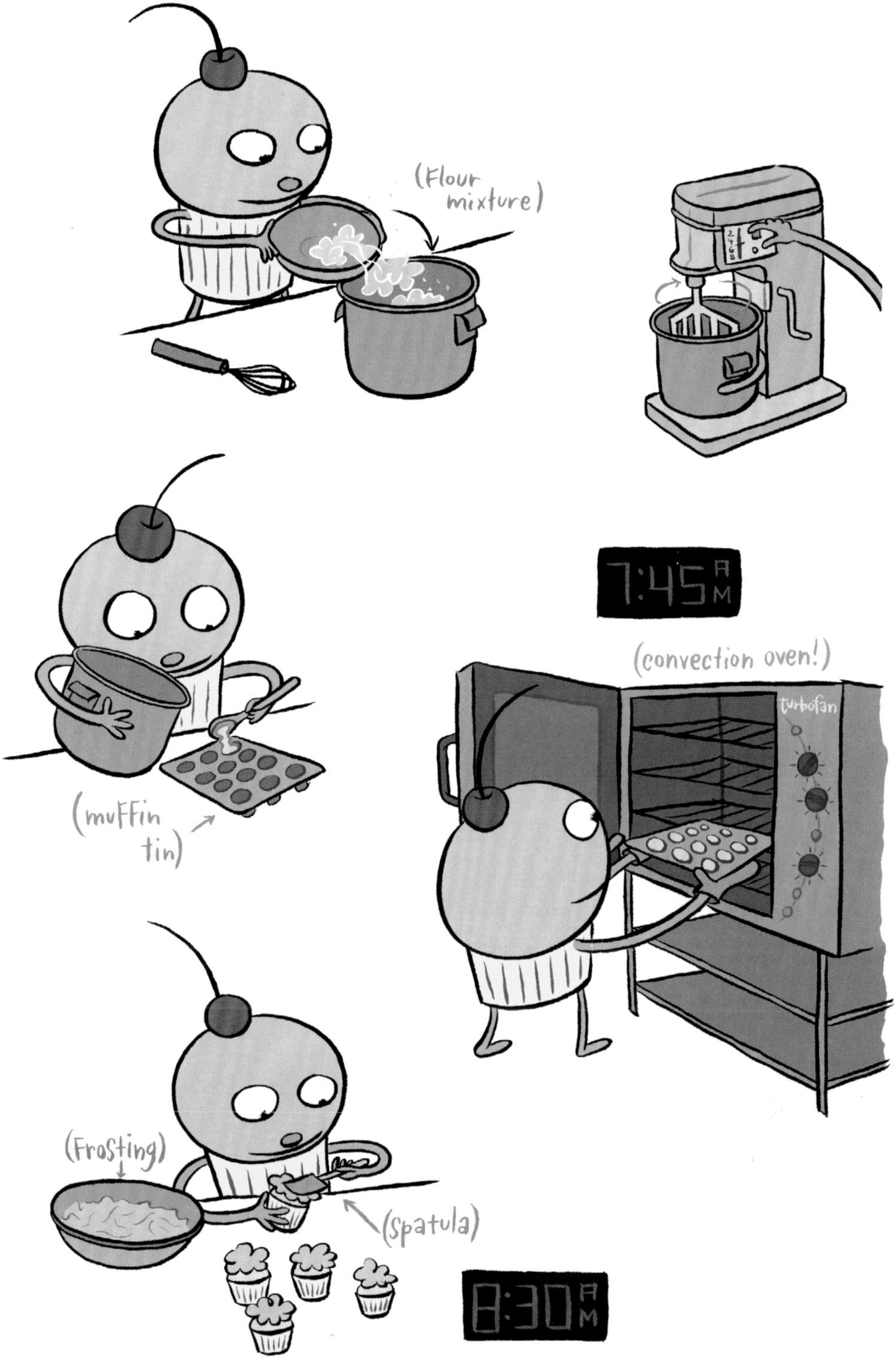
(Flour mixture)
2
4
6
8
7:45 AM
(convection oven!)
turbofan
(muffin tin)
(Frosting)
(spatula)
8:30 AM

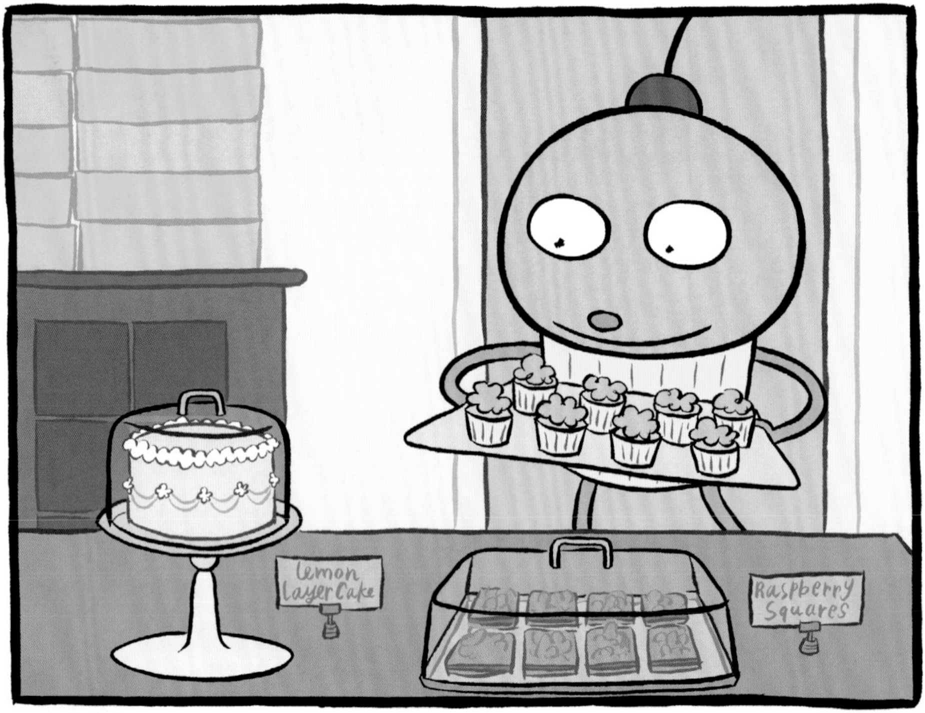
Lemon Layer Cake
Raspberry Squares

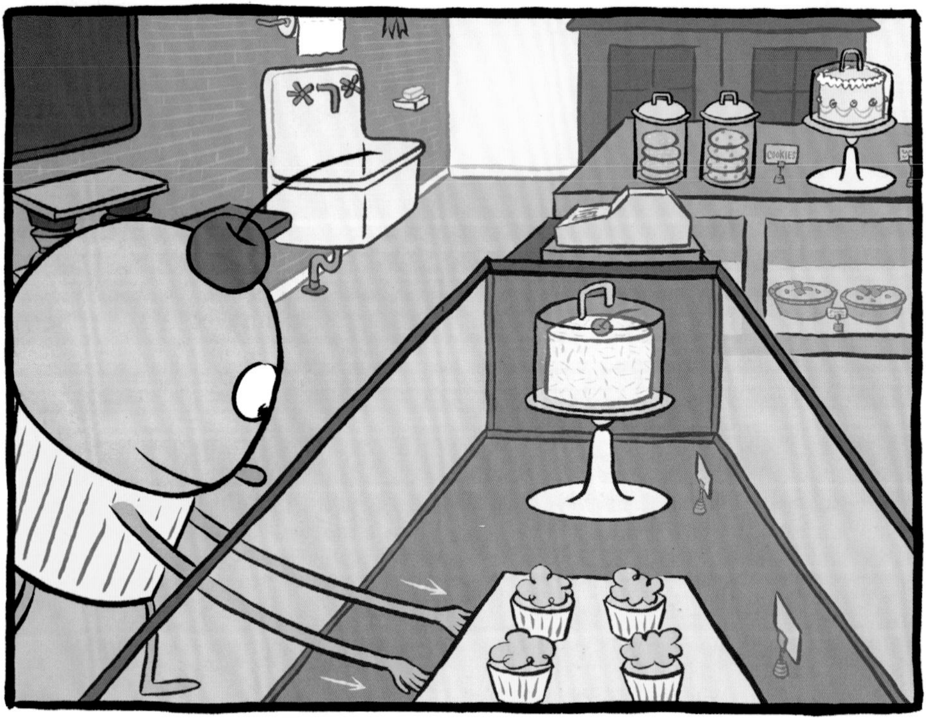
COOKIES

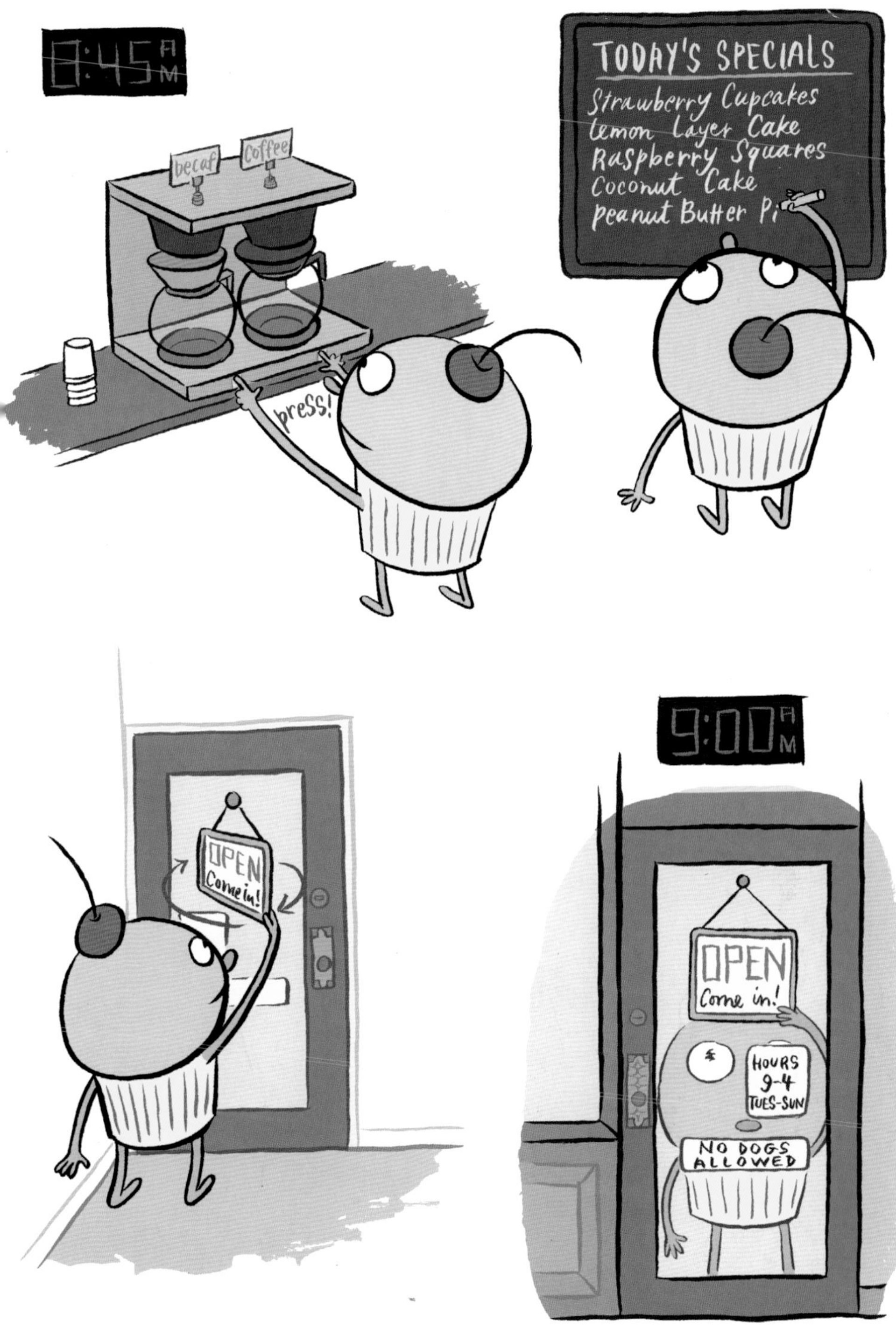
8:45 AM
becaf
Coffee
press!
TODAY'S SPECIALS
Strawberry Cupcakes
Lemon Layer Cake
Raspberry Squares
Coconut Cake
peanut Butter Pi
OPEN
Come in!
9:00 AM
OPEN
Come in!
HOURS
9-4
TUES-SUN
NO DOGS ALLOWED

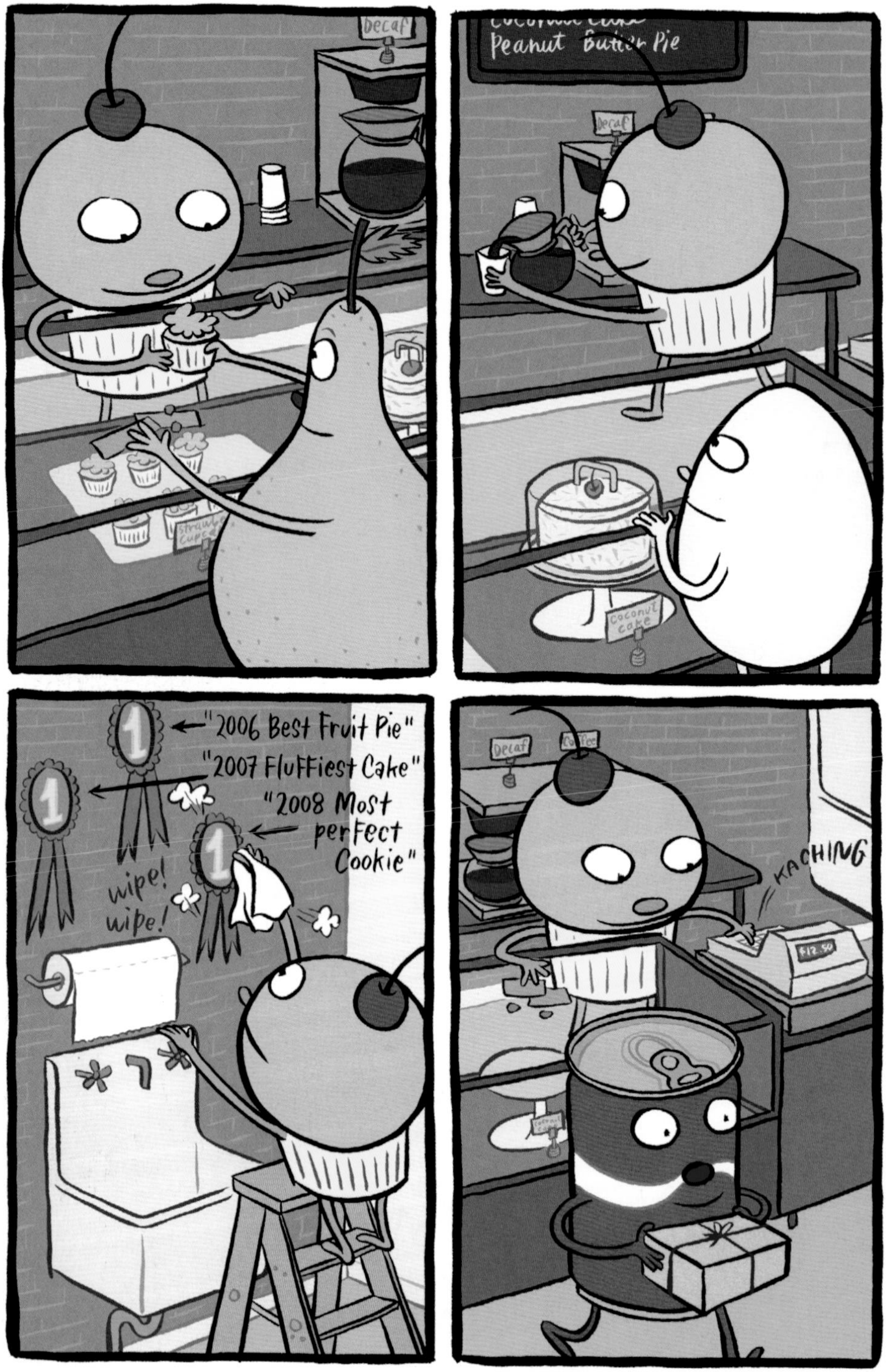
Decaf
Peanut Butter Pie
Decaf
Coconut cake
"2006 Best Fruit Pie"
"2007 Fluffiest Cake"
"2008 Most perfect Cookie"
wipe! wipe!
Decaf
Coffee
KACHING
$12.50

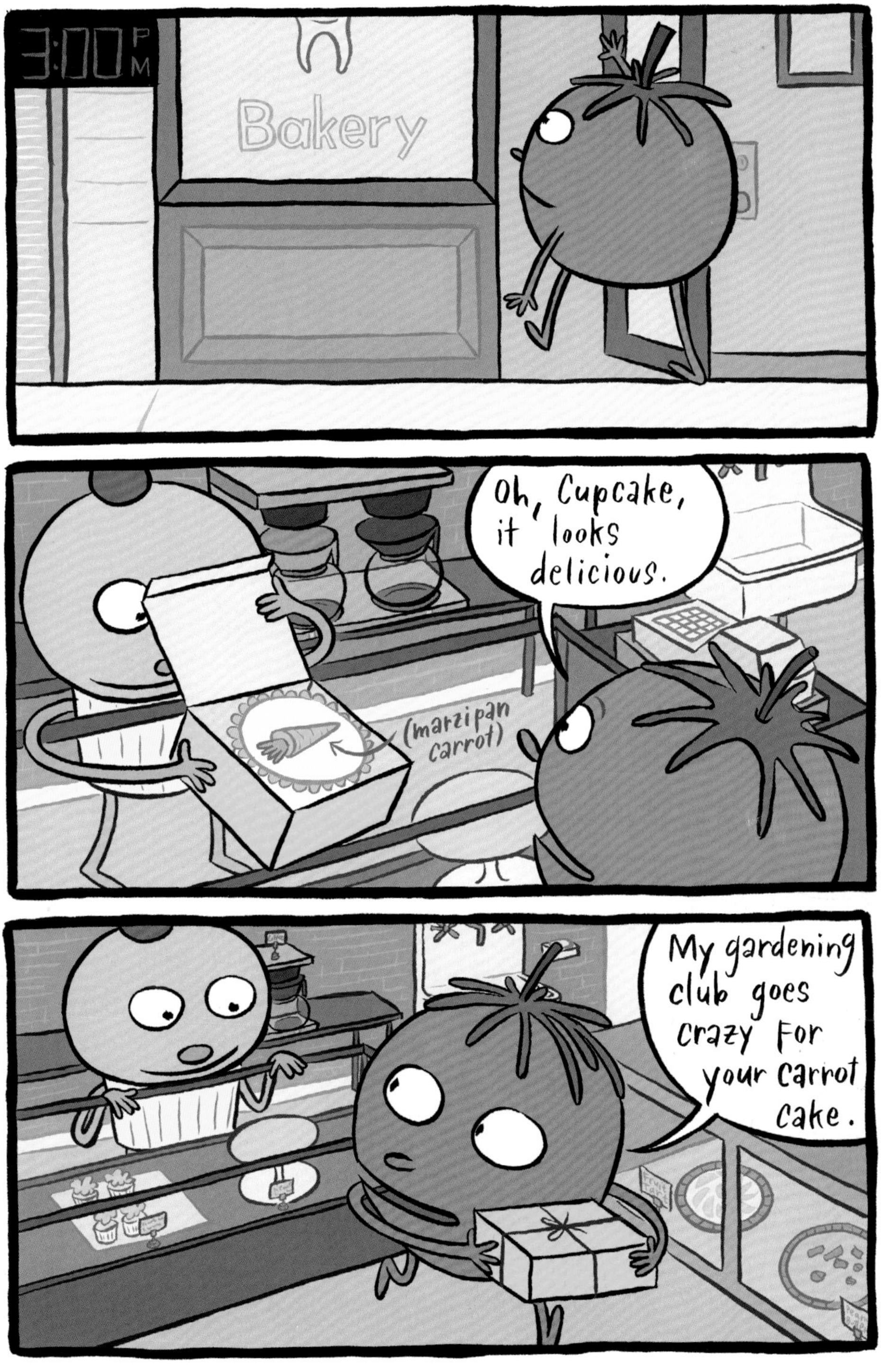
3:00 PM
Bakery
Oh, Cupcake, it looks delicious.
(marzipan carrot)
My gardening club goes crazy for your carrot cake.

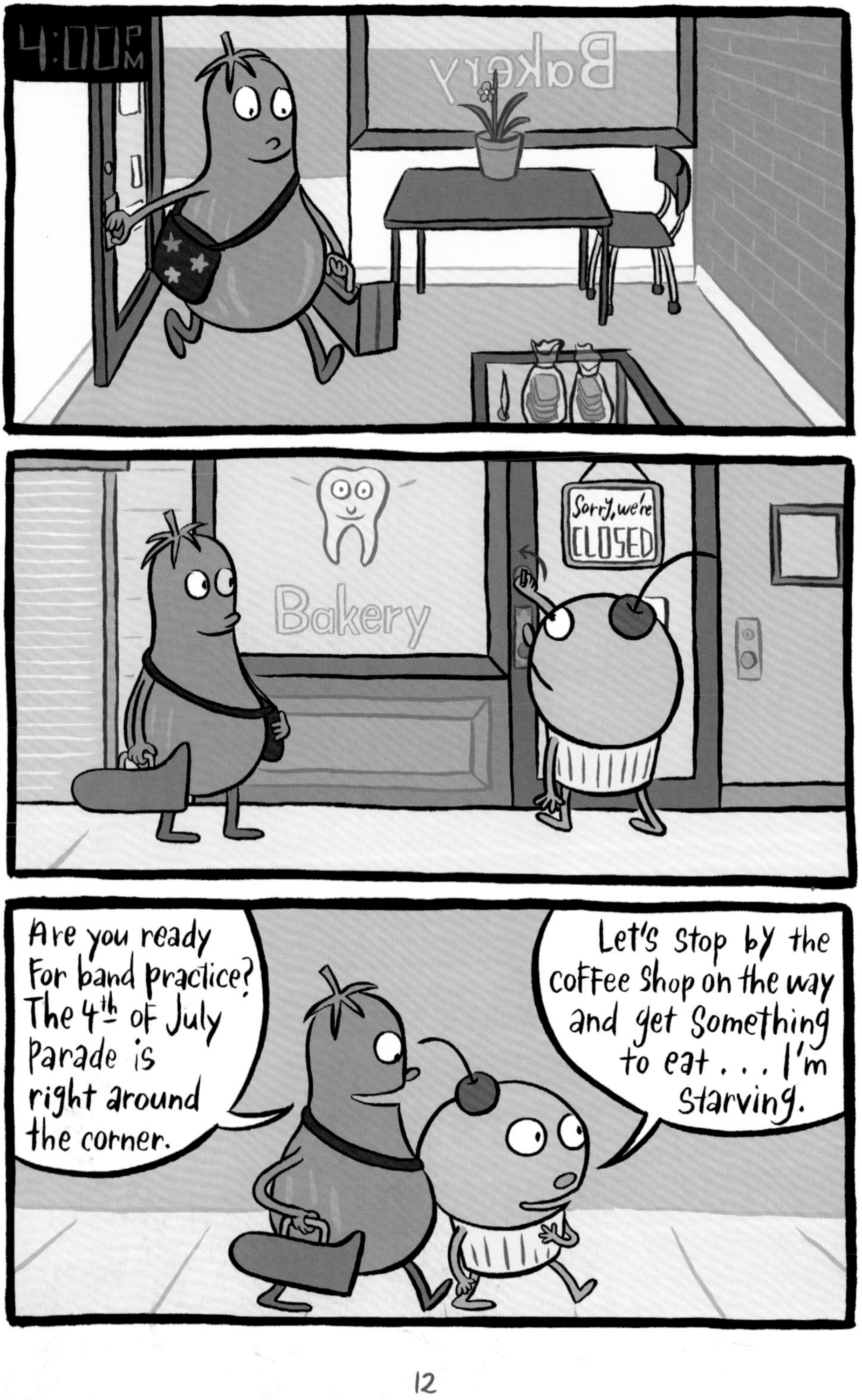
4:00 PM
Bakery
Bakery
Sorry, we're CLOSED
Are you ready for band practice? The 4th of July parade is right around the corner.
Let's stop by the coffee shop on the way and get something to eat . . . I'm starving.

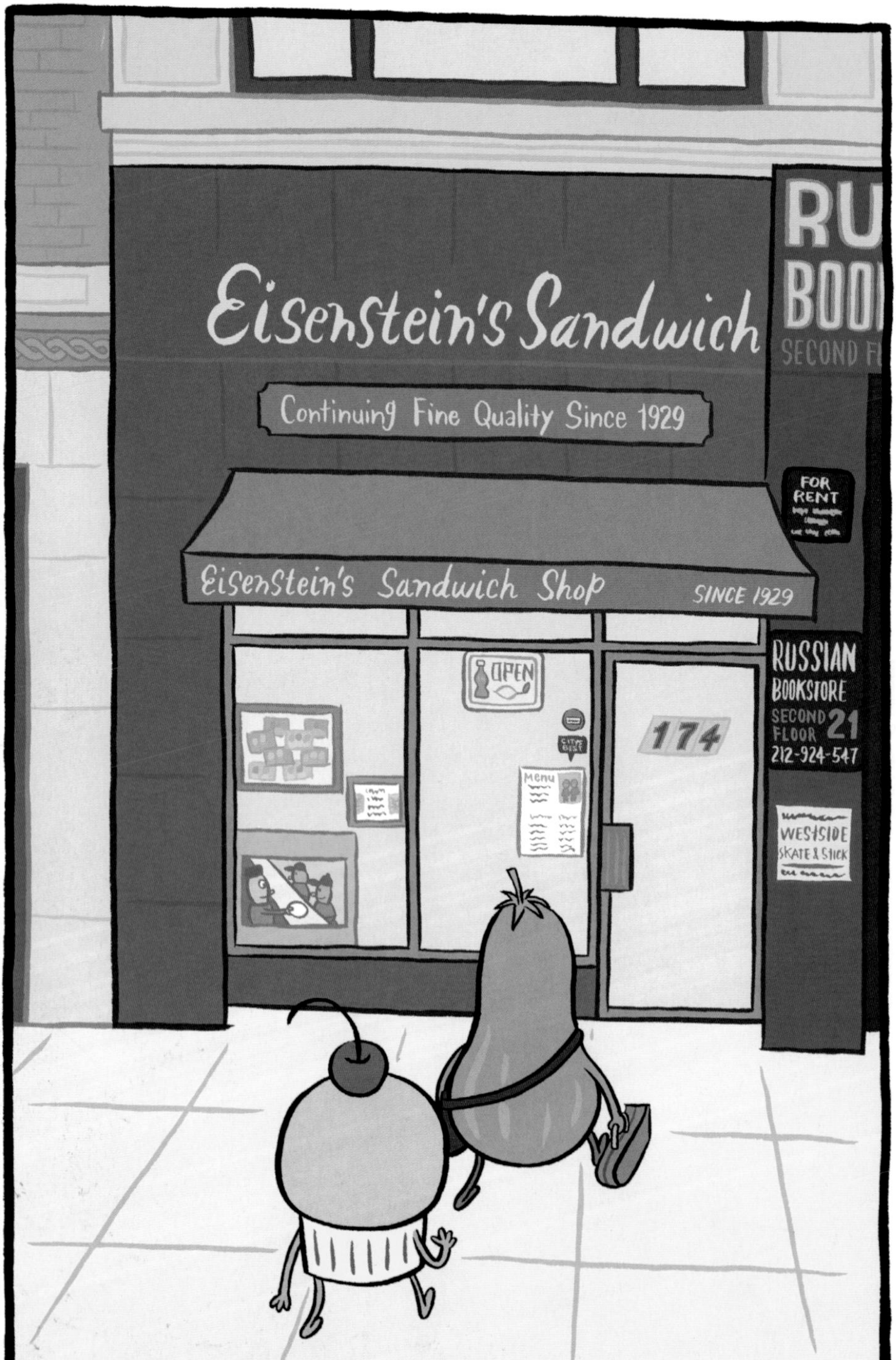

Eisenstein's Sandwich
Continuing Fine Quality Since 1929
Eisenstein's Sandwich Shop
SINCE 1929
OPEN
174
Menu
FOR RENT
RUSSIAN BOOKSTORE SECOND FLOOR 21
212-924-547
WESTSIDE SKATE & STICK
RU
BOO
SECOND F

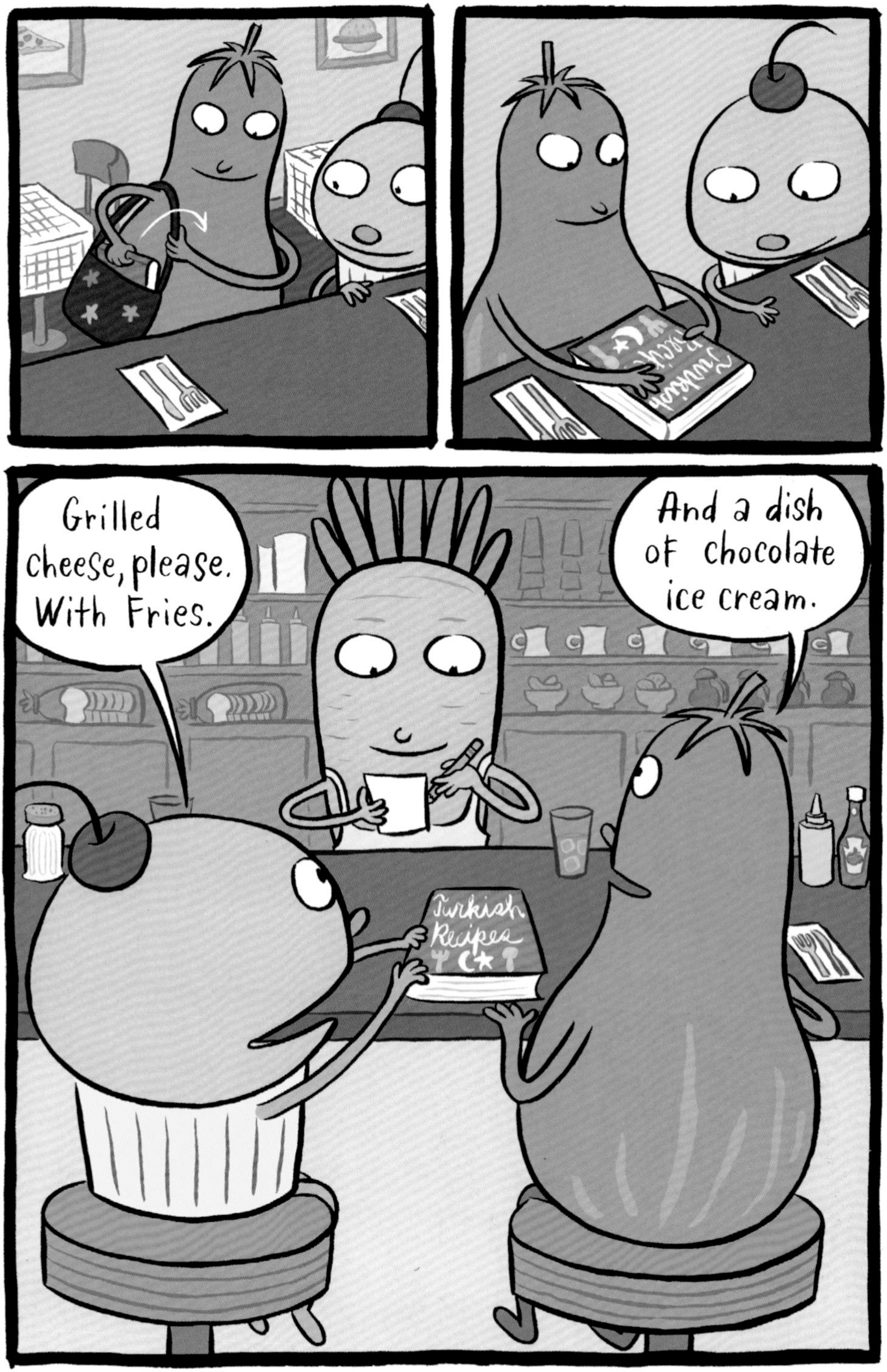
Turkish Recipes
Grilled cheese, please. With Fries.
And a dish of chocolate ice cream.
Turkish Recipes

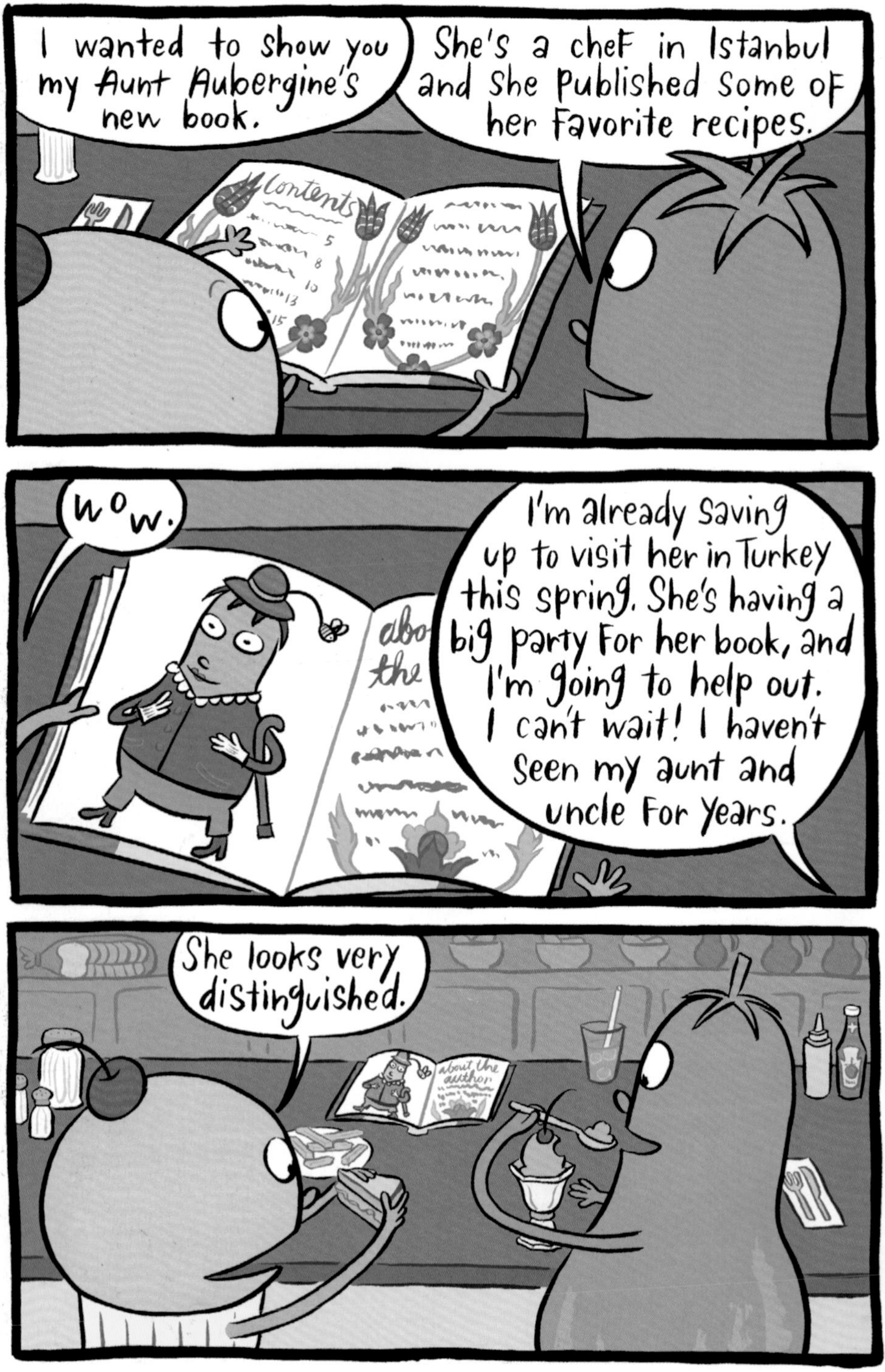
I wanted to show you my Aunt Aubergine's new book.
She's a chef in Istanbul and she published some of her favorite recipes.
Contents
wow.
I'm already saving up to visit her in Turkey this spring. She's having a big party for her book, and I'm going to help out. I can't wait! I haven't seen my aunt and uncle for years.
She looks very distinguished.
about the author

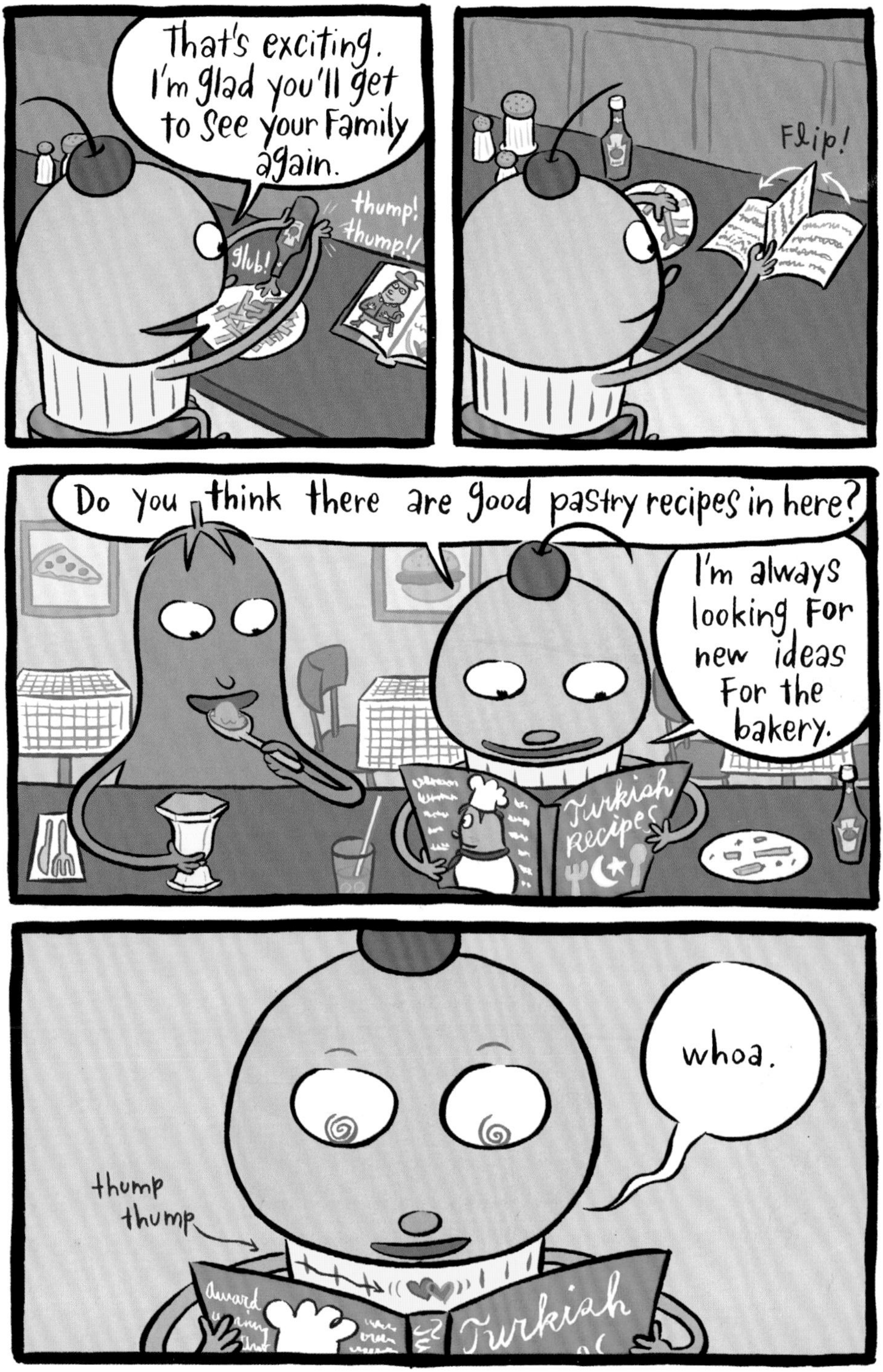
That's exciting. I'm glad you'll get to see your family again.
glub!
thump! thump!!
Flip!
Do you think there are good pastry recipes in here?
I'm always looking for new ideas for the bakery.
Turkish Recipes
whoa.
thump thump
Turkish

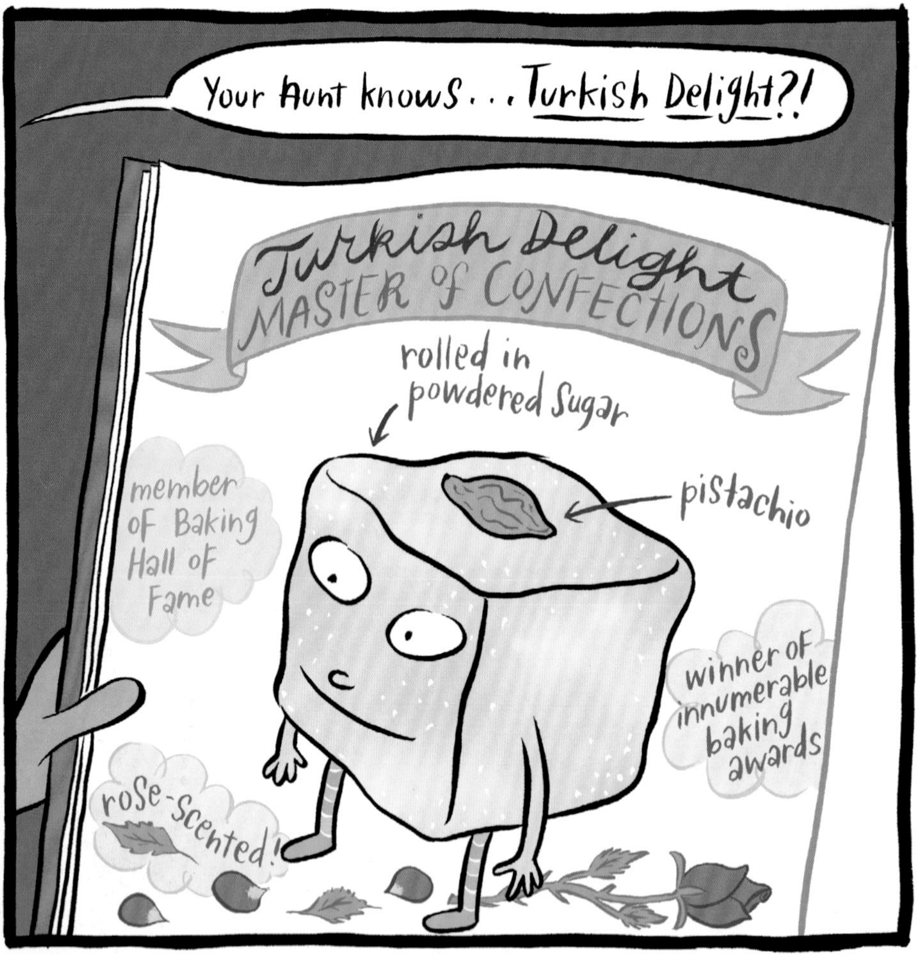
Your Aunt knows . . . Turkish Delight?!
Turkish Delight
MASTER of CONFECTIONS
rolled in powdered sugar
pistachio
member of Baking Hall of Fame
winner of innumerable baking awards
rose-scented!

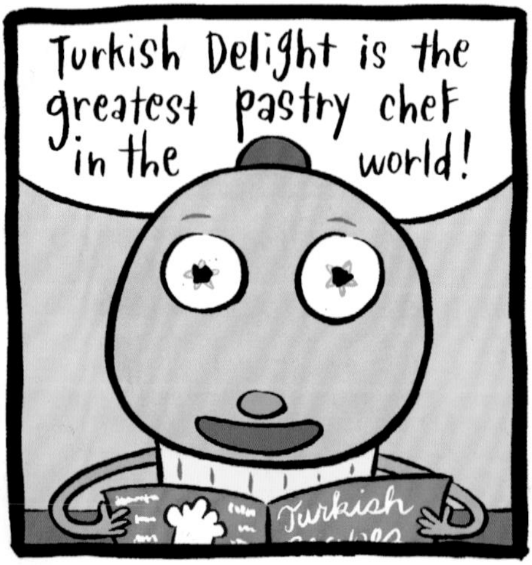
Turkish Delight is the greatest pastry chef in the world!
Turkish

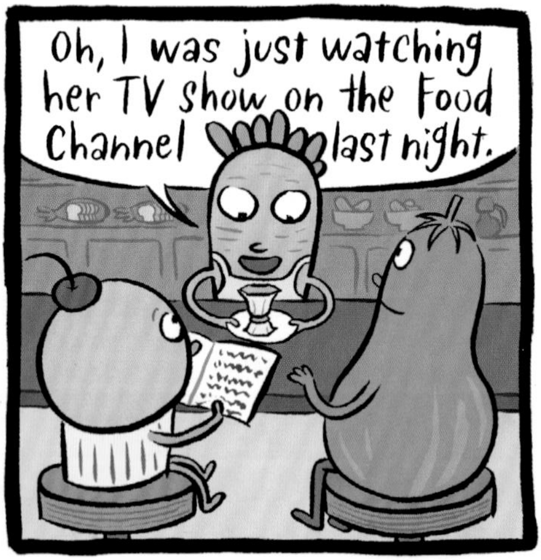
Oh, I was just watching her TV show on the Food Channel last night.

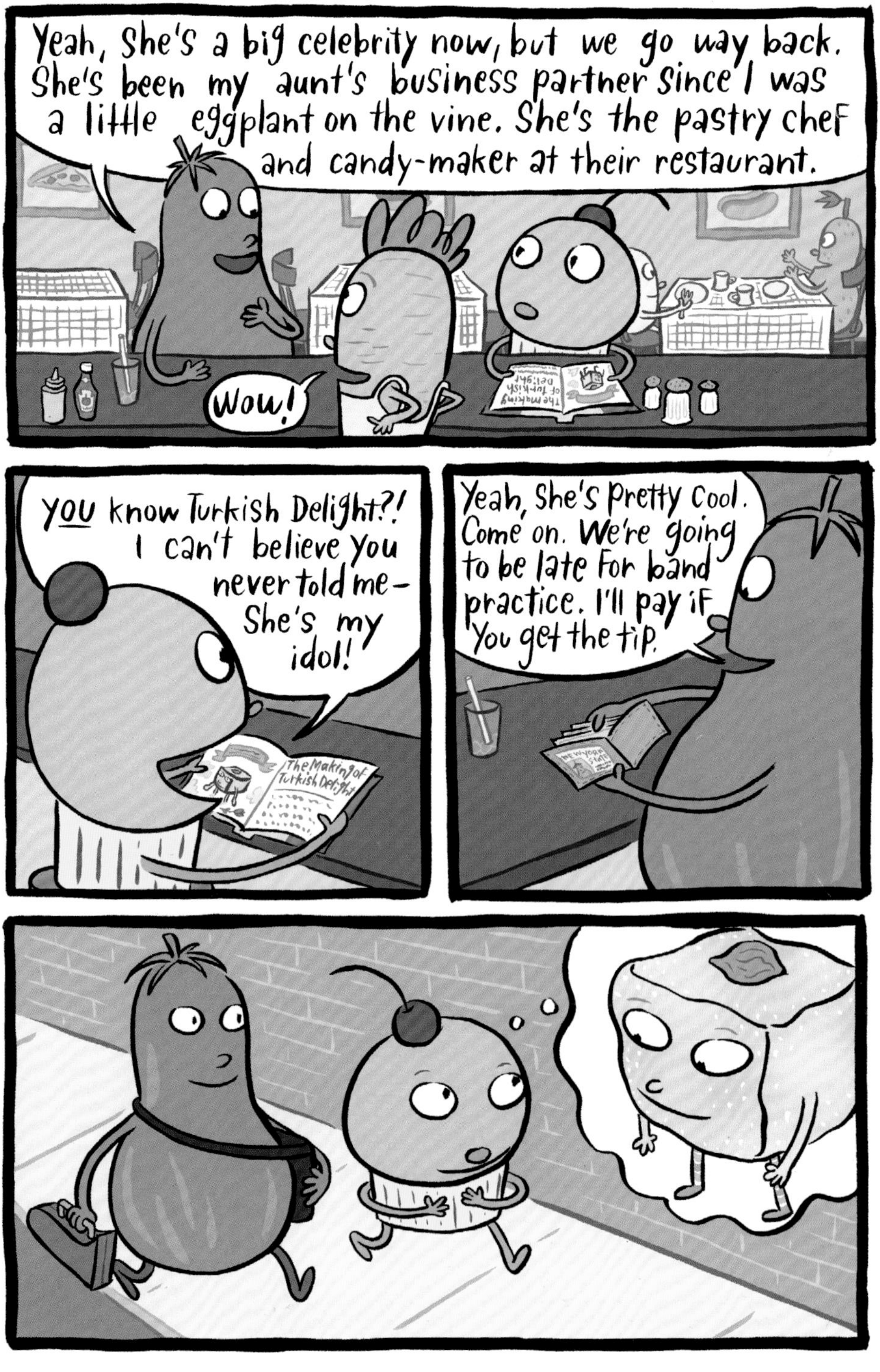

Yeah, She's a big celebrity now, but we go way back. She's been my aunt's business partner since I was a little eggplant on the vine. She's the pastry chef and candy-maker at their restaurant.
Wow!
The making of Turkish Delight
YOU know Turkish Delight?! I can't believe you never told me- She's my idol!
The Making of Turkish Delight
Yeah, She's pretty cool. Come on. We're going to be late for band practice. I'll pay if you get the tip.

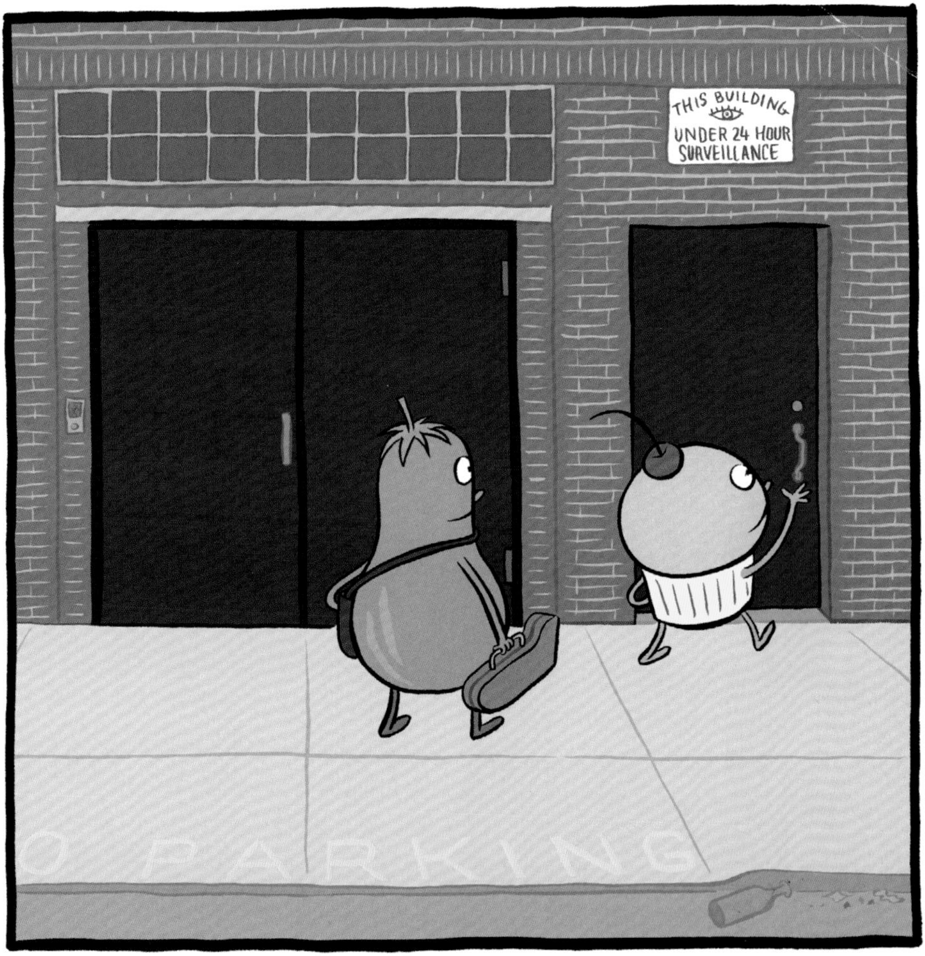
THIS BUILDING
UNDER 24 HOUR SURVEILLANCE
O PARKING
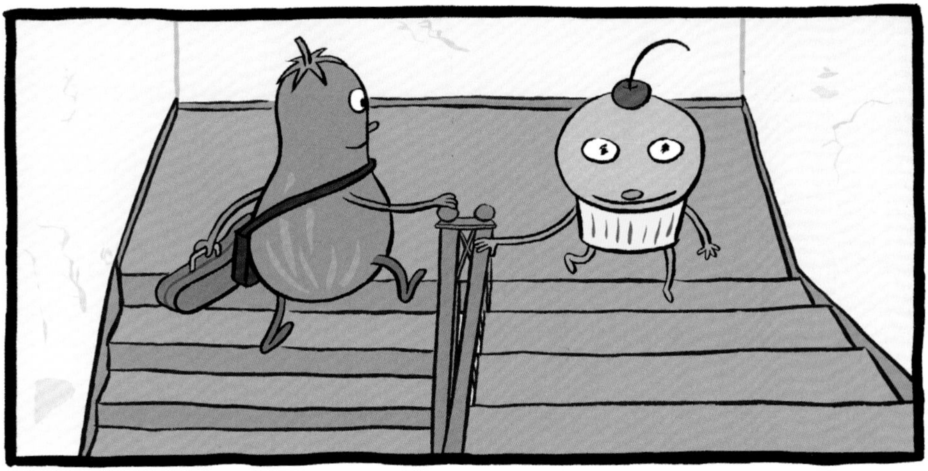

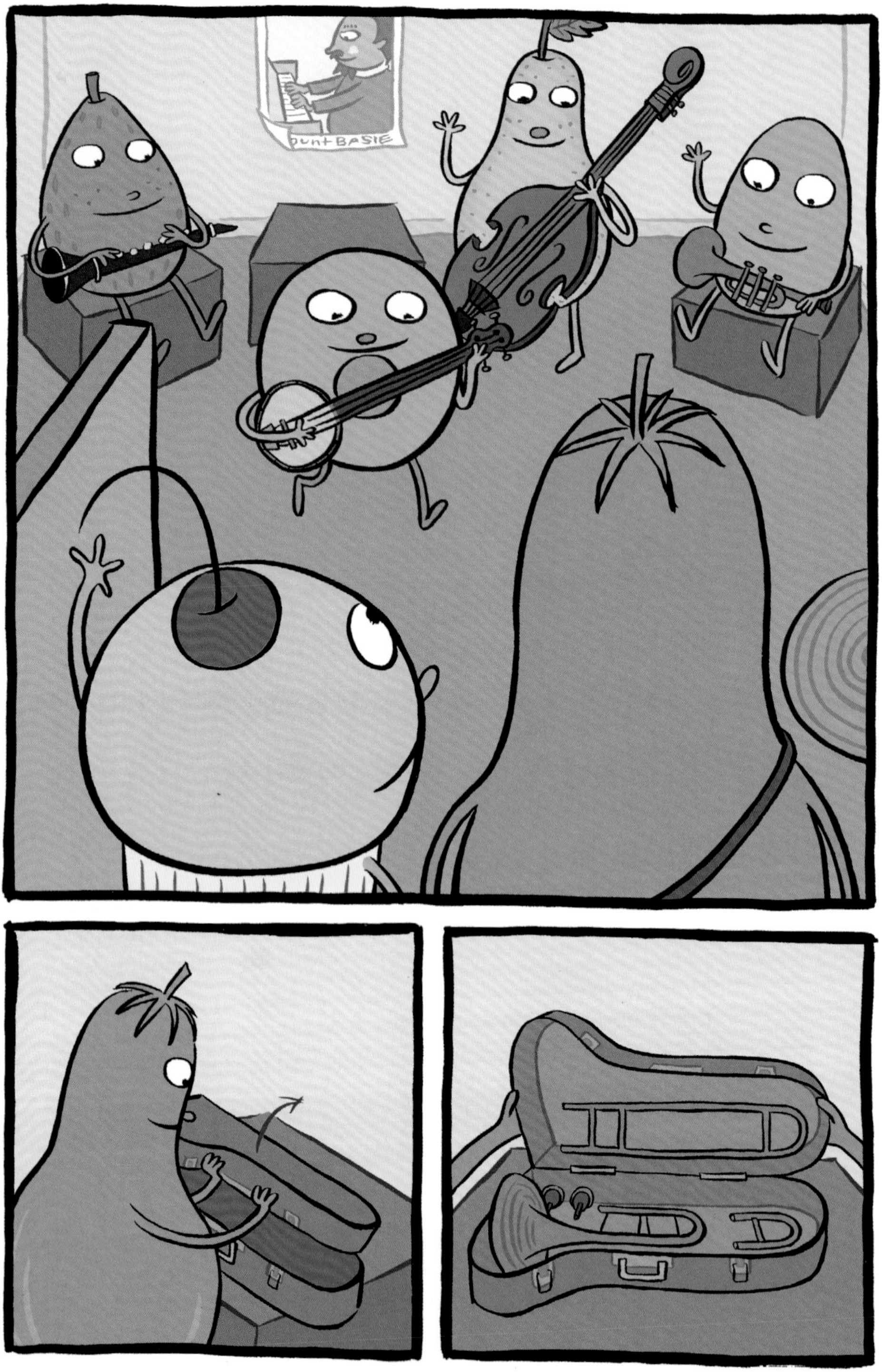
ount BASIE

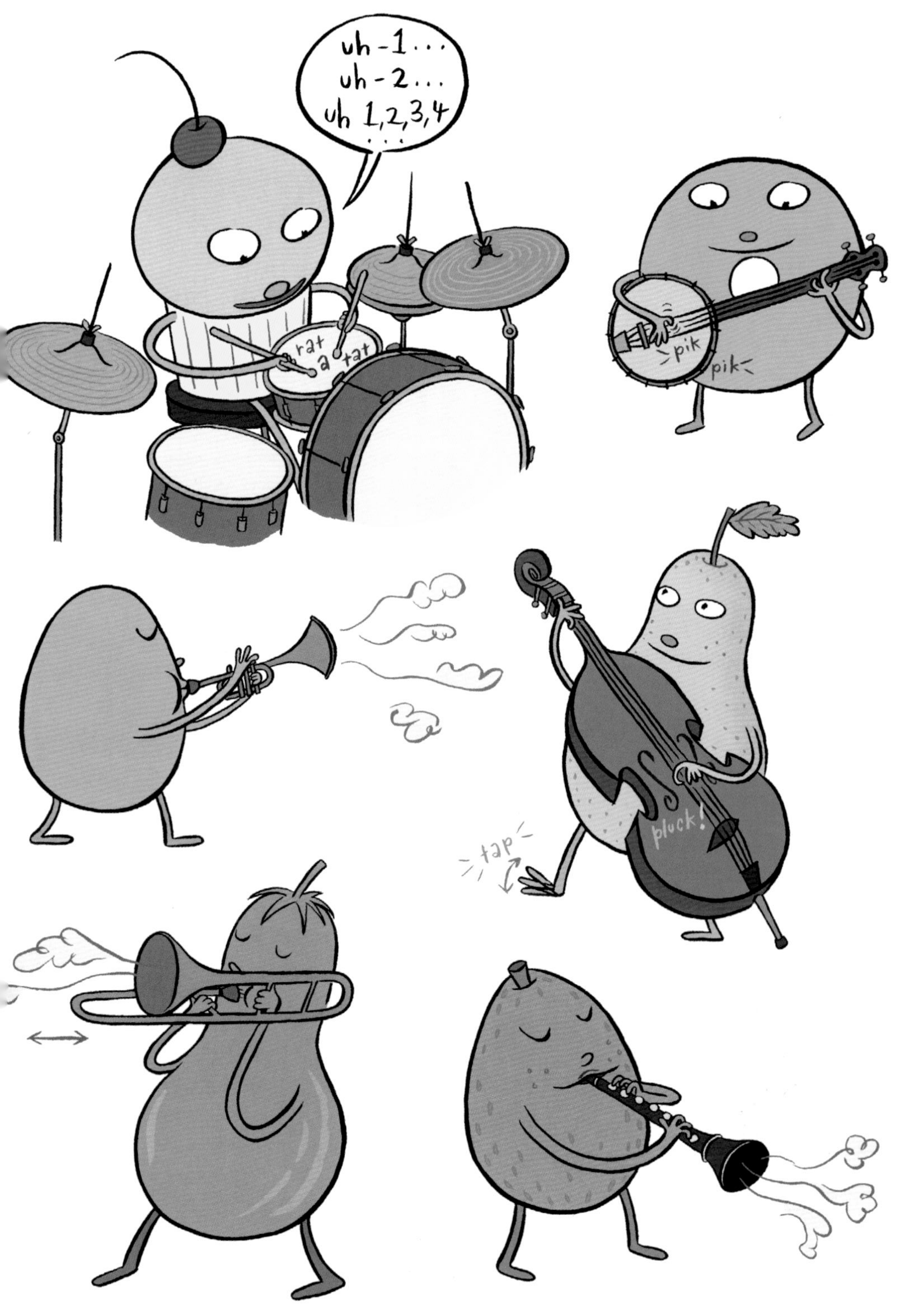
uh-1...
uh-2...
uh 1,2,3,4
...
rat a tat
pik
pik
pluck!
tap

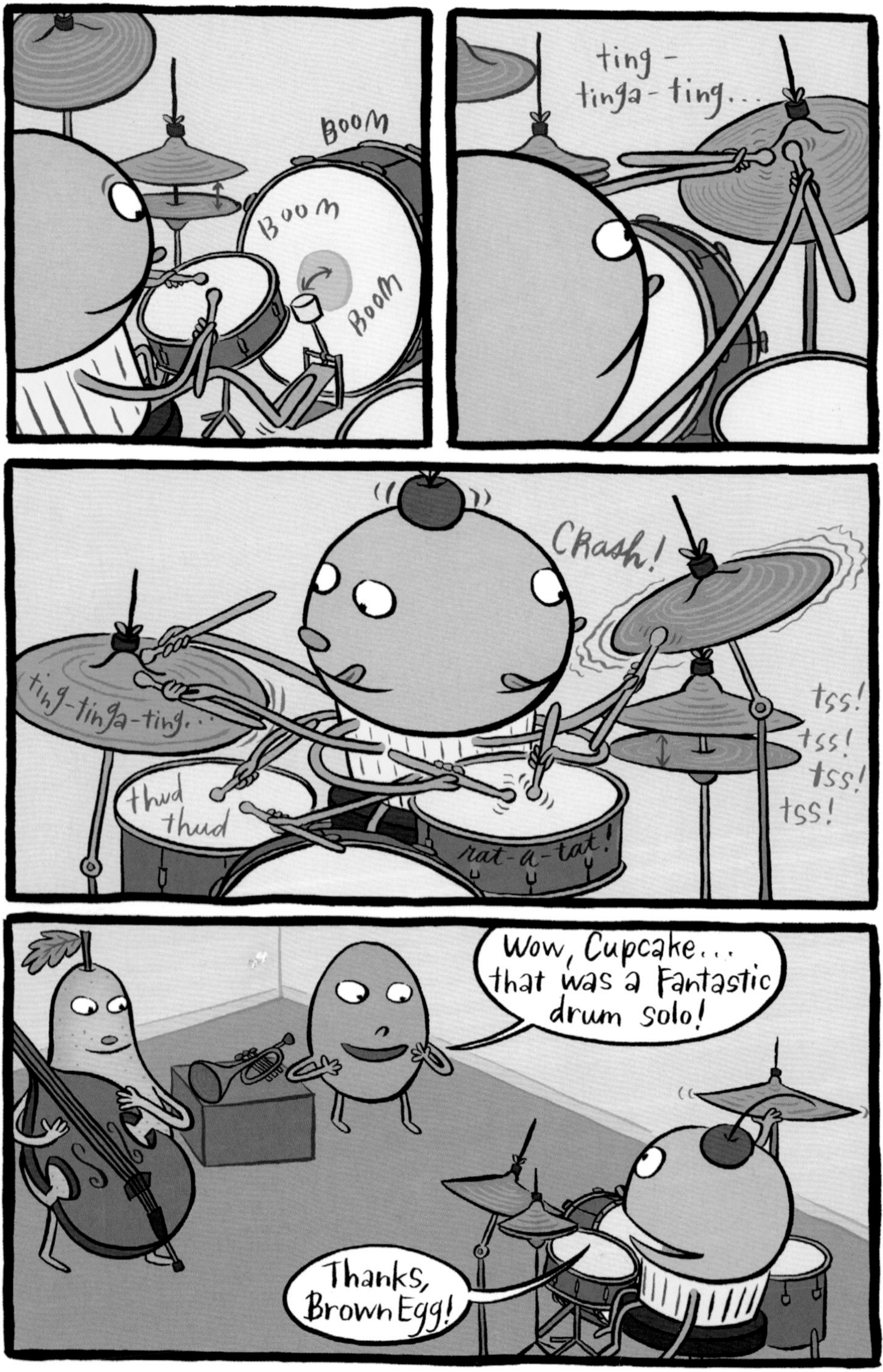
BOOM
BOOM
BOOM
ting-
tinga-ting...
CRASH!
ting-tinga-ting...
thud
thud
rat-a-tat!
tss!
tss!
tss!
tss!
Wow, Cupcake... that was a Fantastic drum solo!
Thanks, Brown Egg!

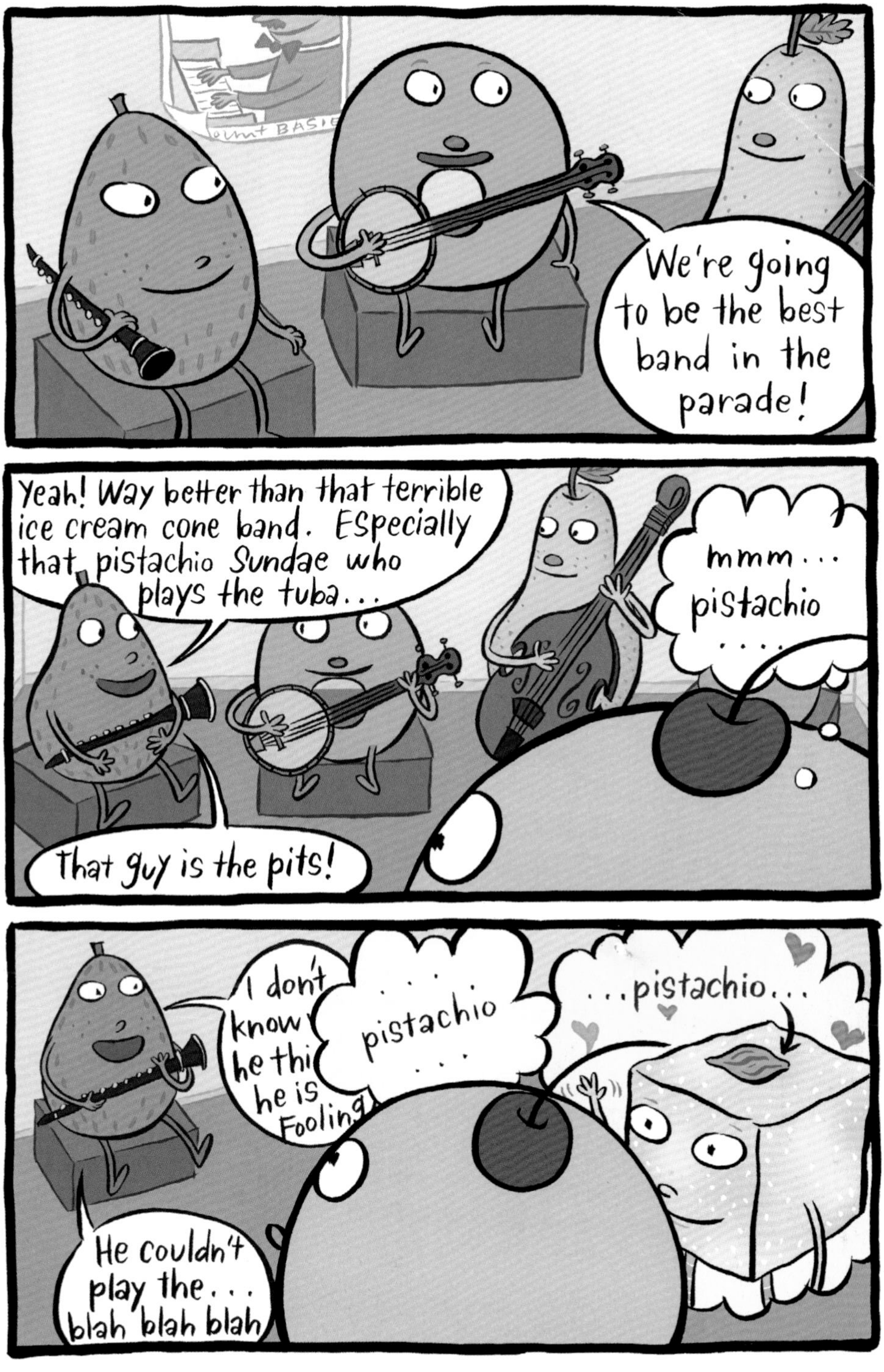

We're going to be the best band in the parade!
Yeah! Way better than that terrible ice cream cone band. Especially that pistachio Sundae who plays the tuba...
mmm... pistachio ....
That guy is the pits!
I don't know he thi he is Fooling
.... pistachio ...
...pistachio...
He couldn't play the... blah blah blah

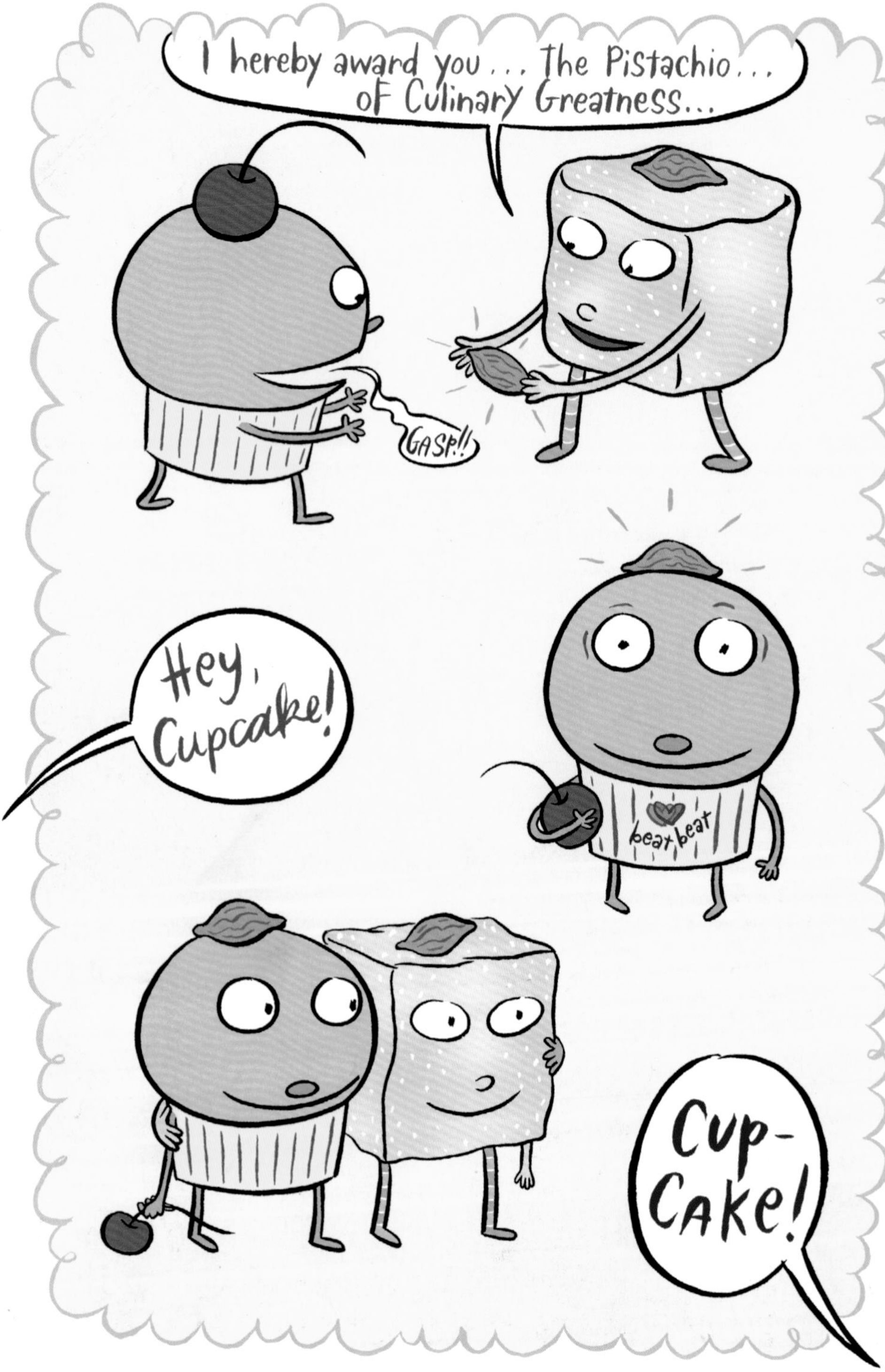
I hereby award you . . . The Pistachio . . . of Culinary Greatness . . .
GASP!!
Hey, Cupcake!
beat beat
Cup-Cake!

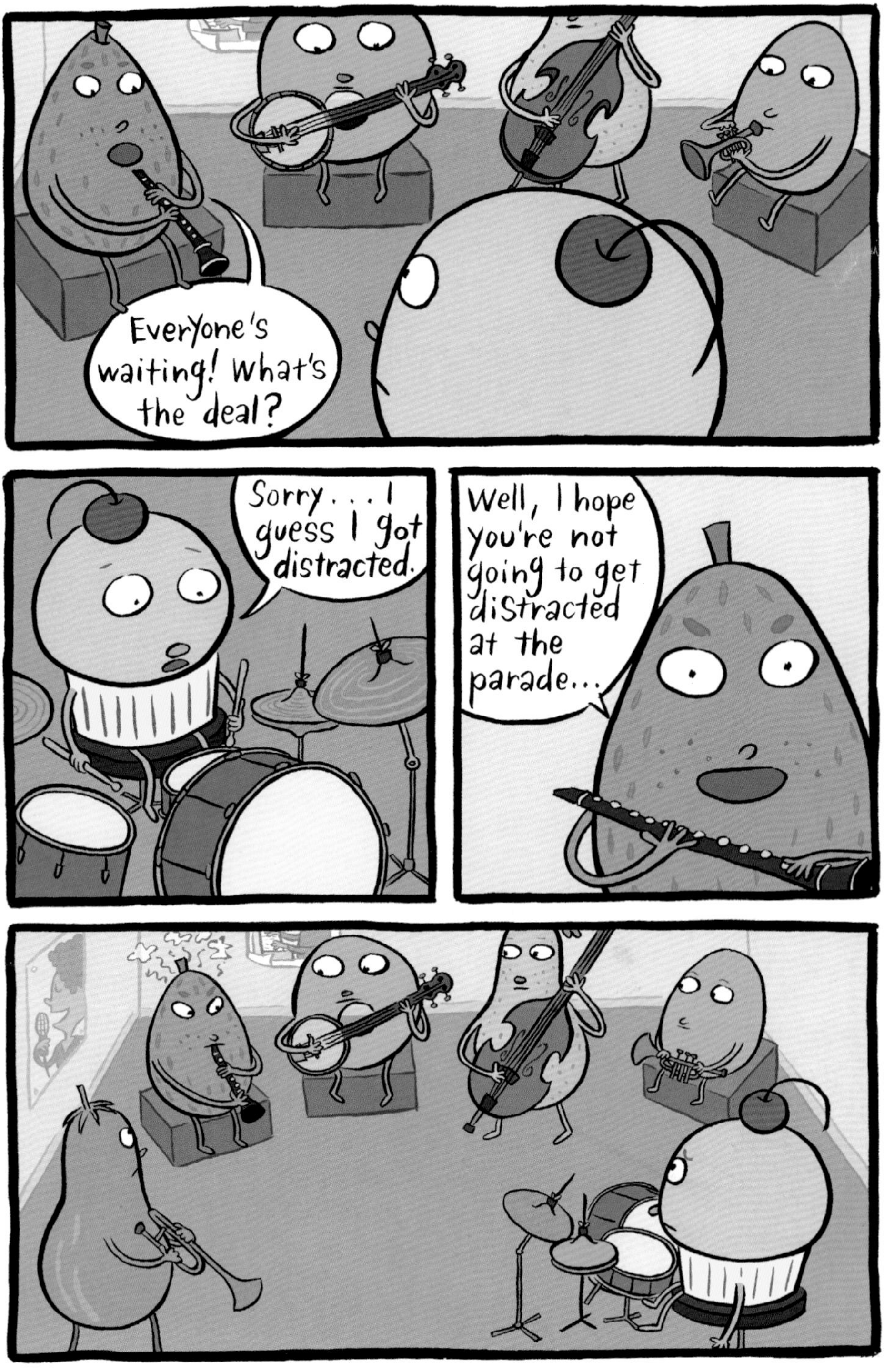
Everyone's waiting! What's the deal?
Sorry . . . I guess I got distracted.
Well, I hope you're not going to get distracted at the parade...

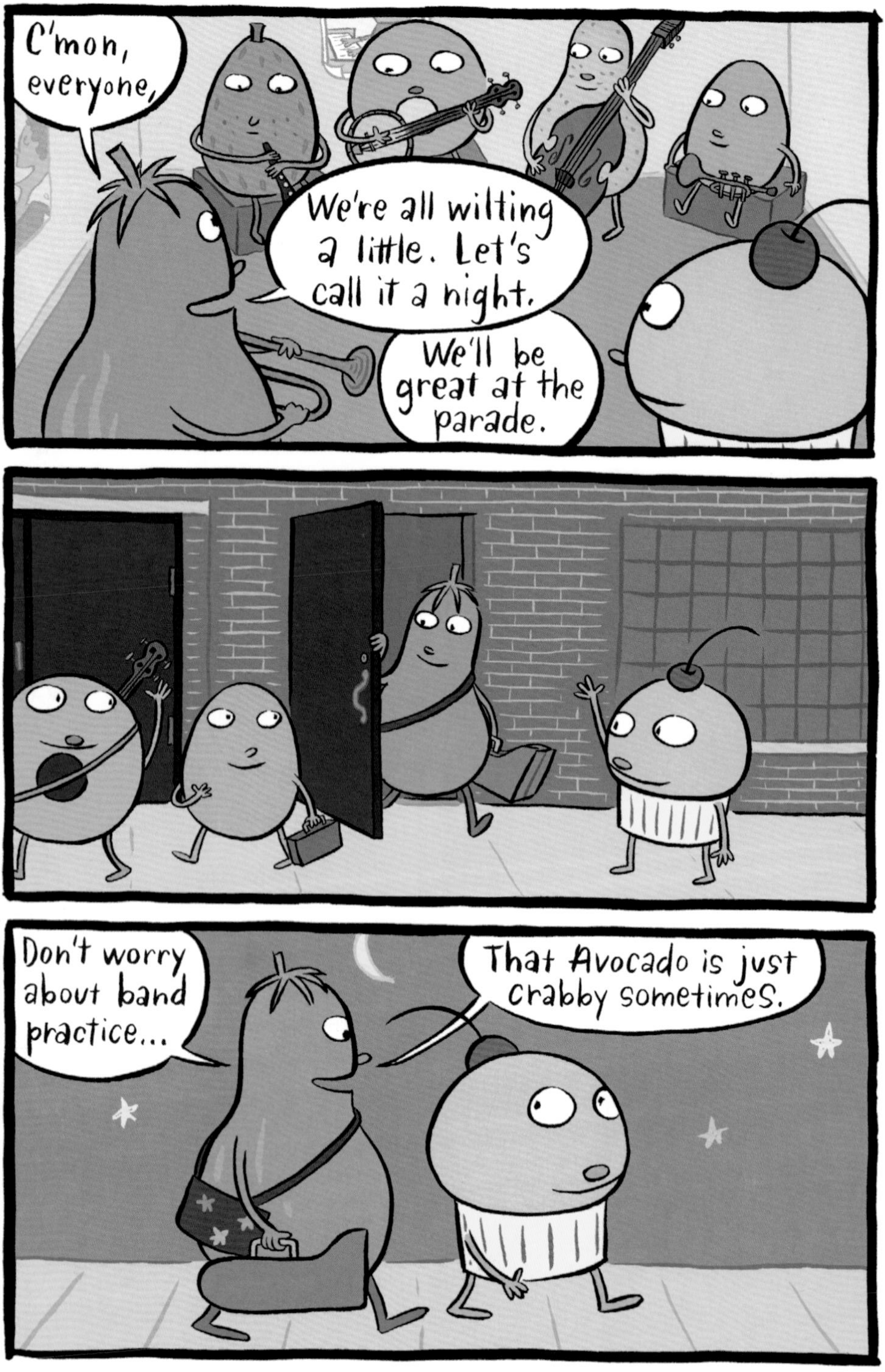
C'mon, everyone,
We're all wilting a little. Let's call it a night.
We'll be great at the parade.
Don't worry about band practice...
That Avocado is just crabby sometimes.

the following week . . .

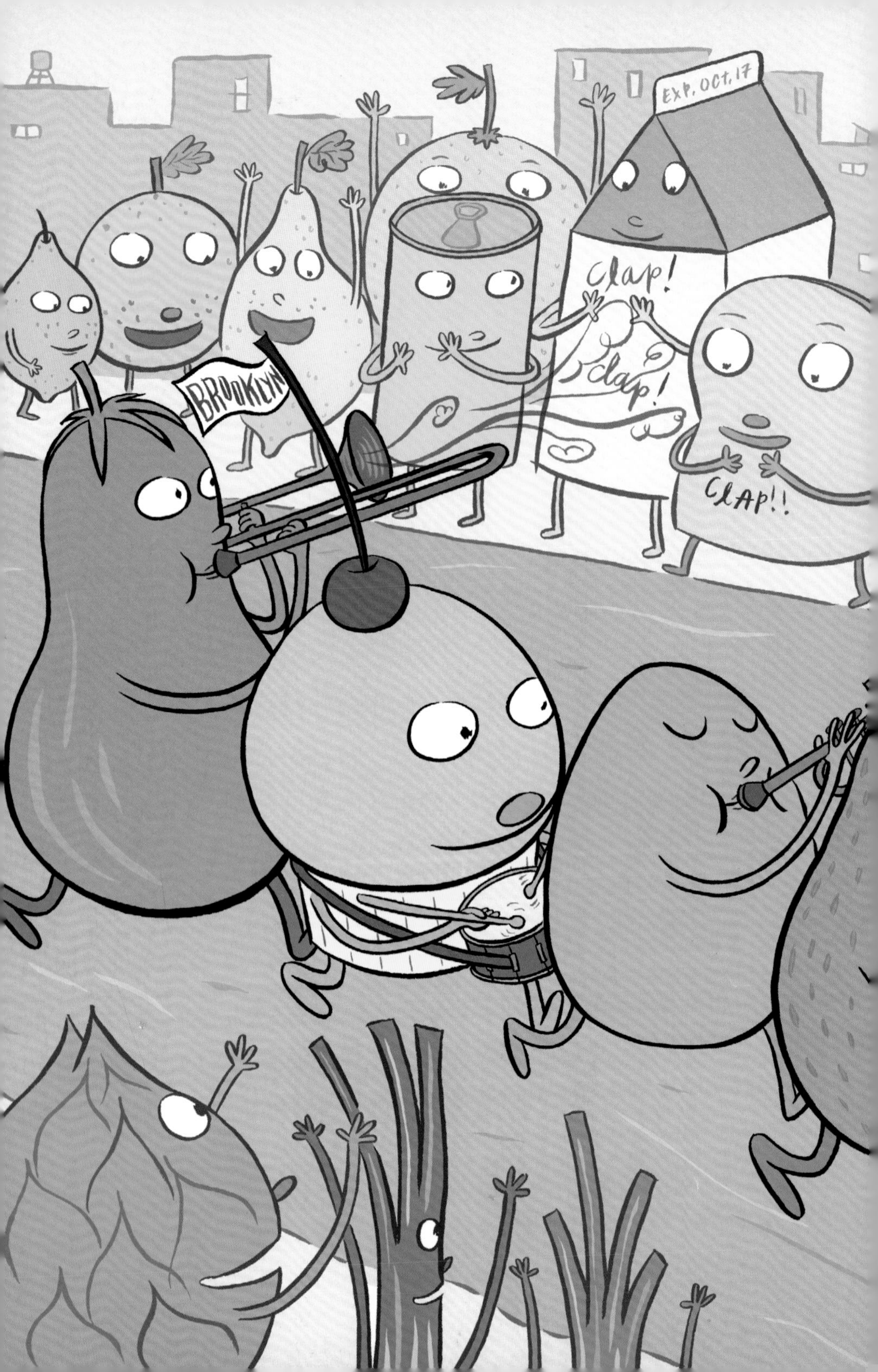
EXP. OCT. 17
BROOKLYN
CLAP!
CLAP!
CLAP!!

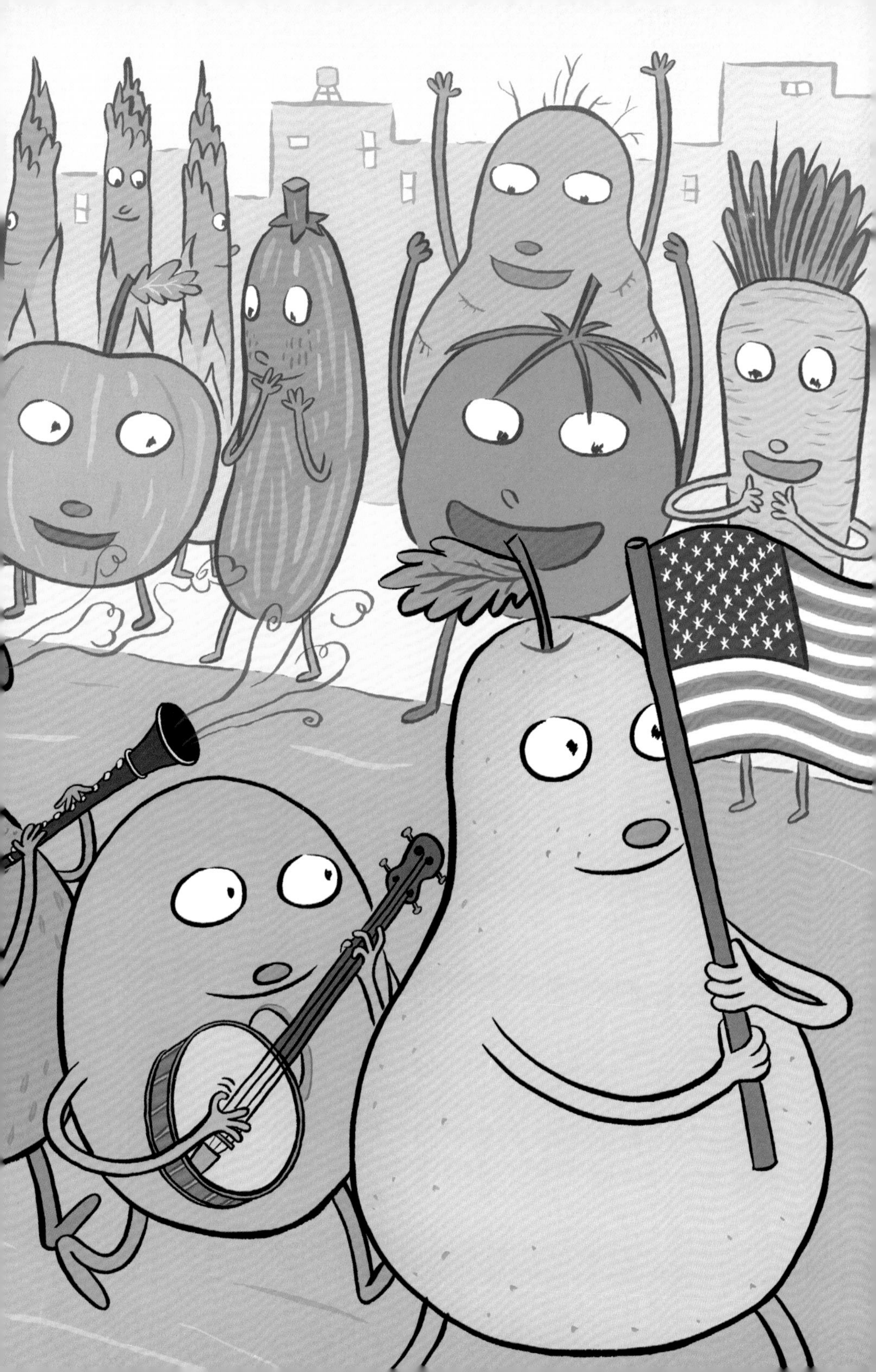

chapter
two

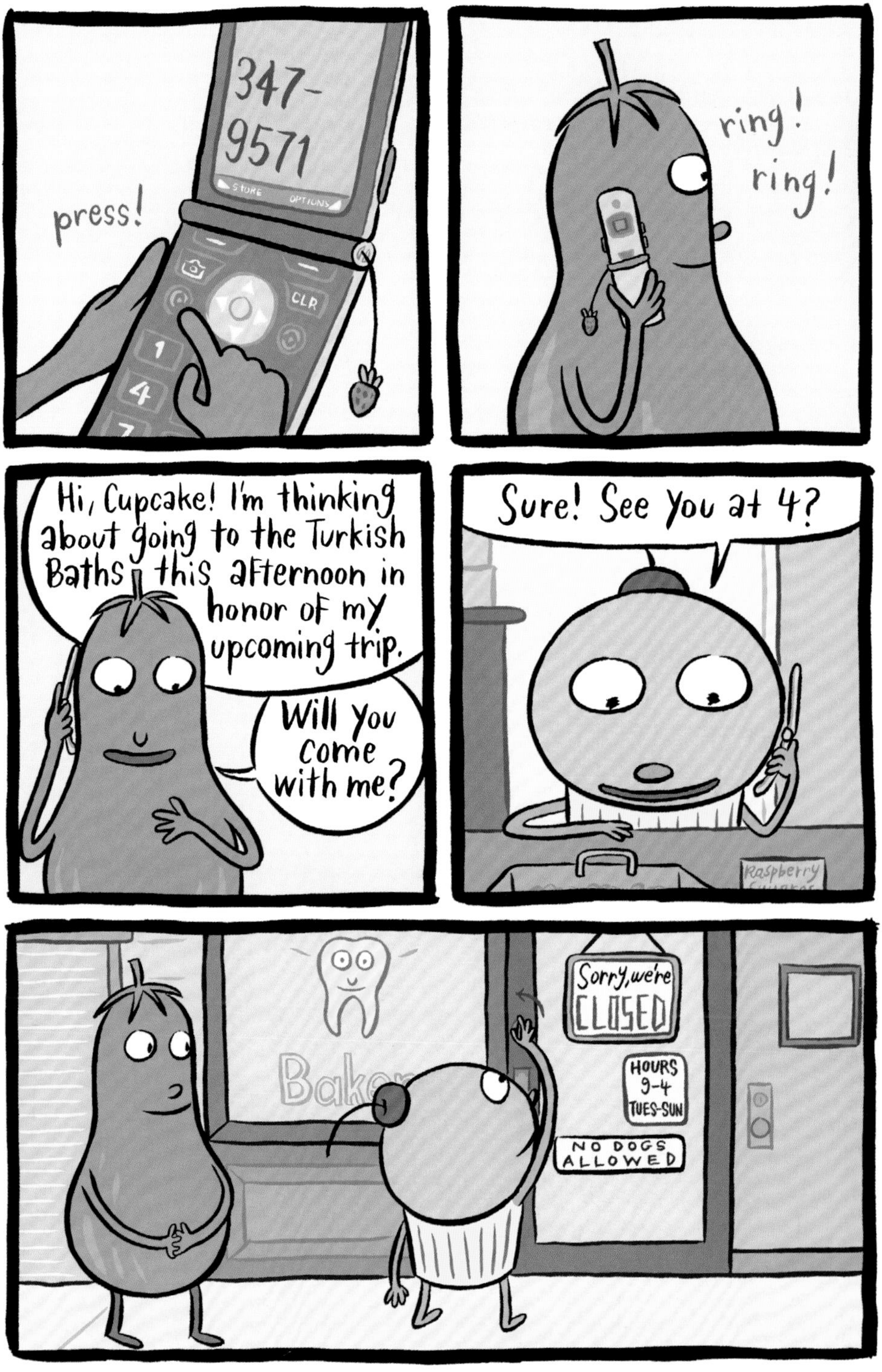
347-
9571
STORE
OPTIONS
CLR
press!
ring!
ring!
Hi, Cupcake! I'm thinking about going to the Turkish Baths this afternoon in honor of my upcoming trip.
Will you come with me?
Sure! See you at 4?
Raspberry
Sorry, we're CLOSED
HOURS 9-4 TUES-SUN
NO DOGS ALLOWED

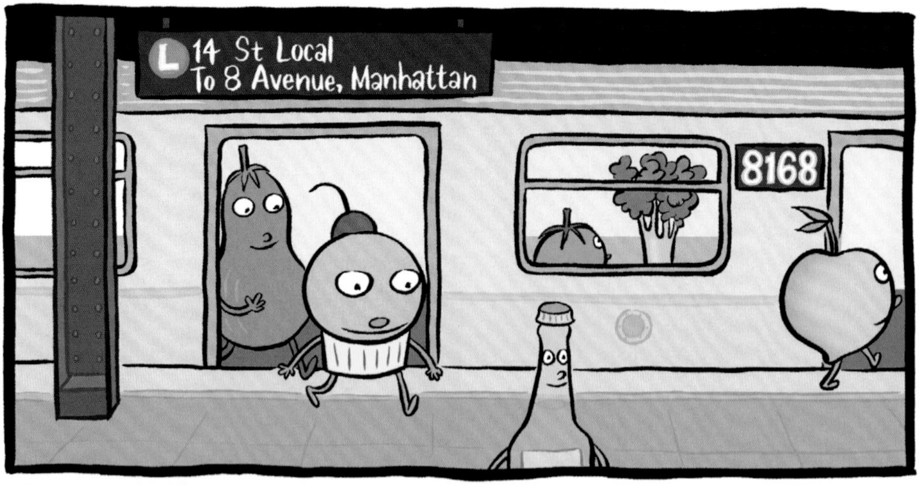
L 14 St Local
To 8 Avenue, Manhattan
8168

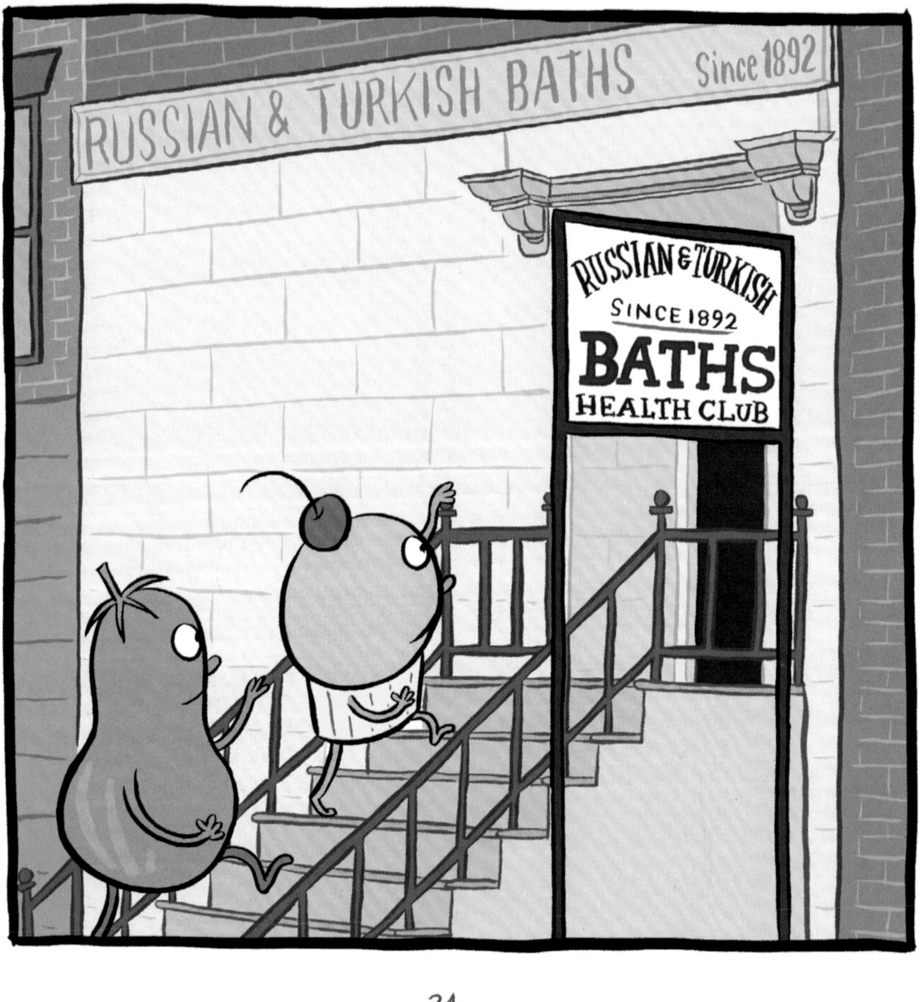
RUSSIAN & TURKISH BATHS Since 1892
RUSSIAN & TURKISH
SINCE 1892
BATHS
HEALTH CLUB

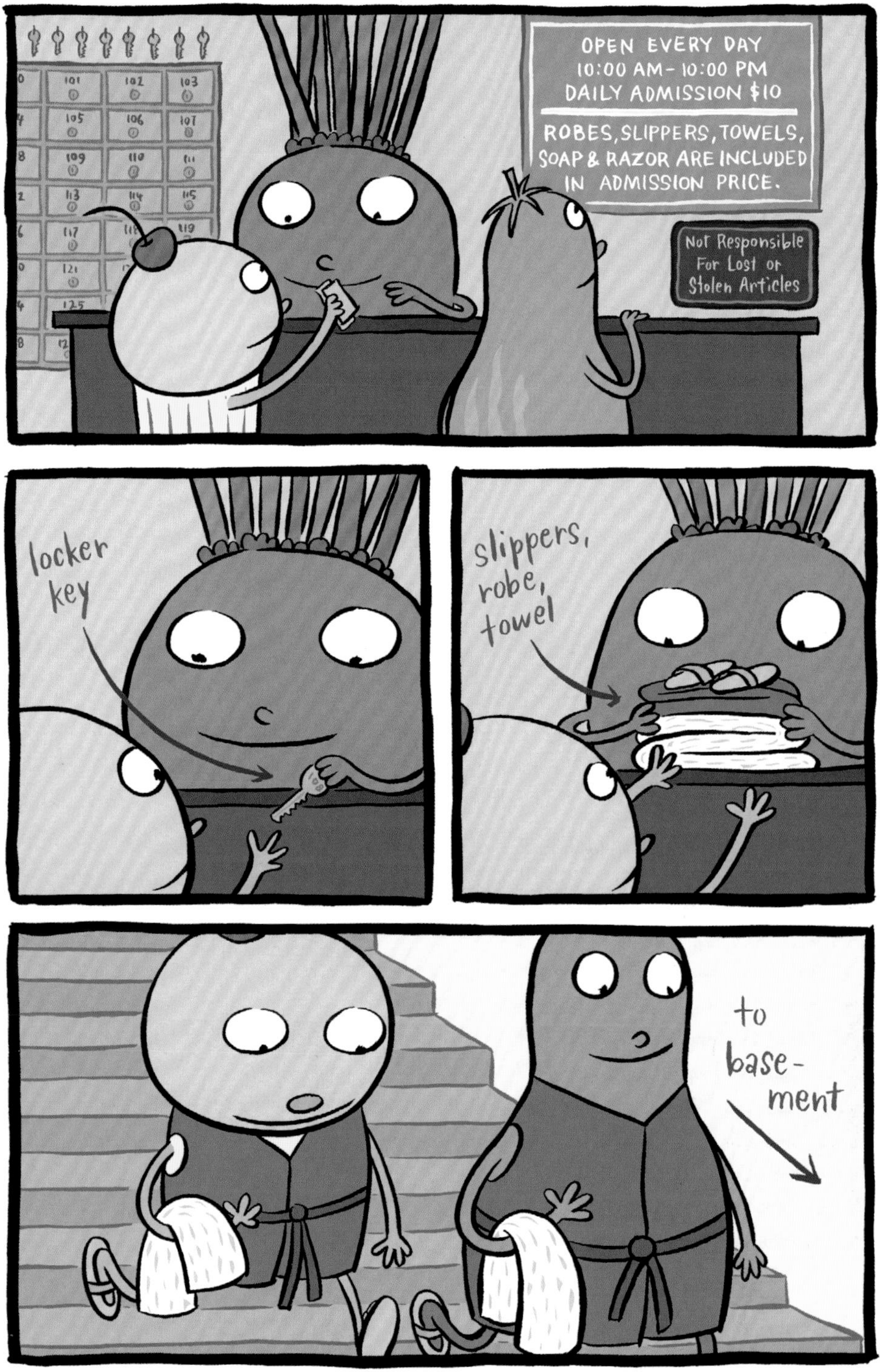
OPEN EVERY DAY
10:00 AM - 10:00 PM
DAILY ADMISSION $10
ROBES, SLIPPERS, TOWELS, SOAP & RAZOR ARE INCLUDED IN ADMISSION PRICE.
Not Responsible For Lost or Stolen Articles
locker key
slippers, robe, towel
to base-ment

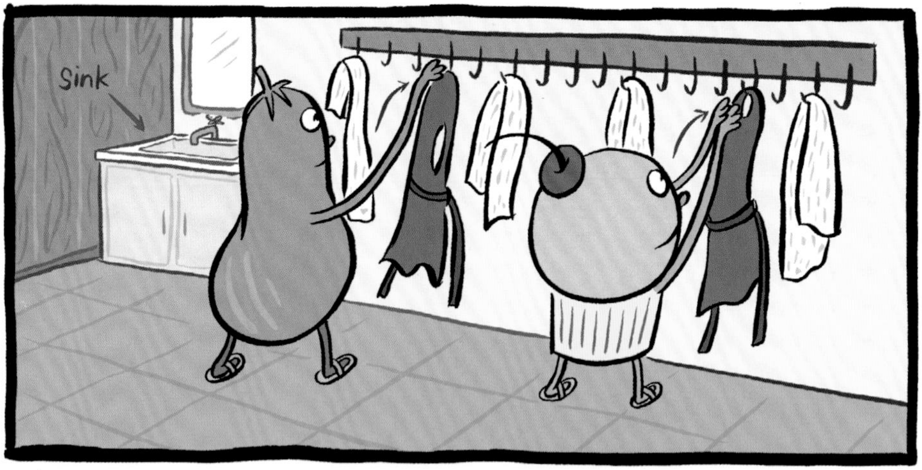
Sink

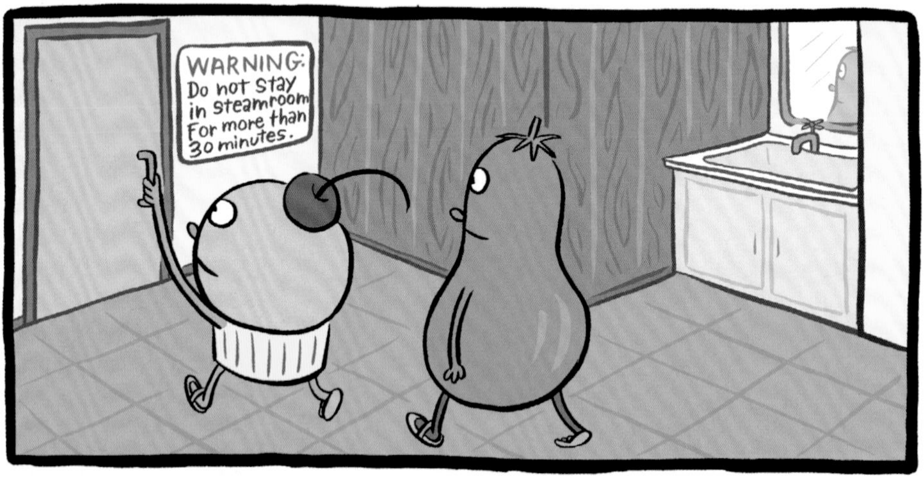
WARNING:
Do not stay in steamroom for more than 30 minutes.

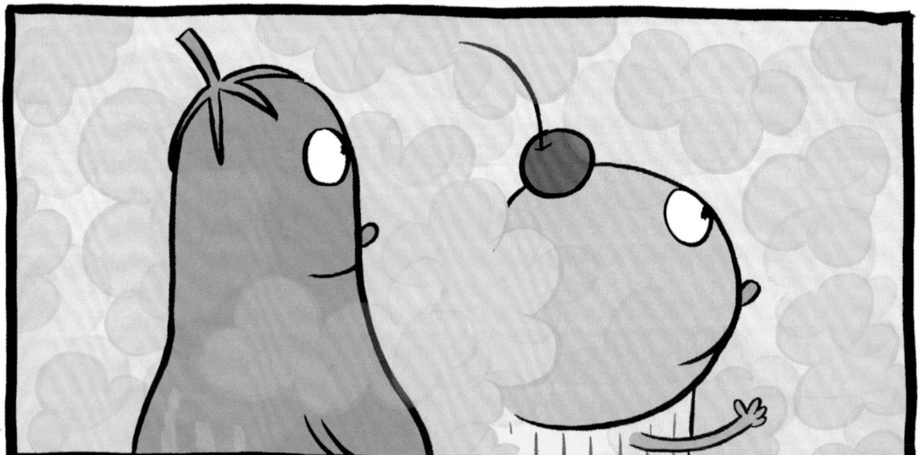

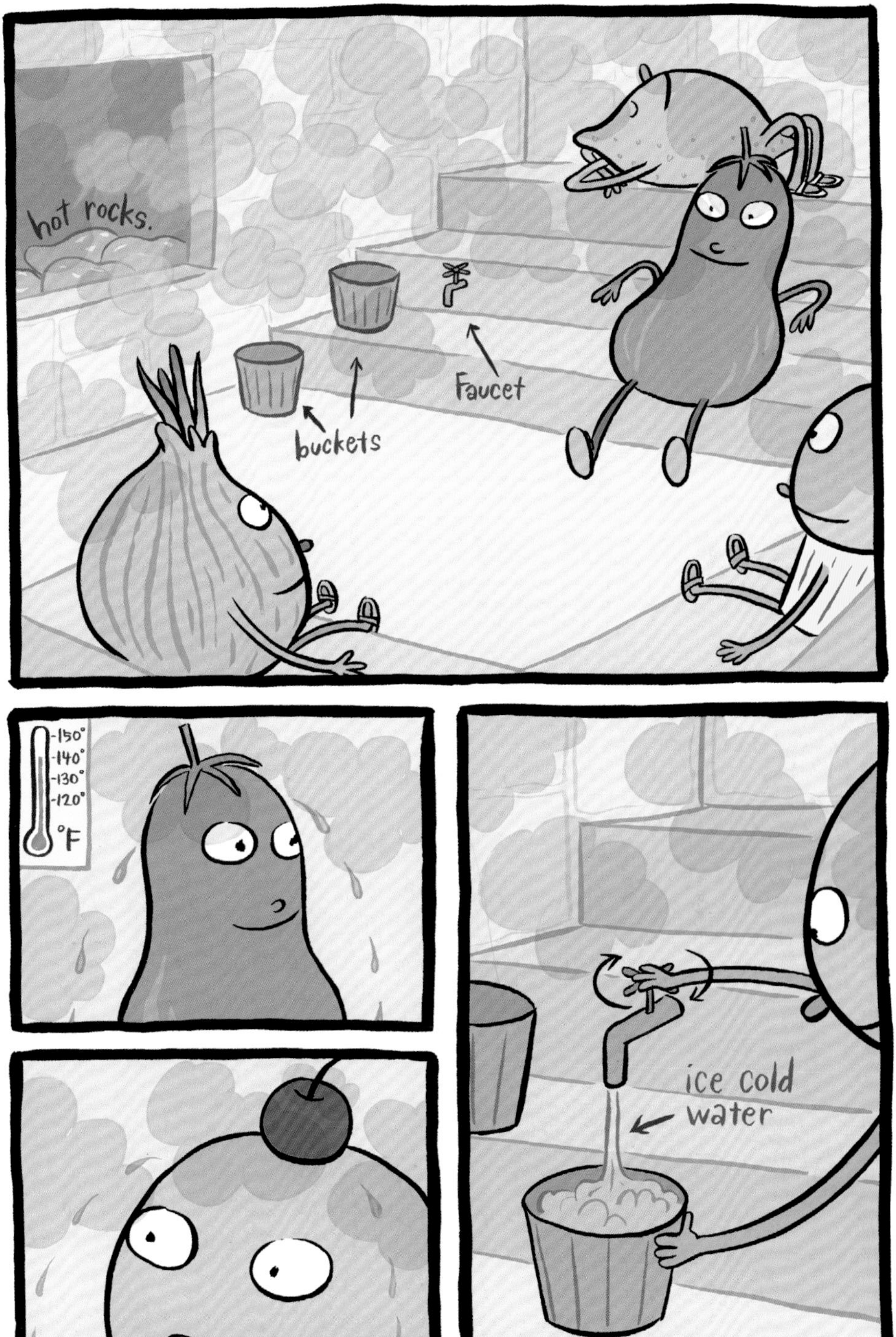
hot rocks.
buckets
Faucet
-150°
-140°
-130°
-120°
°F
ice cold
water

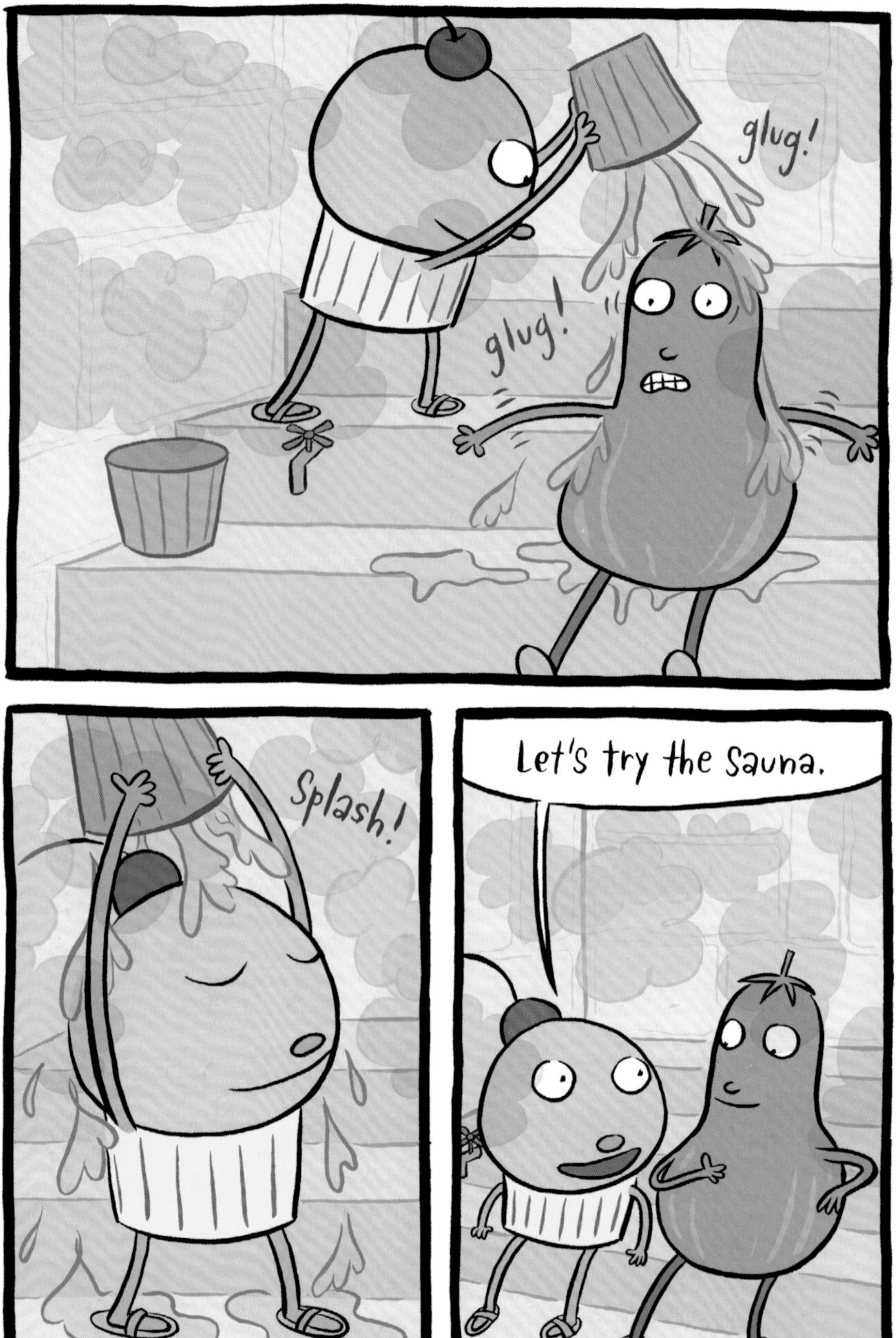
glug!
glug!
Splash!
Let's try the Sauna.

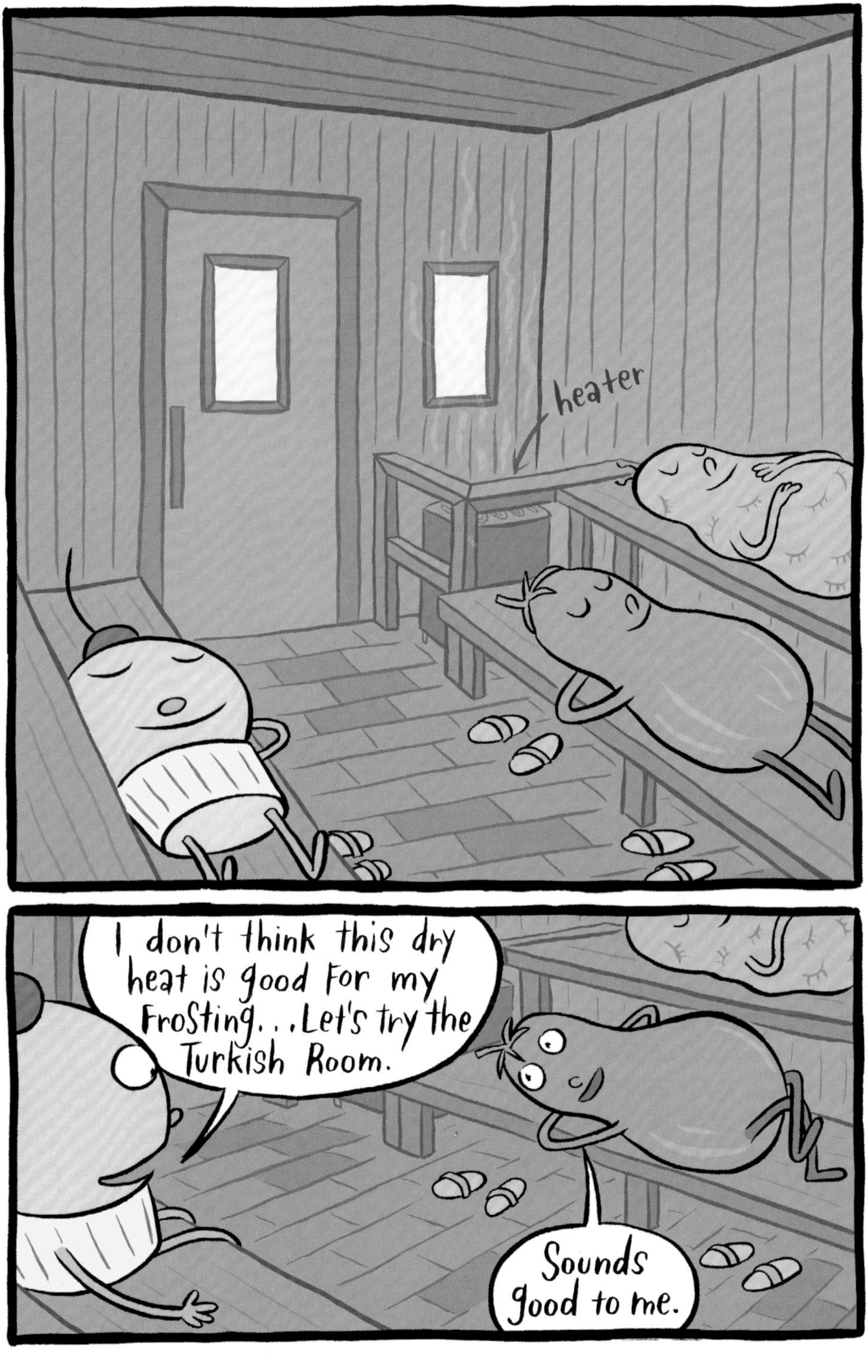
heater
I don't think this dry heat is good for my frosting...Let's try the Turkish Room.
Sounds good to me.

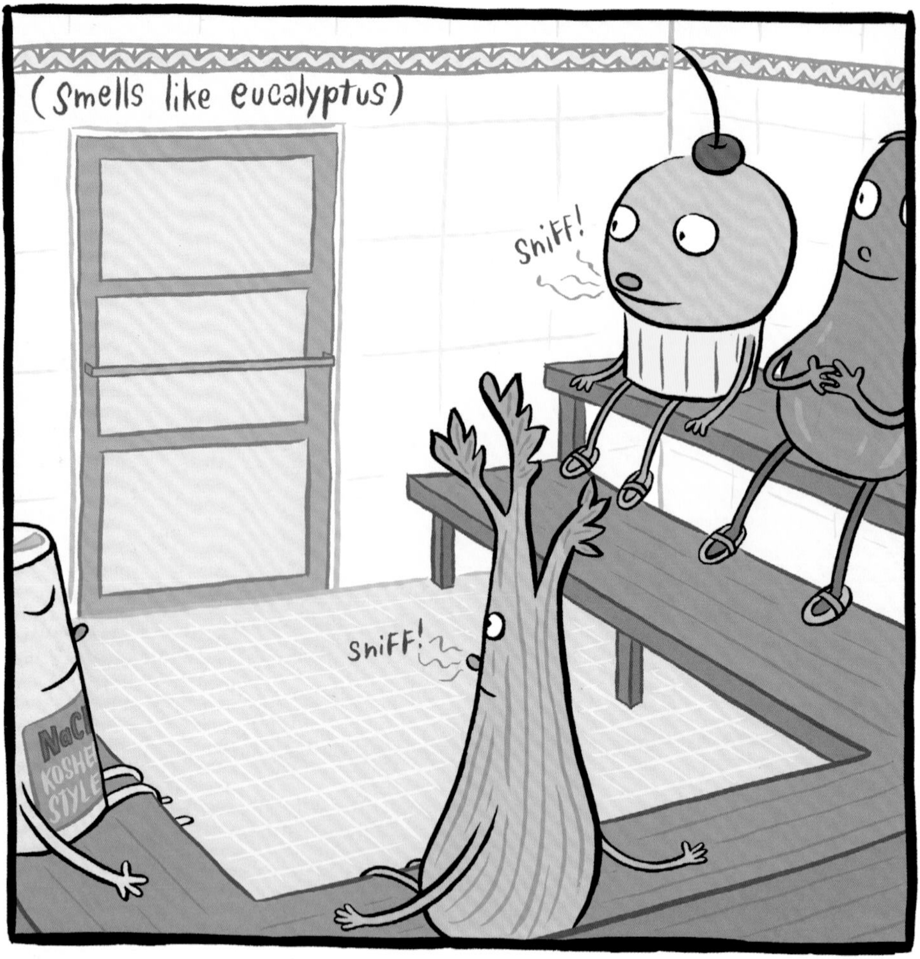
(Smells like eucalyptus)
SNIFF!
SNIFF!
NaCl
KOSHER
STYLE

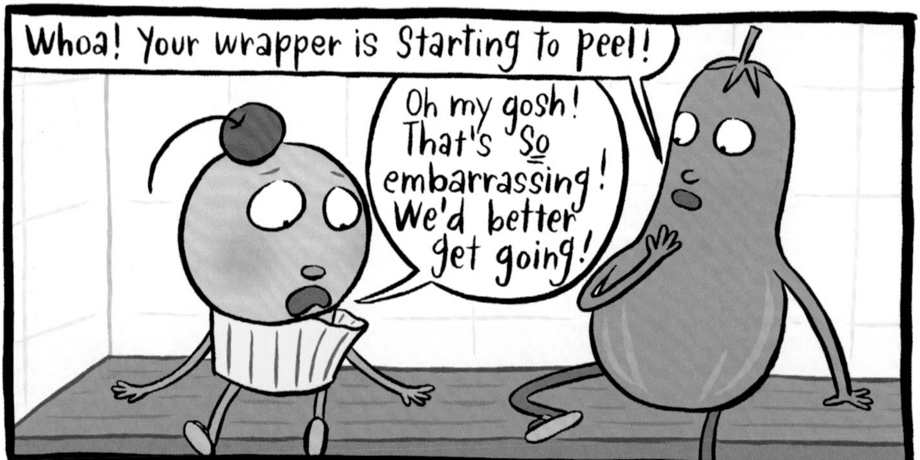
Whoa! Your wrapper is Starting to peel!
Oh my gosh! That's So embarrassing! We'd better get going!

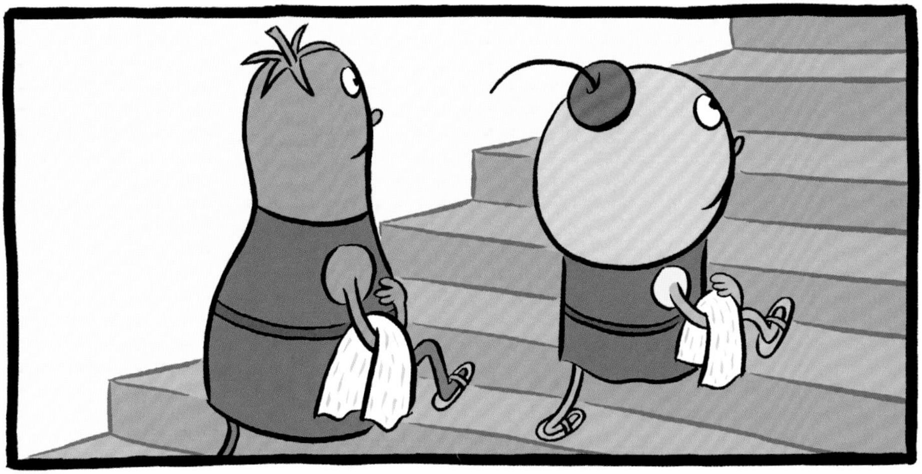

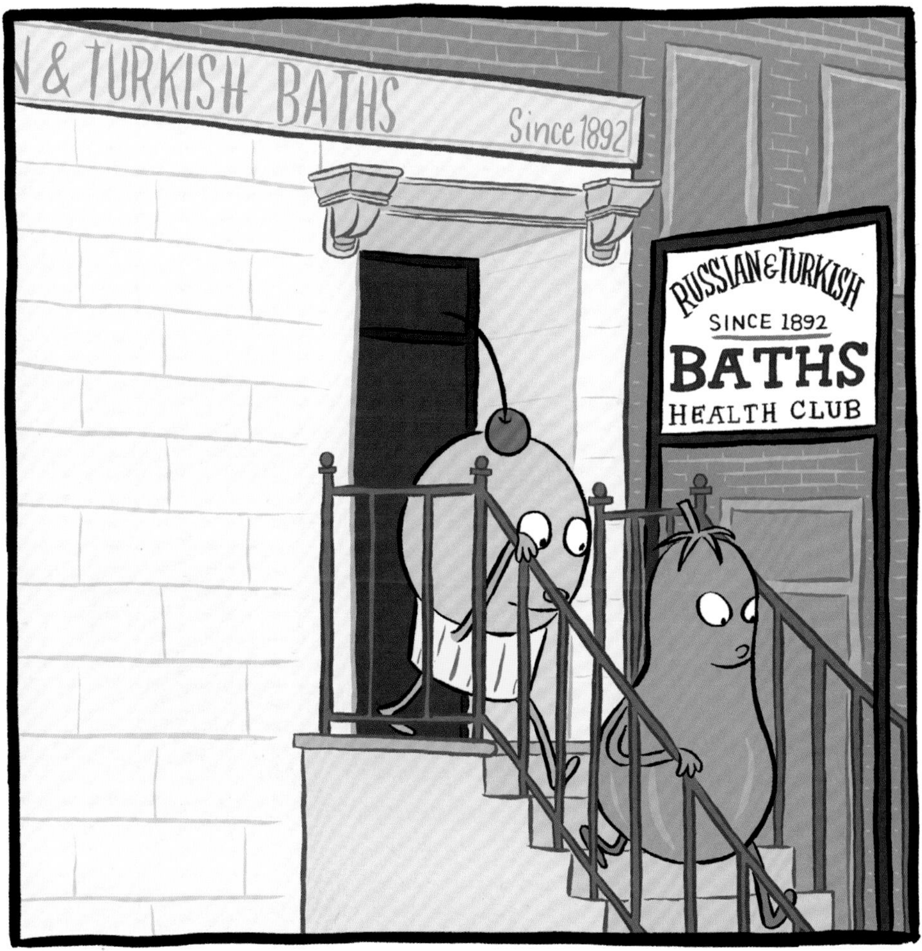
N & TURKISH BATHS
Since 1892
RUSSIAN & TURKISH
SINCE 1892
BATHS
HEALTH CLUB

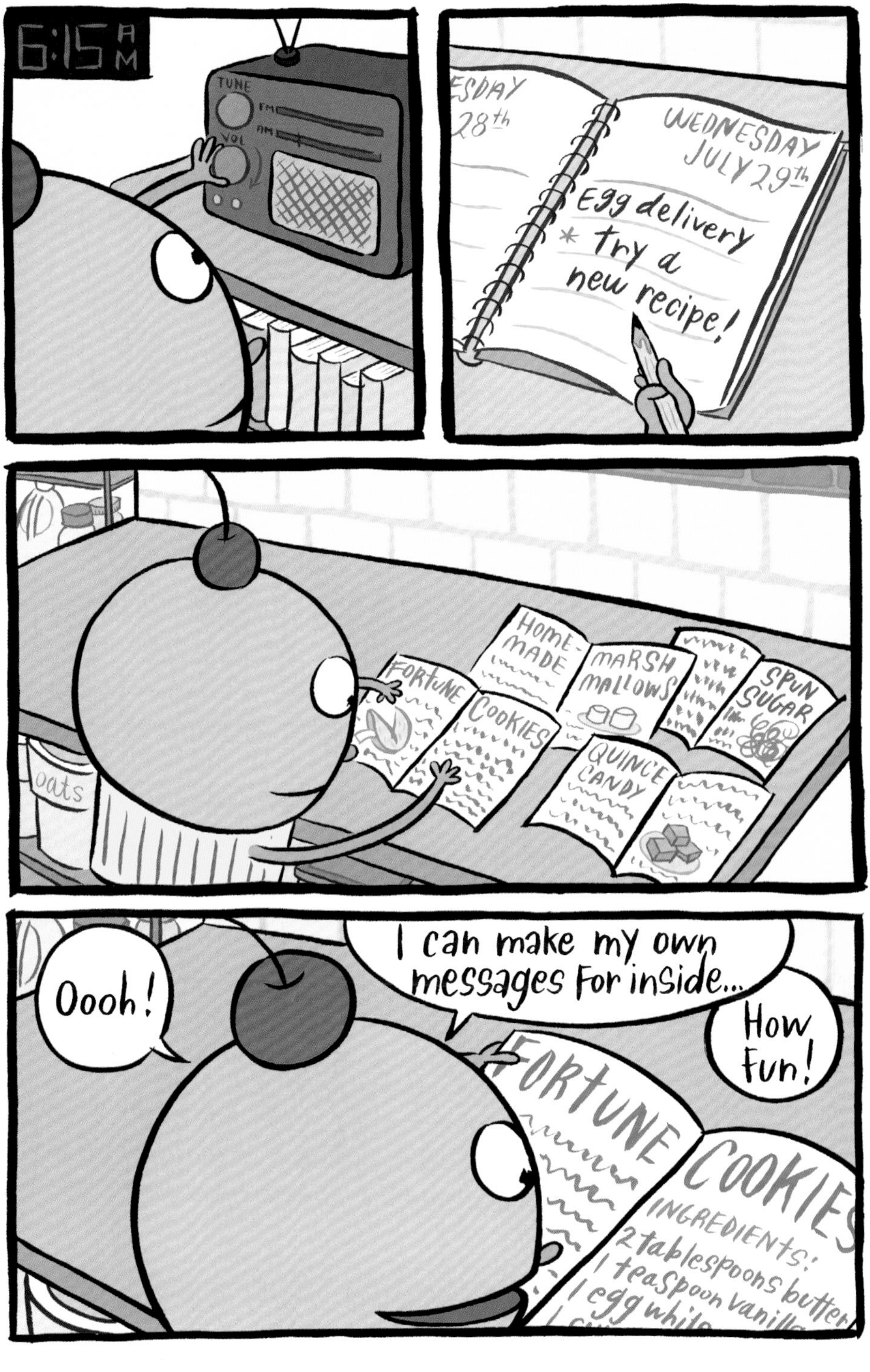
6:15 AM
TUNE
FM
AM
VOL
ESDAY 28th
WEDNESDAY JULY 29th
Egg delivery
* try a new recipe!
FORTUNE COOKIES
HOME-MADE MARSHMALLOWS
SPUN SUGAR
QUINCE CANDY
oats
Oooh!
I can make my own messages for inside...
How fun!
FORTUNE COOKIES
INGREDIENTS:
2 tablespoons butter
1 teaspoon vanilla
1 egg white

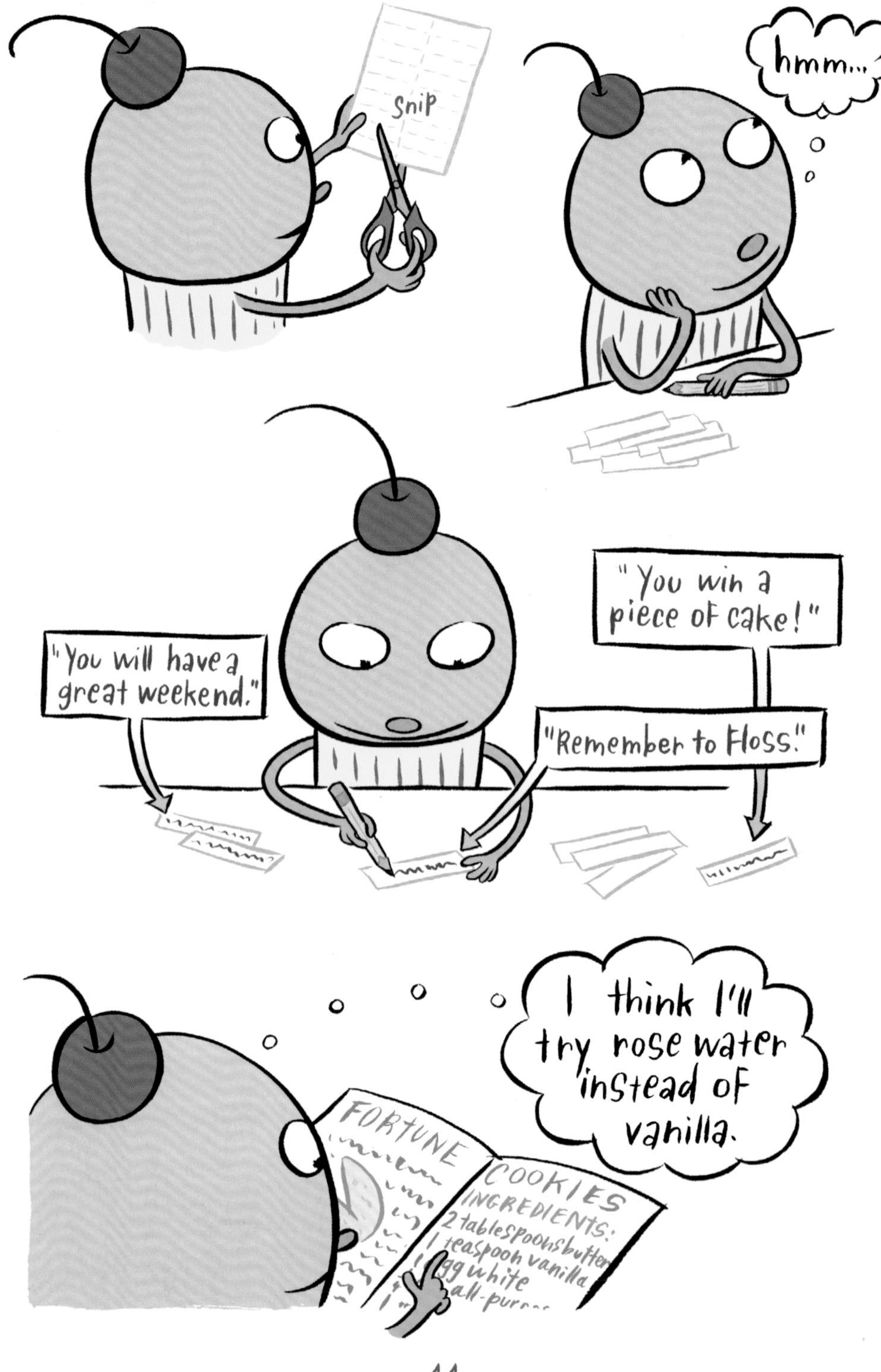
snip
hmm...
"You will have a great weekend."
"You win a piece of cake!"
"Remember to floss."
I think I'll try rose water instead of vanilla.
FORTUNE COOKIES
INGREDIENTS:
2 tablespoons butter
1 teaspoon vanilla
egg white

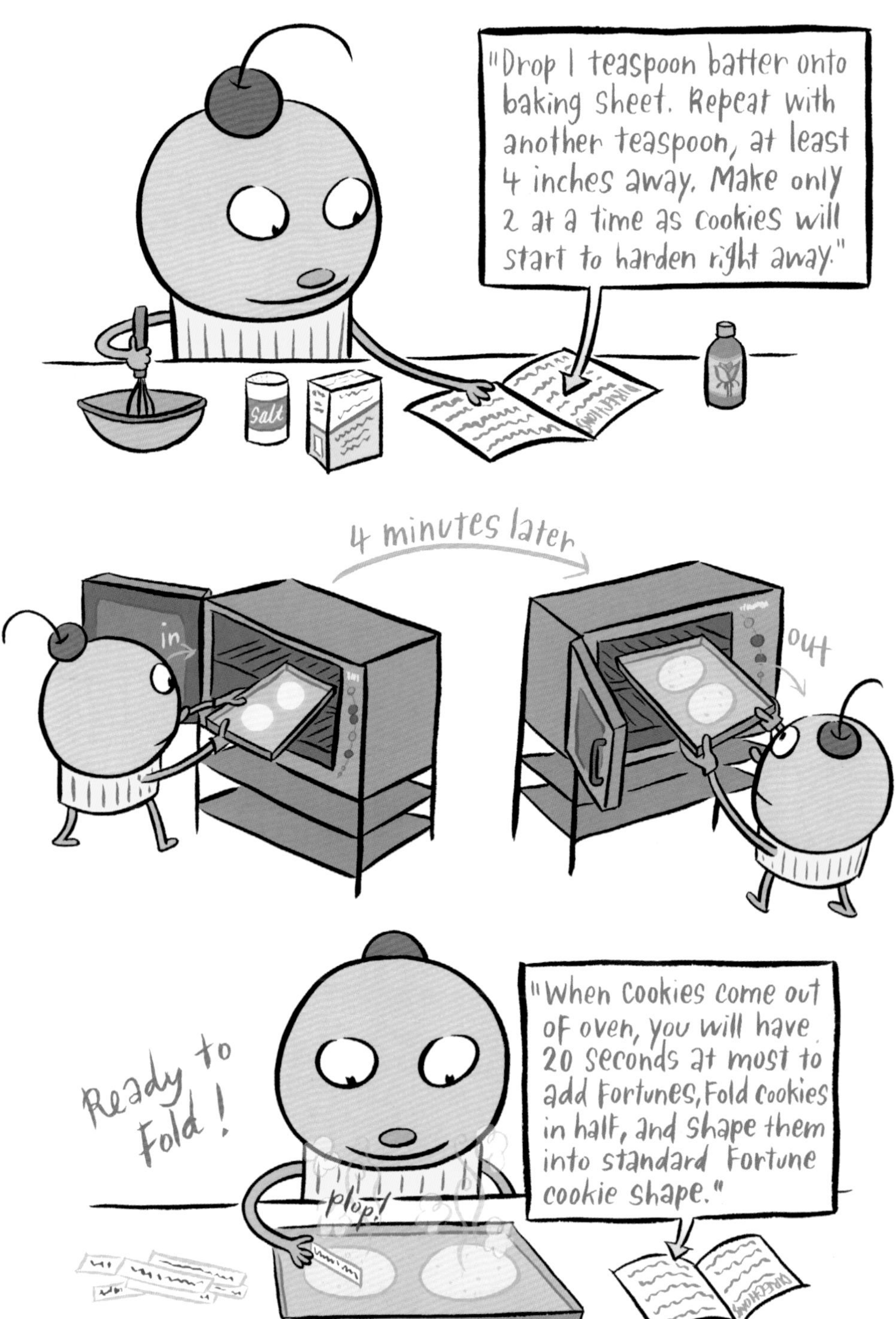
"Drop 1 teaspoon batter onto baking sheet. Repeat with another teaspoon, at least 4 inches away. Make only 2 at a time as cookies will start to harden right away."
Salt
4 minutes later
in
out
Ready to Fold!
"When cookies come out of oven, you will have 20 seconds at most to add fortunes, fold cookies in half, and shape them into standard fortune cookie shape."
plop!

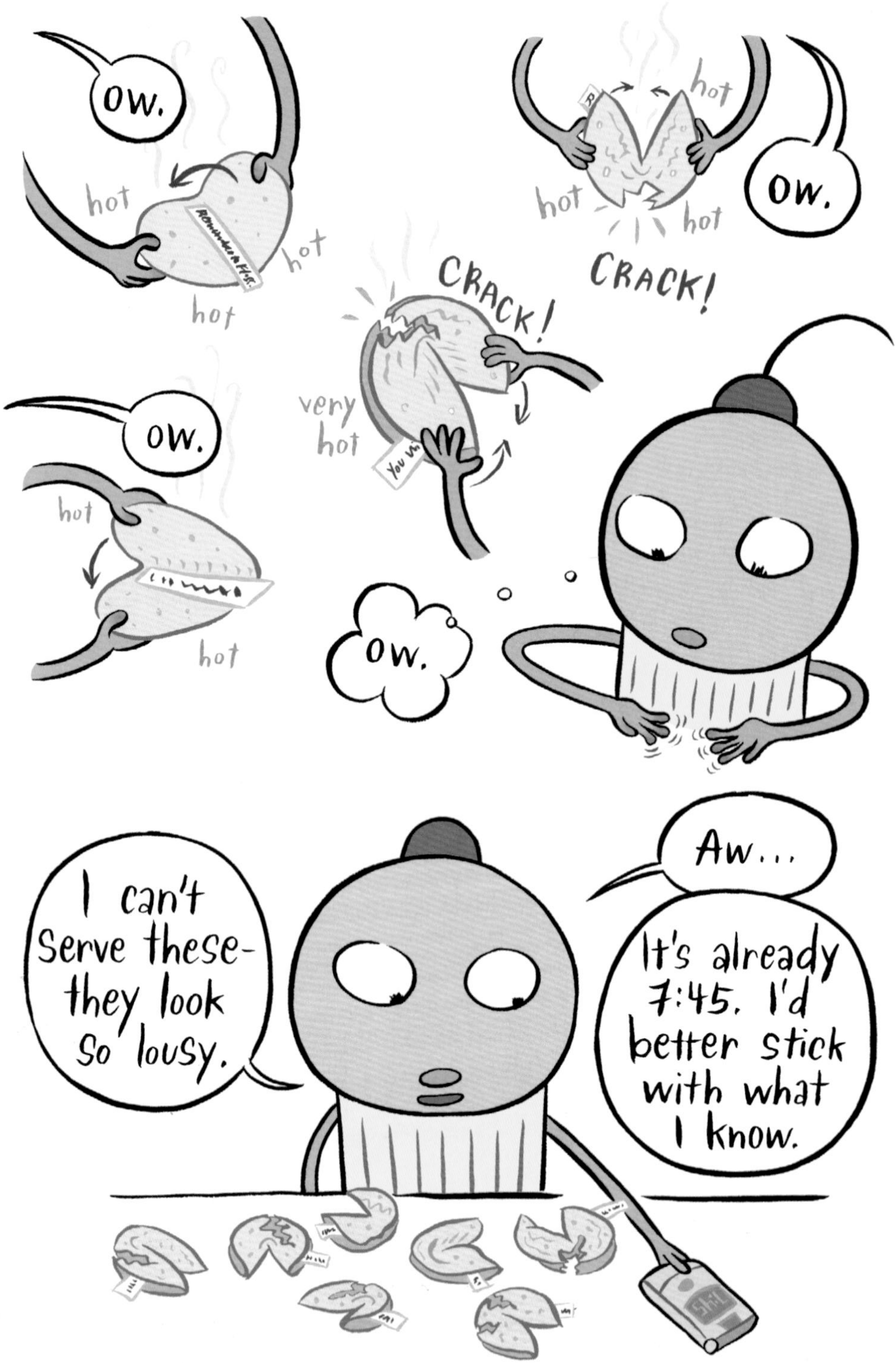
OW.
hot
hot
hot
hot
hot
OW.
CRACK!
CRACK!
very hot
OW.
hot
hot
OW.
I can't serve these- they look so lousy.
Aw...
It's already 7:45. I'd better stick with what I know.

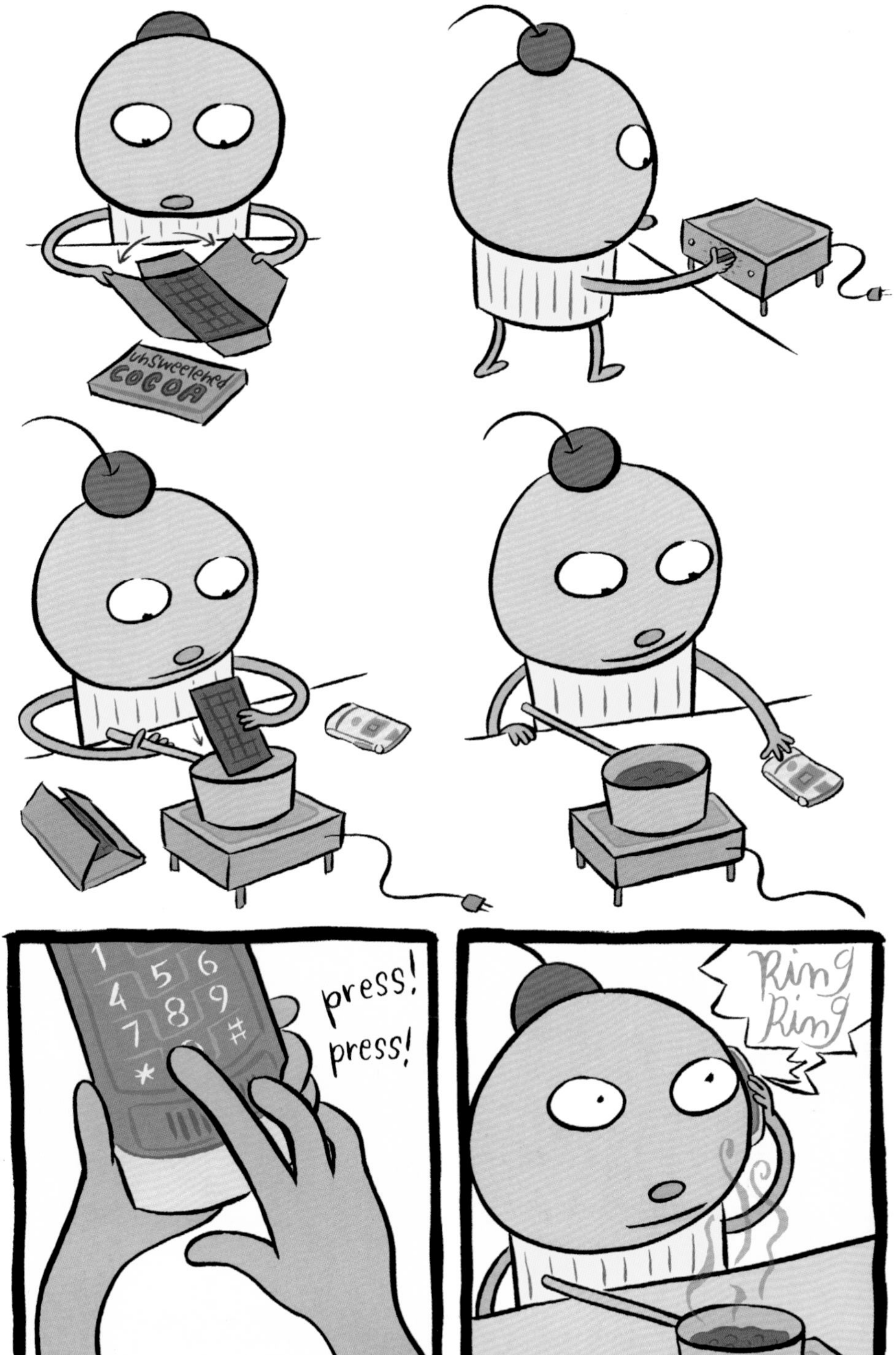
unsweetened
COCOA
press!
press!
Ring
Ring

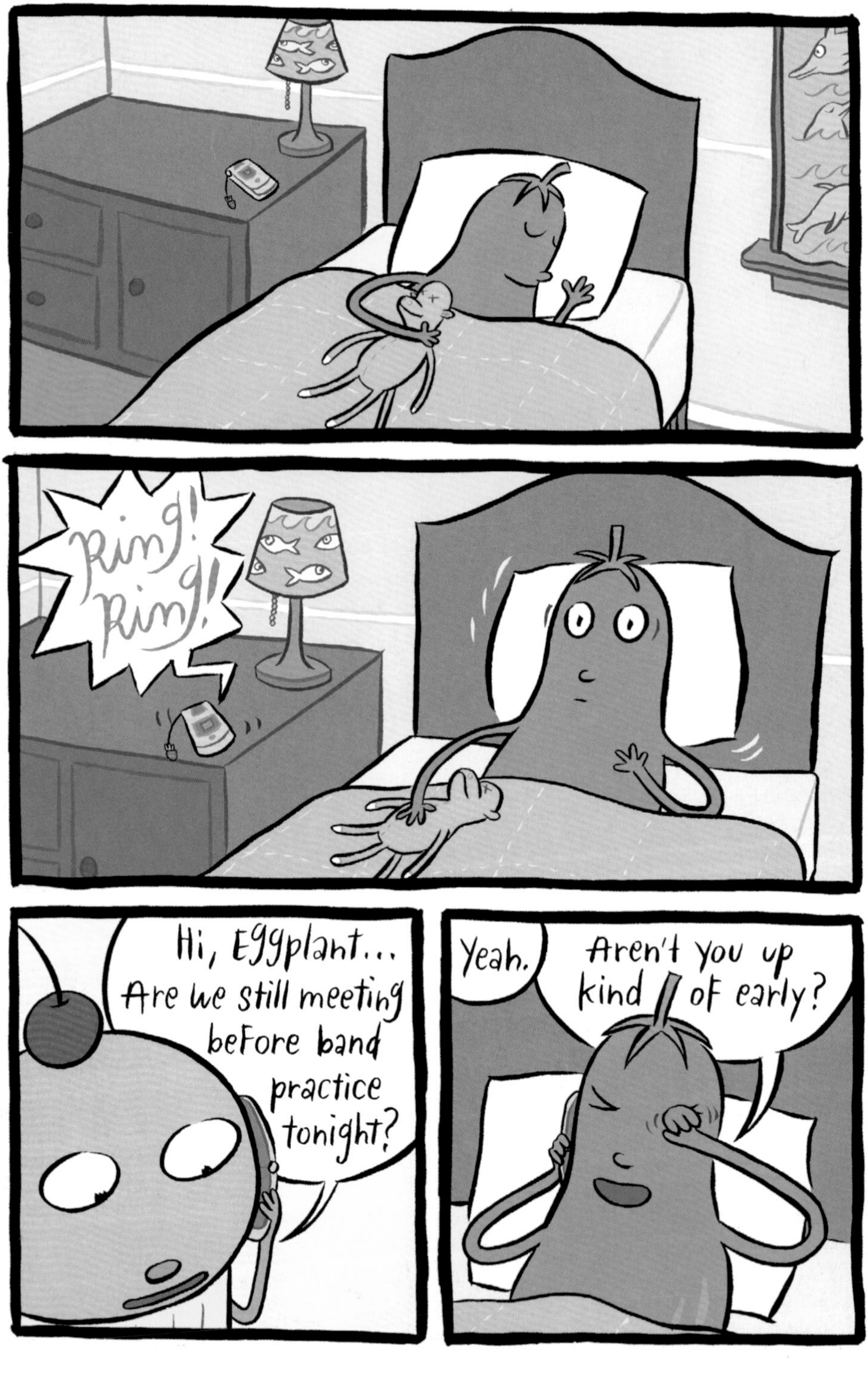
Ring! Ring!
Hi, Eggplant... Are we still meeting before band practice tonight?
Yeah.
Aren't you up kind of early?

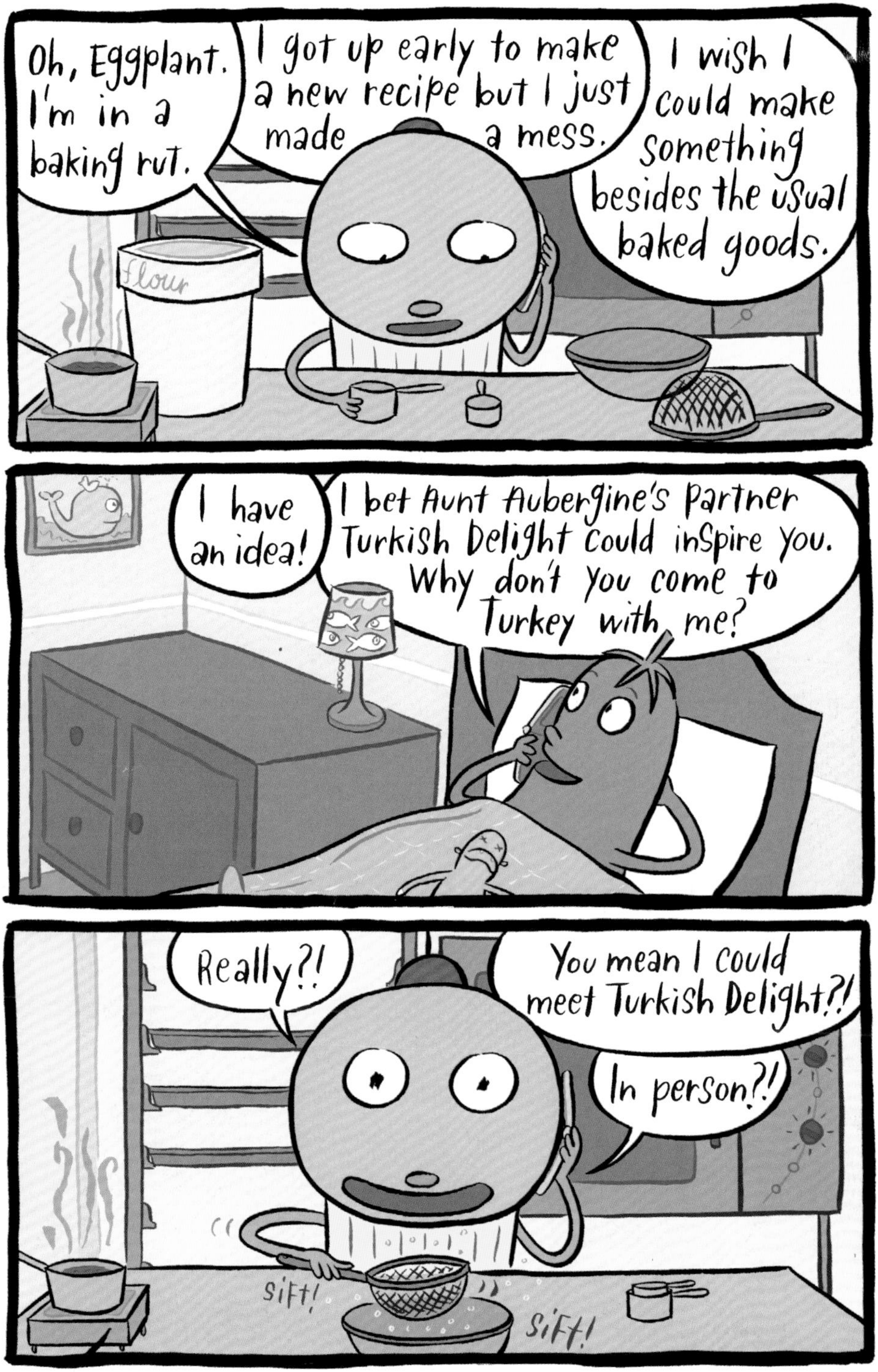
Oh, Eggplant. I'm in a baking rut.
I got up early to make a new recipe but I just made a mess.
I wish I could make something besides the usual baked goods.
Flour
I have an idea!
I bet Aunt Aubergine's Partner Turkish Delight could inspire you. Why don't you come to Turkey with me?
Really?!
You mean I could meet Turkish Delight?!
In person?!
SIFT!
SIFT!

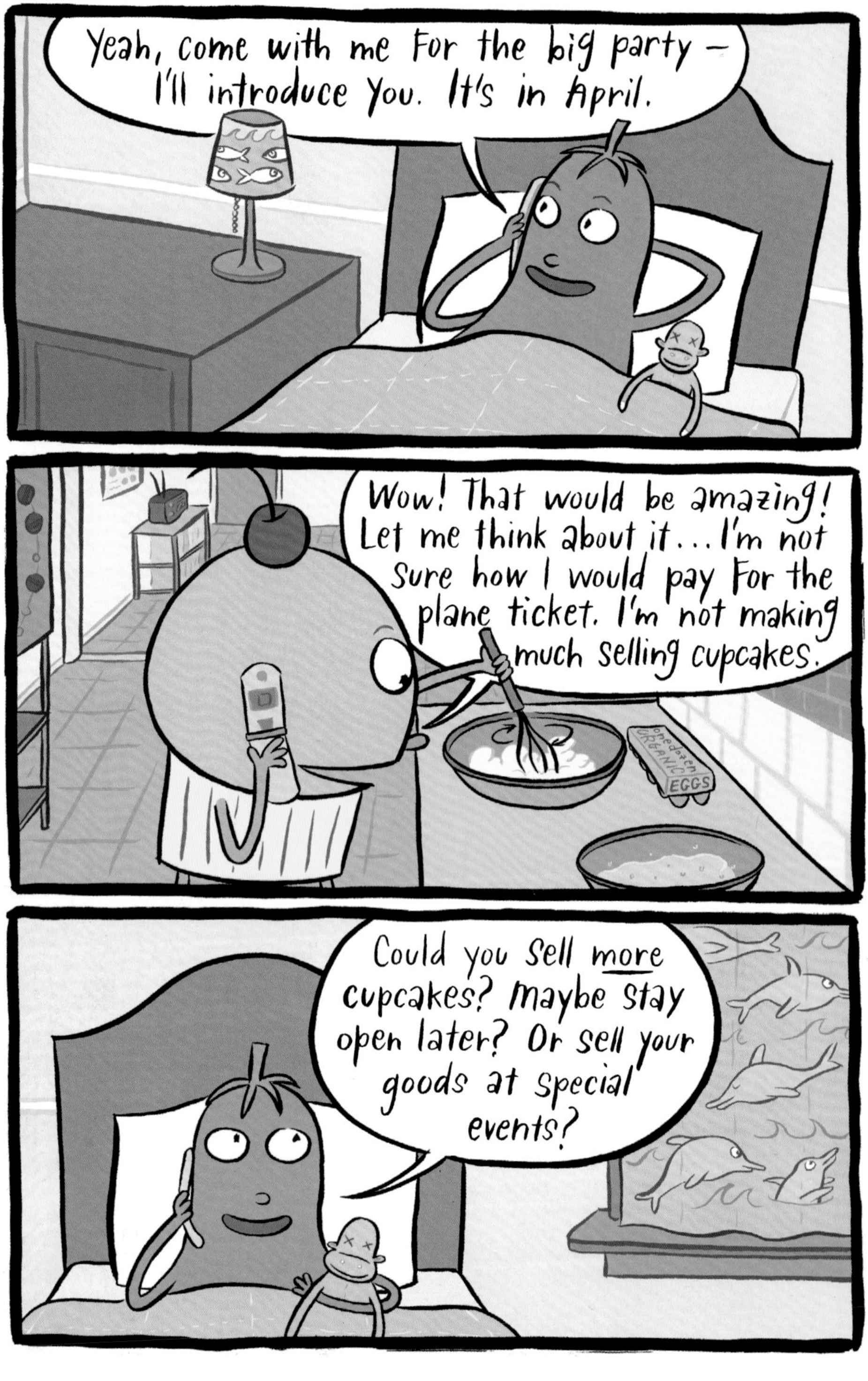
Yeah, come with me for the big party – I'll introduce you. It's in April.
Wow! That would be amazing! Let me think about it... I'm not sure how I would pay for the plane ticket. I'm not making much selling cupcakes.
EGGS
Could you sell more cupcakes? Maybe stay open later? Or sell your goods at special events?

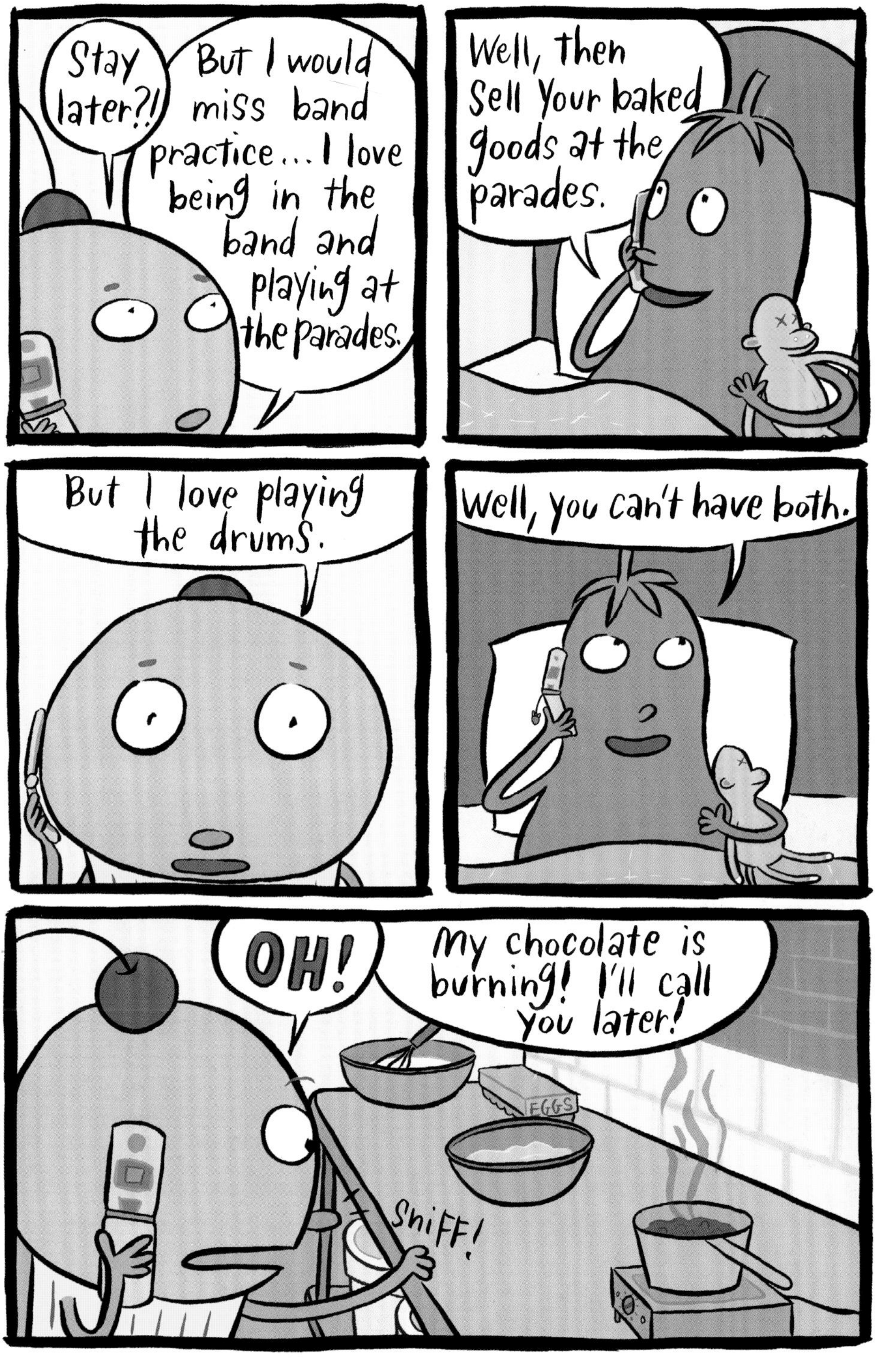
Stay later?!
But I would miss band practice... I love being in the band and playing at the parades.
Well, then sell your baked goods at the parades.
But I love playing the drums.
Well, you can't have both.
OH!
My chocolate is burning! I'll call you later!
EGGS
SNIFF!

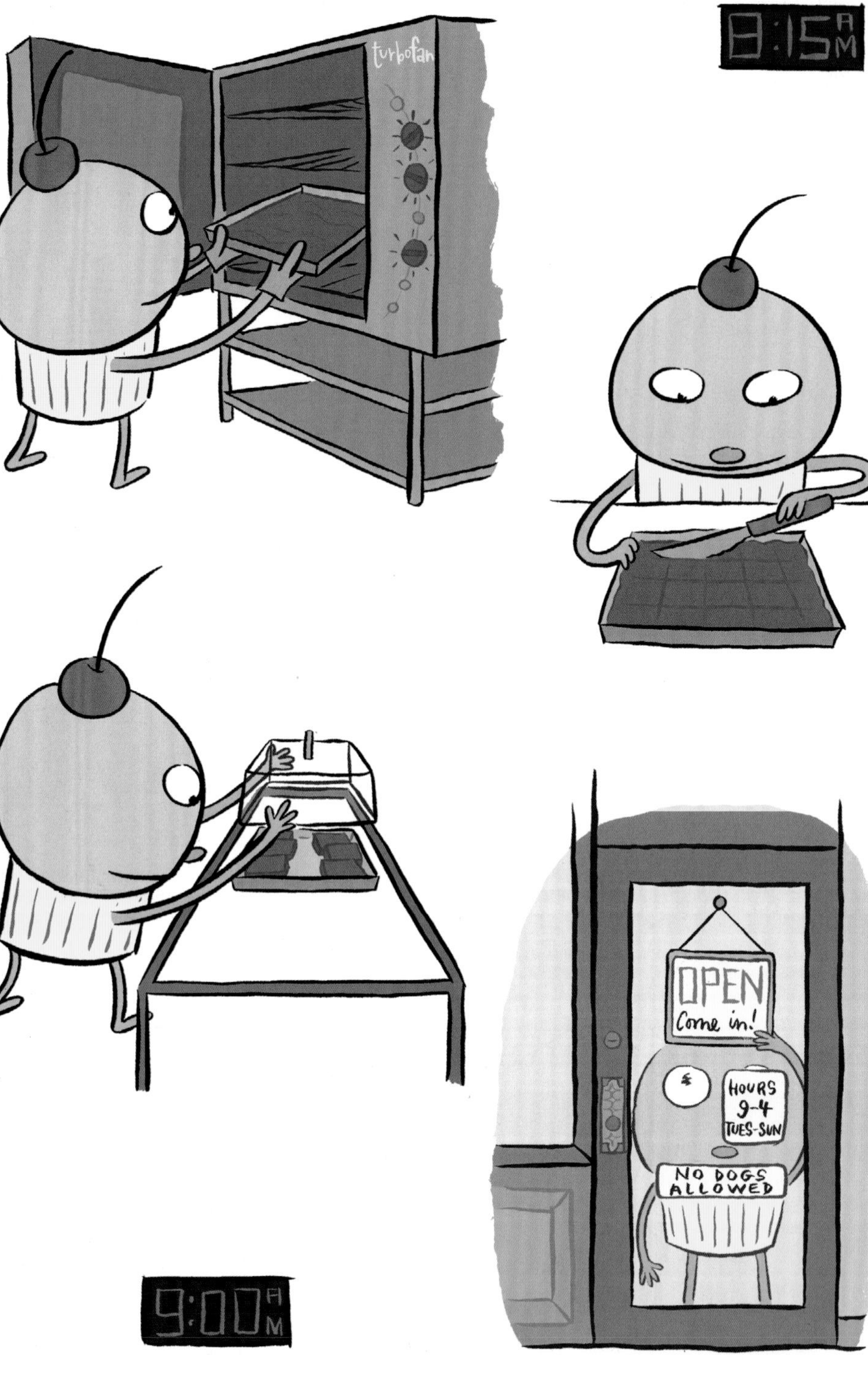
8:15 AM
turbofan
9:00 AM
OPEN
Come in!
HOURS
9-4
TUES-SUN
NO DOGS
ALLOWED

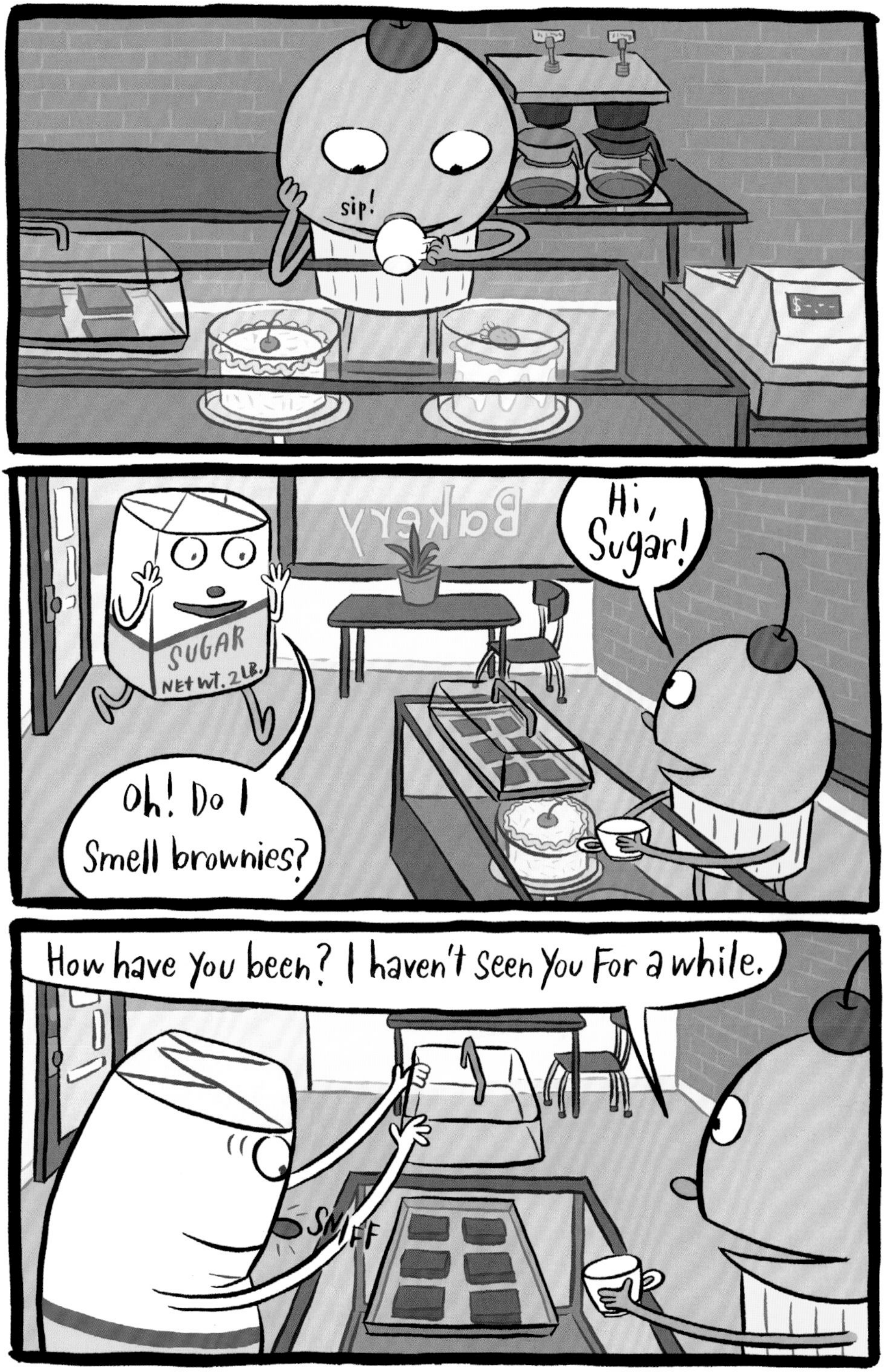
sip!
Bakery
SUGAR
NET WT. 2 LB.
Hi, Sugar!
Oh! Do I smell brownies?
How have you been? I haven't seen you for a while.
SNIFF

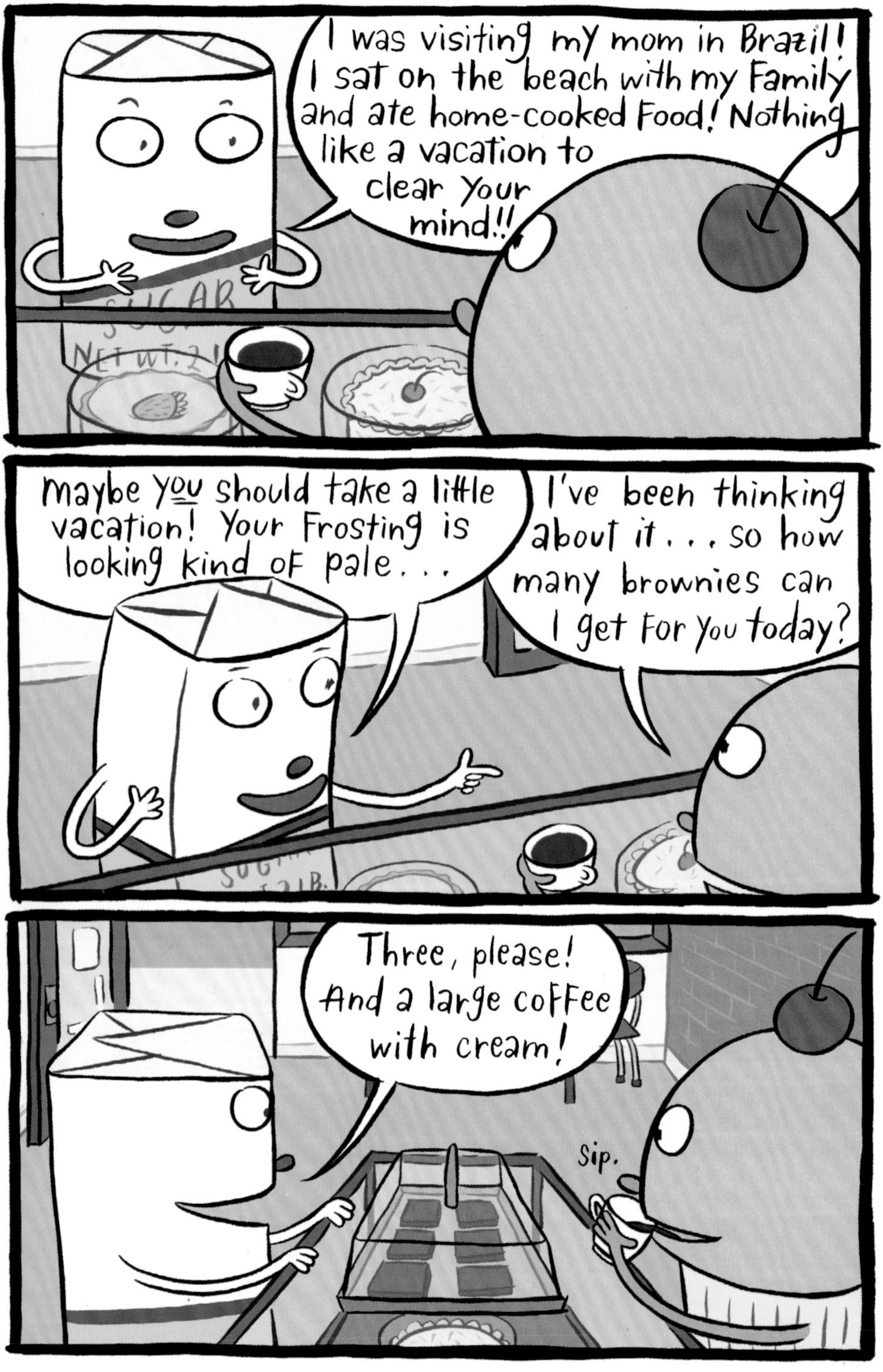
I was visiting my mom in Brazil! I sat on the beach with my Family and ate home-cooked Food! Nothing like a vacation to clear your mind!!
Maybe you should take a little vacation! Your Frosting is looking kind of pale...
I've been thinking about it... so how many brownies can I get For you today?
Three, please! And a large coFFee with cream!
Sip.

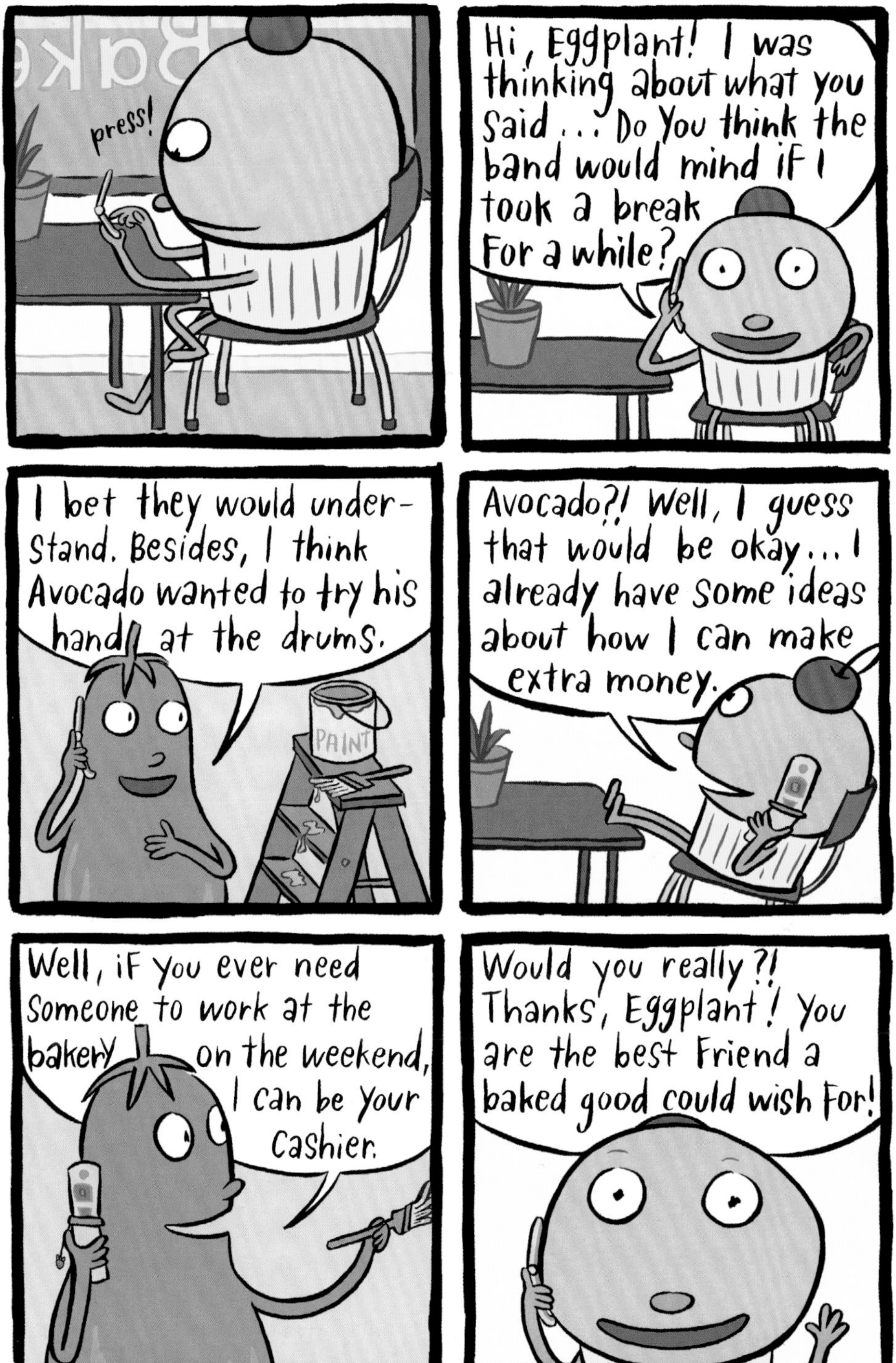
press!
Hi, Eggplant! I was thinking about what you said... Do you think the band would mind if I took a break for a while?
I bet they would understand. Besides, I think Avocado wanted to try his hand at the drums.
PAINT
Avocado?! Well, I guess that would be okay... I already have some ideas about how I can make extra money.
Well, if you ever need someone to work at the bakery on the weekend, I can be your cashier.
Would you really?! Thanks, Eggplant! You are the best friend a baked good could wish for!

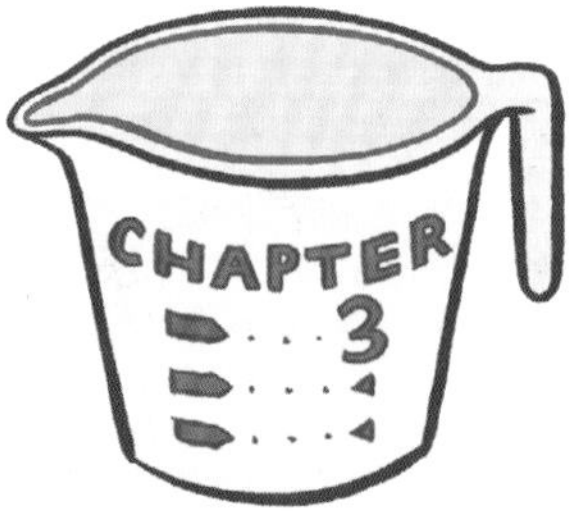
CHAPTER
3

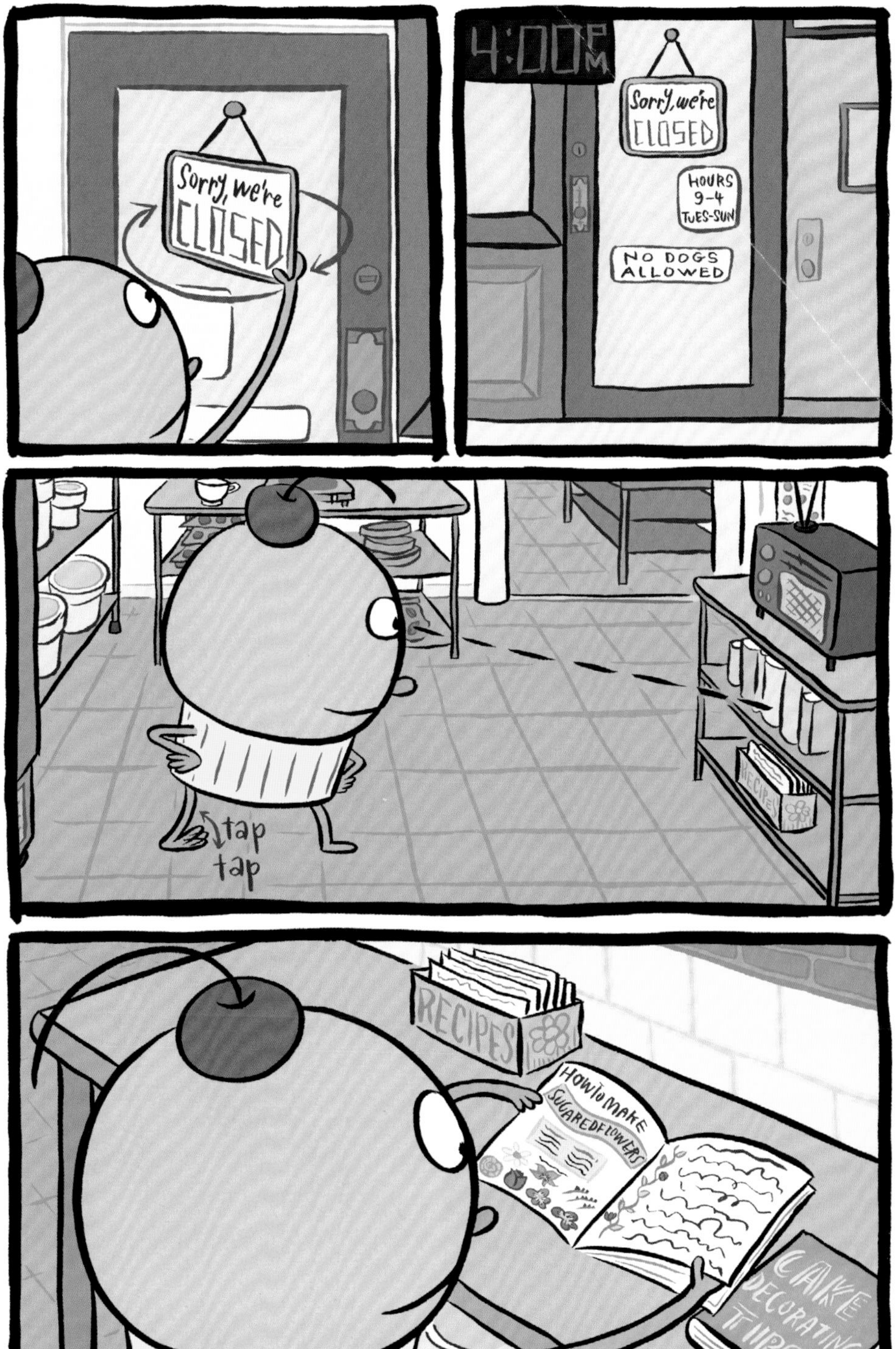
Sorry, we're CLOSED
4:00 PM
Sorry, we're CLOSED
HOURS 9-4 TUES-SUN
NO DOGS ALLOWED
RECIPES
tap tap
RECIPES
HOW TO MAKE SUGARED FLOWERS
CAKE DECORATING TIPS

HOW TO MAKE SUGARED FLOWERS

ingredients

1. One dozen freshly cut, pesticide-free, edible flowers
2. 4 teaspoons meringue powder
3. One cup superfine sugar
4. water

You will also need:

scissors, tweezers, small bowl, container for mixing meringue powder, wax paper, watercolor paint-brush, and a tray or cookie sheet for drying your flowers

Some common edible flowers:
(NOTE: Be sure they are pesticide-free)

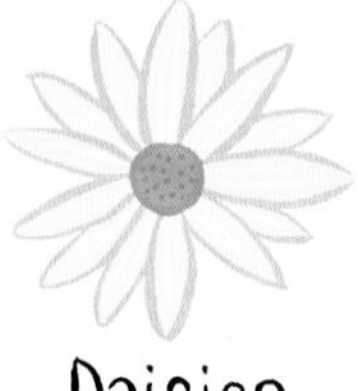

Daisies

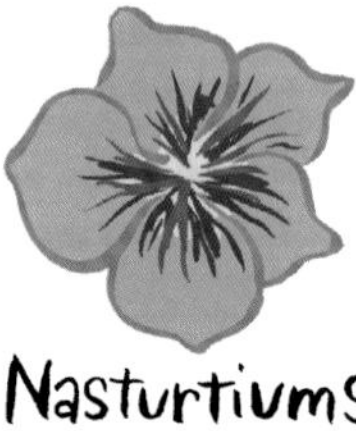

Nasturtiums

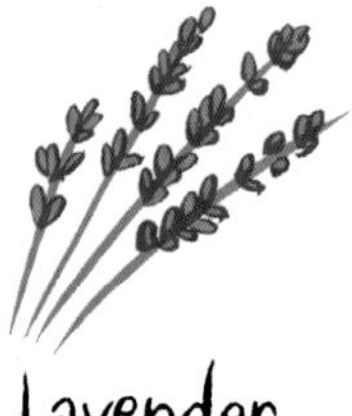

Lavender

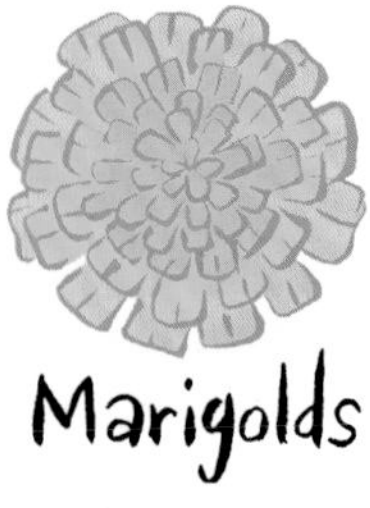

Marigolds

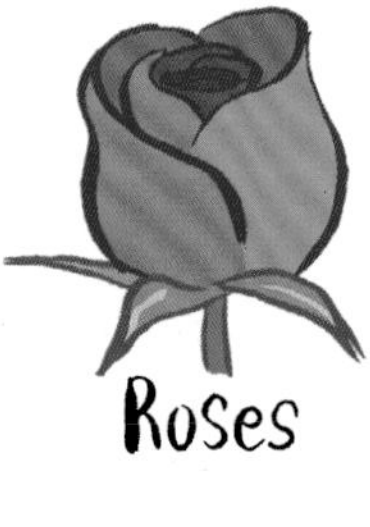

Roses

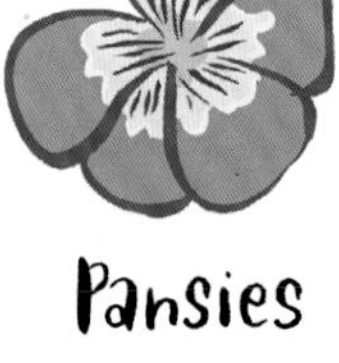

Pansies

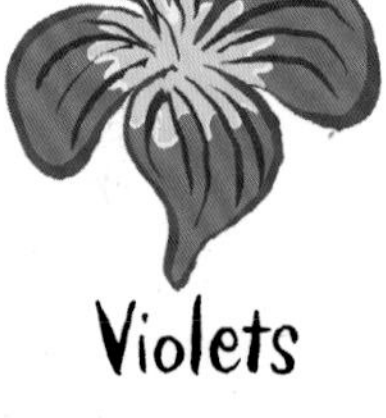

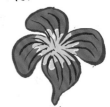

Violets

1. Pull petals from flowers. The white bases of the petals (especially on roses) may be bitter, so trim them off.

2. Rinse flowers to remove dirt and check for insects. To rinse, fill small bowl with lightly salted cool water and dip each petal. Afterwards, quickly dip petals in very cold water to perk them up. Air dry on paper towel. Petals must be completely dry before proceeding.

3. In a small bowl, dissolve 4 teaspoons of meringue powder in 4 tablespoons of water.

4. Hold flower petals with tweezers. Apply thin, even layer of meringue mixture with paint brush. Any places not coated will turn brown.

5. With tweezers, hold petal over bowl and sprinkle with superfine sugar. Tap the tweezers to remove excess sugar, and repeat on other side.

6. Place on superfine sugar-coated wax paper to dry. Let dry in a cool place for 2-4 hours, longer if humidity is high.

7. When dry, pick up petals with tweezers and set into frosting. Sugared flowers can be made in advance and stored in an airtight container (for up to a year) in a cool dry place.

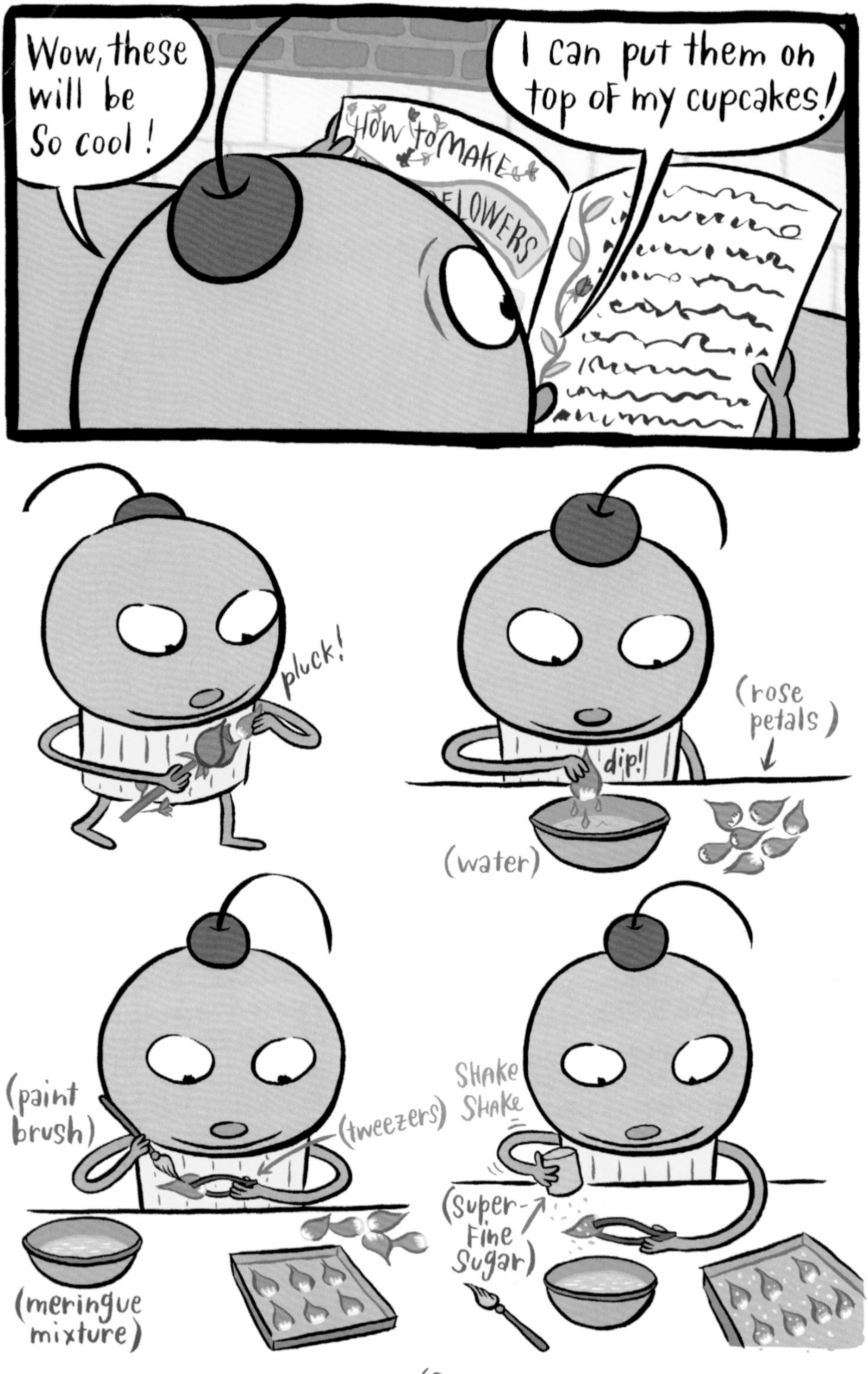

Wow, these will be So cool!
I can put them on top of my cupcakes!
HOW TO MAKE ...FLOWERS
pluck!
dip!
(rose petals)
(water)
(paint brush)
(tweezers)
(meringue mixture)
SHAKE SHAKE
(super-fine sugar)

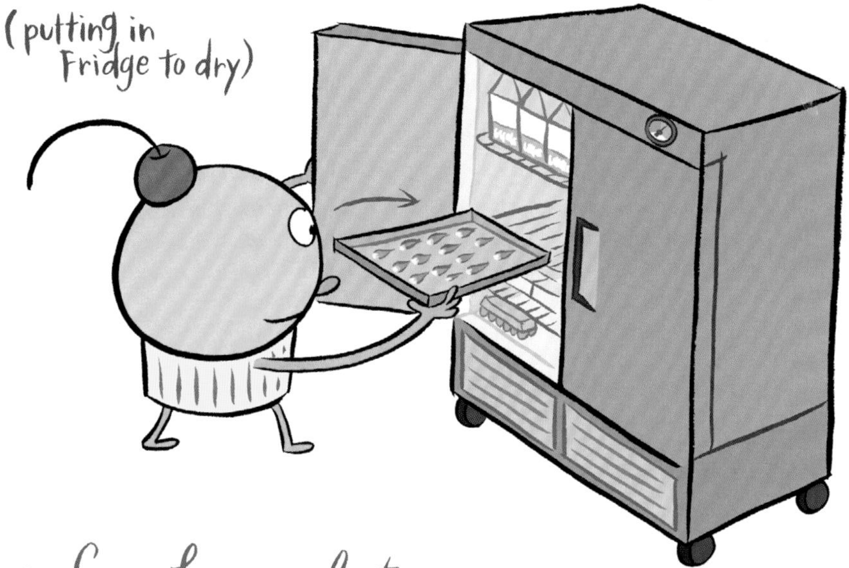
(putting in Fridge to dry)

a few hours later:

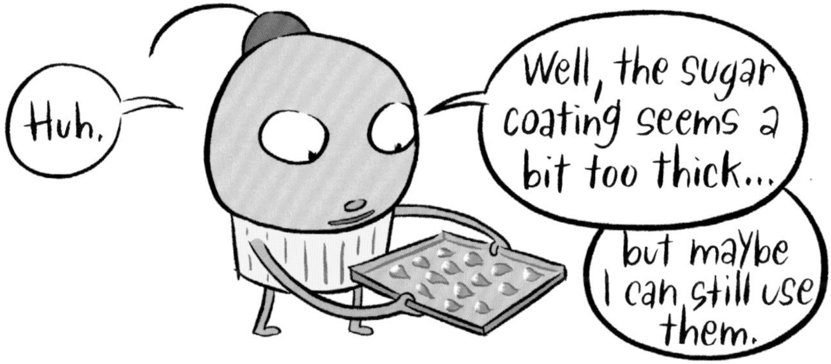
Huh.
Well, the sugar coating seems a bit too thick...
but maybe I can still use them.

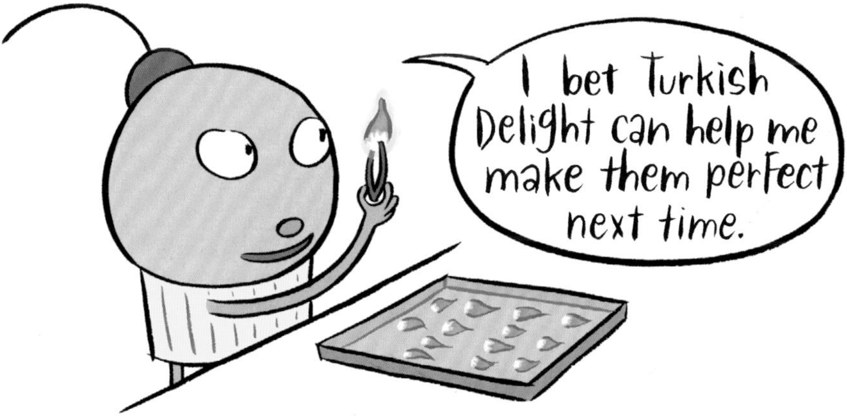
I bet Turkish Delight can help me make them perfect next time.

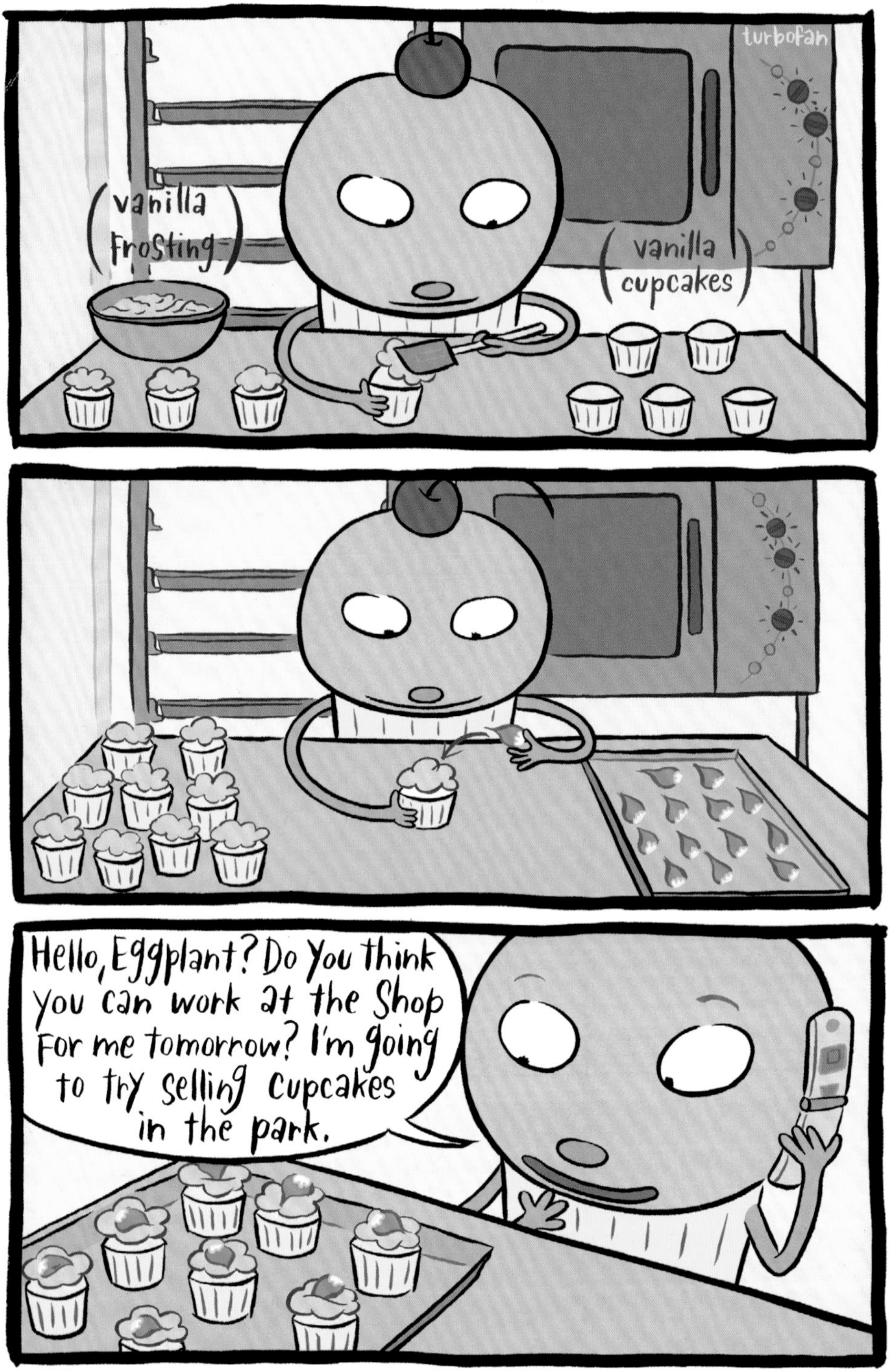
turbofan
vanilla frosting
vanilla cupcakes
Hello, Eggplant? Do you think you can work at the shop for me tomorrow? I'm going to try selling cupcakes in the park.

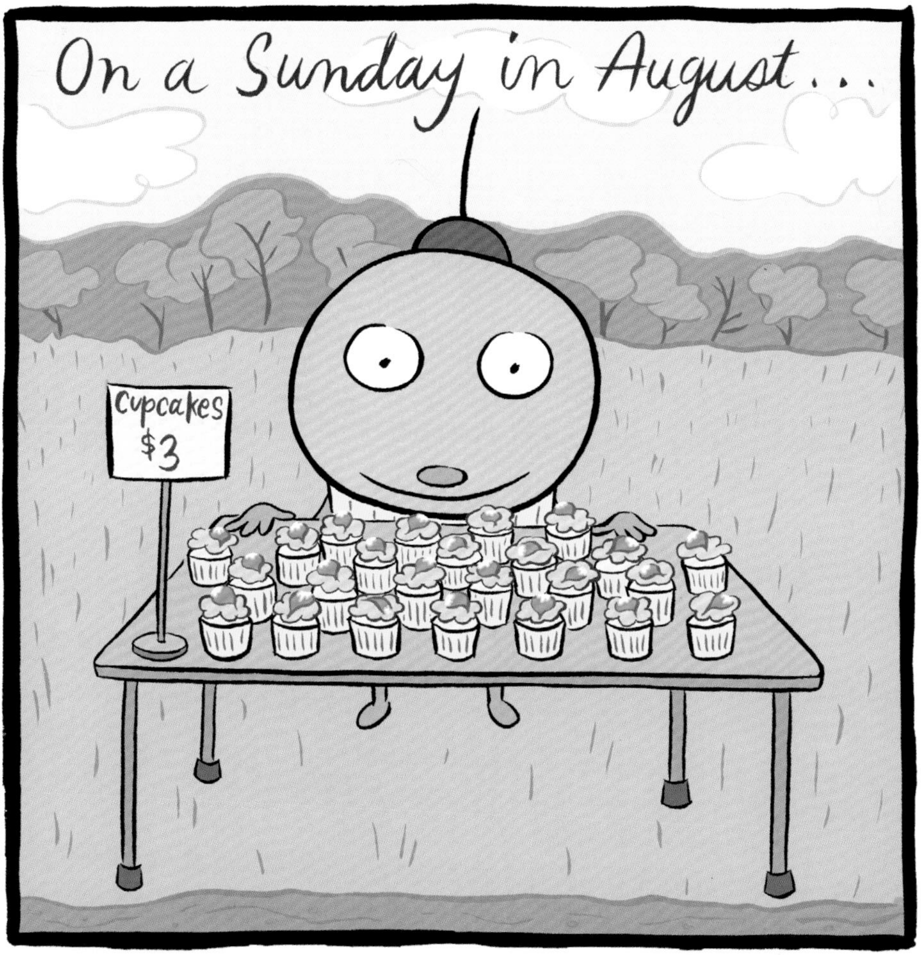
On a Sunday in August...
Cupcakes
$3

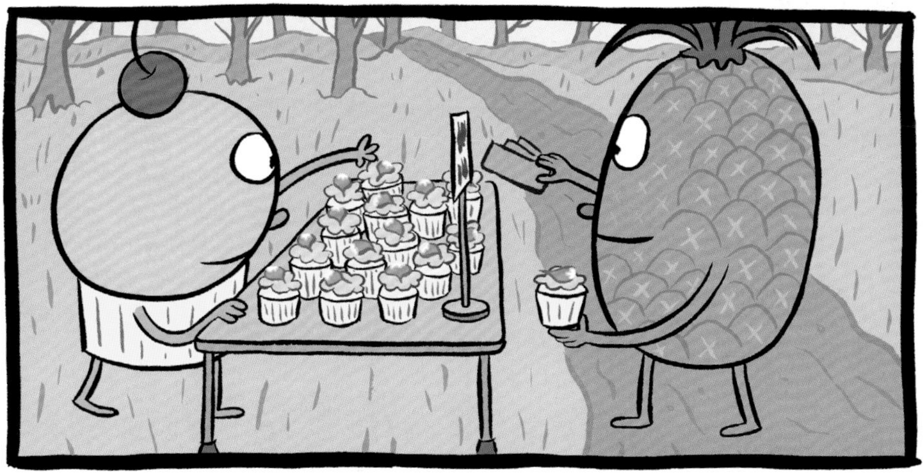

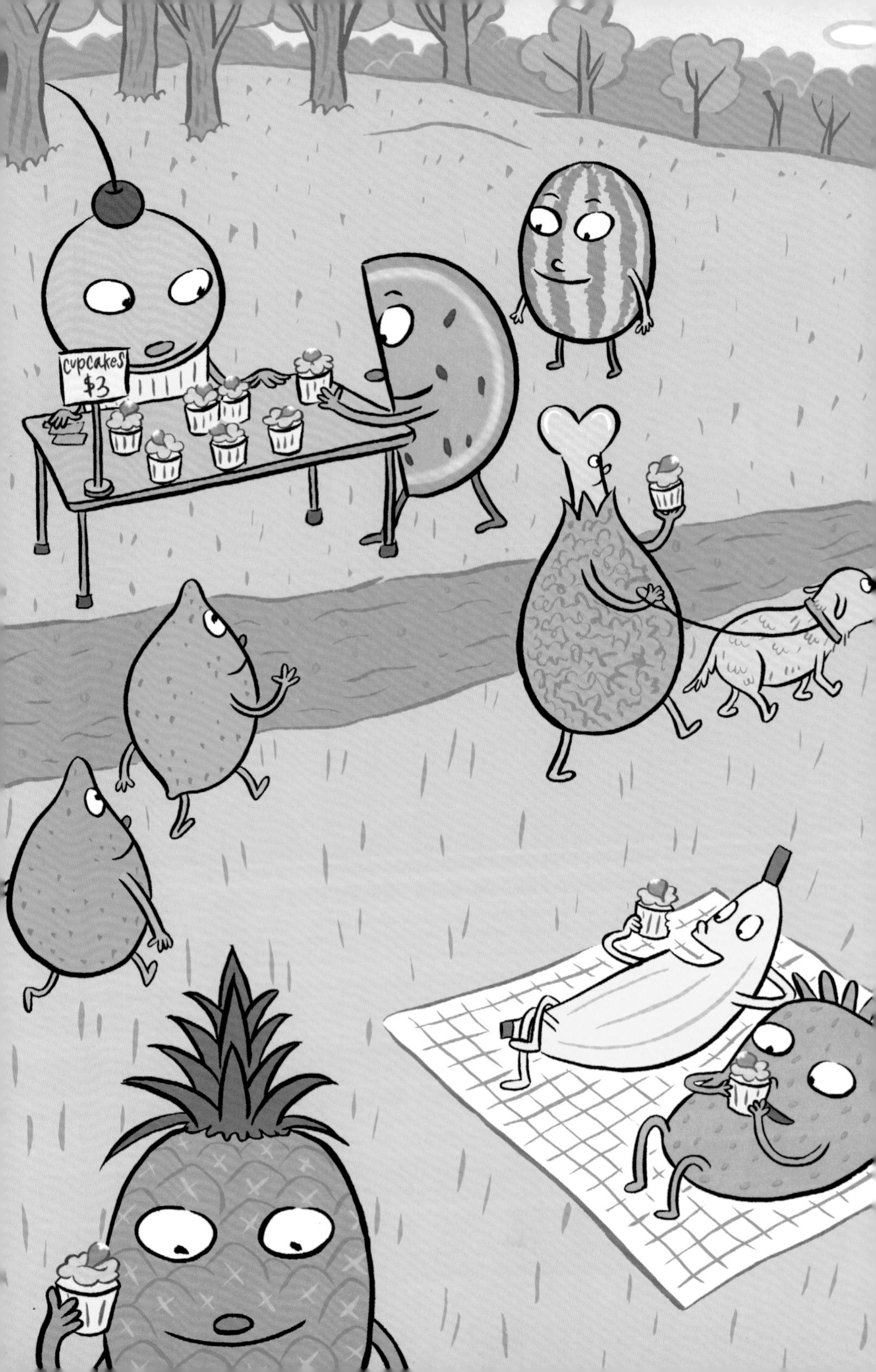
Cupcakes
$3

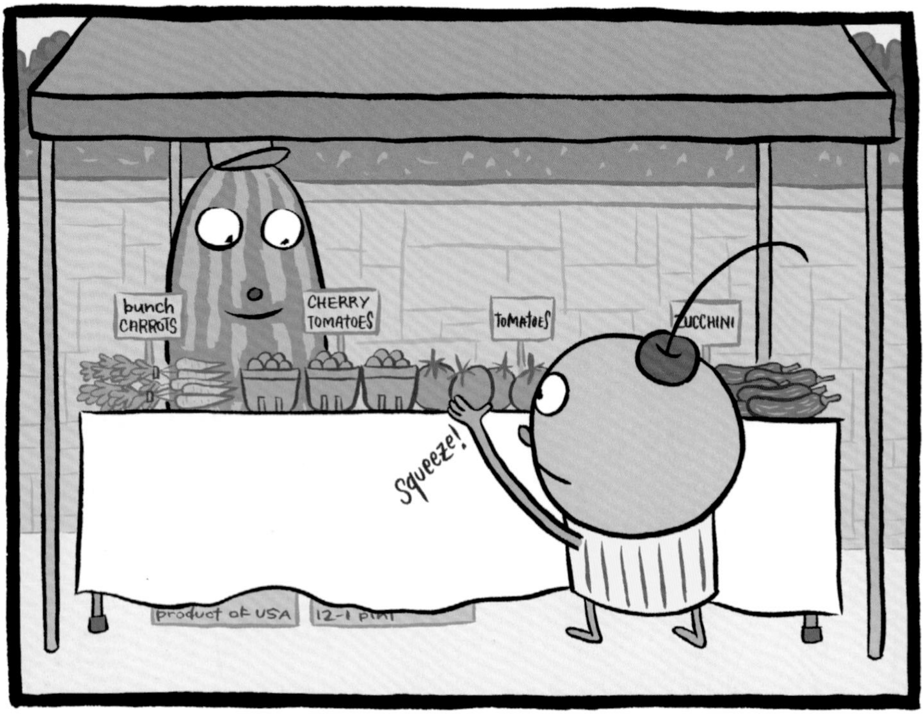
bunch CARROTS
CHERRY TOMATOES
TOMATOES
ZUCCHINI
Squeeze!
product of USA
12-1 pint

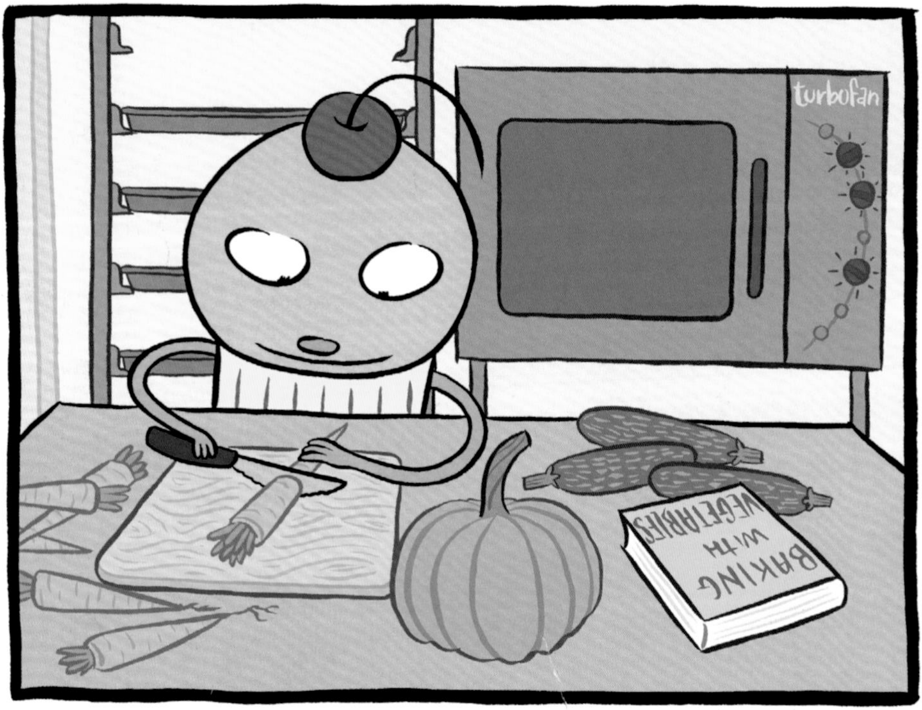
turbofan
BAKING with VEGETABLES

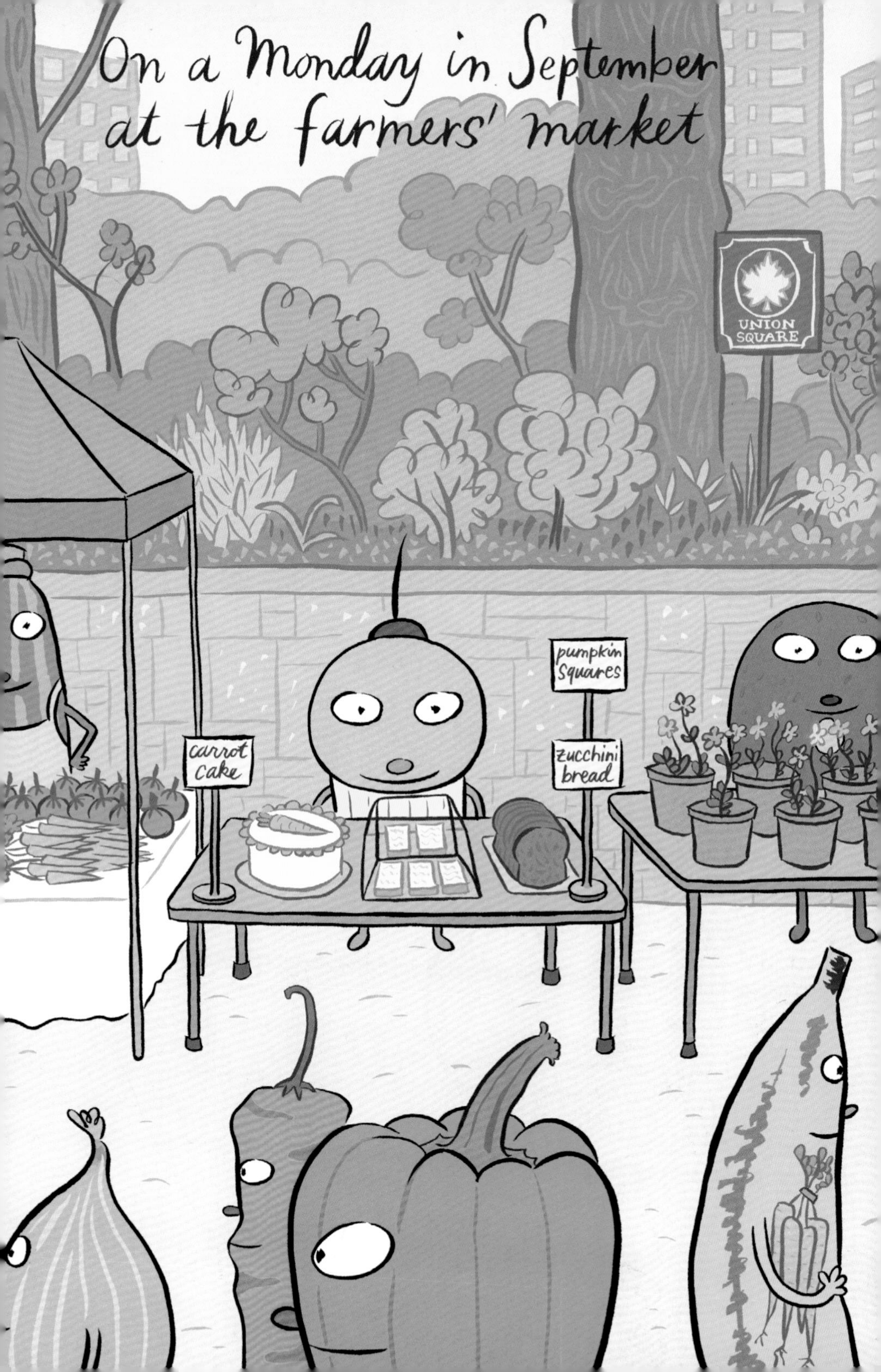

On a Monday in September at the farmers' market
UNION SQUARE
carrot cake
pumpkin squares
zucchini bread

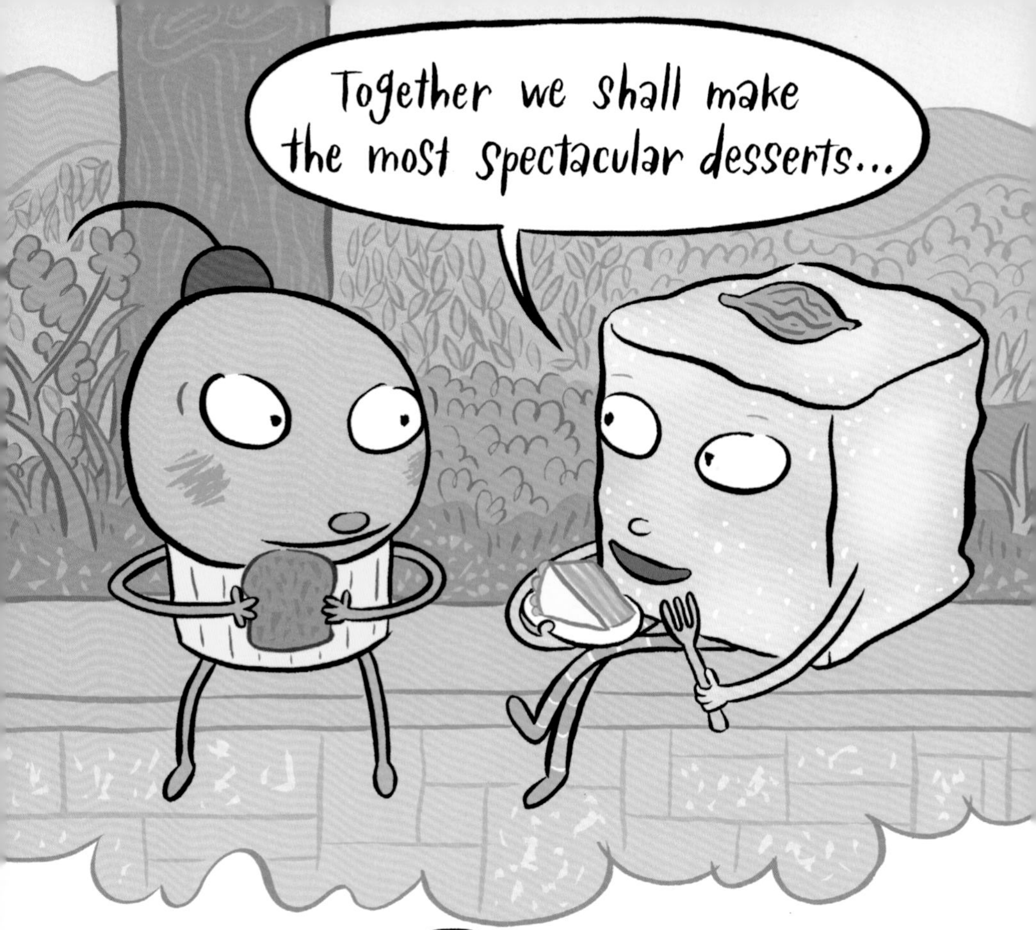
Together we shall make the most spectacular desserts...

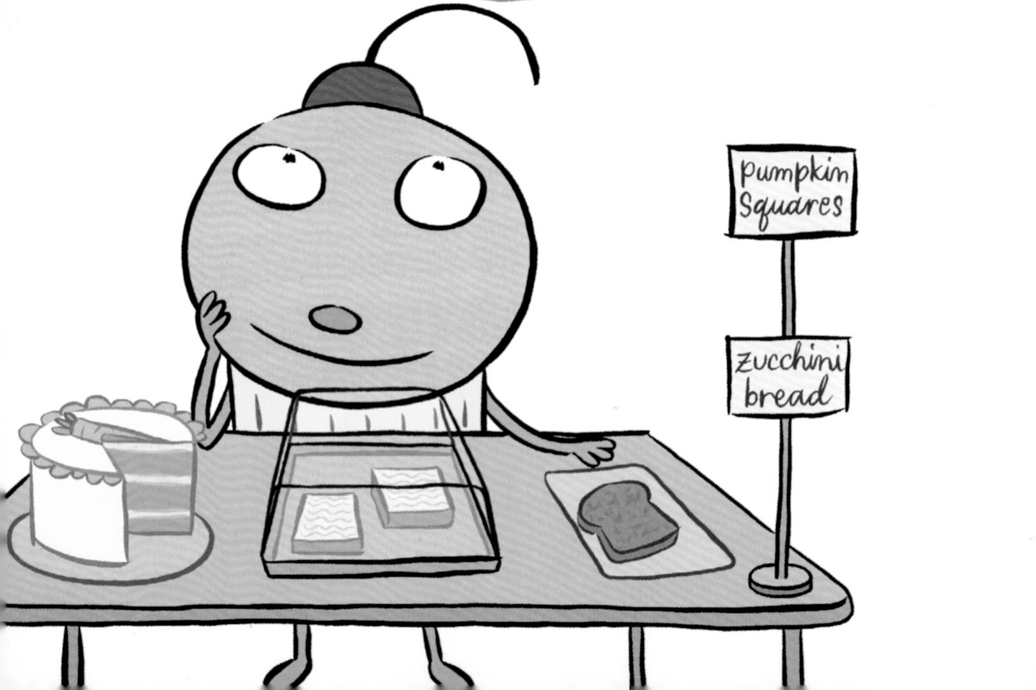
pumpkin Squares
zucchini bread

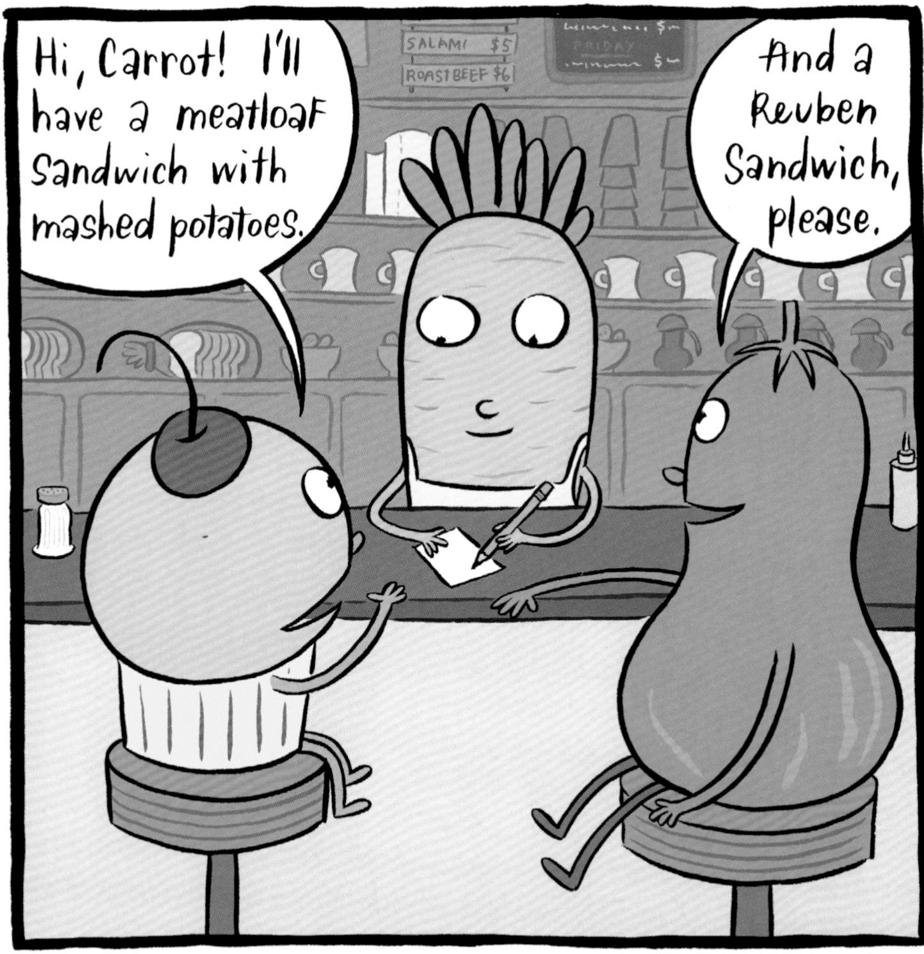
SALAMI $5
ROASTBEEF $6
FRIDAY
Hi, Carrot! I'll have a meatloaf sandwich with mashed potatoes.
And a Reuben Sandwich, please.

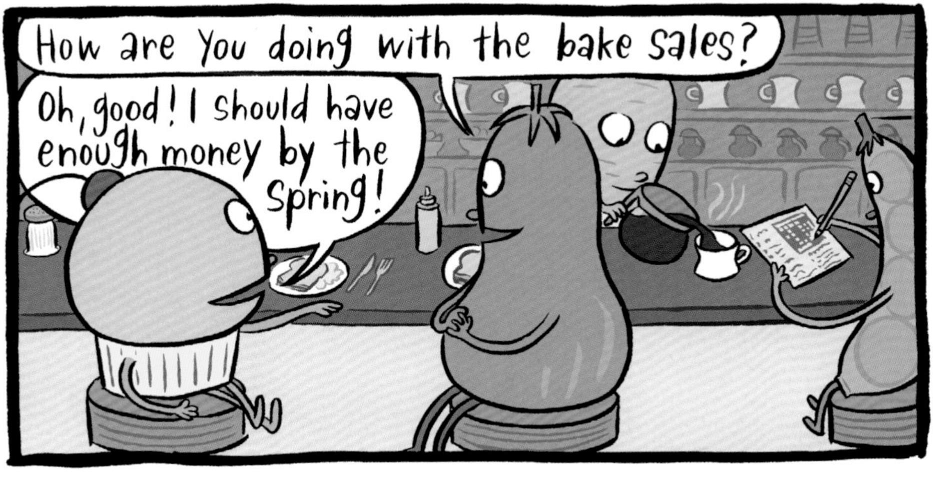
How are you doing with the bake sales?
Oh, good! I should have enough money by the spring!

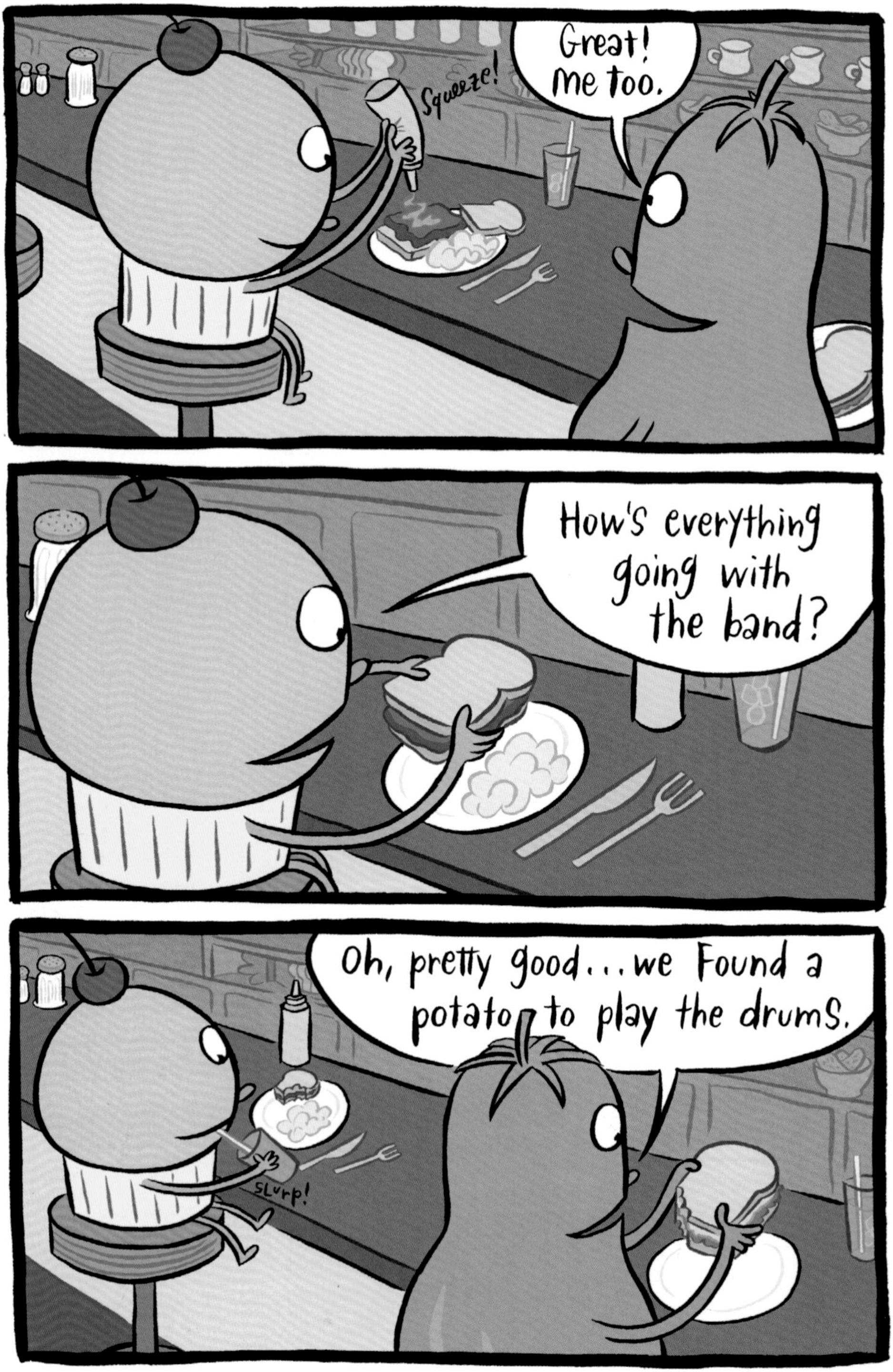
Squeeze!
Great! Me too.
How's everything going with the band?
Oh, pretty good...we Found a potato to play the drums.
SLurp!

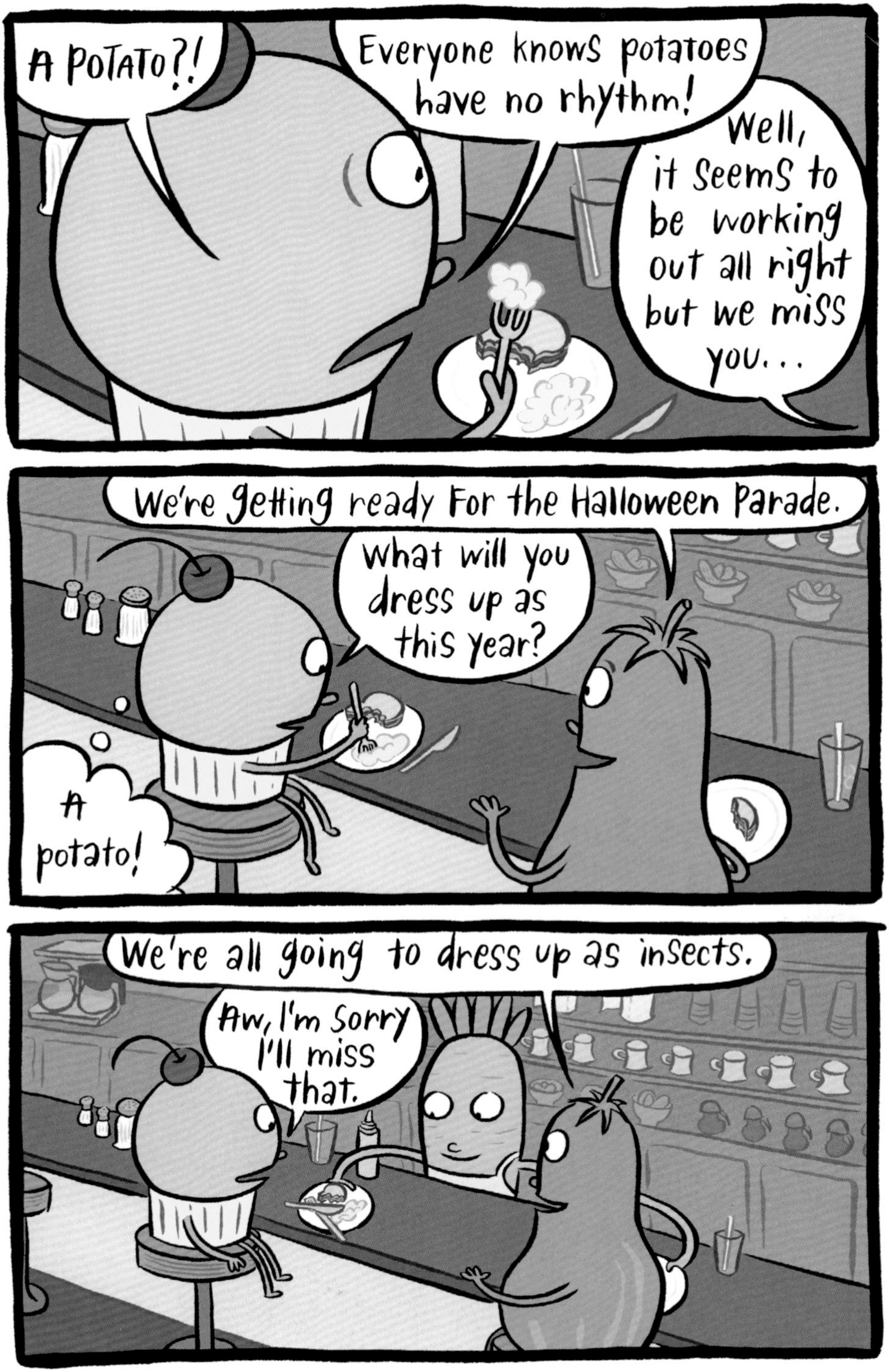
A POTATO?!
Everyone knows potatoes have no rhythm!
Well, it seems to be working out all right but we miss you...
We're getting ready for the Halloween Parade.
What will you dress up as this year?
A potato!
We're all going to dress up as insects.
Aw, I'm sorry I'll miss that.

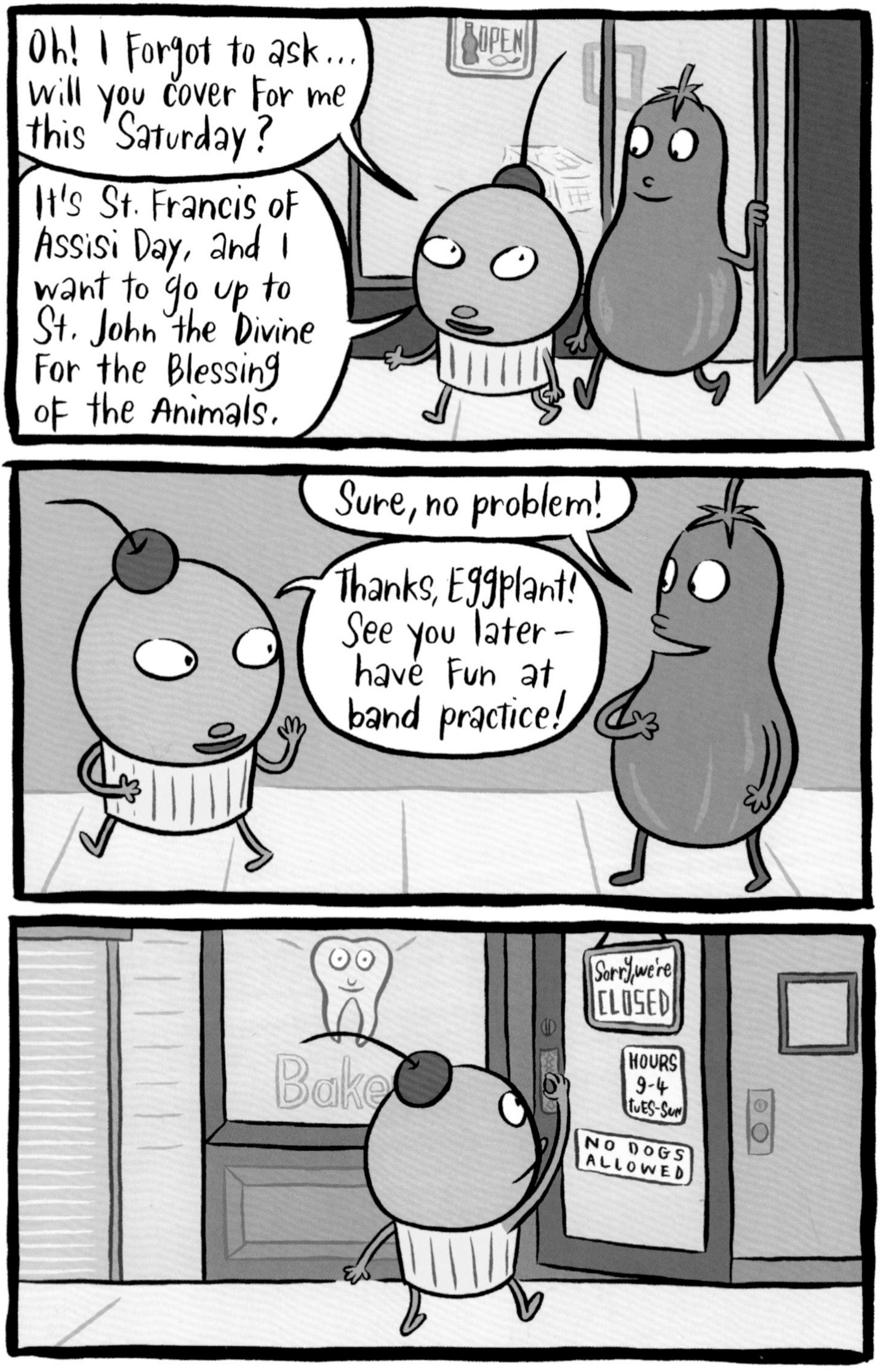
Oh! I forgot to ask... will you cover for me this Saturday?
It's St. Francis of Assisi Day, and I want to go up to St. John the Divine for the Blessing of the Animals.
OPEN
Sure, no problem!
Thanks, Eggplant! See you later— have fun at band practice!
Sorry, we're CLOSED
HOURS 9-4 TUES-SUN
NO DOGS ALLOWED
Bake

6:00 PM

How to Make marzipan
Yield: 2 lbs.

INGREDIENTS:
1 pound almond paste
1 pound confectioners sugar

1. Cut up almond paste and mix on low speed for 30
2. Add half the sugar and continue mixing while slowly pouring in corn syrup and vanilla. Mix until dough sticks together. ...the remaining sugar counter...

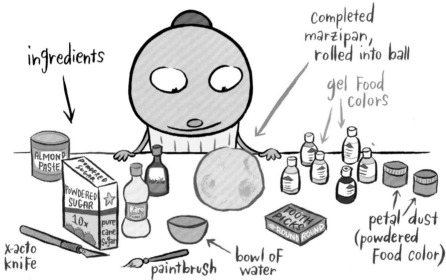

ingredients

completed marzipan, rolled into ball

gel Food colors

ALMOND PASTE

POWDERED SUGAR 10x pure cane sugar

vanilla

Karo LIGHT

TOOTH PICKS ROUND ROUND

petal dust (powdered Food color)

x-acto knife

paintbrush

bowl of water

(kneading gel Food color into smaller blobs of marzipan:)

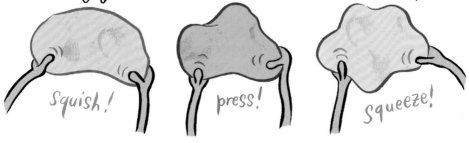

Squish!

press!

squeeze!

Roll marzipan into small spheres and hemispheres.

Brush with water where shapes will attach.

Attach head to body.

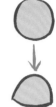

Roll out flat pieces of marzipan and cut shapes for ears and noses.

Brush with water where shapes will attach.

Attach shapes to head.

push!

Roll out flat pieces of marzipan and cut long rectangle for collar.

Brush with water on one side.

Attach around neck.

Paint on eyes with white gel food color and then use toothpick dipped in black gel color to make pupils.

Use toothpick dipped in red gel color (or color of your choice) to make freckles.

poke!

marzipan dog!

Use brush or toothpick and black gel food color to paint mouth.

Use brush and pink or red petal dust to put blush on cheeks...

marzipan cat!

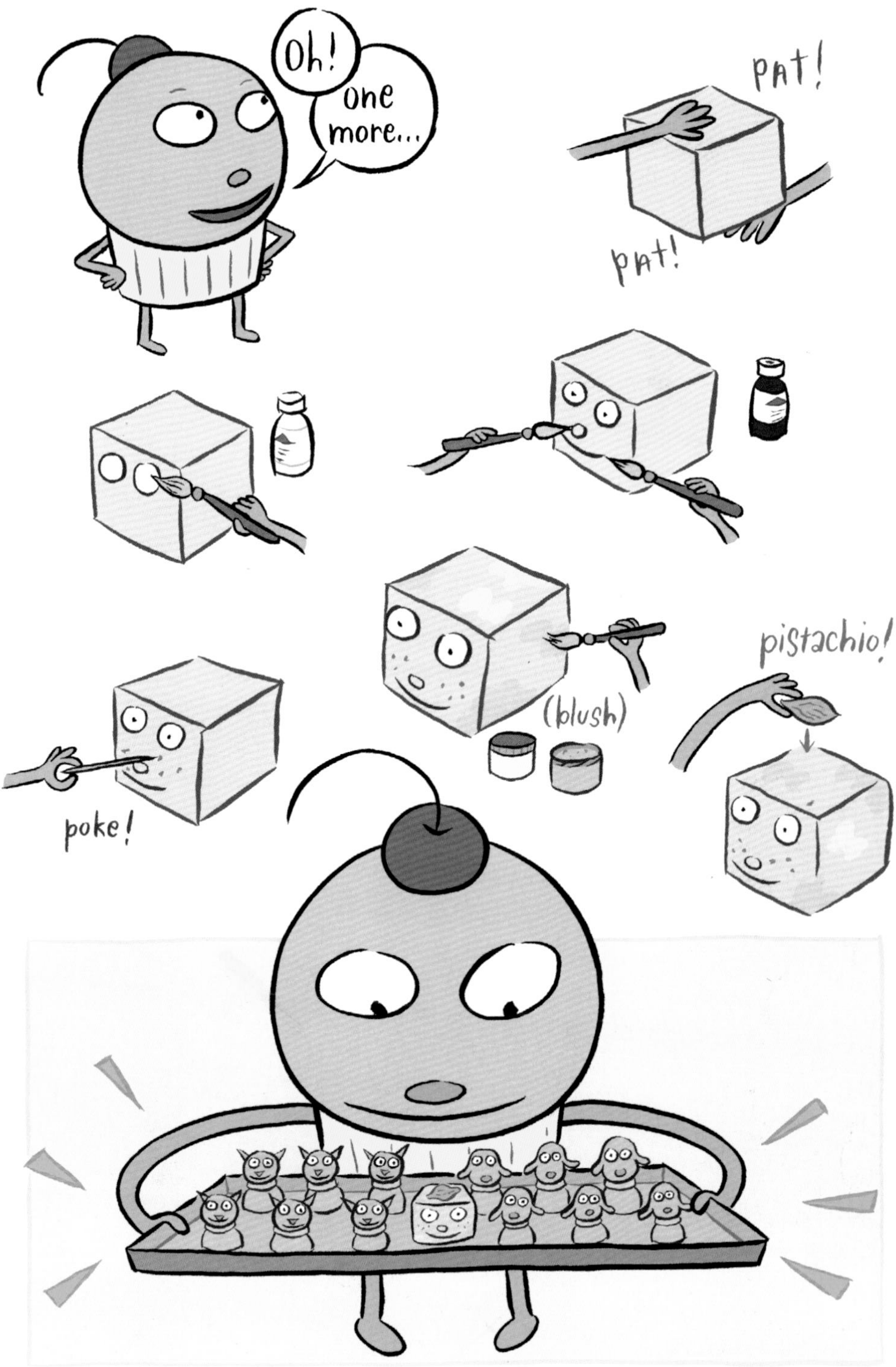
Oh!
One more...
PAT!
PAT!
pistachio!
(blush)
poke!

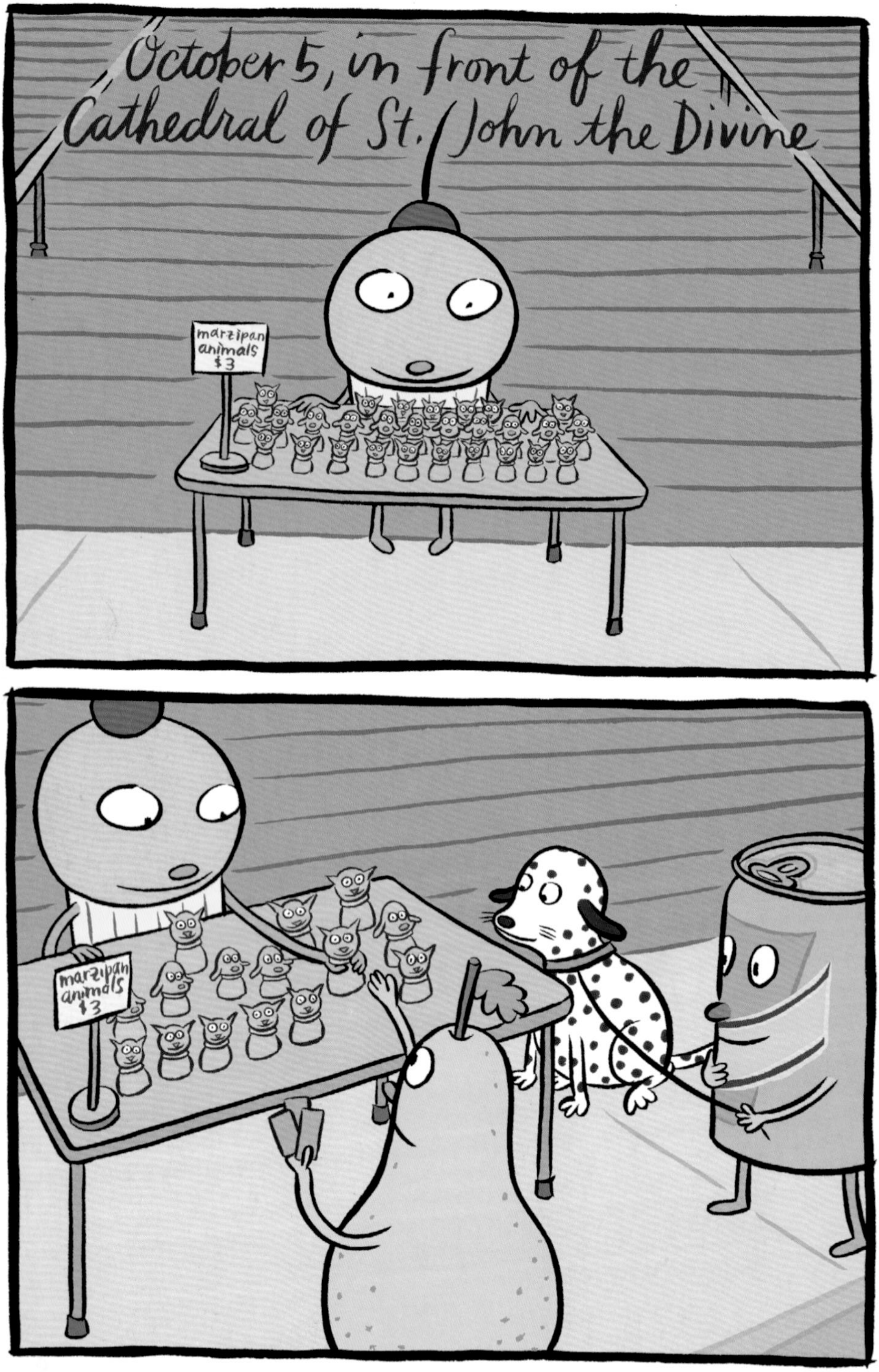
October 5, in front of the Cathedral of St. John the Divine
marzipan animals $3
marzipan animals $3

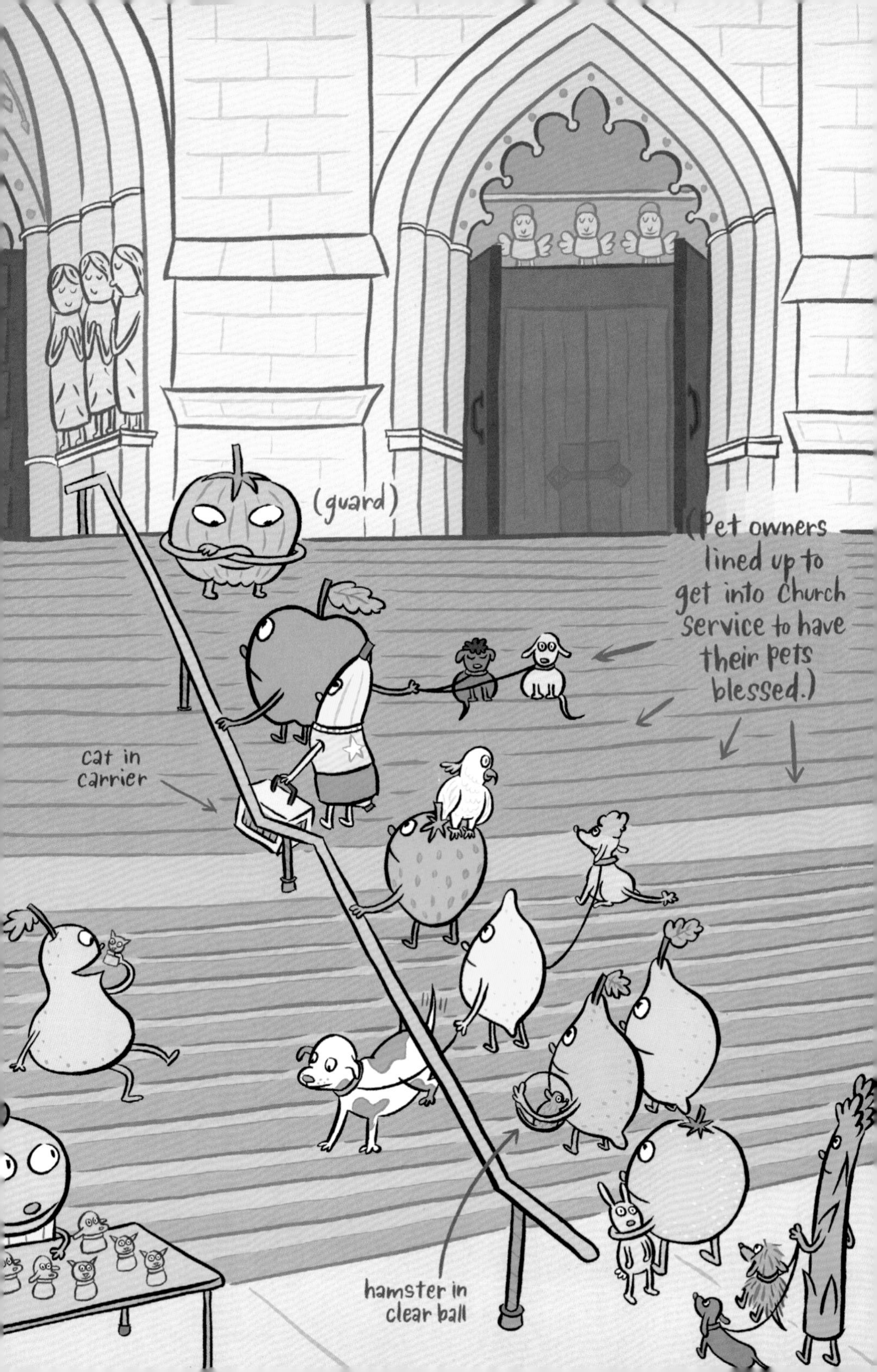
(guard)
(Pet owners lined up to get into Church service to have their pets blessed.)
cat in carrier
hamster in clear ball

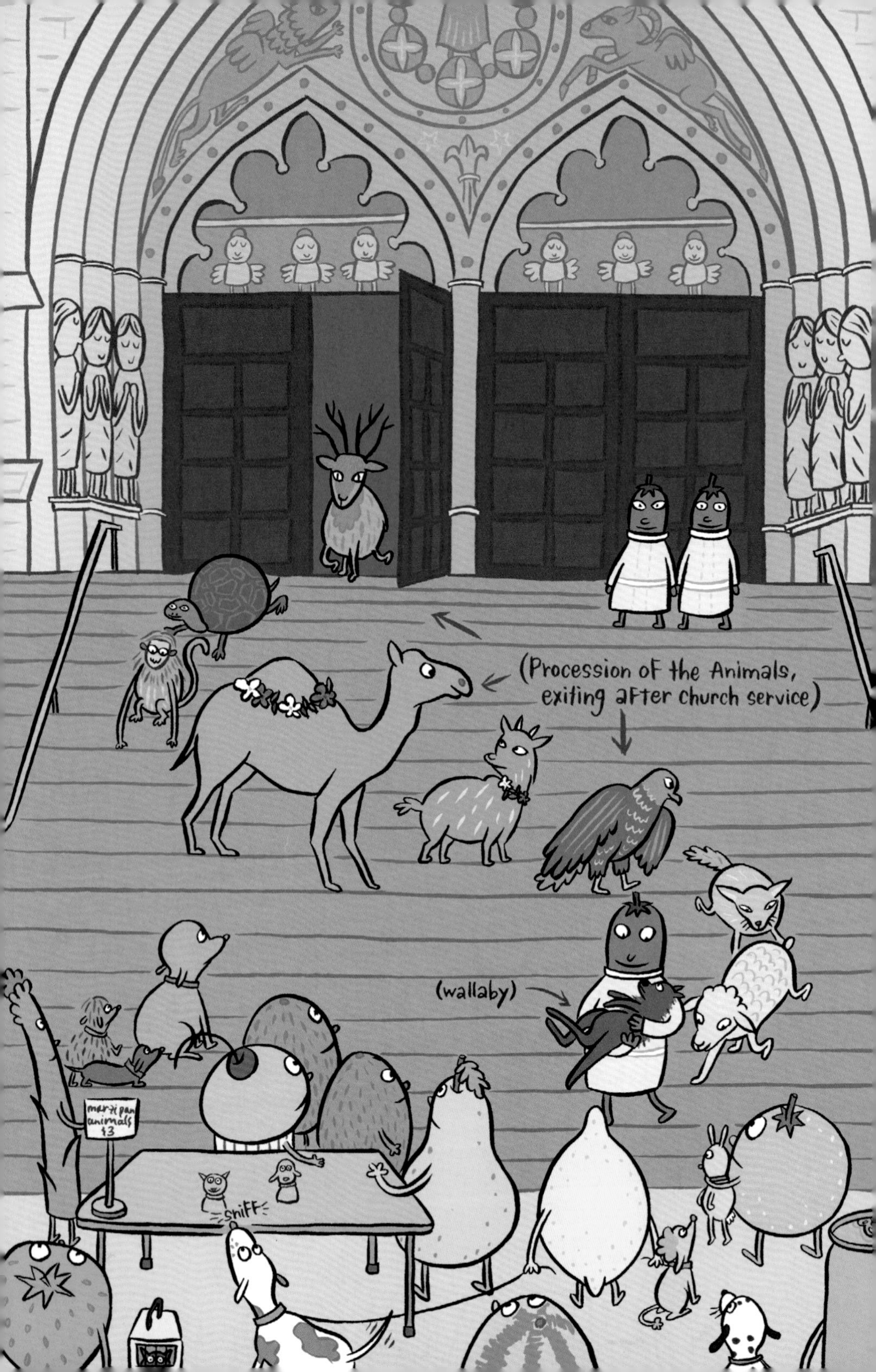
(Procession of the Animals, exiting after church service)
(wallaby)
marzipan animals £3
sniff

a few weeks later...

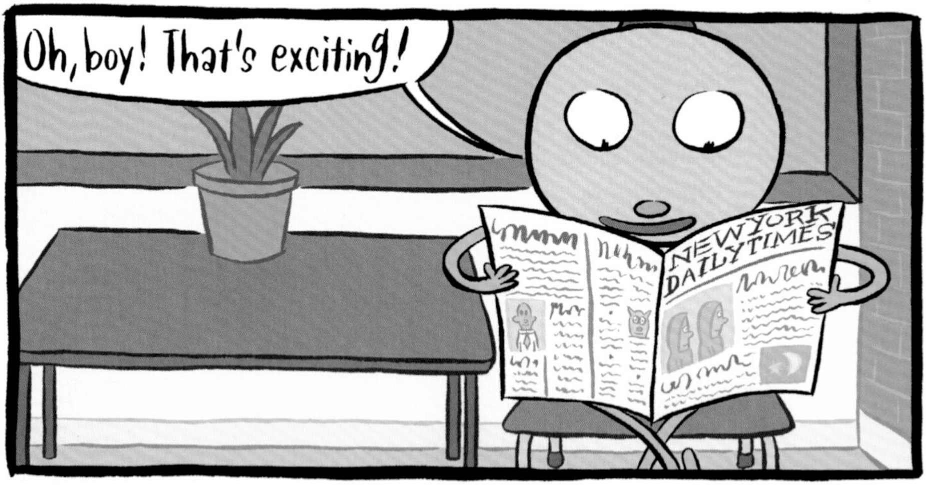
Oh, boy! That's exciting!
NEW YORK DAILY TIMES

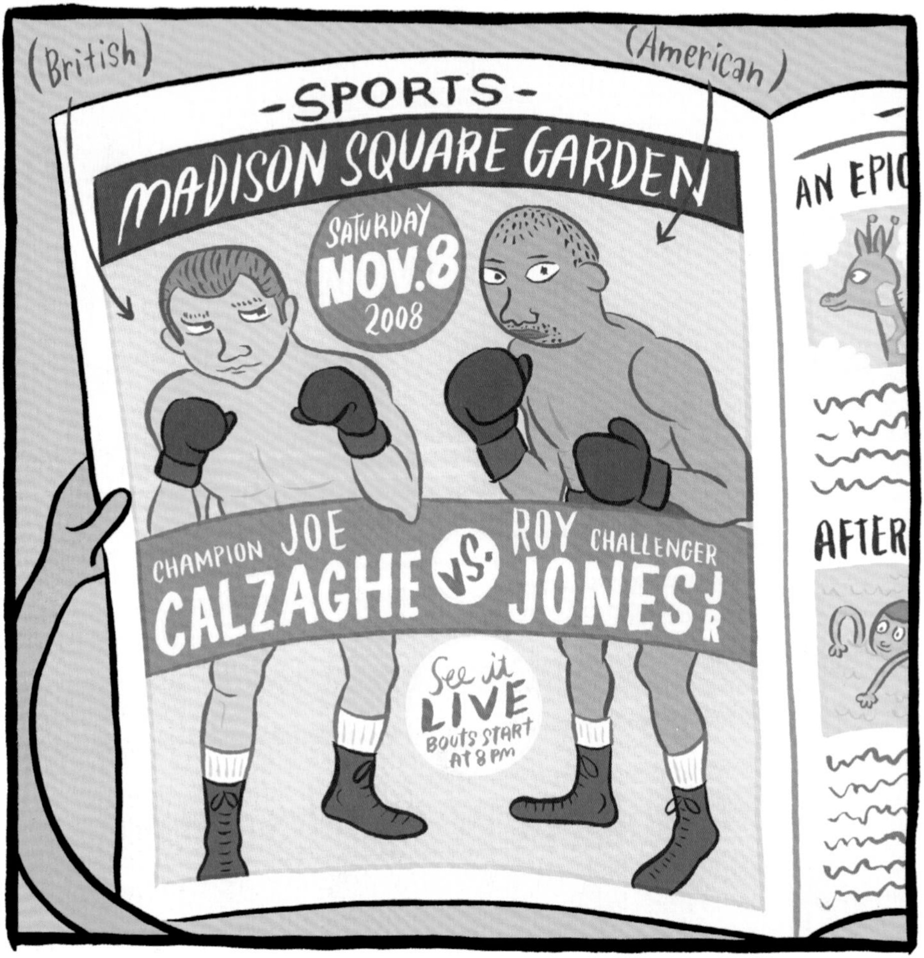
(British)
(American)
-SPORTS-
MADISON SQUARE GARDEN
SATURDAY NOV. 8 2008
CHAMPION JOE CALZAGHE
VS.
ROY CHALLENGER JONES JR
See it LIVE BOUTS START AT 8 PM
AN EPIC
AFTER

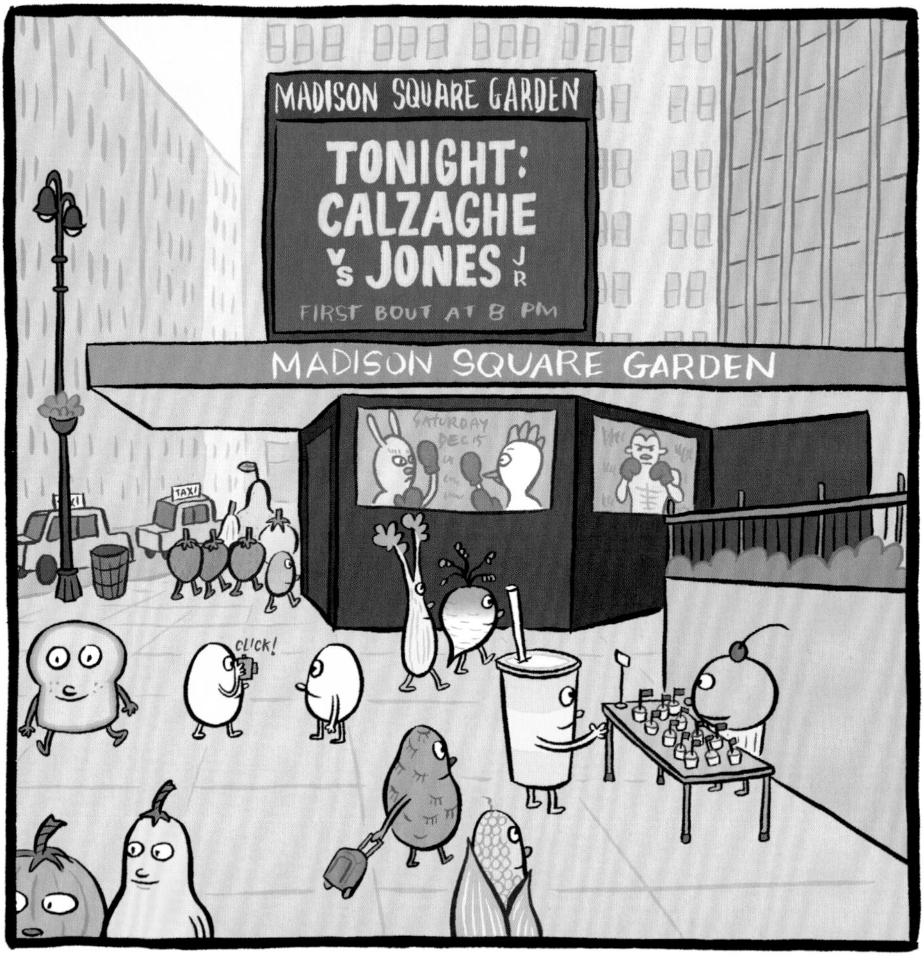
MADISON SQUARE GARDEN
TONIGHT:
CALZAGHE
VS JONES JR
FIRST BOUT AT 8 PM
MADISON SQUARE GARDEN
TAXI
TAXI
CLICK!

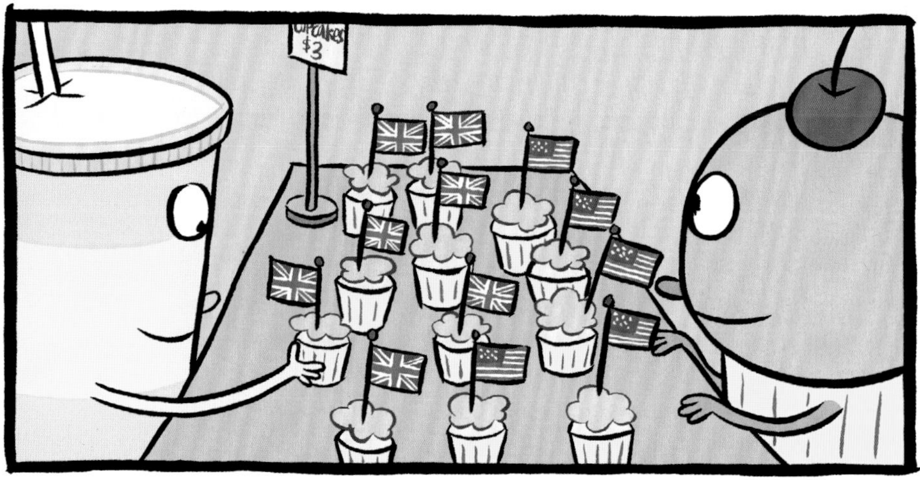
CUPCAKES
$3

and a few months later...

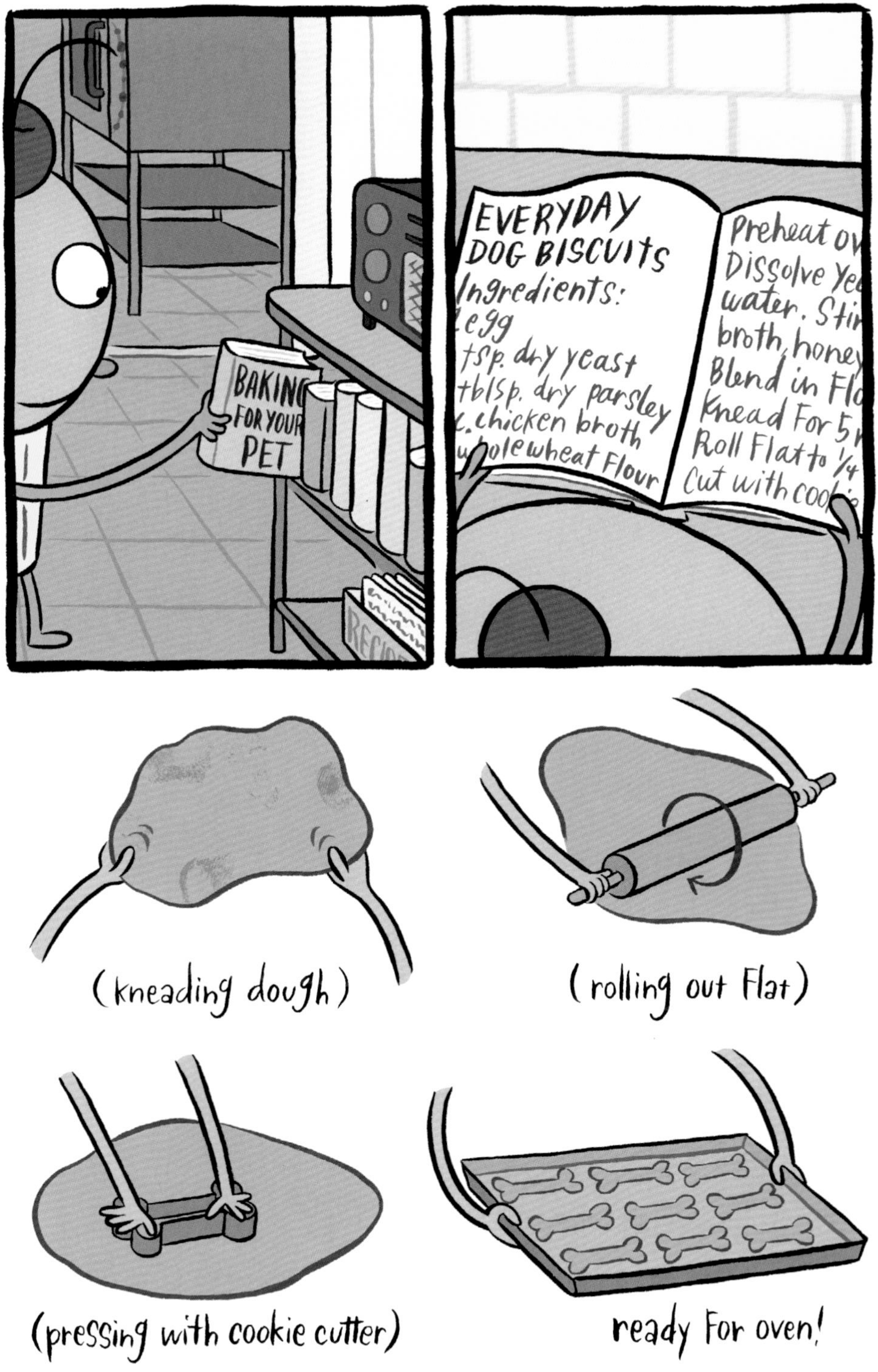
BAKING FOR YOUR PET
EVERYDAY DOG BISCUITS
Ingredients:
egg
tsp. dry yeast
tblsp. dry parsley
c. chicken broth
wholewheat Flour
Preheat ov
Dissolve Ye
water. Stir
broth, honey
Blend in Flo
Knead For 5
Roll Flat to 1/4
Cut with coo
(kneading dough)
(rolling out Flat)
(pressing with cookie cutter)
ready For oven!

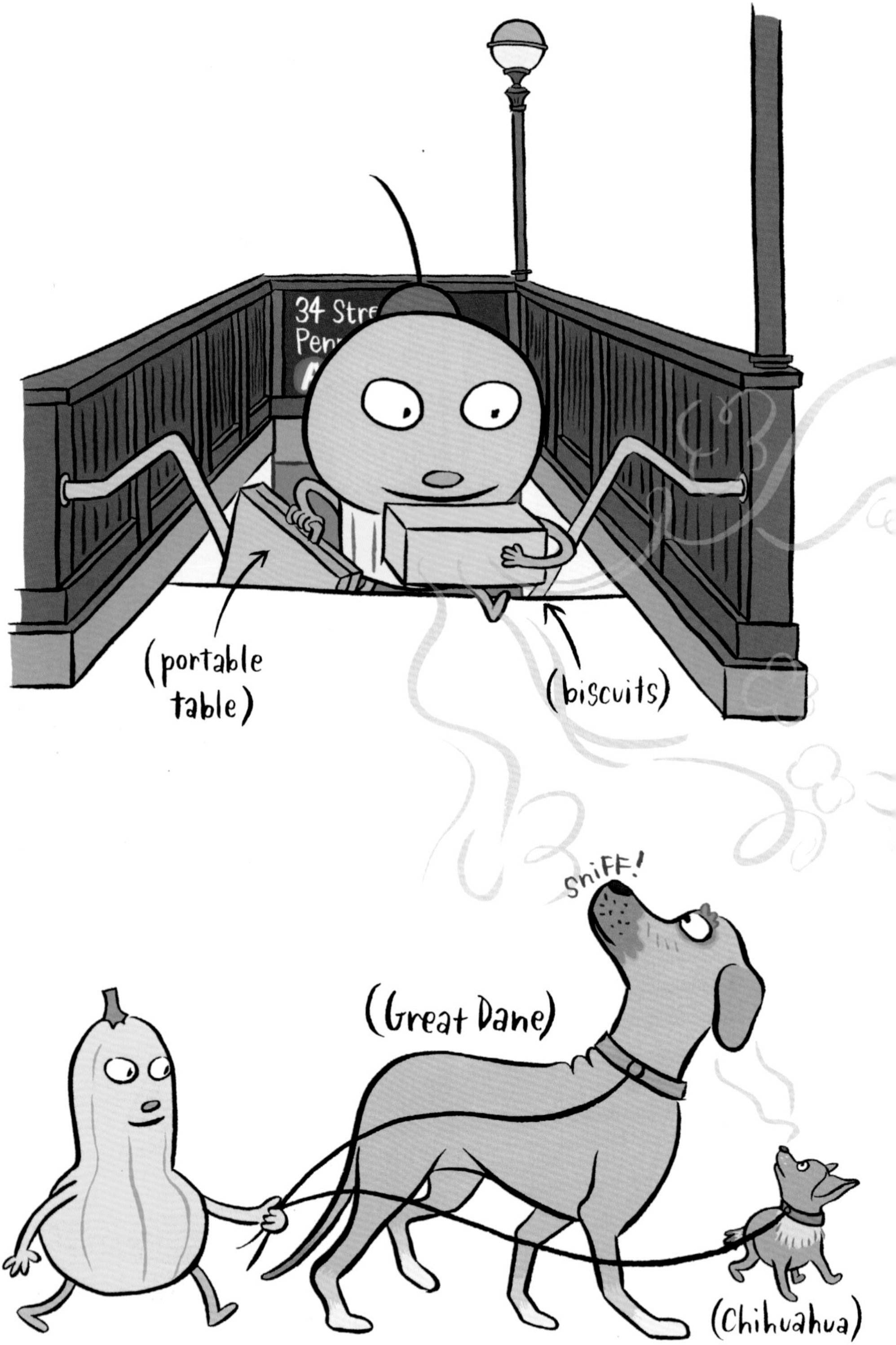
34 Stre
Penn
(portable table)
(biscuits)
SNIFF!
(Great Dane)
(Chihuahua)

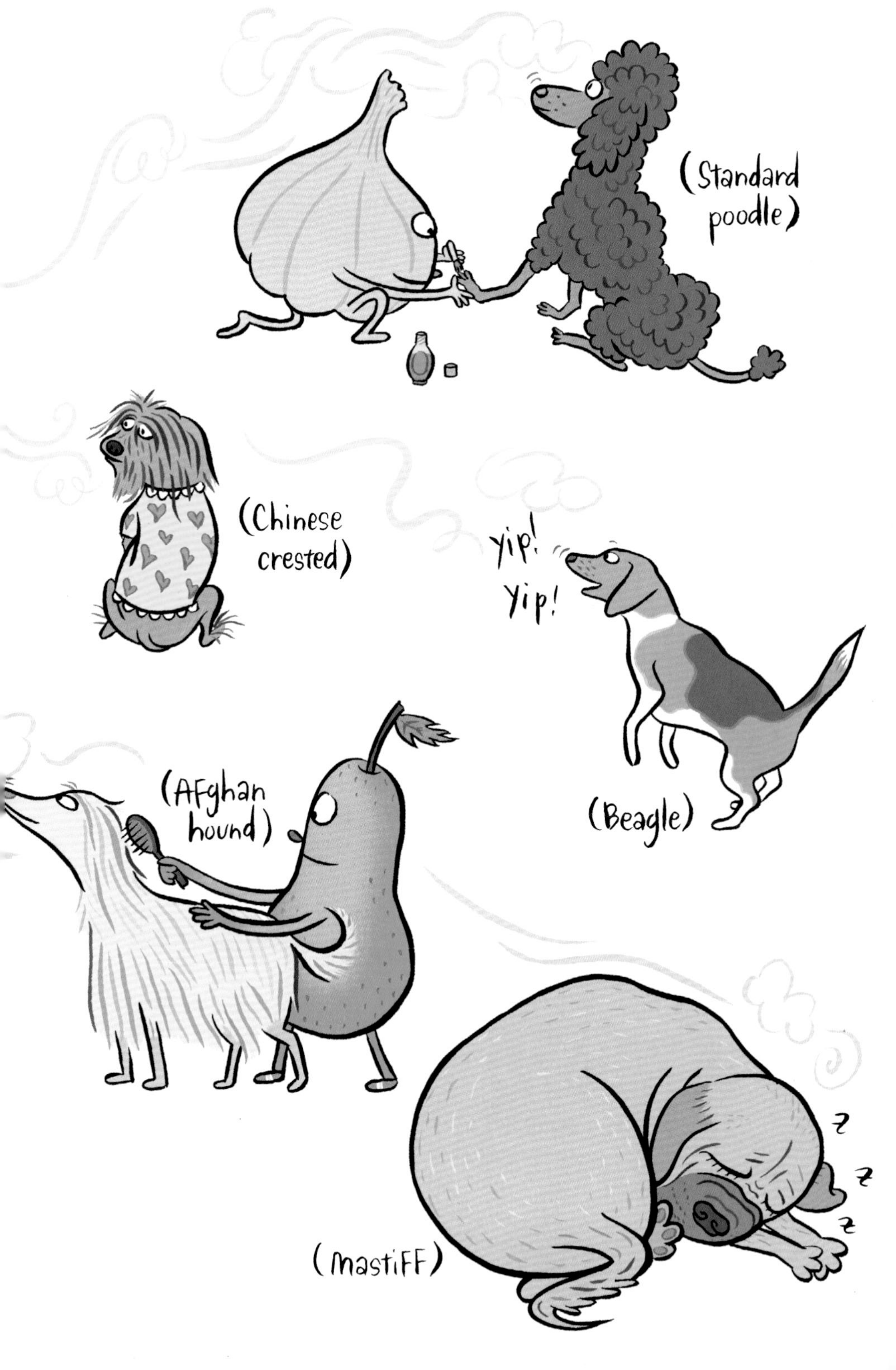
(Standard poodle)
(Chinese crested)
Yip! Yip!
(Beagle)
(Afghan hound)
(mastiff)
z z z

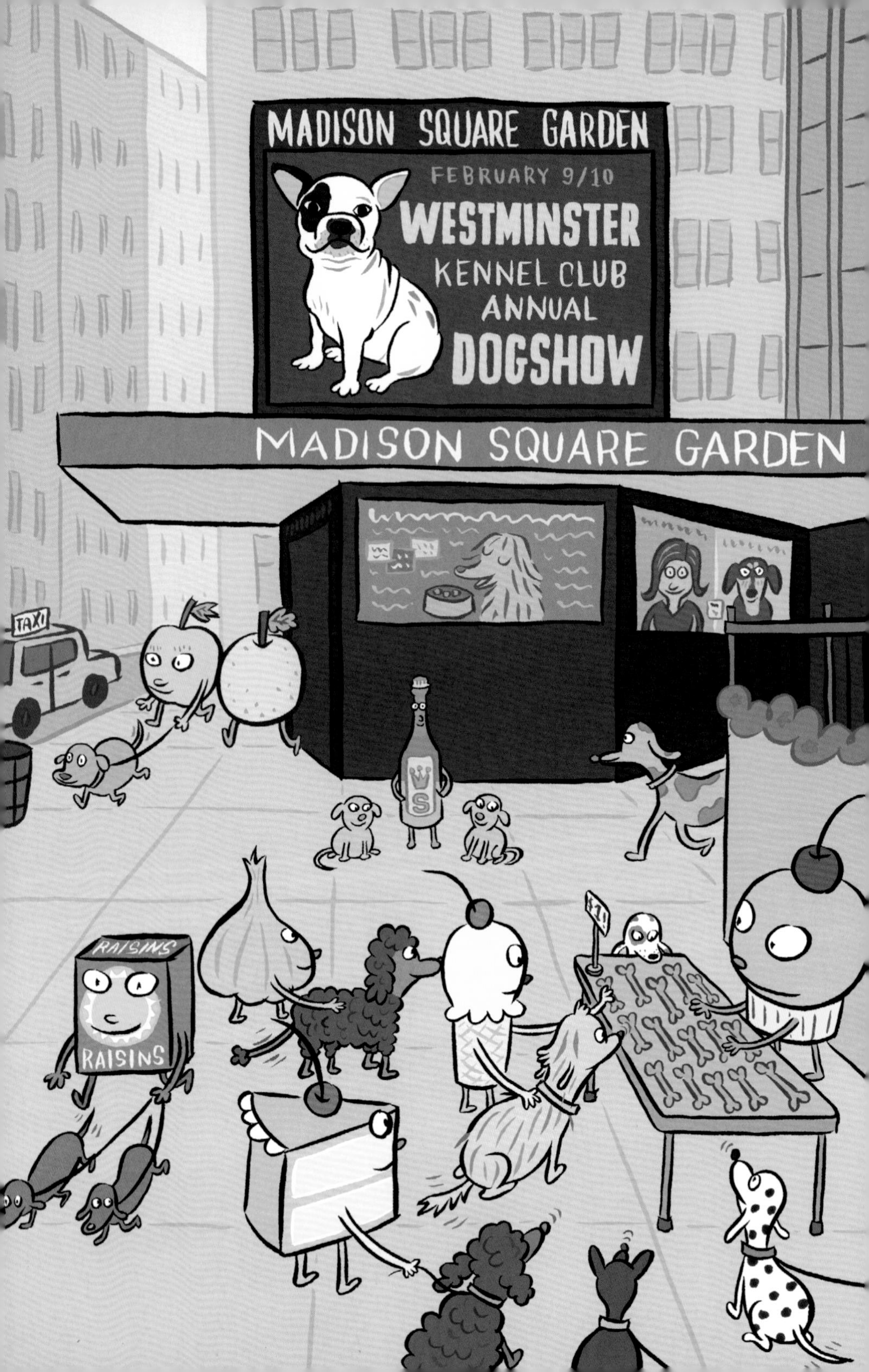

MADISON SQUARE GARDEN
FEBRUARY 9/10
WESTMINSTER
KENNEL CLUB
ANNUAL
DOGSHOW
MADISON SQUARE GARDEN
TAXI
S
$1!
RAISINS
RAISINS

Finally . . .

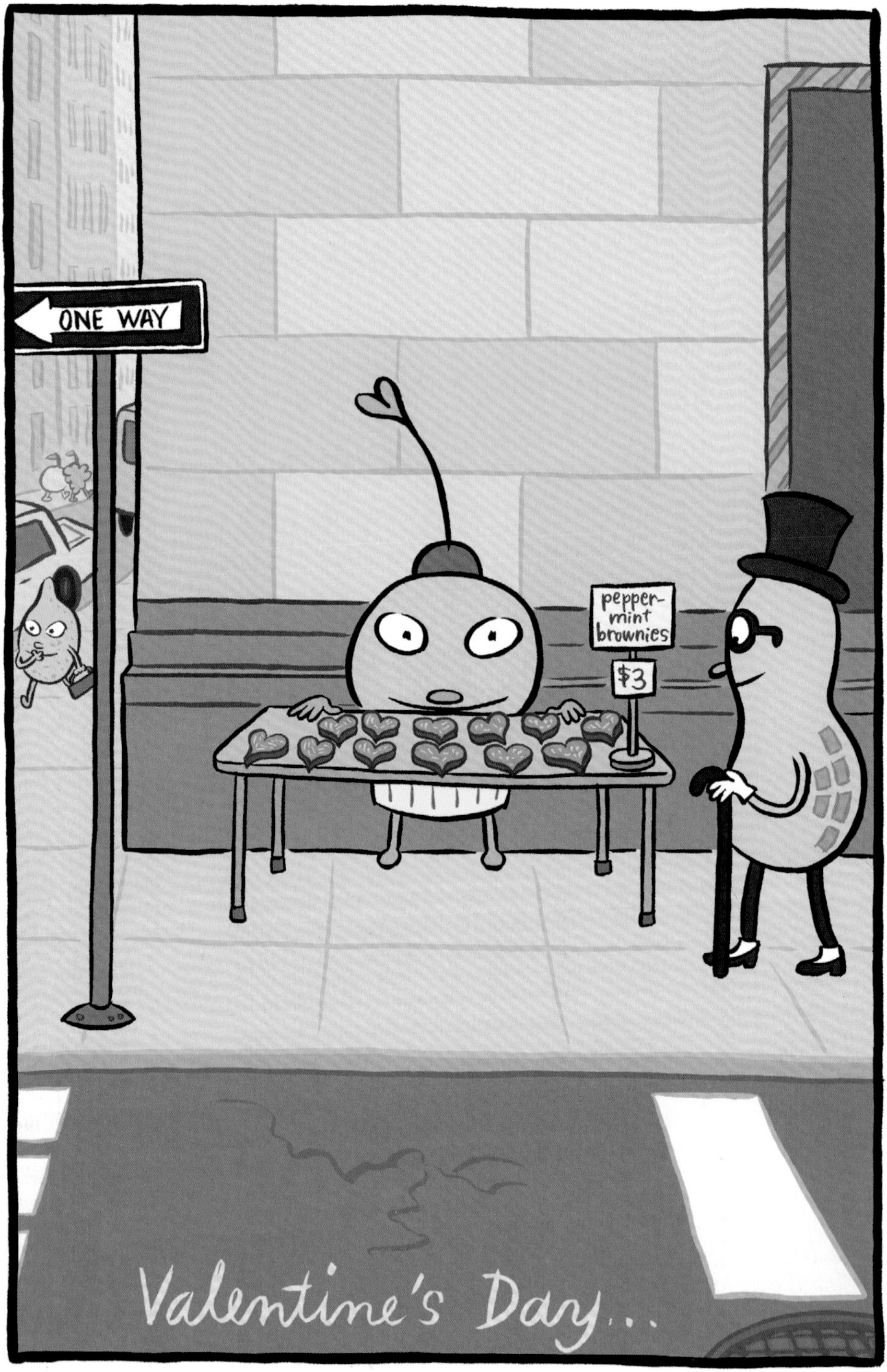
ONE WAY
pepper-
mint
brownies
$3
Valentine's Day...

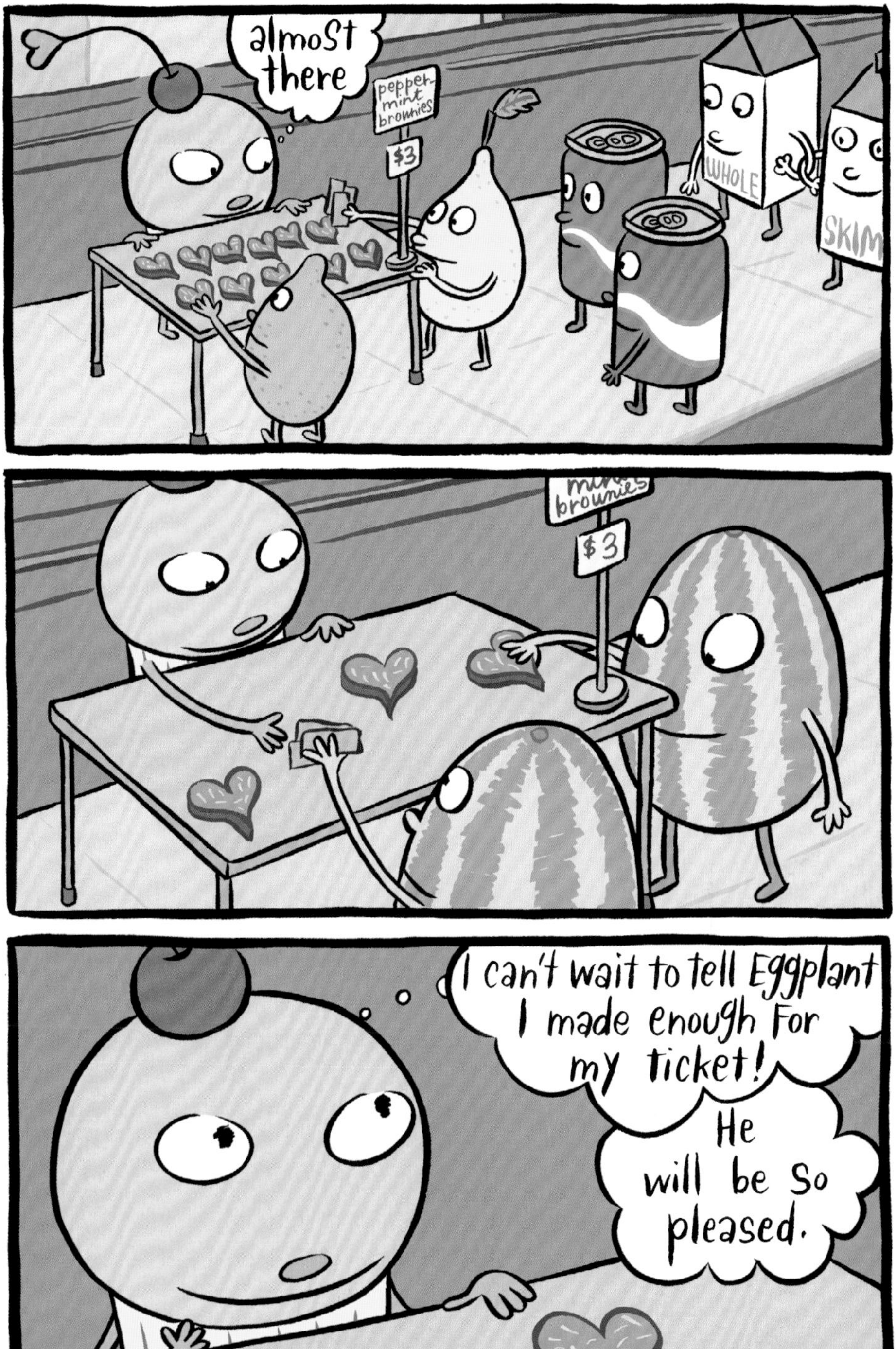
almost there
pepper-mint brownies
$3
WHOLE
SKIM
mint brownies
$3
I can't wait to tell Eggplant I made enough for my ticket!
He will be so pleased.

chapter 4

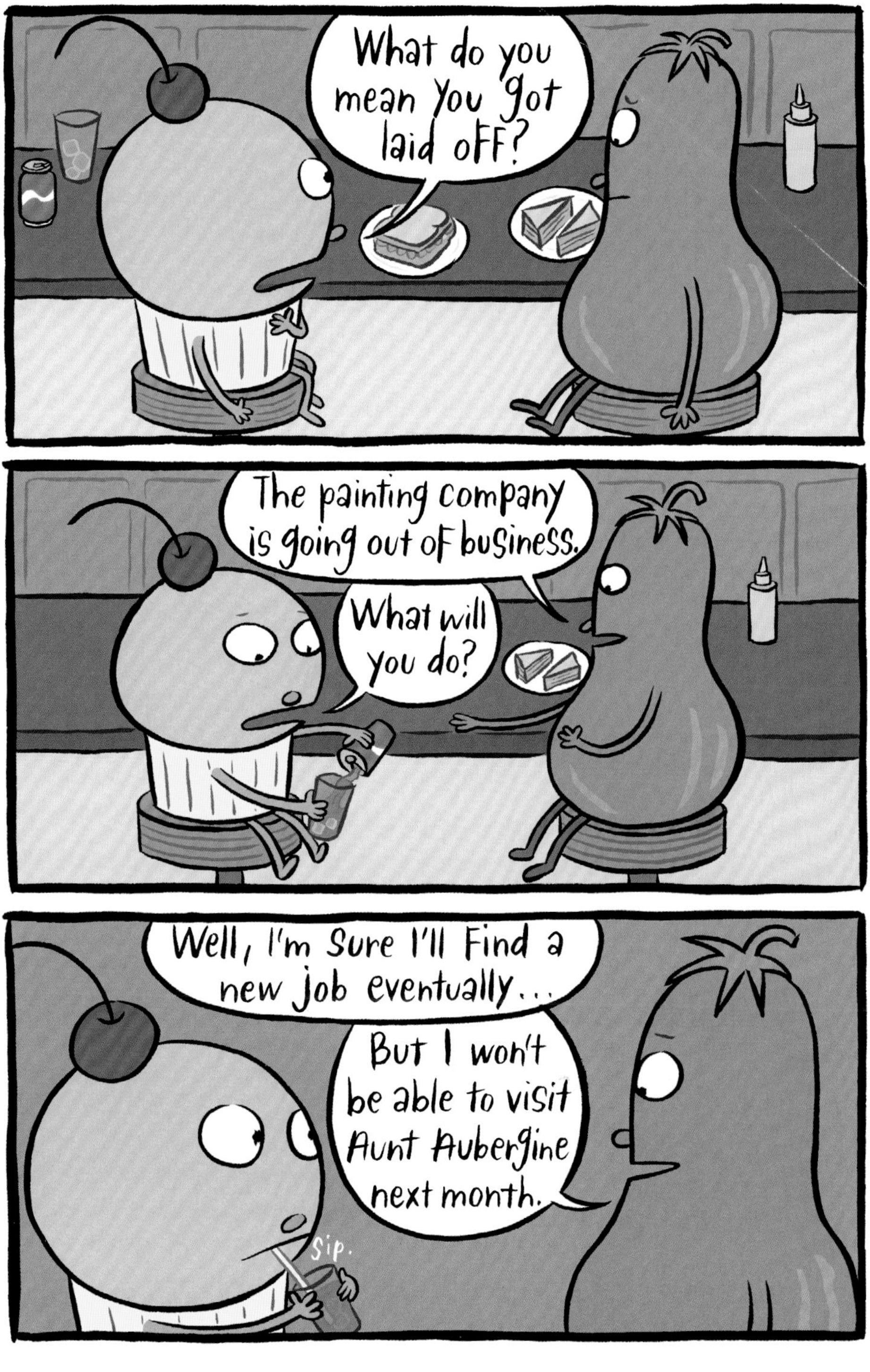
What do you mean you got laid off?
The painting company is going out of business.
What will you do?
Well, I'm sure I'll find a new job eventually...
But I won't be able to visit Aunt Aubergine next month.
sip.

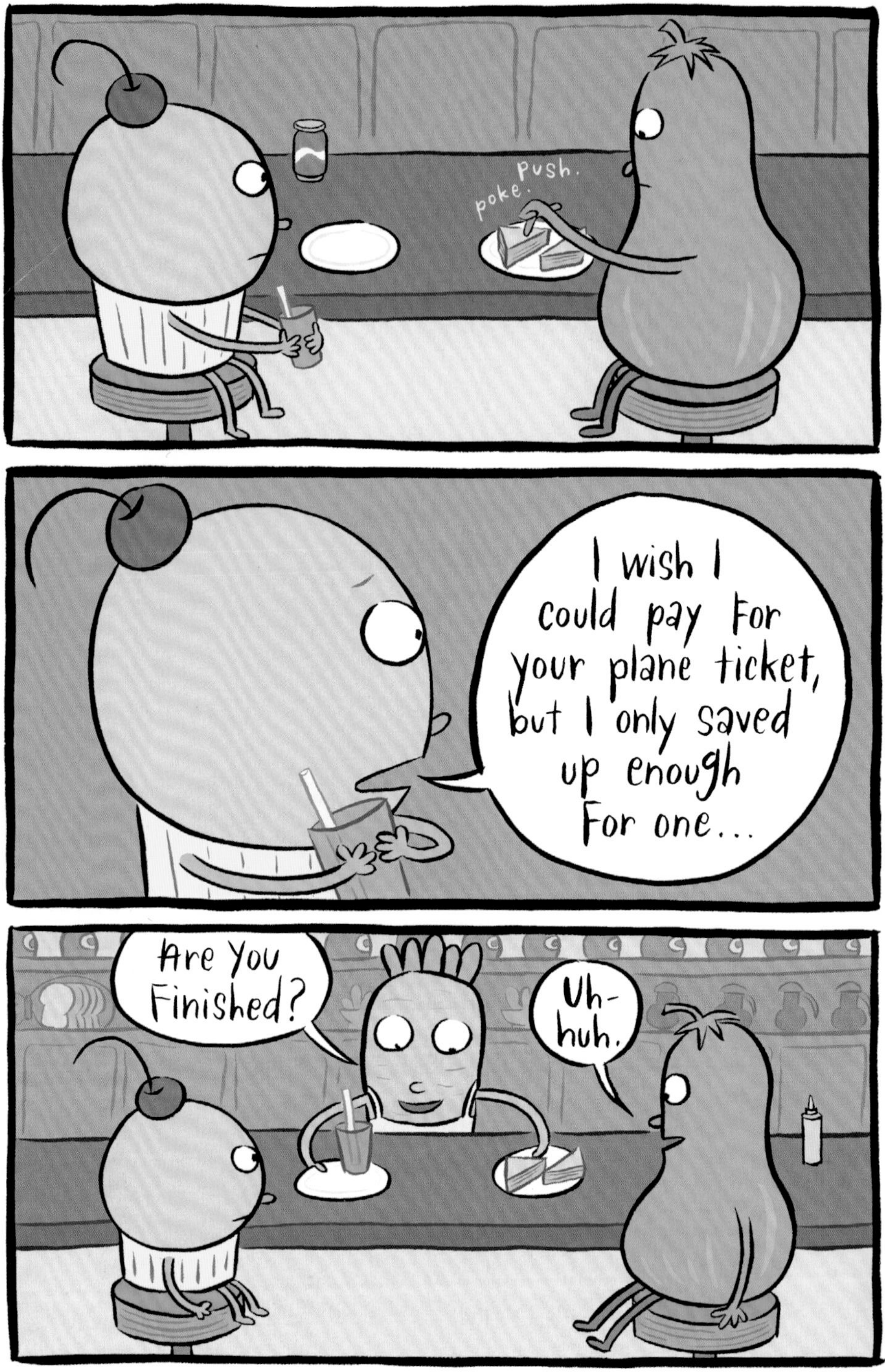
poke.
Push.
I wish I could pay For your plane ticket, but I only saved up enough For one...
Are You Finished?
Uh-huh.

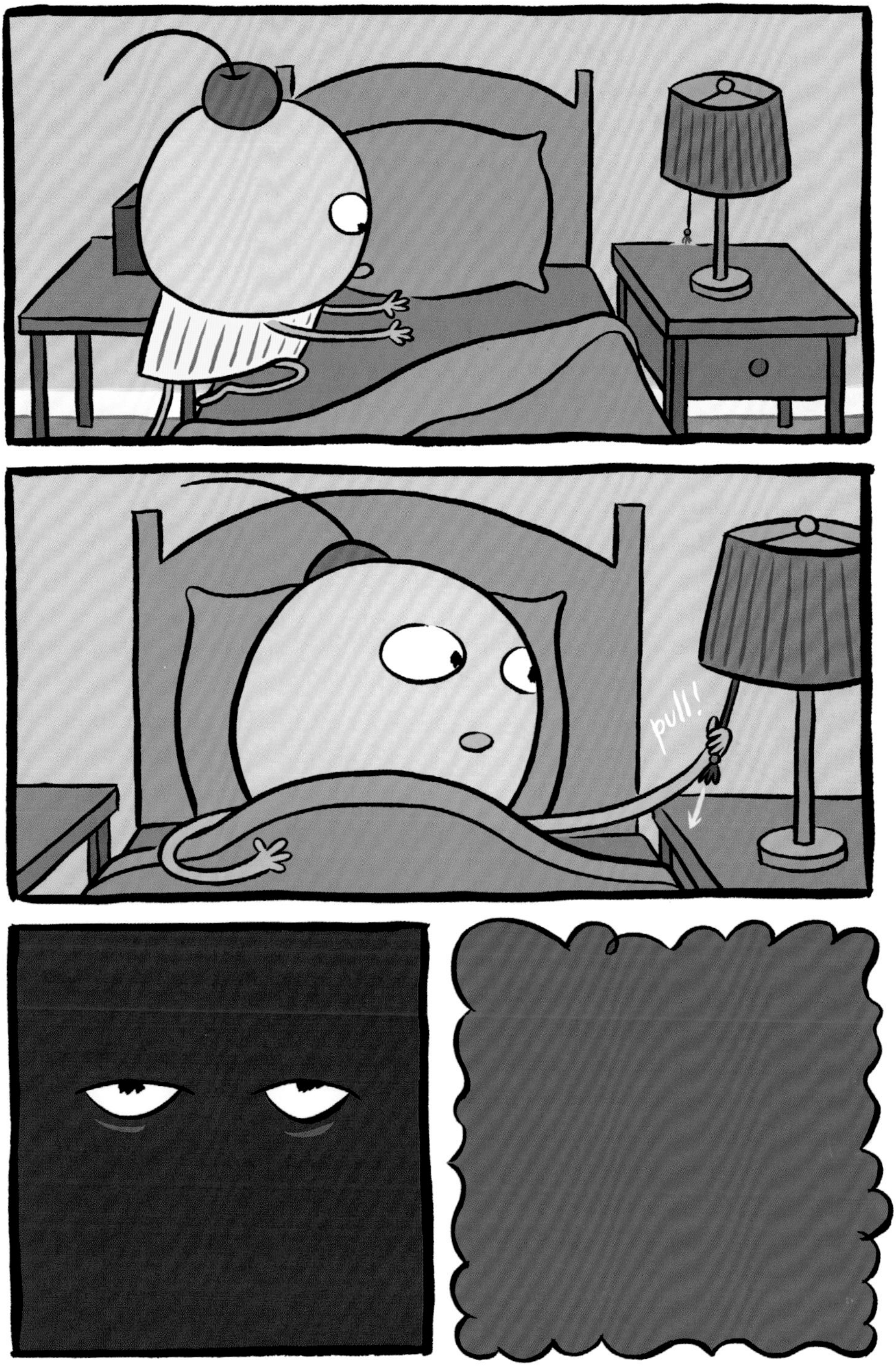
pull!

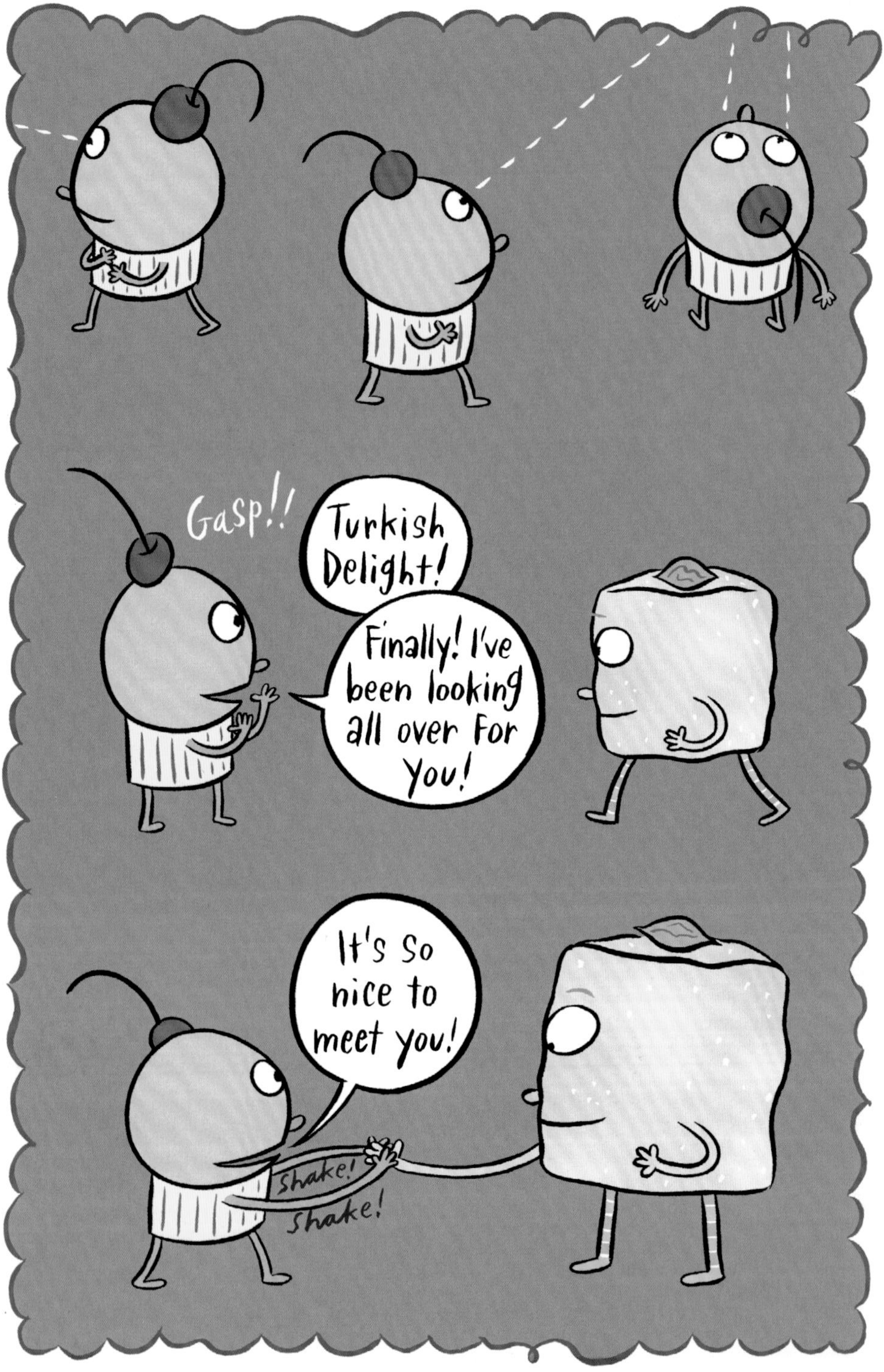
Gasp!!
Turkish Delight!
Finally! I've been looking all over for you!
It's so nice to meet you!
Shake!
Shake!

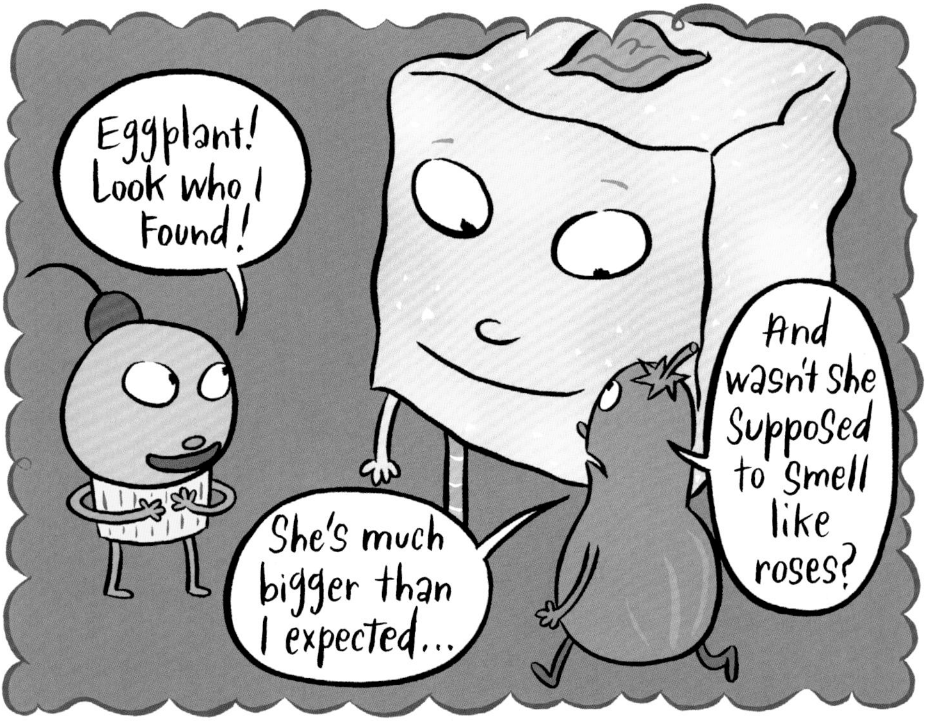
Eggplant! Look who I Found!
And wasn't she Supposed to Smell like roses?
She's much bigger than I expected...

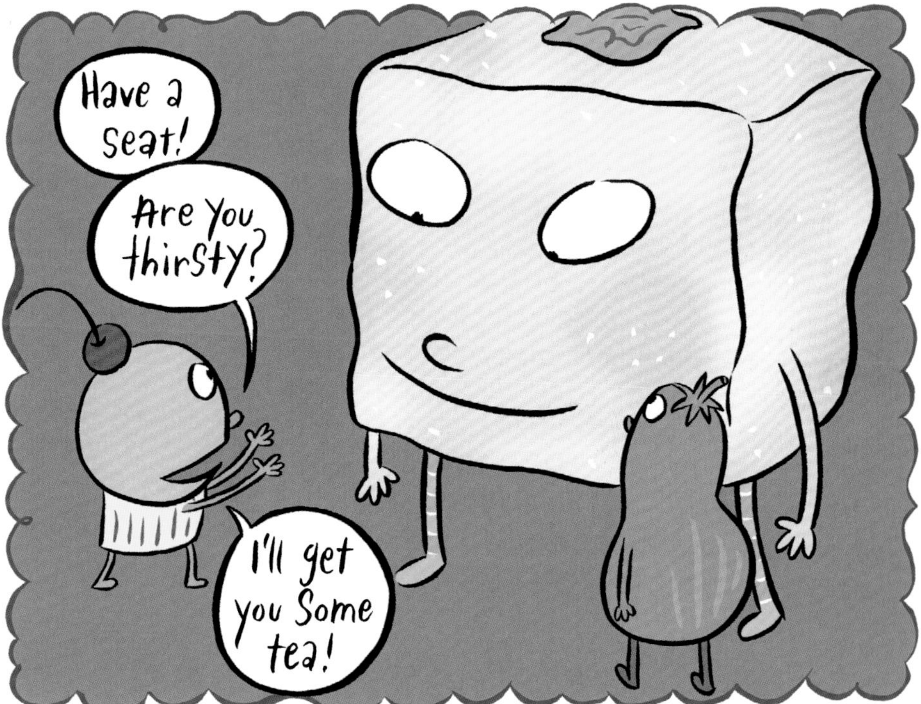
Have a seat!
Are you thirsty?
I'll get you Some tea!

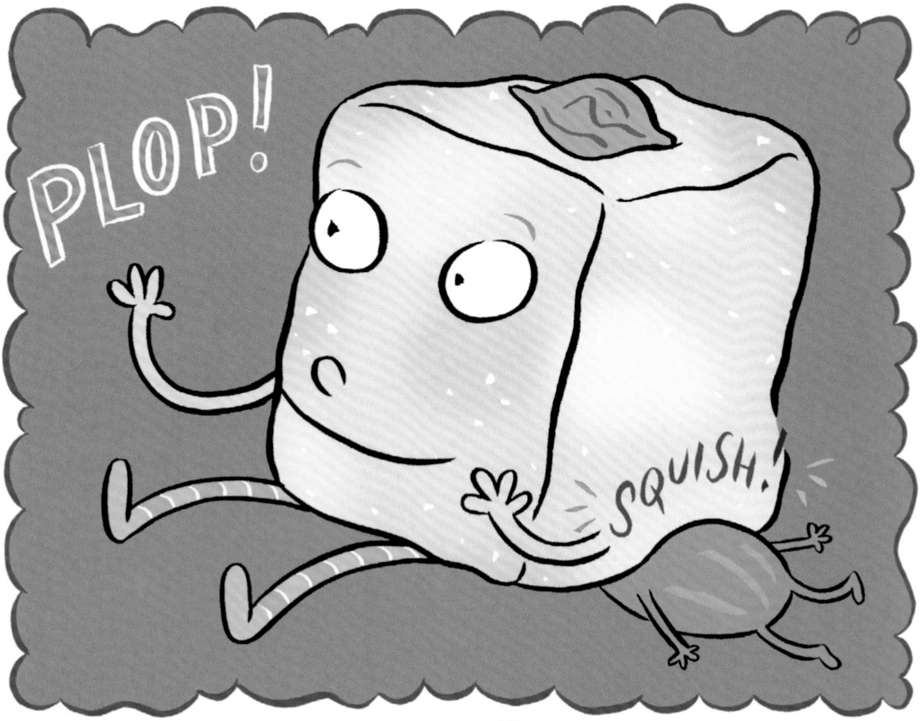
PLOP!
SQUISH!

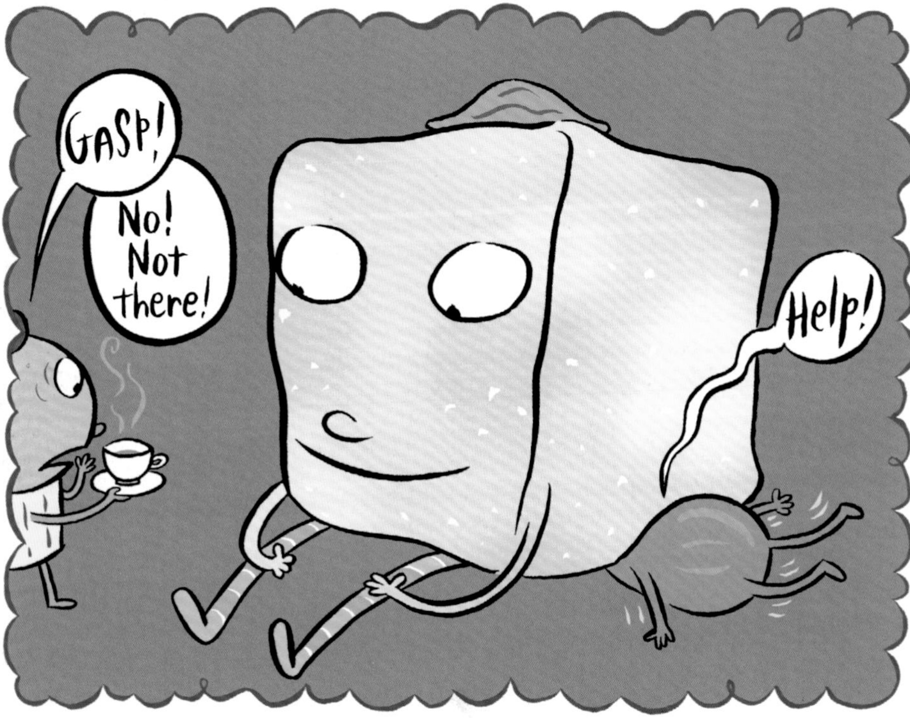
GASP!
No! Not there!
Help!

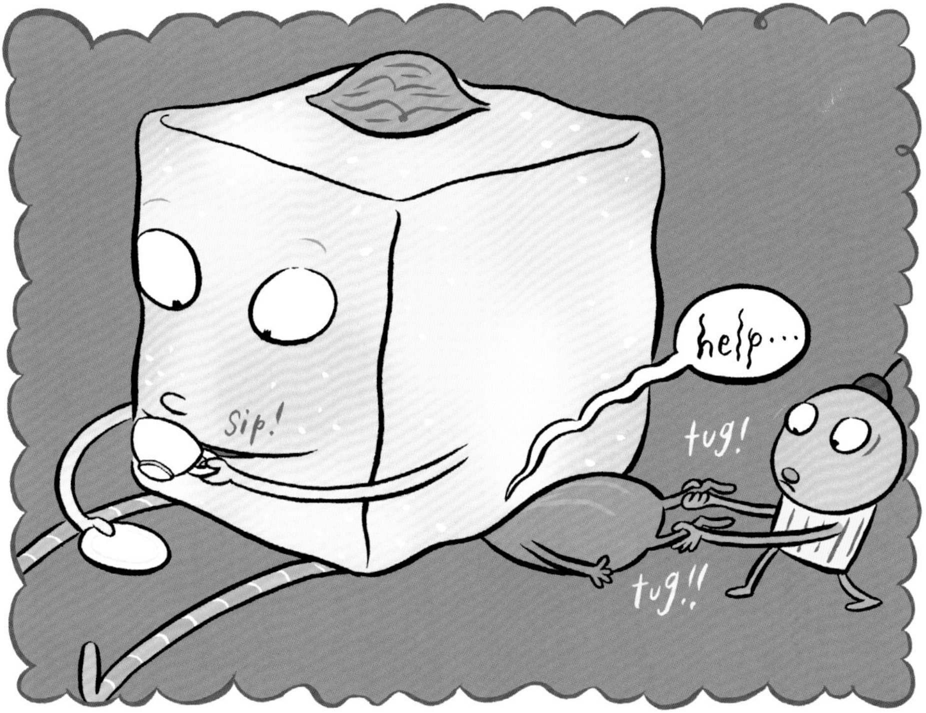
help...
Sip!
tug!
tug!!

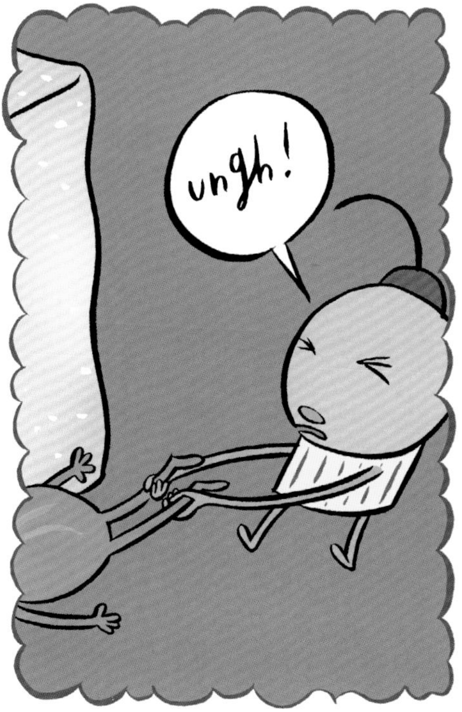
ungh!

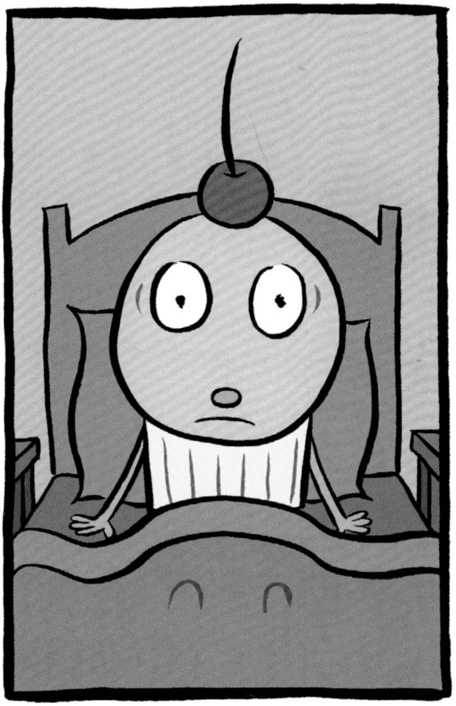

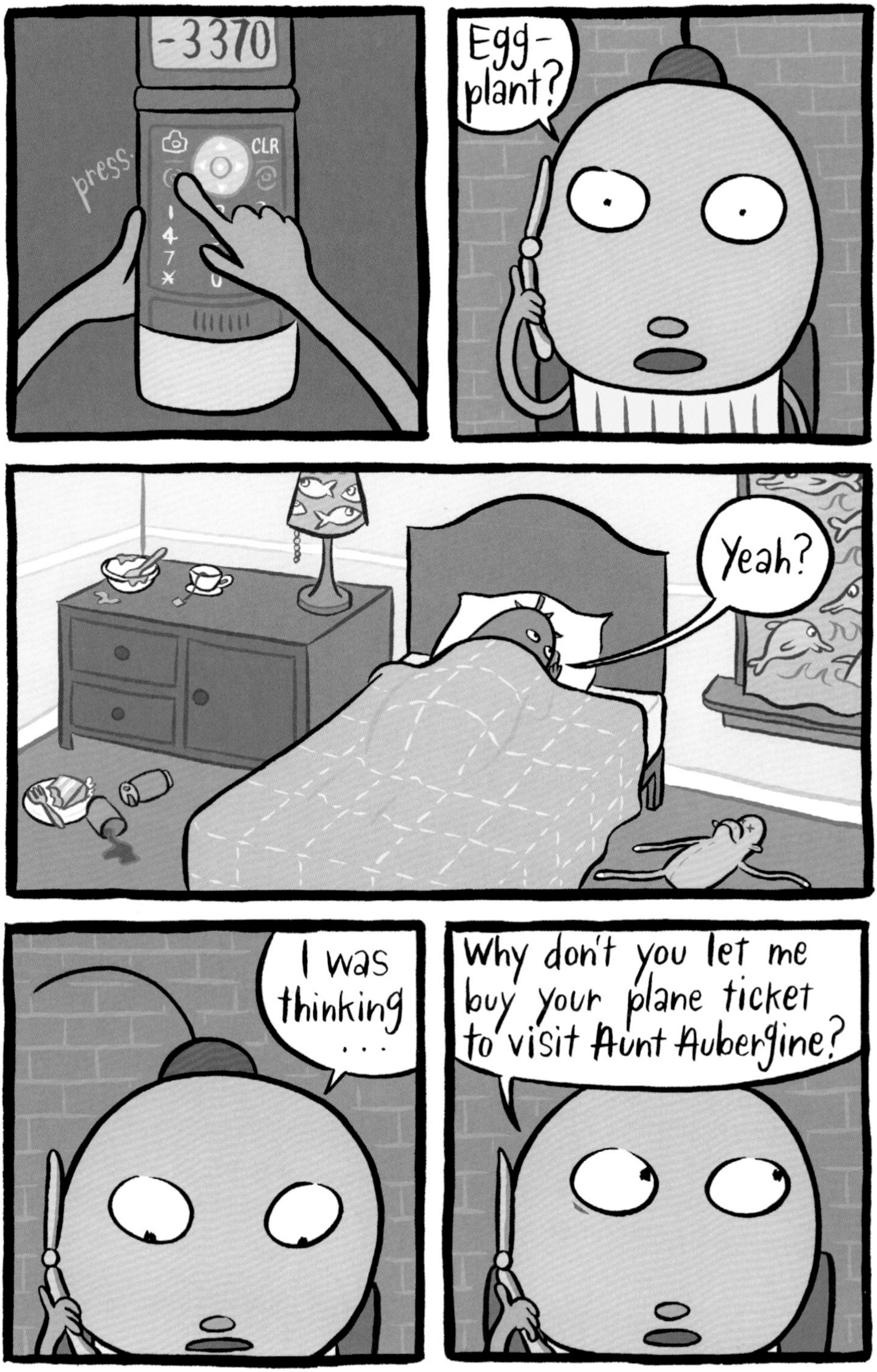
-3370
CLR
press.
Egg-plant?
Yeah?
I was thinking . . .
Why don't you let me buy your plane ticket to visit Aunt Aubergine?

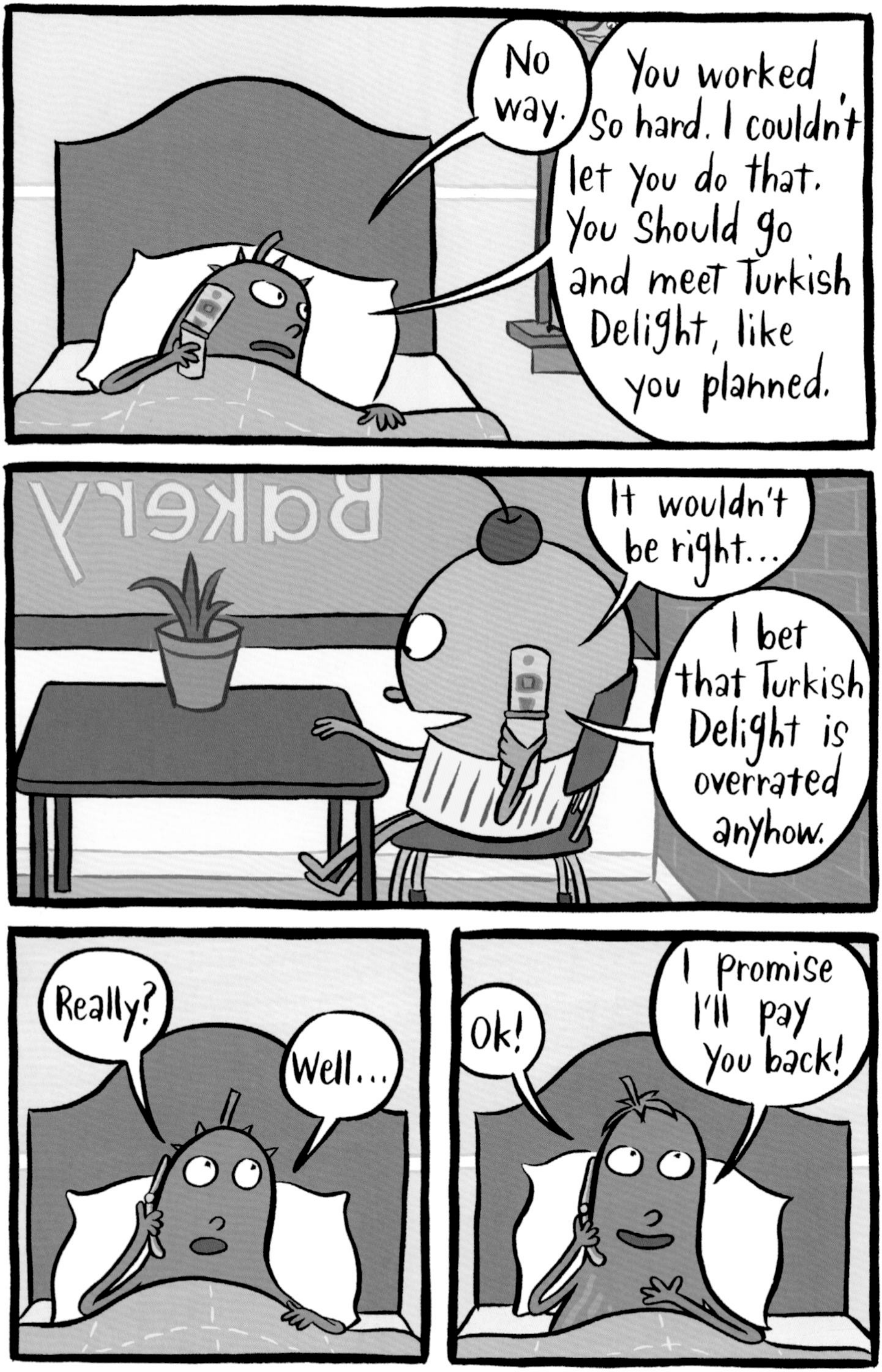
No way.
You worked so hard. I couldn't let you do that. You should go and meet Turkish Delight, like you planned.
Bakery
It wouldn't be right...
I bet that Turkish Delight is overrated anyhow.
Really?
Well...
Ok!
I promise I'll pay you back!

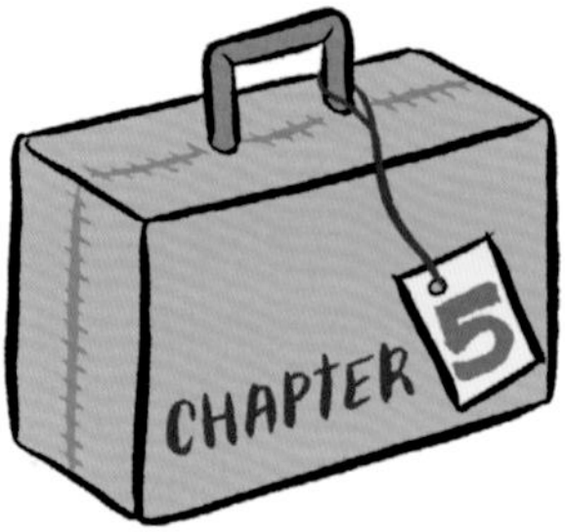
CHAPTER
5

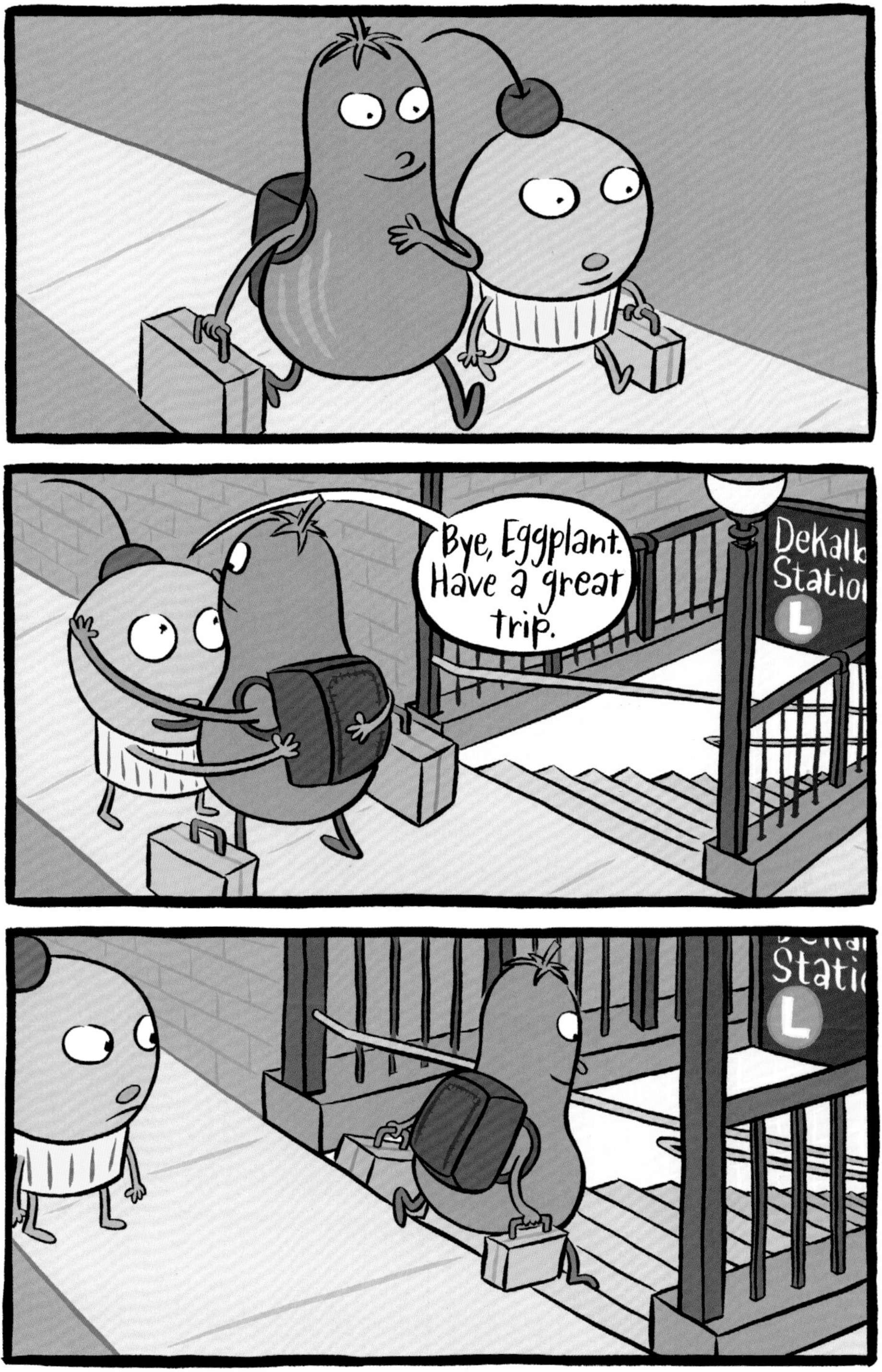
Bye, Eggplant. Have a great trip.
DeKalb Station
L
Statio
L

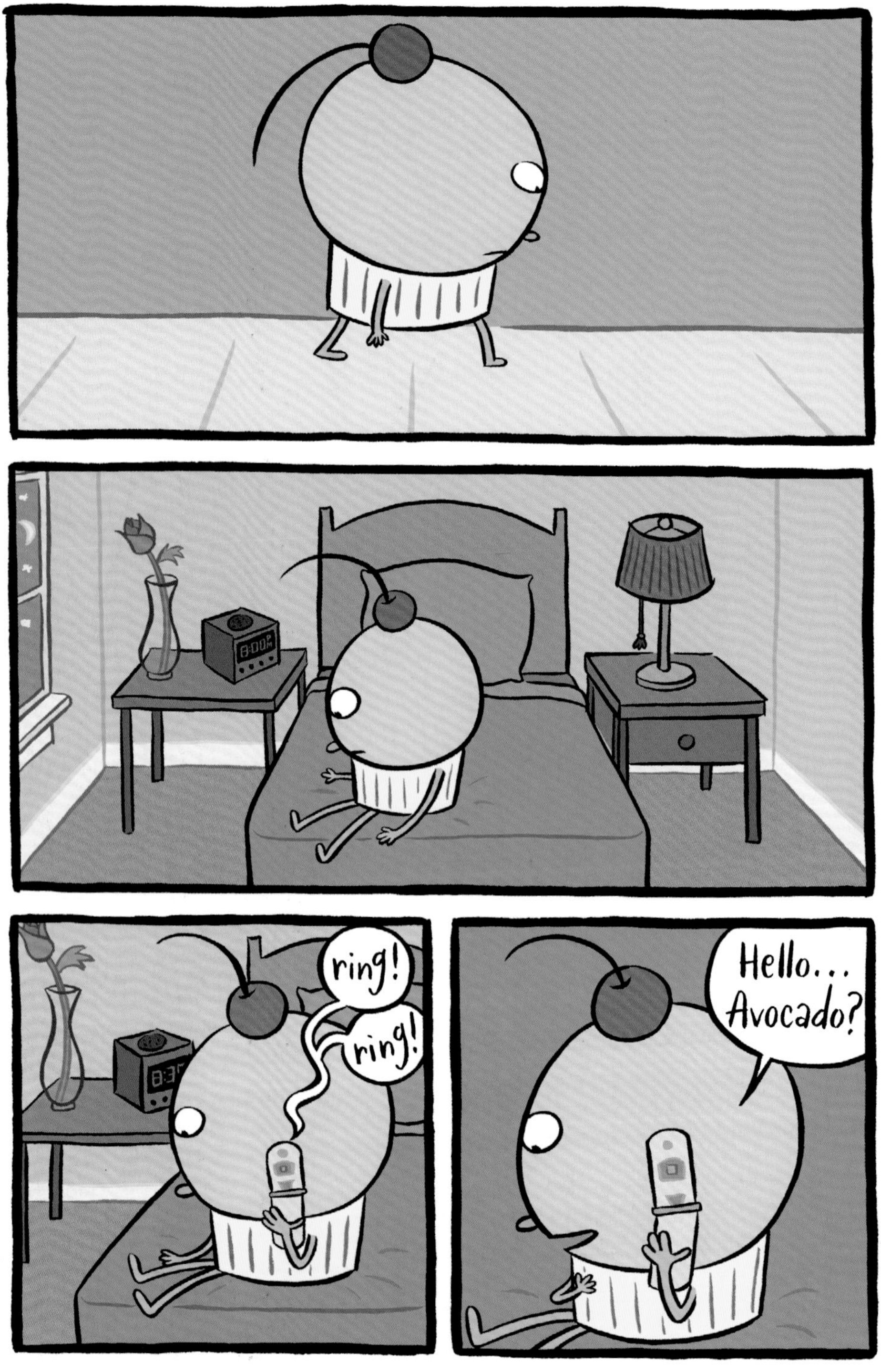
ring!
ring!
Hello...
Avocado?

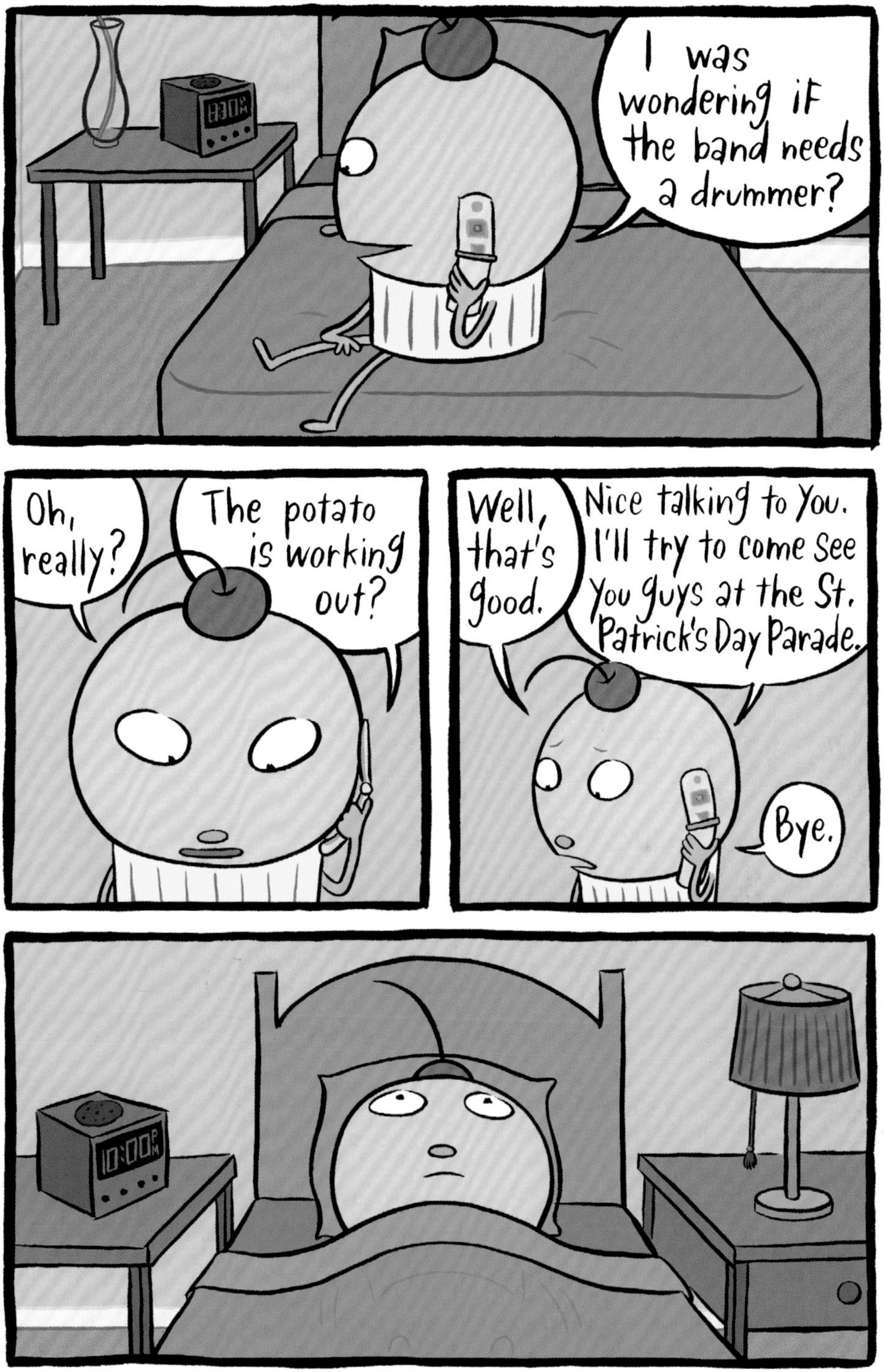
I was wondering if the band needs a drummer?
Oh, really?
The potato is working out?
Well, that's good.
Nice talking to You. I'll try to come see You guys at the St. Patrick's Day Parade.
Bye.

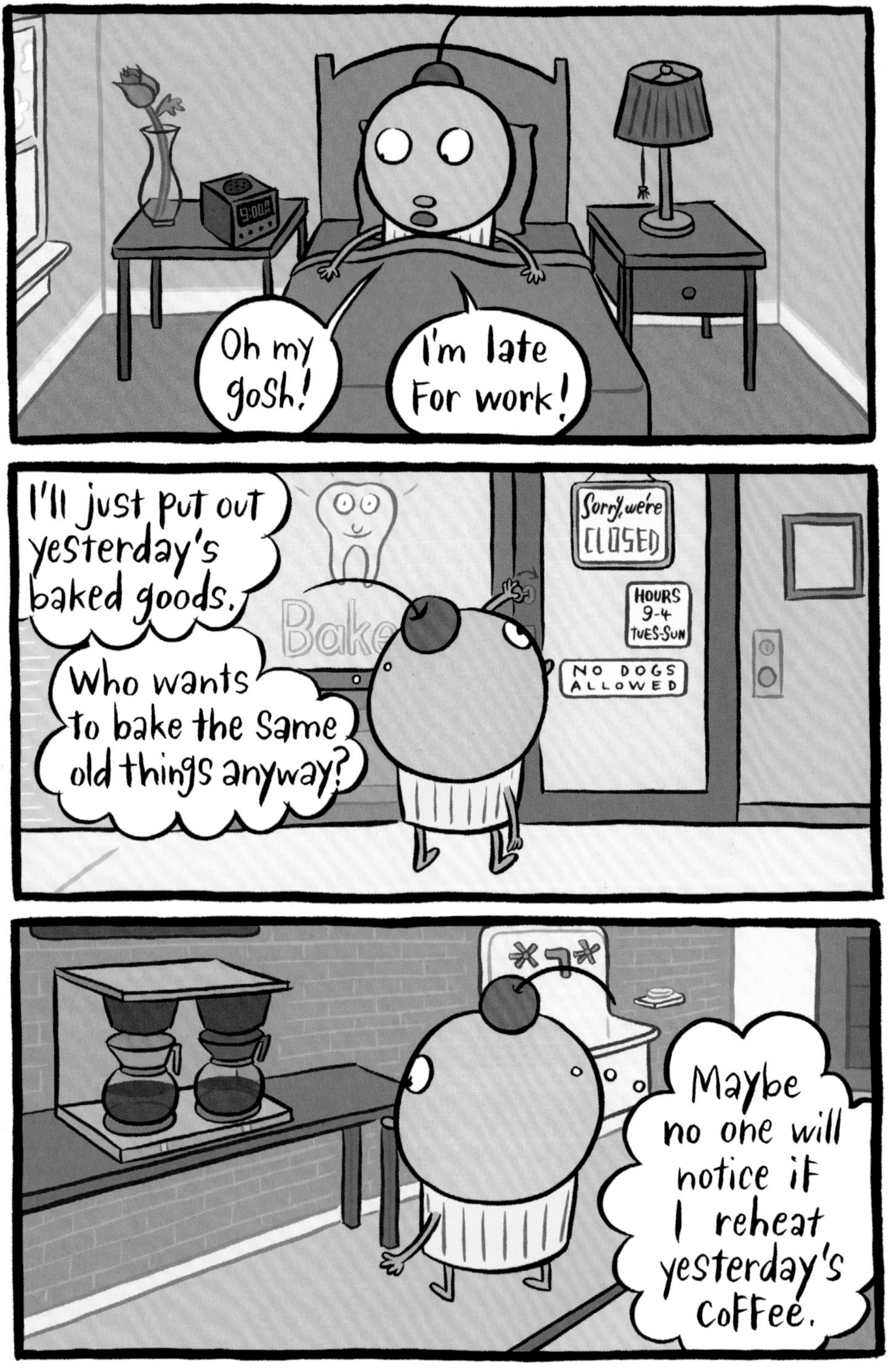

9:00A
Oh my gosh!
I'm late For work!
I'll just put out yesterday's baked goods.
Who wants to bake the same old things anyway?
Sorry, we're CLOSED
HOURS 9-4 TUES-SUN
NO DOGS ALLOWED
Maybe no one will notice iF I reheat yesterday's coFFee.

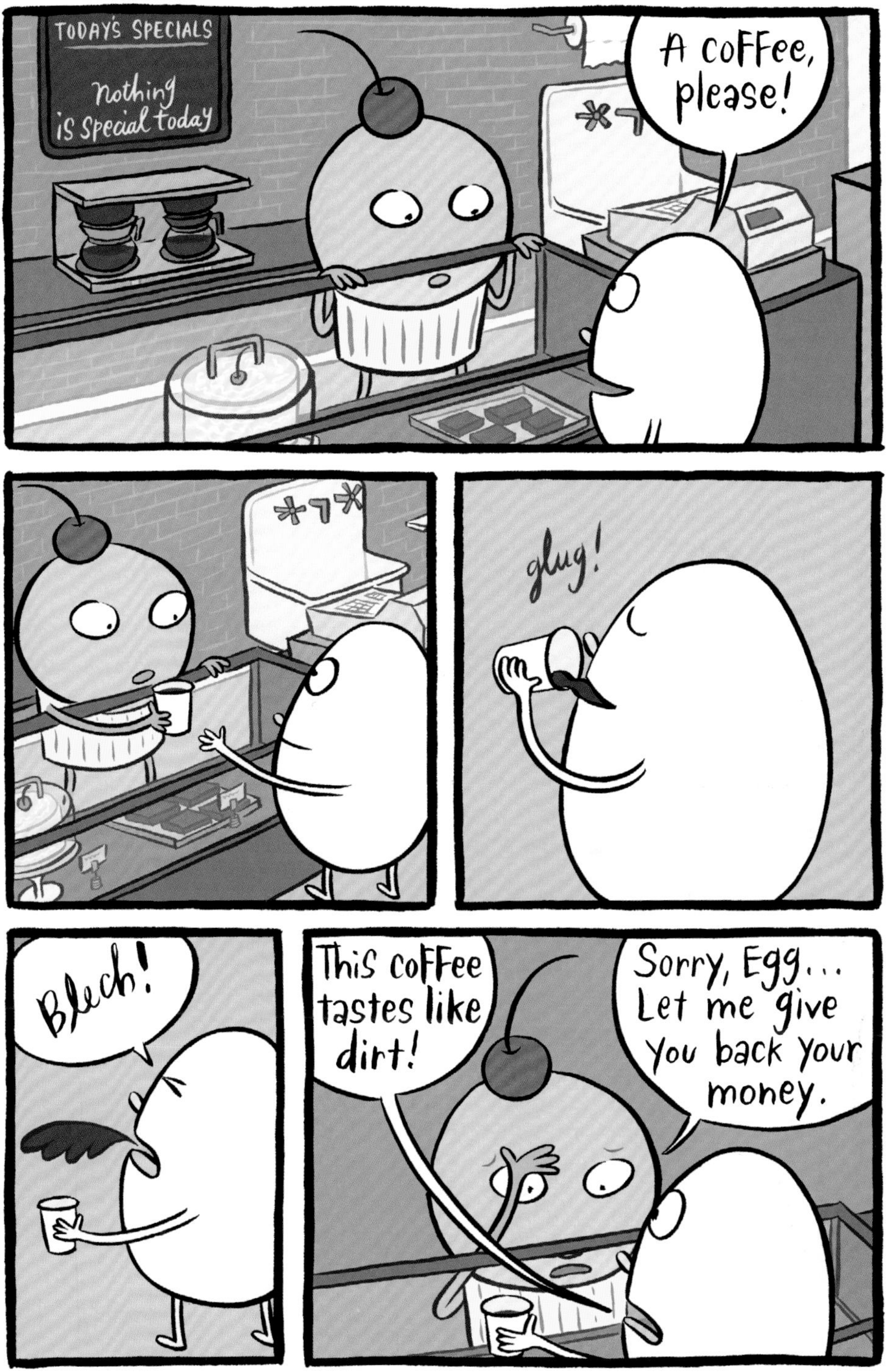
TODAY'S SPECIALS
Nothing is special today
A coffee, please!
glug!
Blech!
This coffee tastes like dirt!
Sorry, Egg... Let me give you back your money.

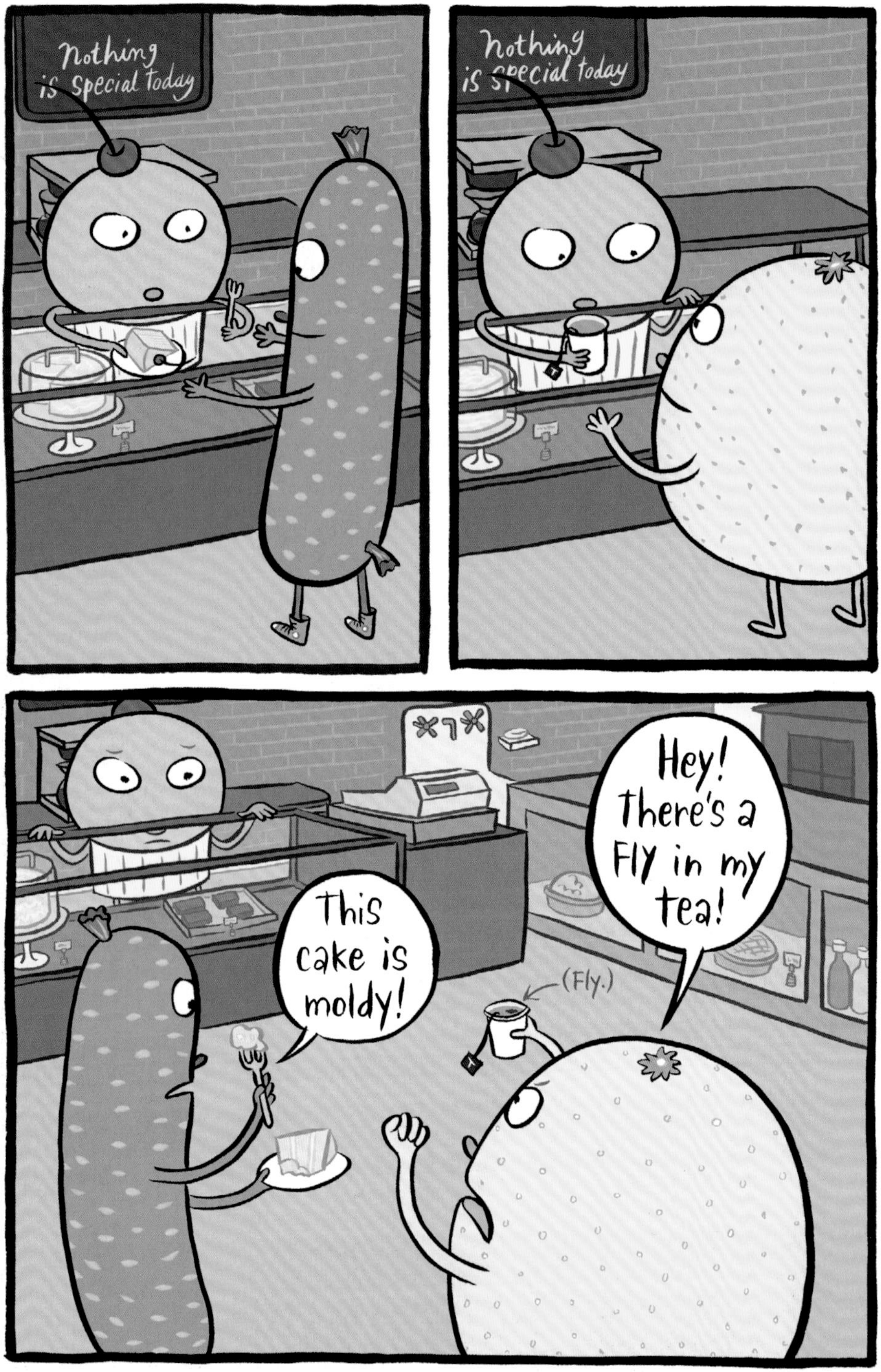

Nothing is special today
Nothing is special today
This cake is moldy!
(Fly.)
Hey! there's a FLY in my tea!

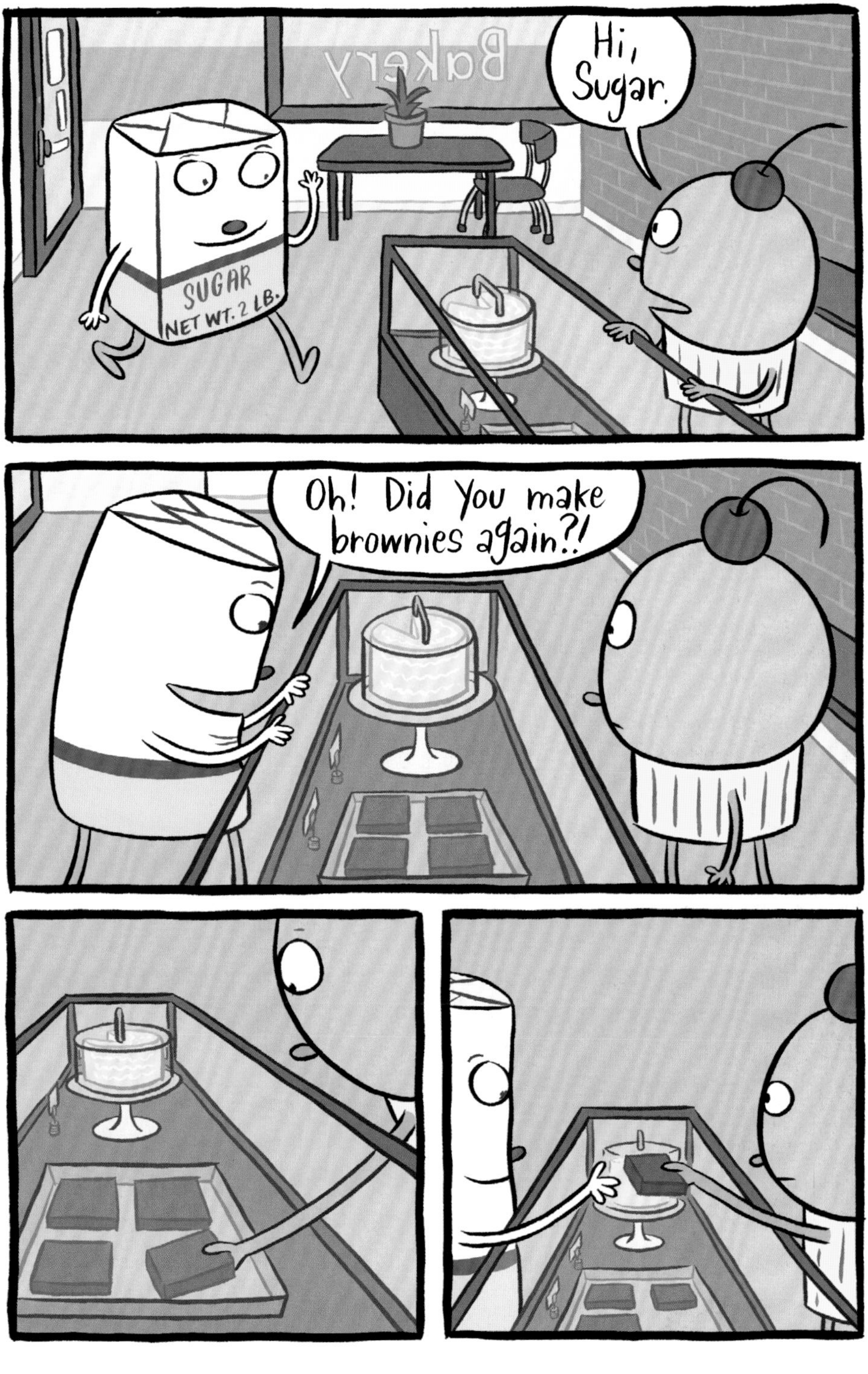
Bakery
Hi, Sugar.
SUGAR
NET WT. 2 LB.
Oh! Did you make brownies again?!

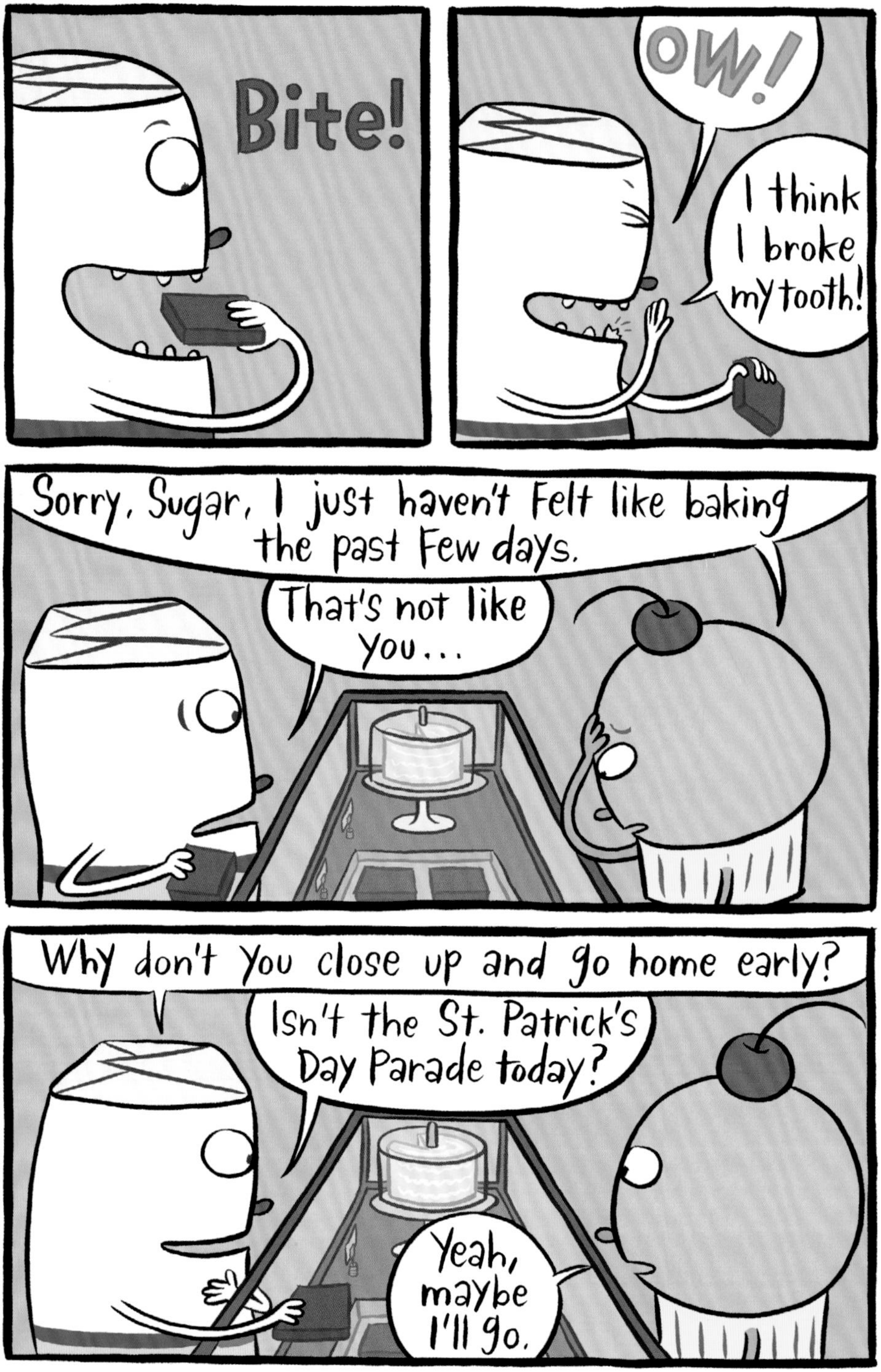
Bite!
OW!
I think I broke my tooth!
Sorry, Sugar, I just haven't Felt like baking the past Few days.
That's not like you...
Why don't you close up and go home early?
Isn't the St. Patrick's Day Parade today?
Yeah, maybe I'll go.

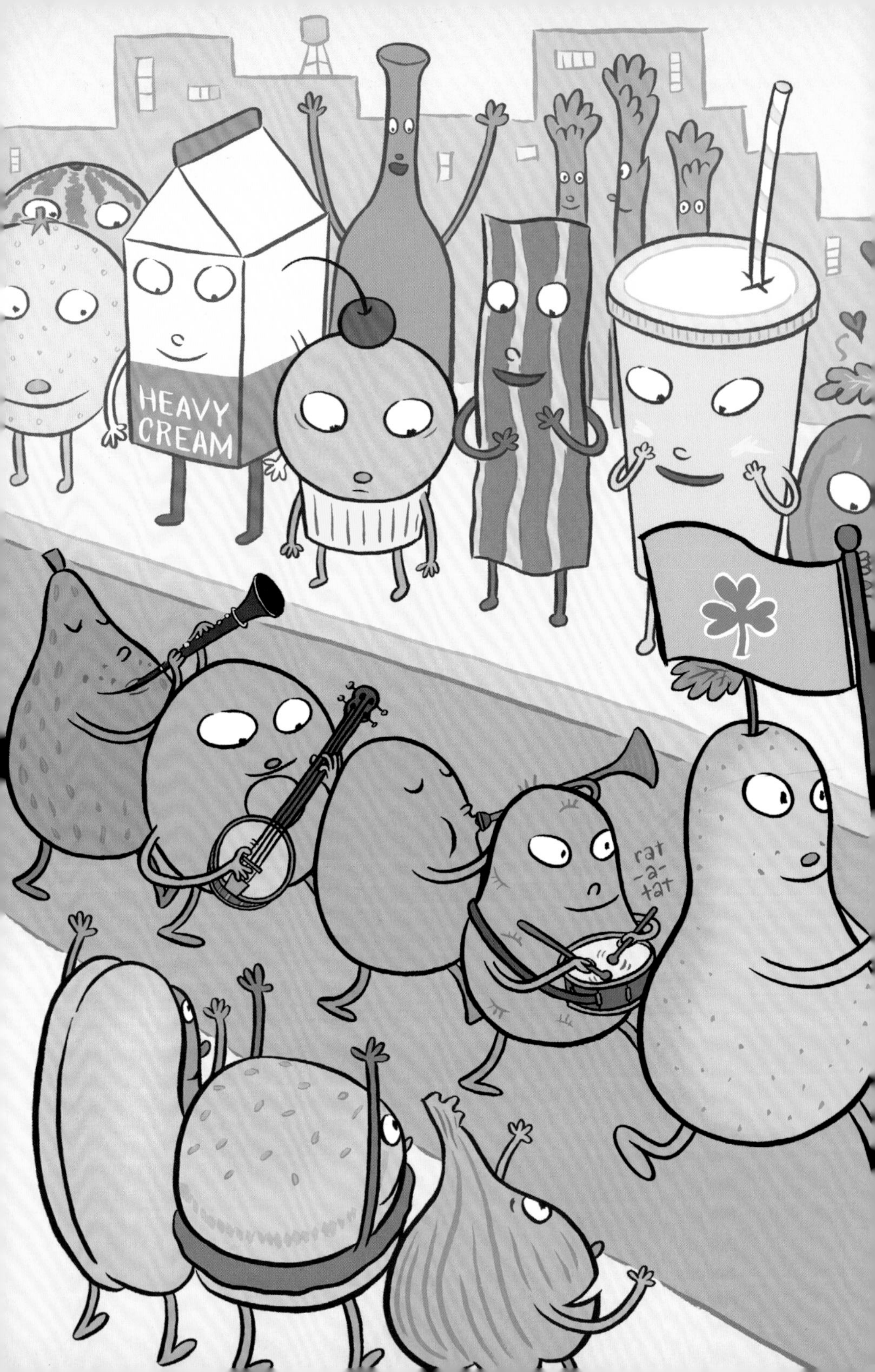
HEAVY CREAM
rat-a-tat

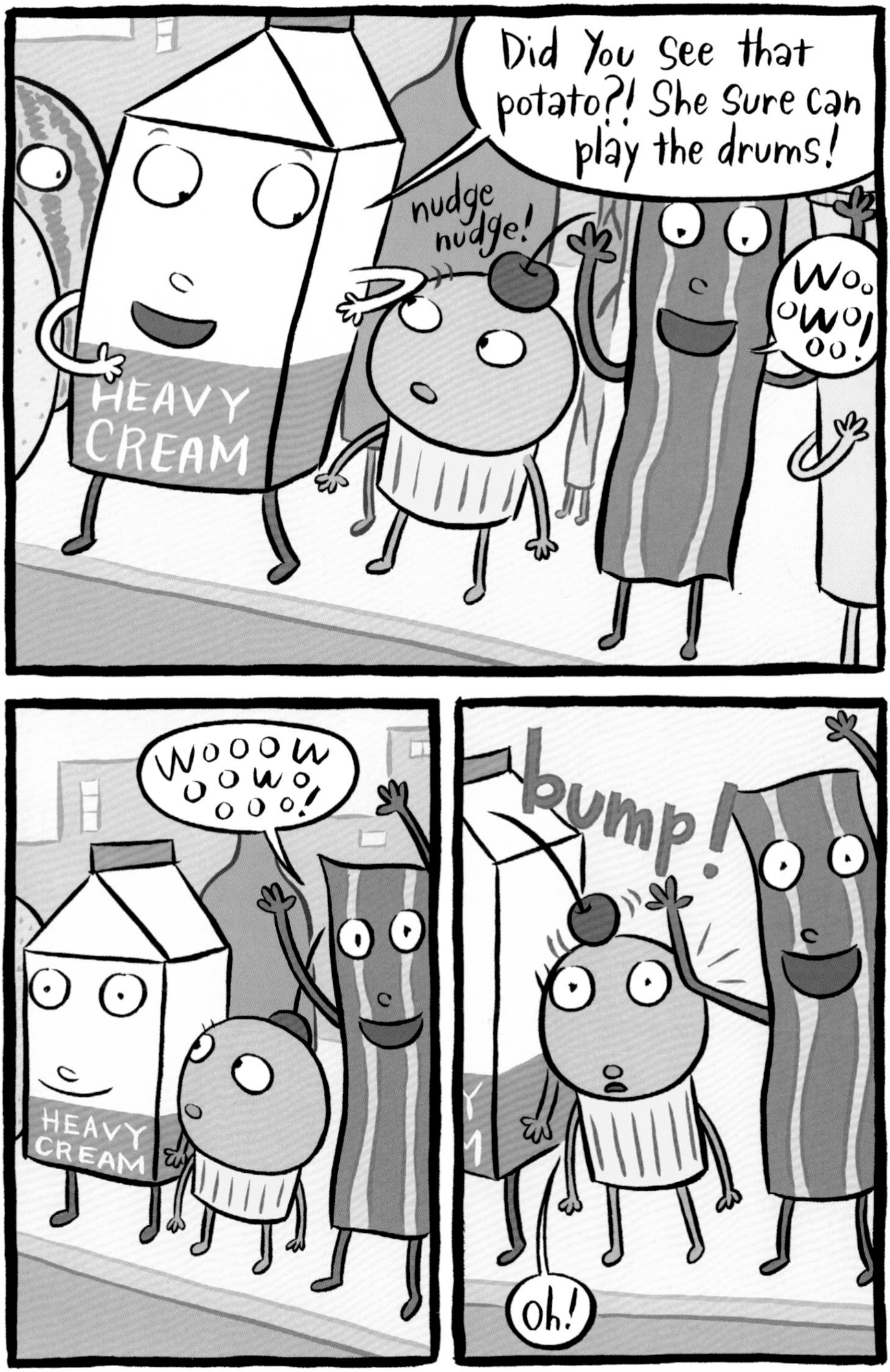
Did You see that potato?! She sure can play the drums!
nudge nudge!
Wooowoooo!
WoooWoooWoooooo!
bump!
Oh!

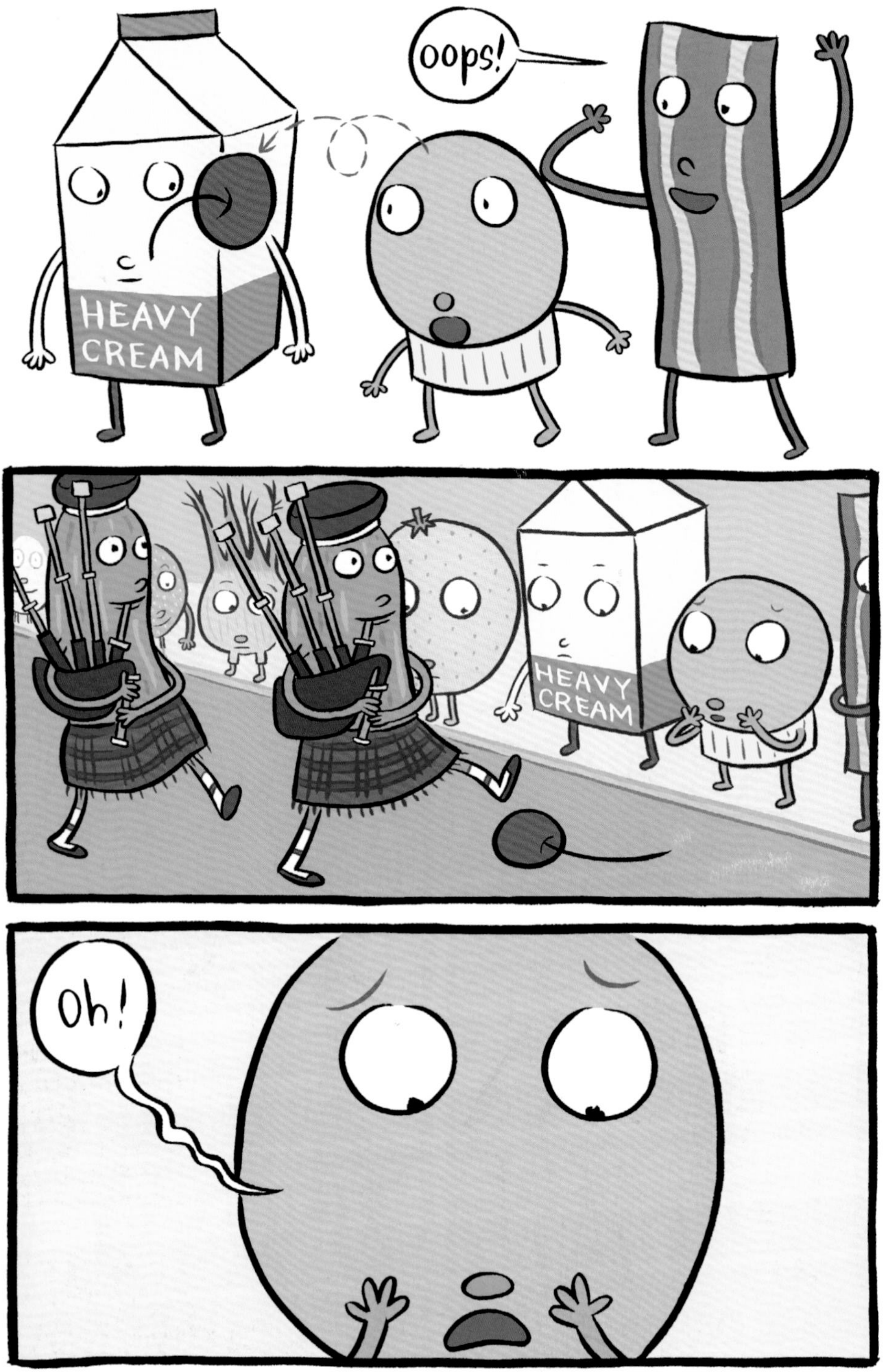
oops!
HEAVY CREAM
HEAVY CREAM
Oh!

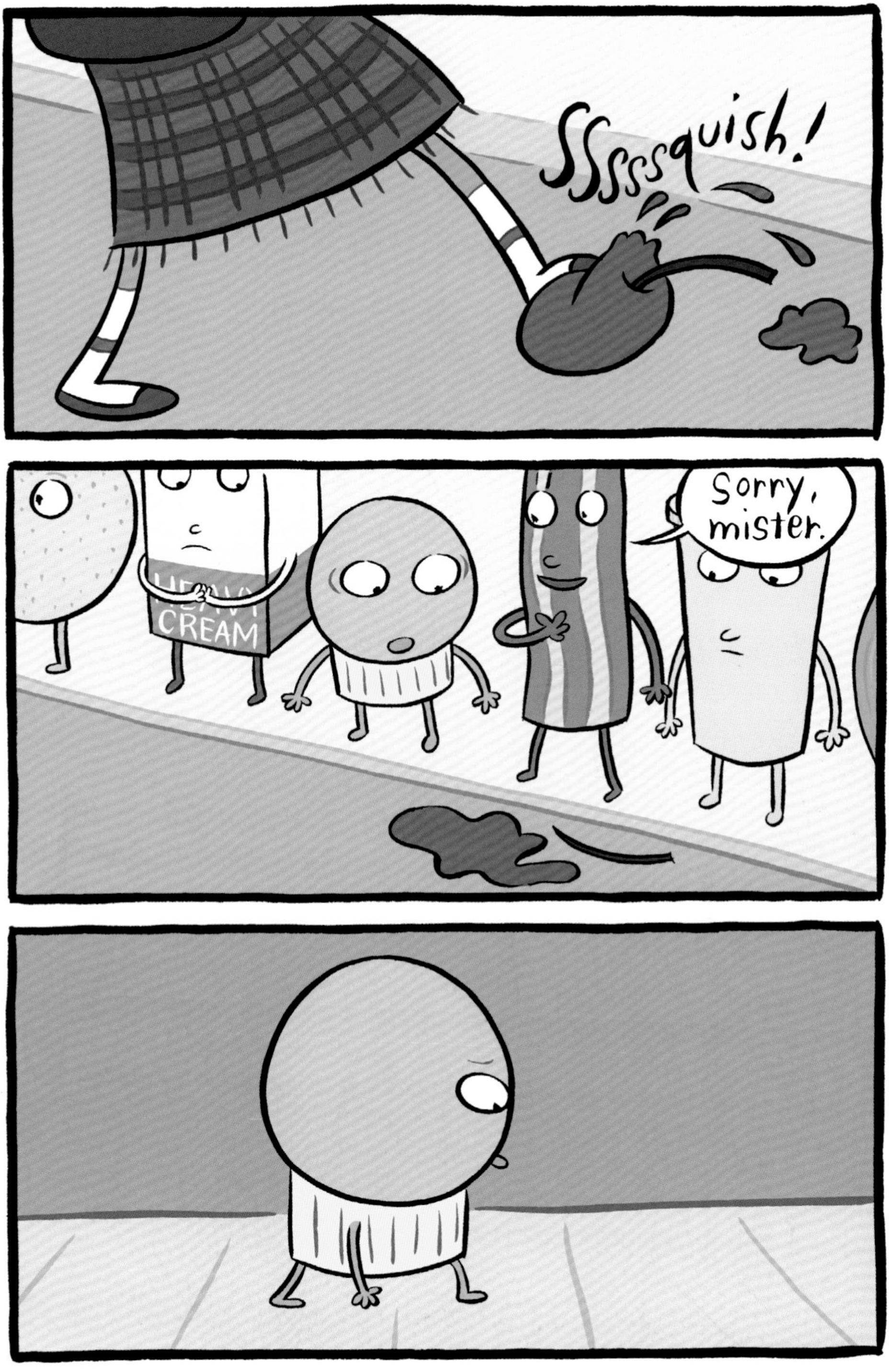
Ssssquish!
CREAM
Sorry, mister.

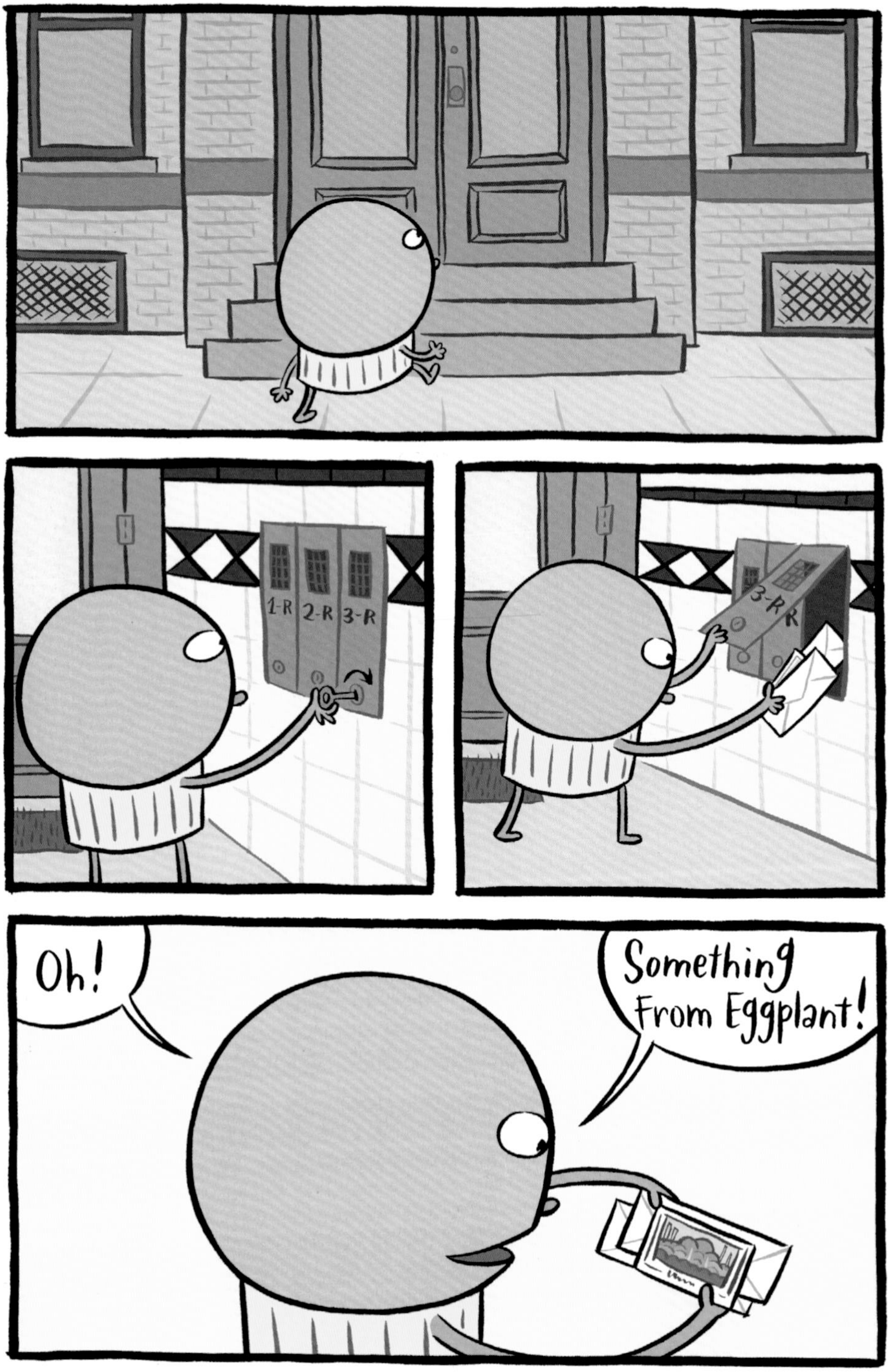
1-R
2-R
3-R
3-R
Oh!
Something From Eggplant!

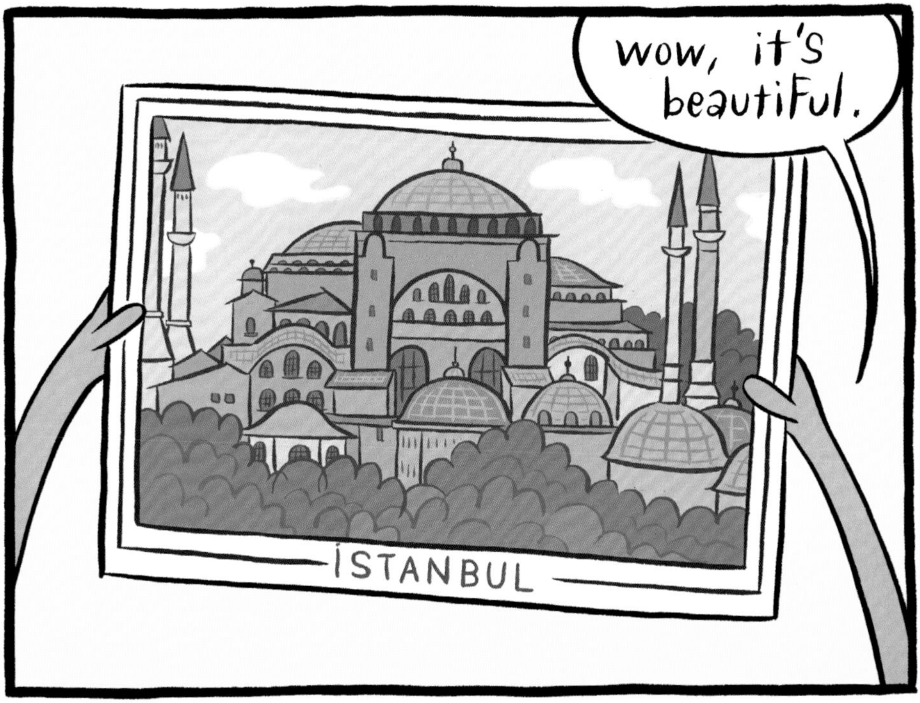
ISTANBUL
wow, it's beautiful.

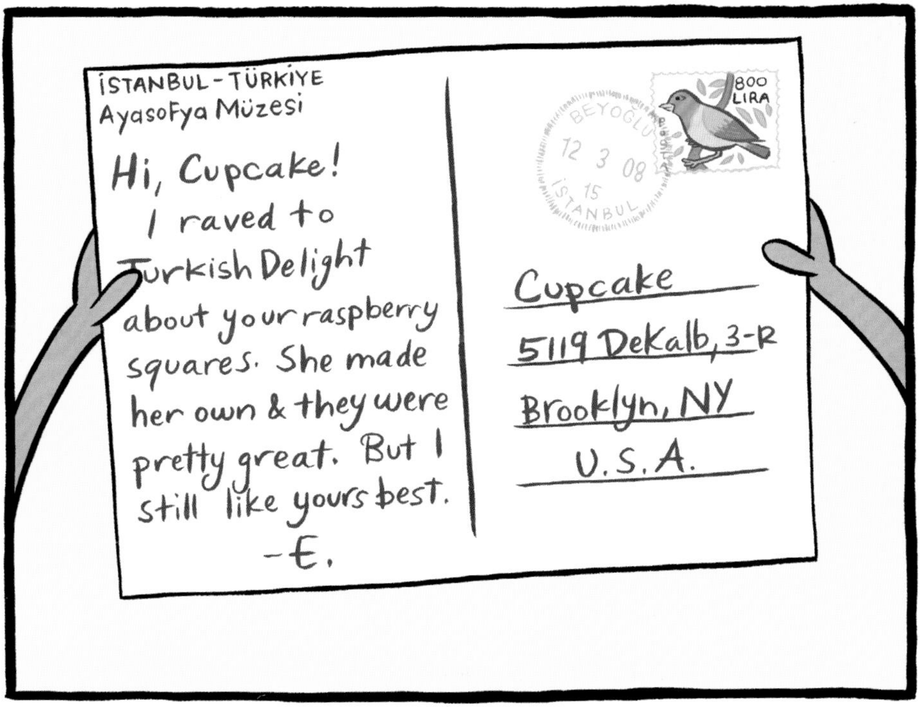
ISTANBUL-TÜRKIYE
AyasoFya Müzesi
Hi, Cupcake!
I raved to Turkish Delight about your raspberry squares. She made her own & they were pretty great. But I still like yours best.
-E.
800 LIRA
BEYOĞLU
12 3 08
15
ISTANBUL
Cupcake
5119 DeKalb, 3-R
Brooklyn, NY
U.S.A.

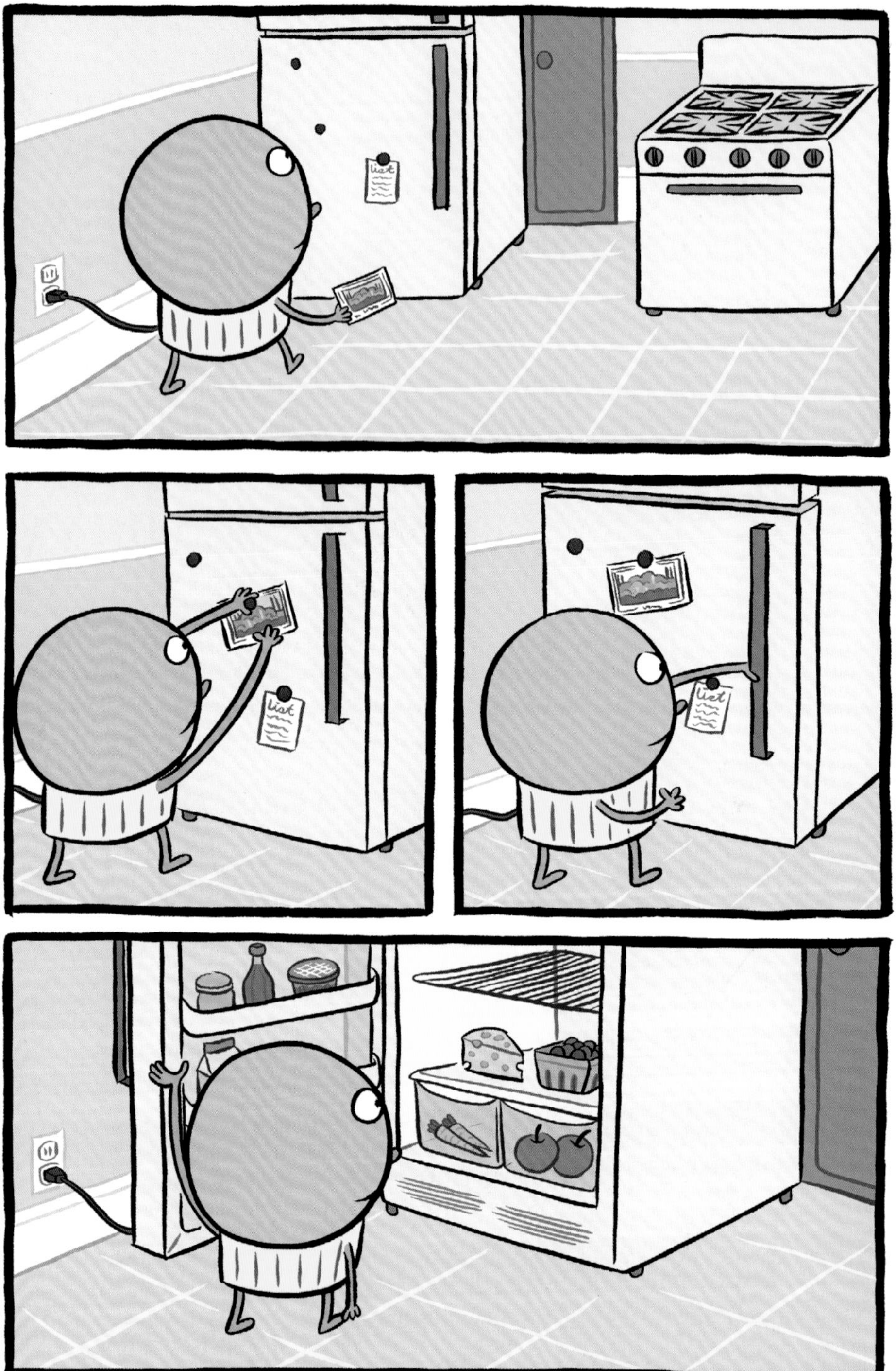
List
List
List

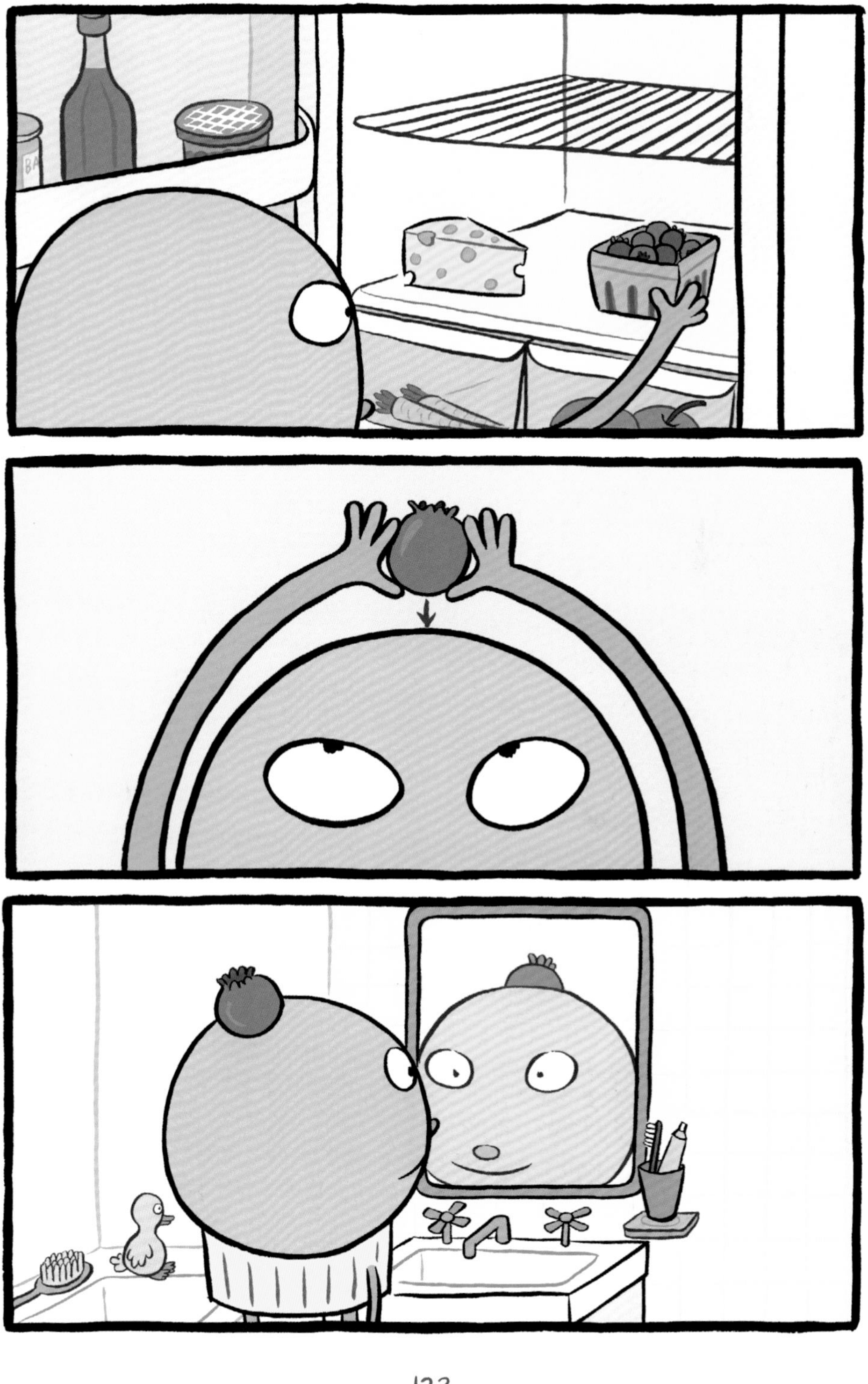

chapter 6

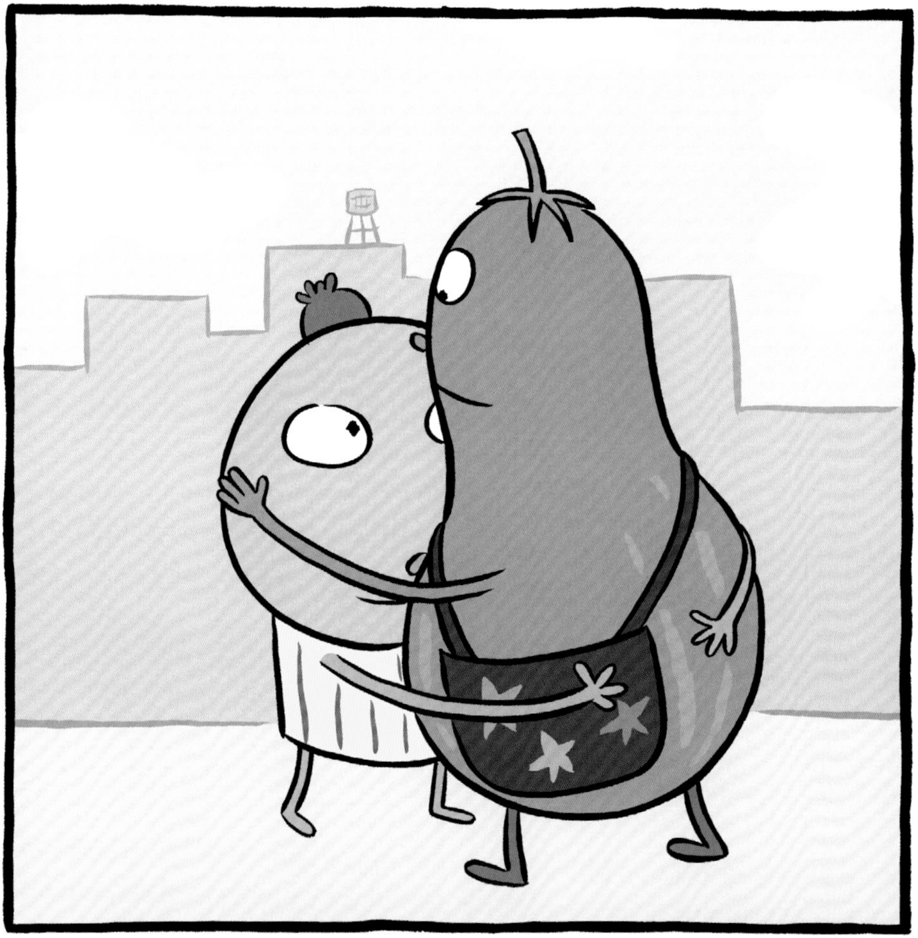

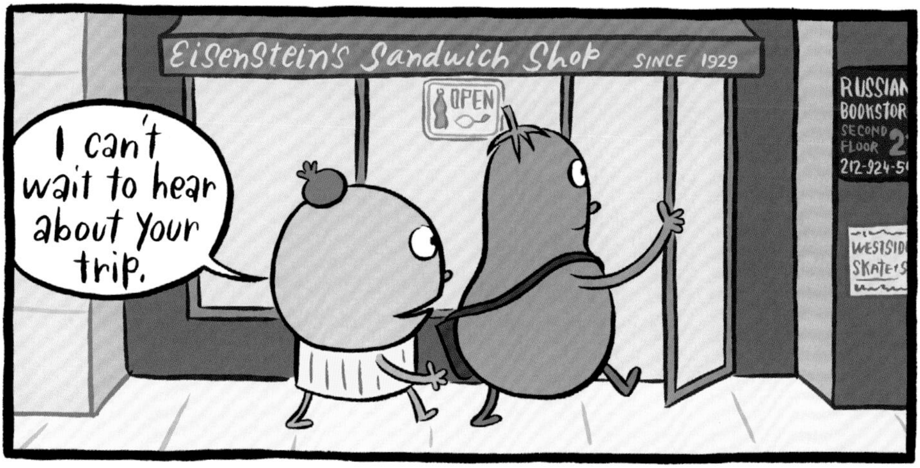
Eisenstein's Sandwich Shop SINCE 1929
OPEN
I can't wait to hear about your trip.
RUSSIAN BOOKSTOR
SECOND FLOOR
212-924-5

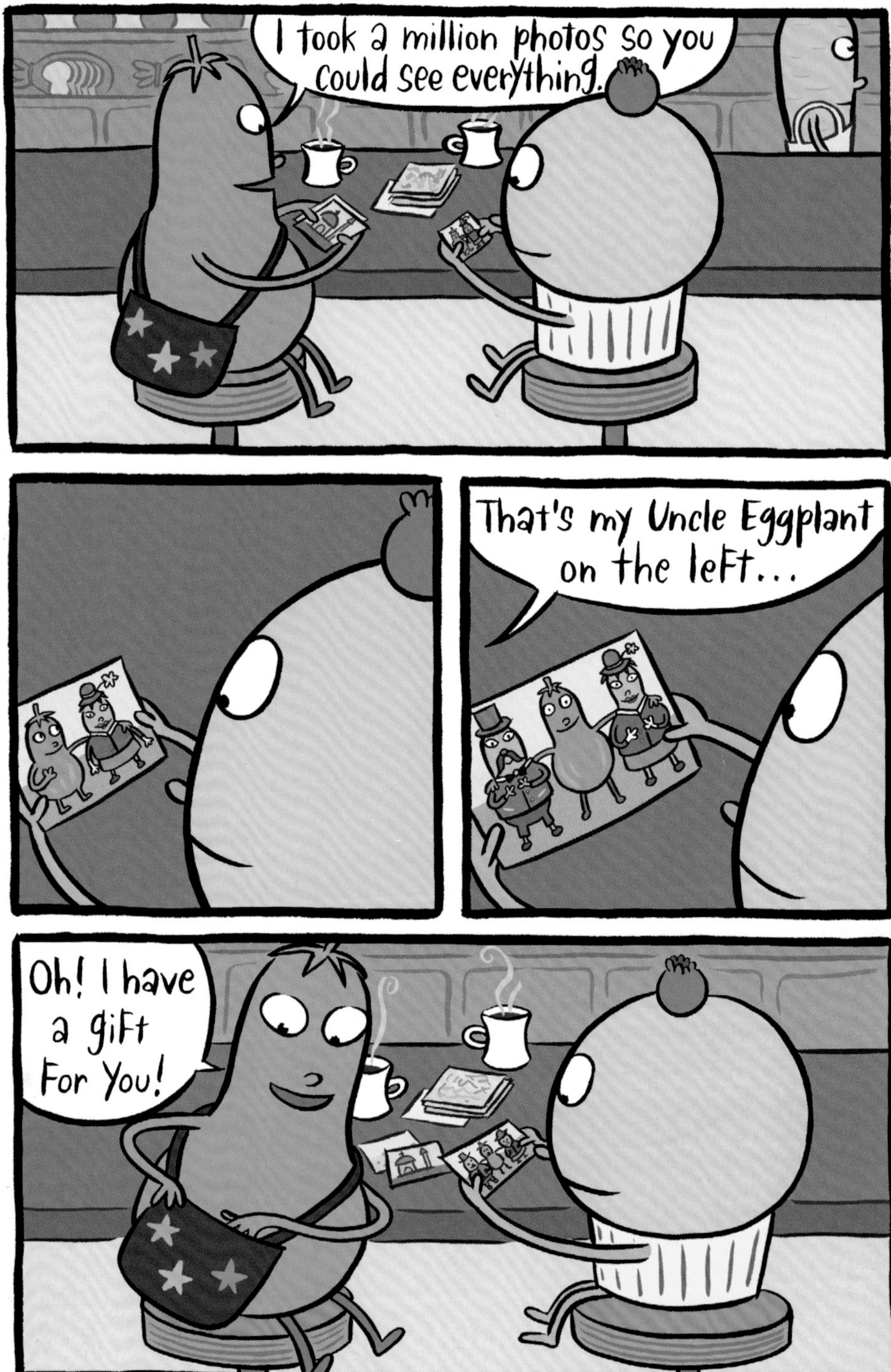
I took a million photos so you could see everything.
That's my Uncle Eggplant on the left...
Oh! I have a gift for you!

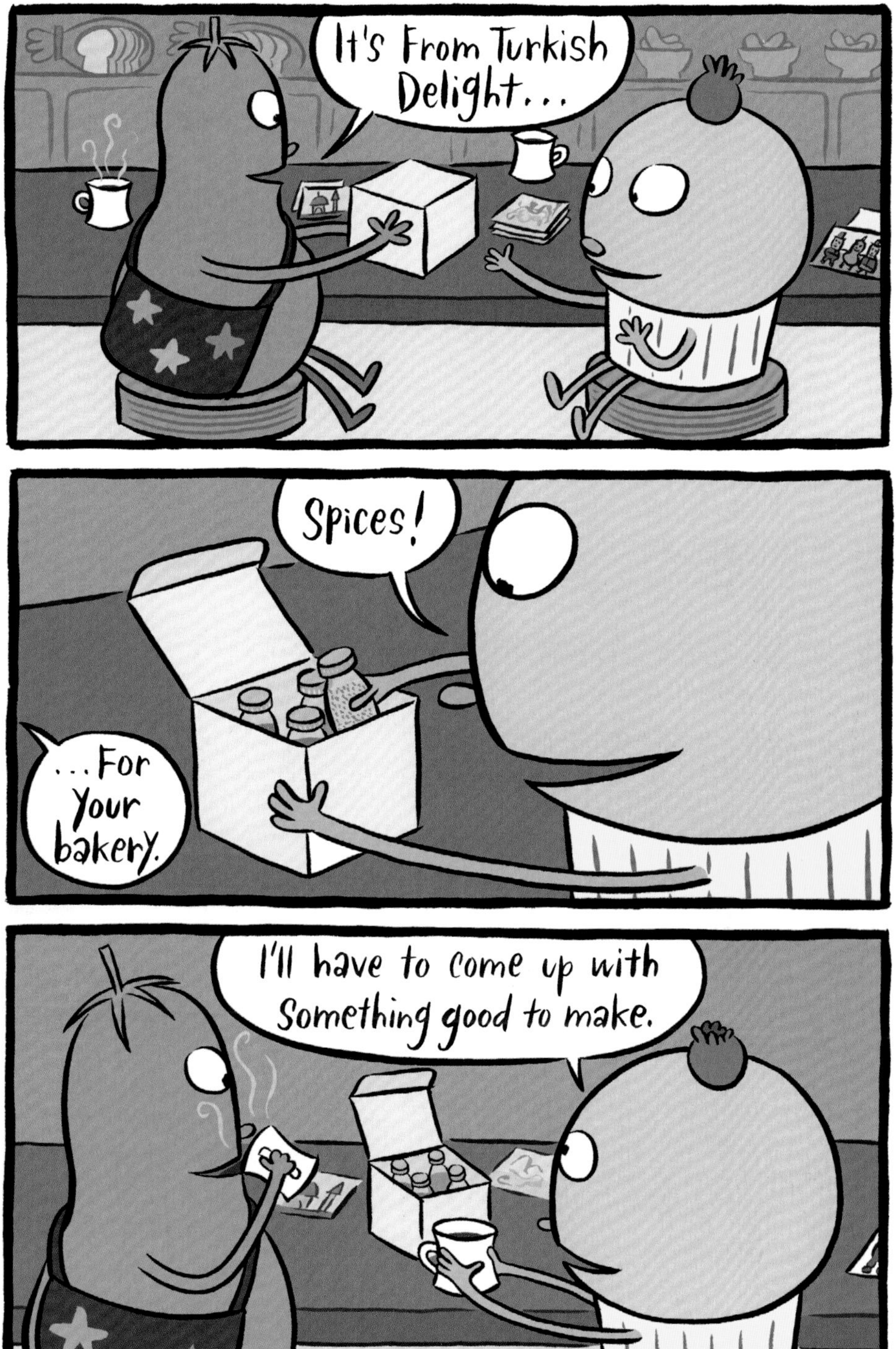
It's From Turkish Delight...
Spices!
...For your bakery.
I'll have to come up with Something good to make.

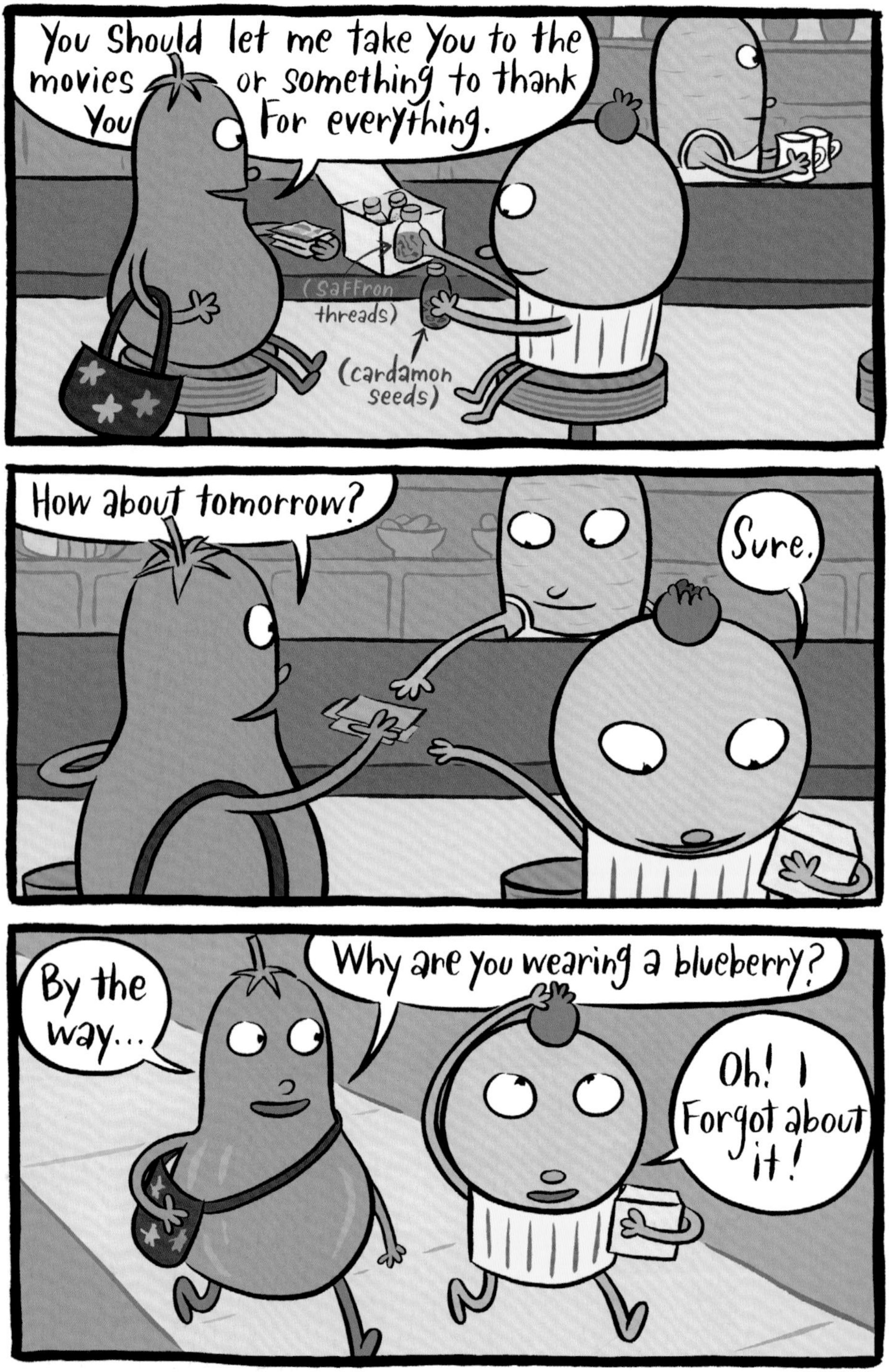
You Should let me take You to the movies or something to thank You For everything.
(SaFFron threads)
(cardamon seeds)
How about tomorrow?
Sure.
By the way...
Why are you wearing a blueberry?
Oh! I Forgot about it!

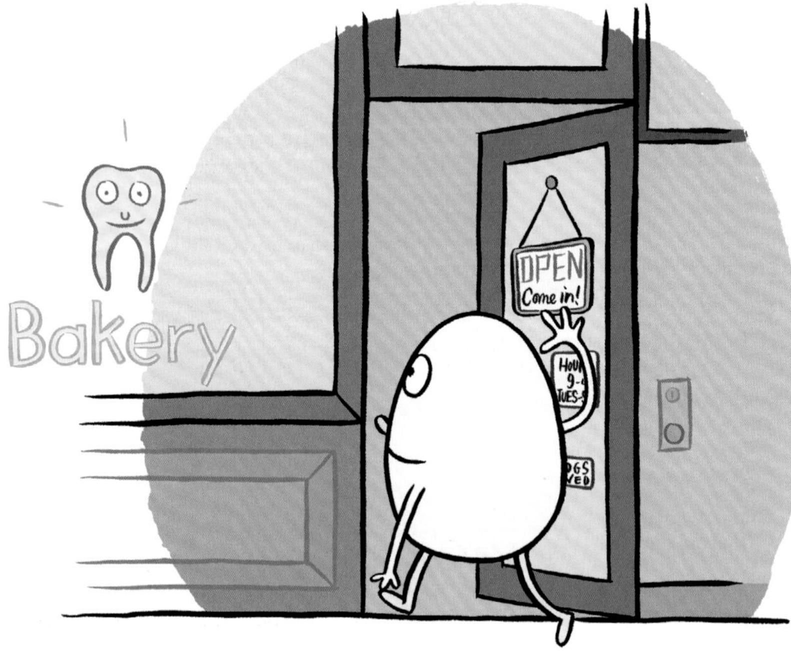

Bakery
OPEN
Come in!

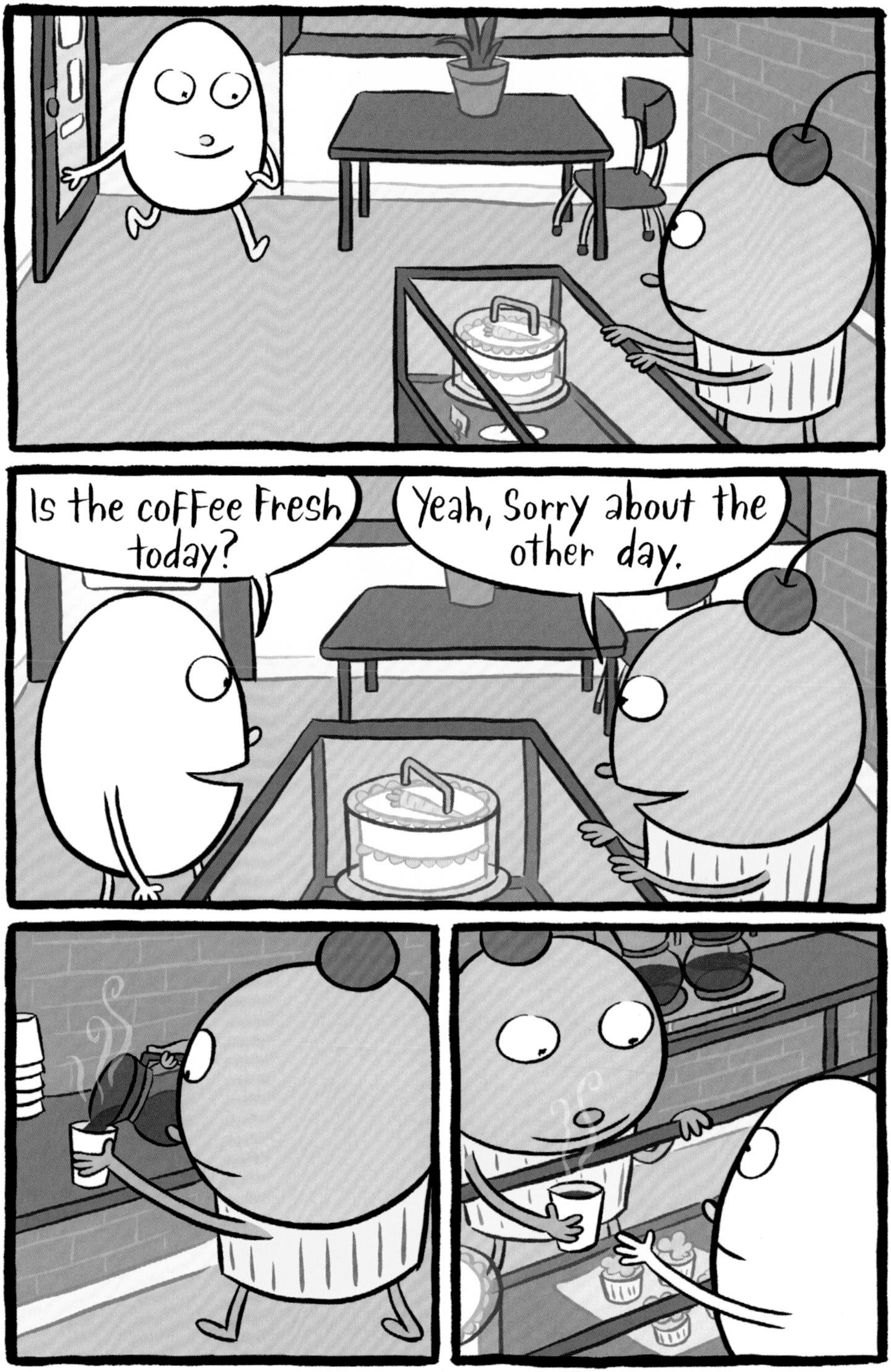
Is the coffee fresh today?
Yeah, Sorry about the other day.

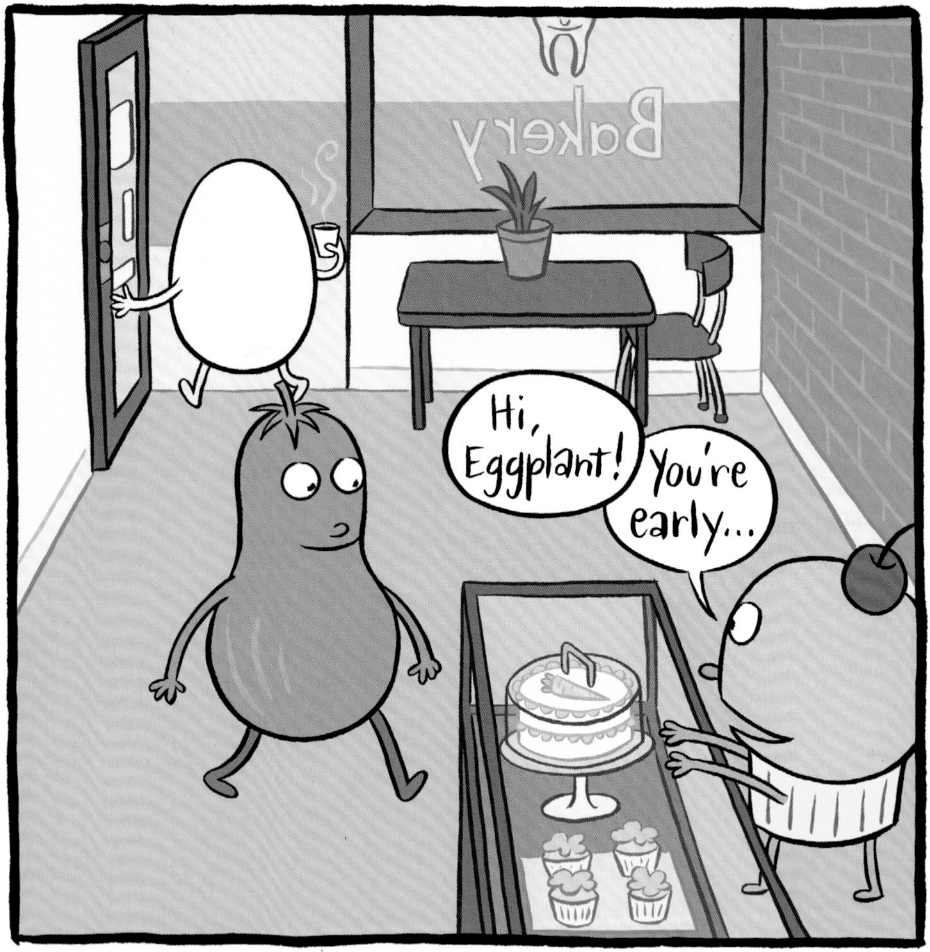
Bakery
Hi, Eggplant!
You're early...

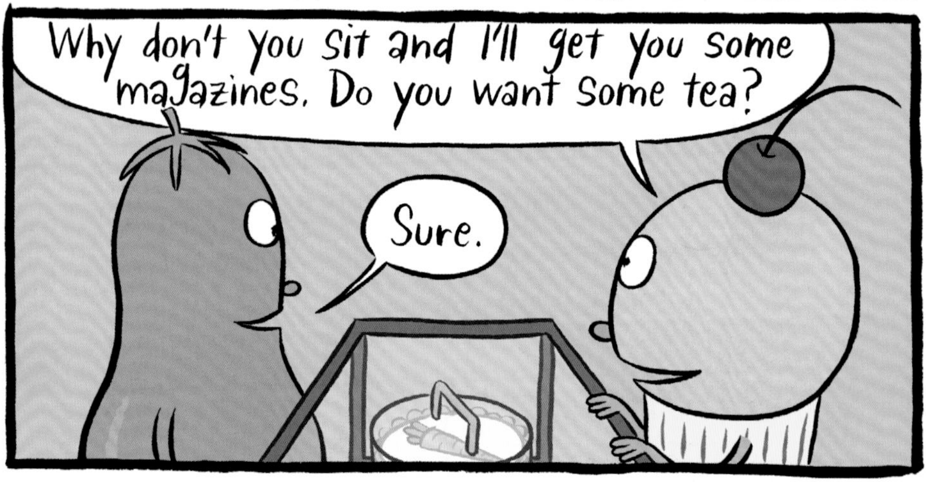
Why don't you sit and I'll get you some magazines. Do you want some tea?
Sure.

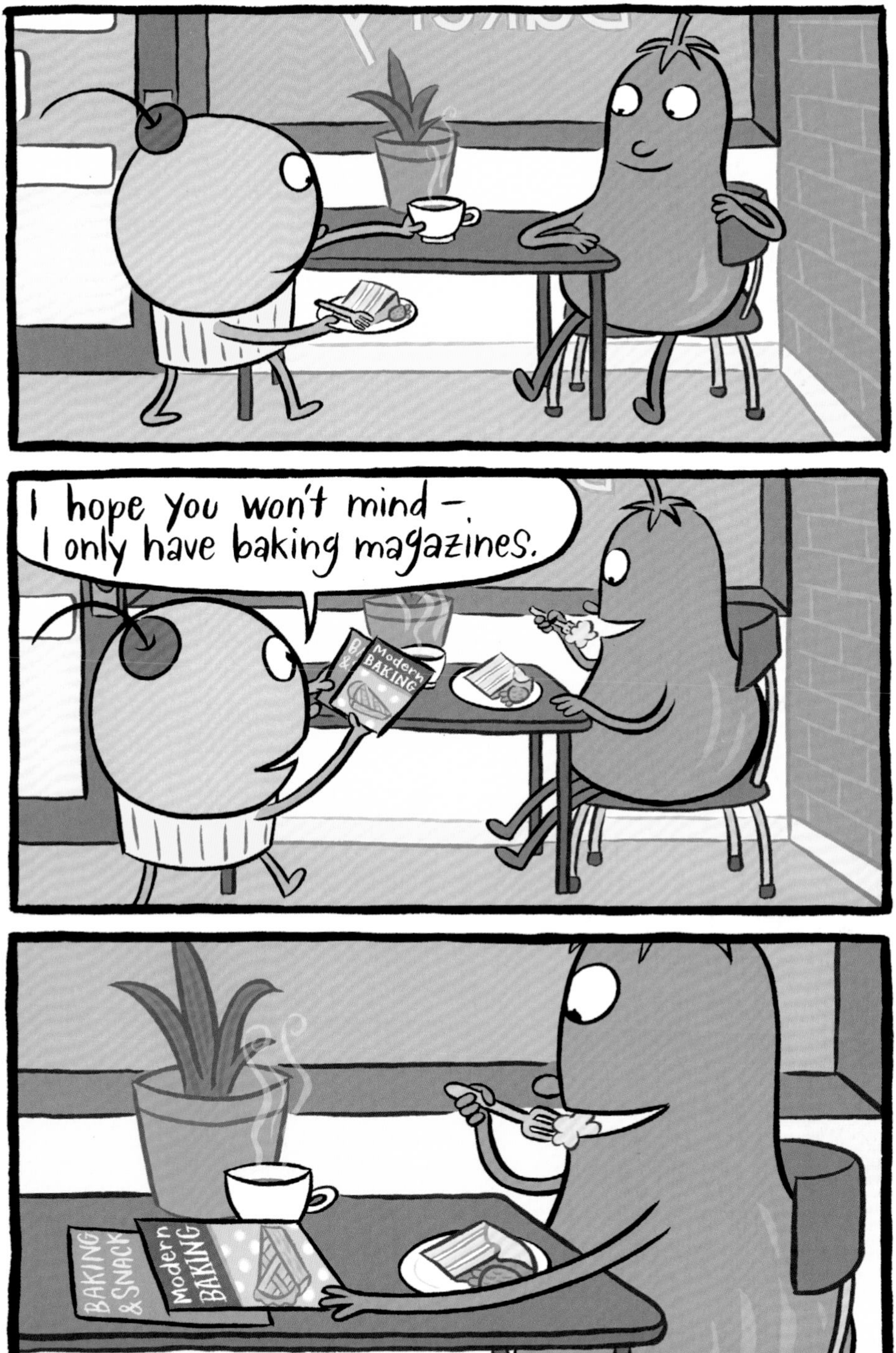
I hope you won't mind -
I only have baking magazines.
Modern BAKING
BAKING & SNACK
Modern BAKING

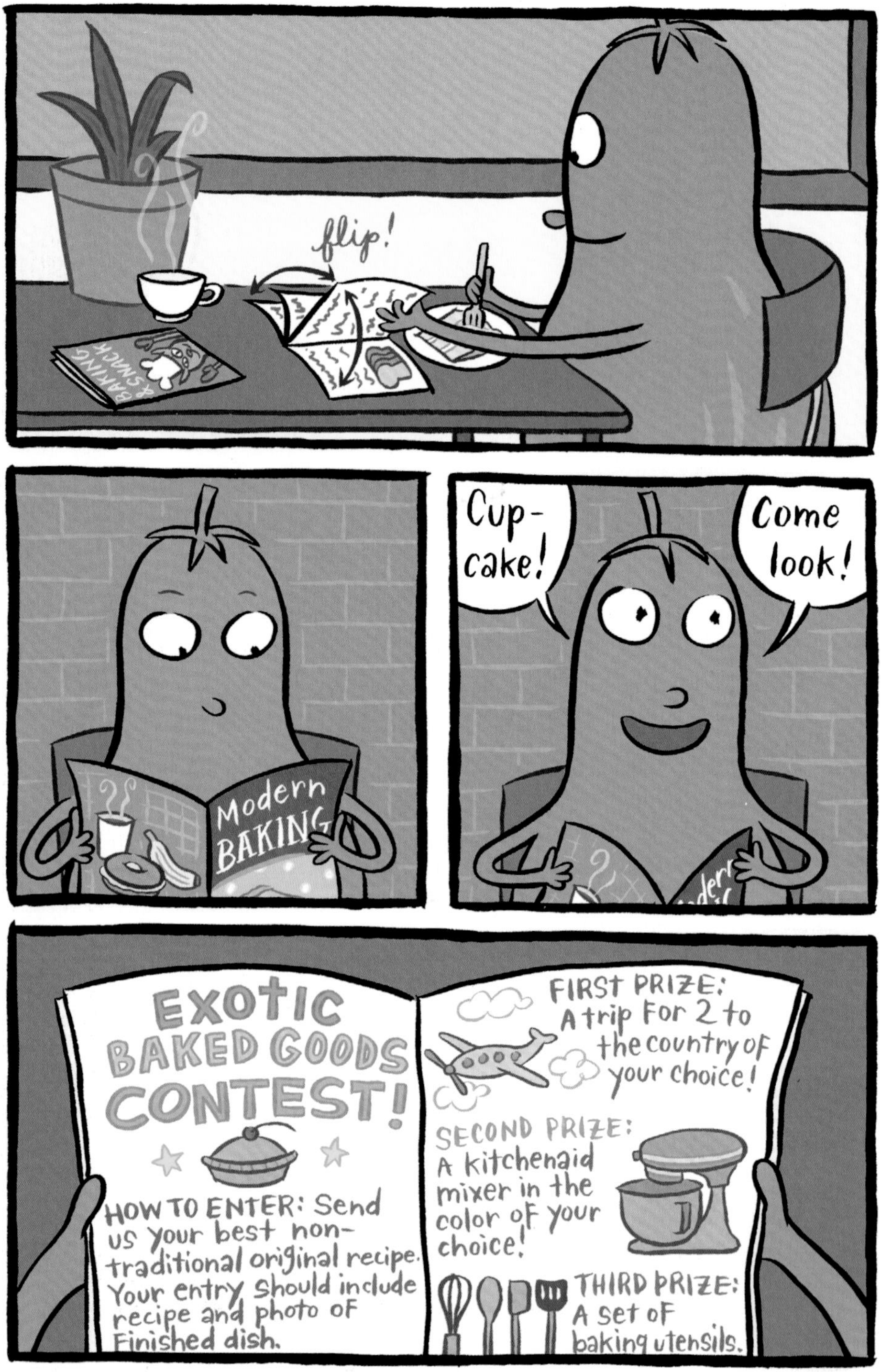
flip!
BAKING & SNACK
Modern BAKING
Cup-cake!
Come look!
EXOTIC BAKED GOODS CONTEST!
HOW TO ENTER: Send us your best non-traditional original recipe. Your entry should include recipe and photo of finished dish.
FIRST PRIZE: A trip for 2 to the country of your choice!
SECOND PRIZE: A kitchenaid mixer in the color of your choice!
THIRD PRIZE: A set of baking utensils.

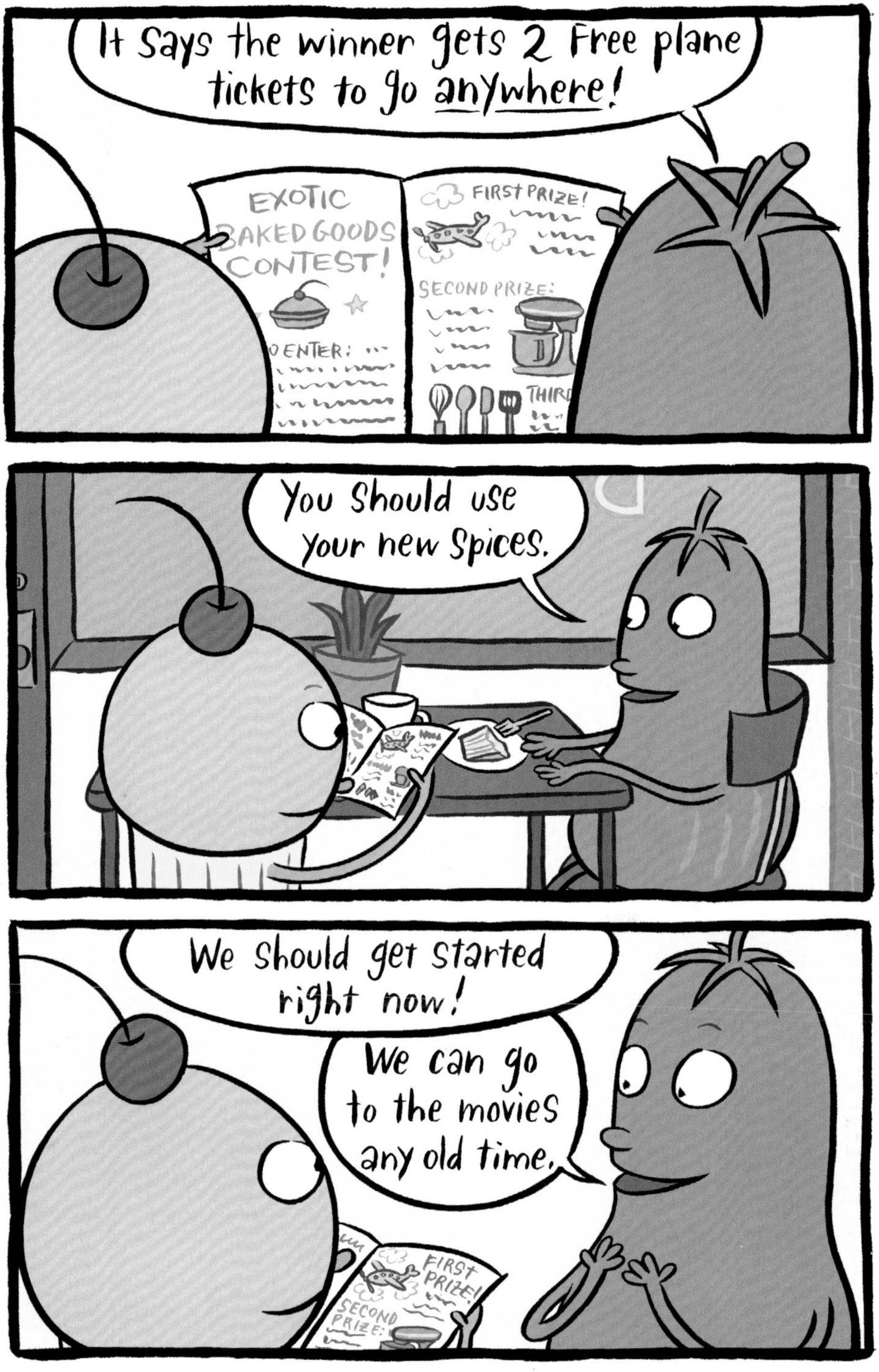

It says the winner gets 2 free plane tickets to go anywhere!
EXOTIC BAKED GOODS CONTEST!
FIRST PRIZE!
SECOND PRIZE:
You should use your new spices.
We should get started right now!
We can go to the movies any old time.
FIRST PRIZE!
SECOND PRIZE:

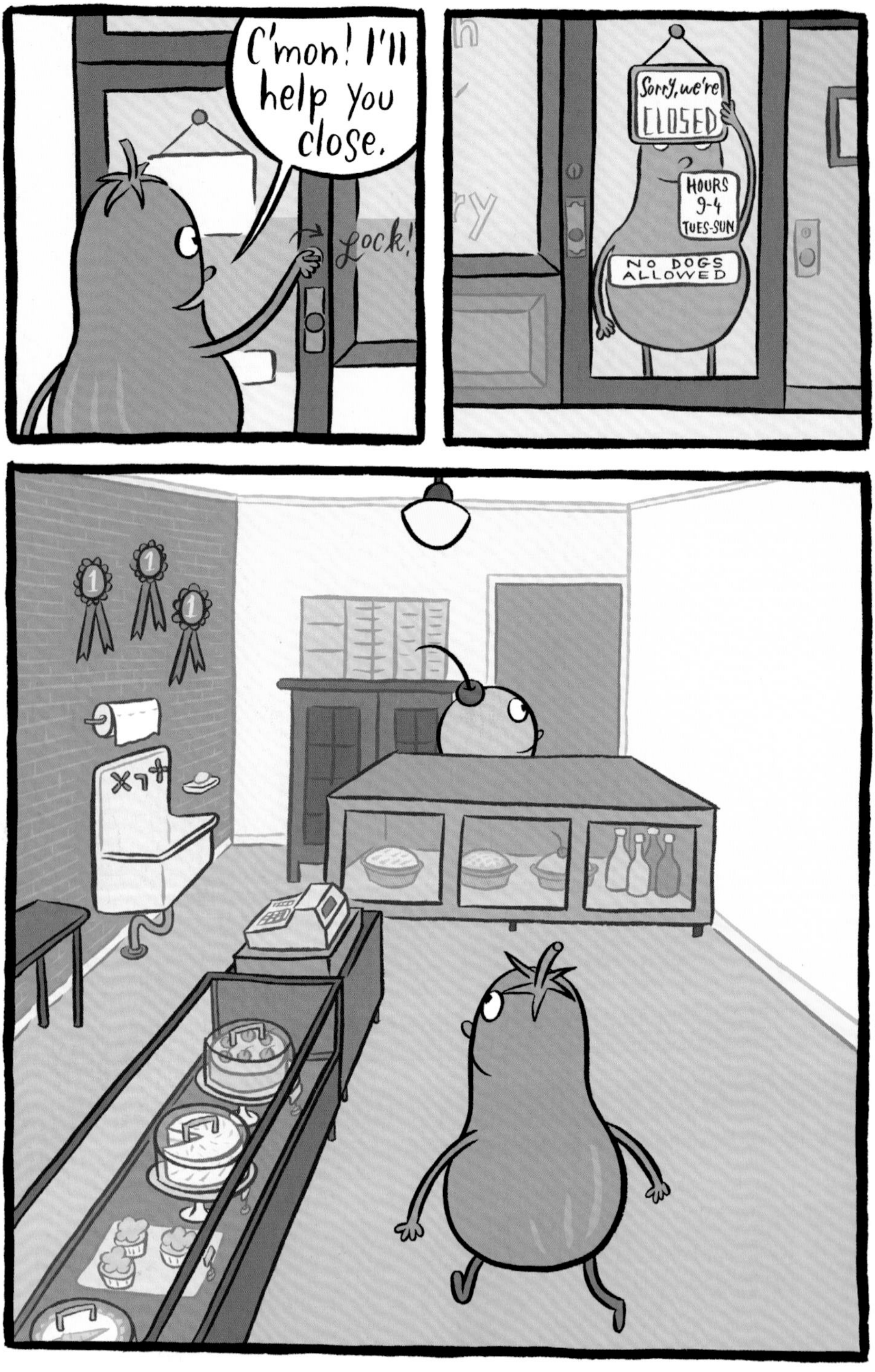
C'mon! I'll help you close.
Lock!
Sorry, we're CLOSED
HOURS 9-4 TUES-SUN
NO DOGS ALLOWED

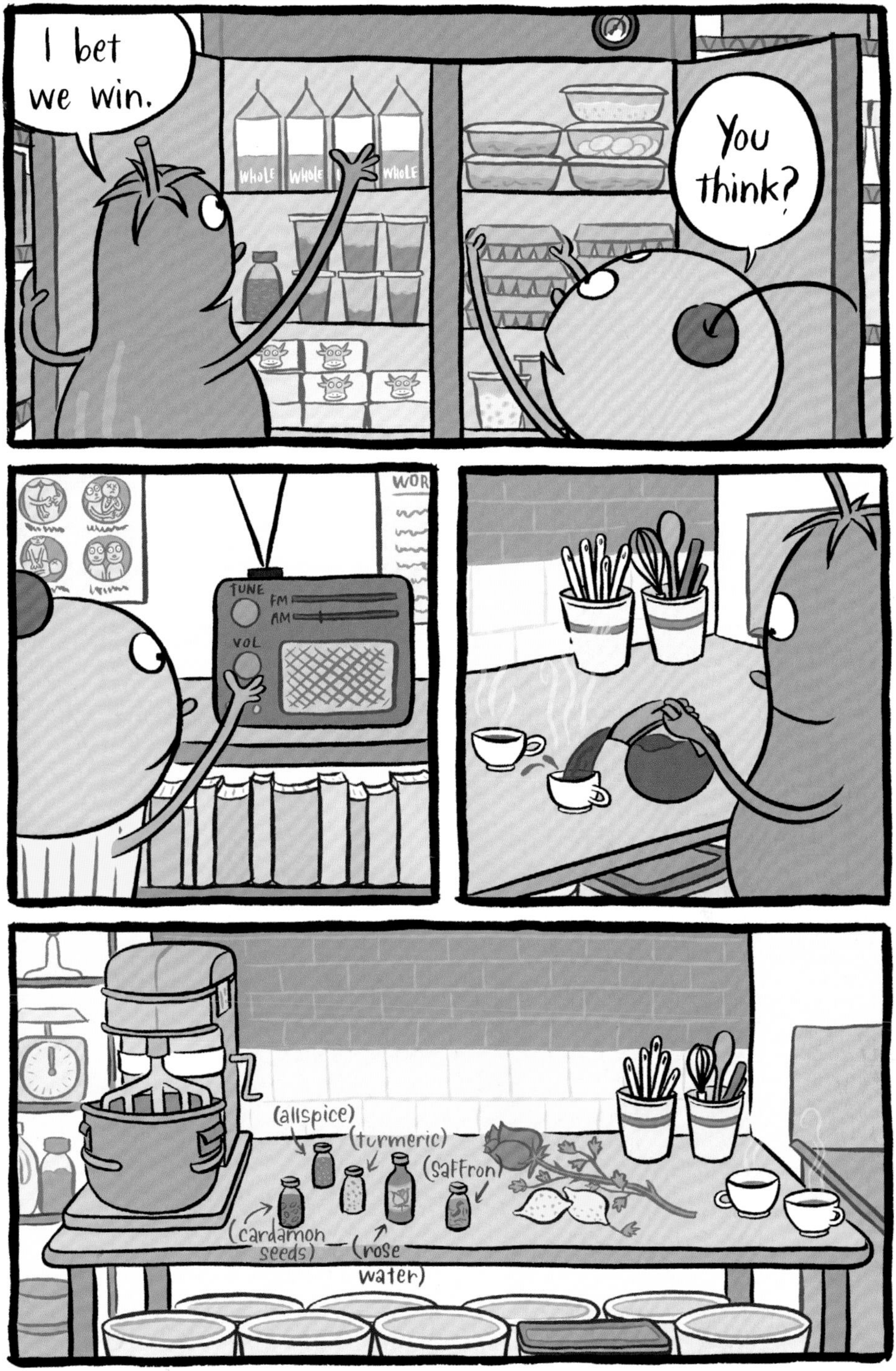
I bet we win.
You think?
WHOLE
WHOLE
WHOLE
TUNE
FM
AM
VOL
WOR
(allspice)
(turmeric)
(saffron)
(cardamon seeds)
(rose water)

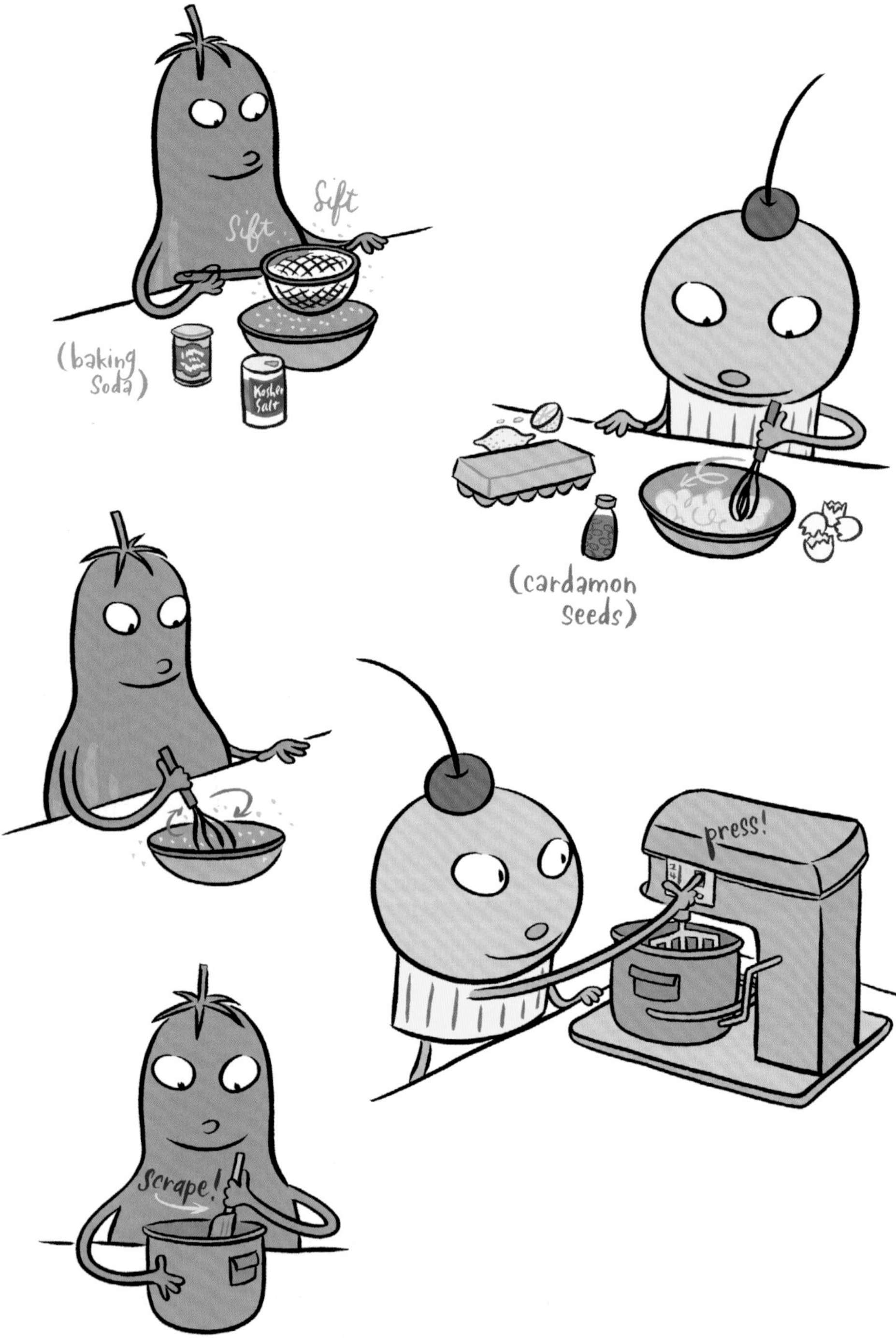
sift
sift
(baking soda)
Kosher Salt
(cardamon seeds)
press!
scrape!

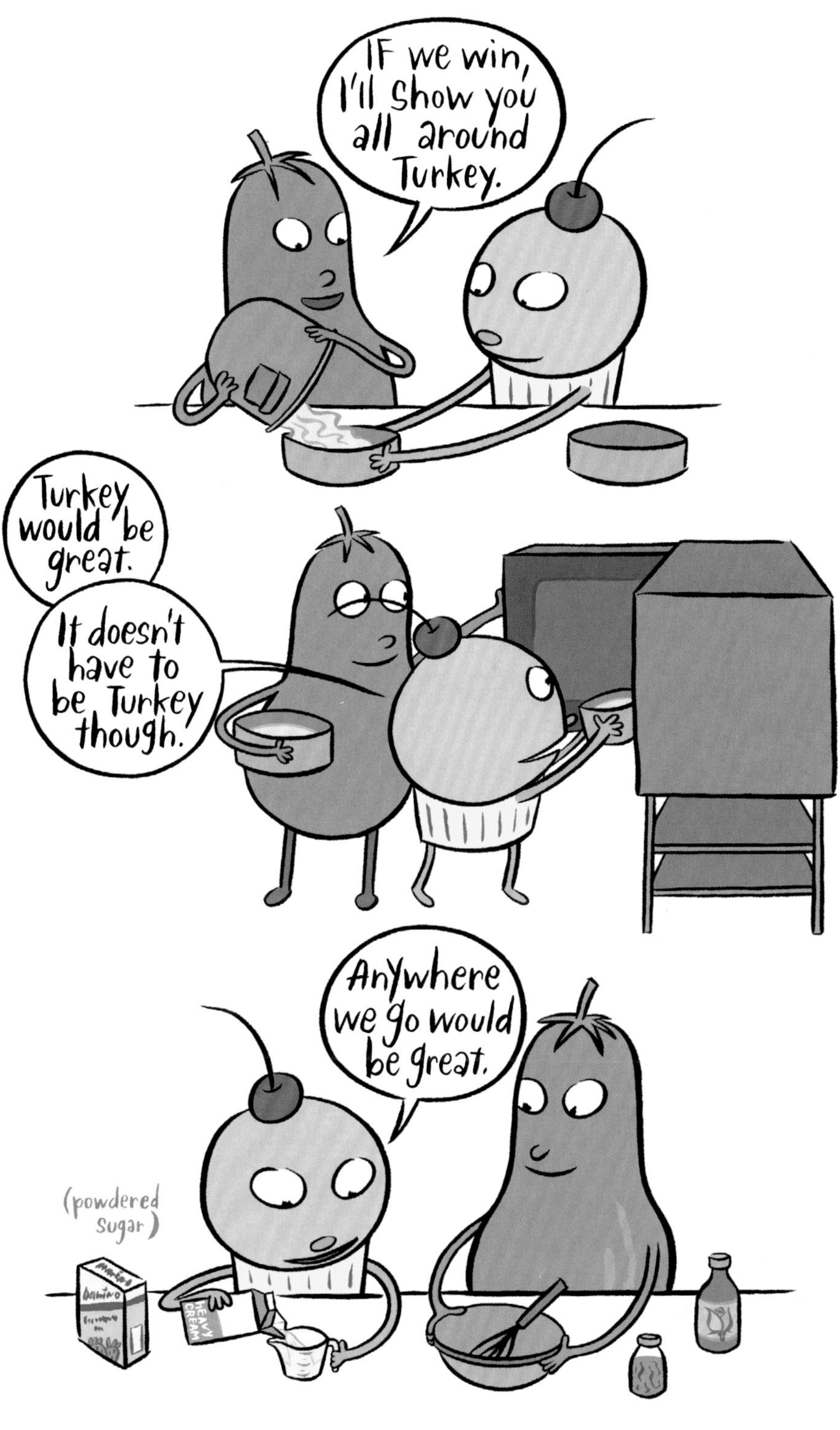
If we win, I'll show you all around Turkey.
Turkey would be great.
It doesn't have to be Turkey though.
Anywhere we go would be great.
(powdered sugar)
HEAVY CREAM

Cupcake's

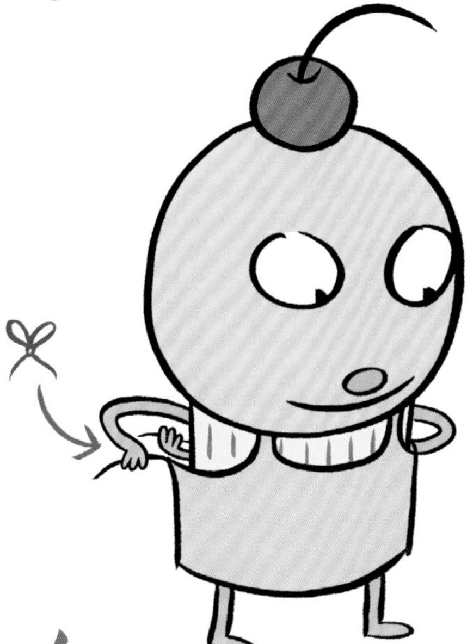

Repertoire

Raspberry Squares (From page 8)

ingredients:

Crust:

2 sticks unsalted butter, melted

2 cups all-purpose Flour

Filling:

1 cup raspberry preserves

topping:

2 1/4 cups all-purpose Flour

1 1/2 cups unpacked light brown sugar

2 sticks unsalted butter at room temperature, cut into smallish pieces

9 by 13 inch glass baking dish

1. Preheat oven to 350° F

2. For the crust, combine butter and Flour in a large bowl, until it becomes doughy.

3. Spread dough evenly into a 9 by 13 inch glass baking dish. You can use a large piece of waxed paper to press down the crust so it is Flat and even.

4. Bake the crust For 17 minutes. Let it cool completely beFore covering it with the Filling. As the crust cools, you can prepare the topping.

5. In a large bowl, mix the flour and the brown sugar.

6. Cut the butter into the flour and sugar with a pastry blender (or a fork,) until the mixture has the texture of coarse crumbs. Don't overmix it!

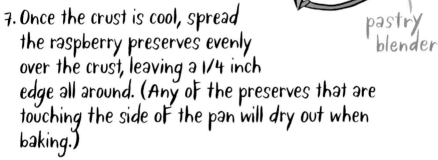

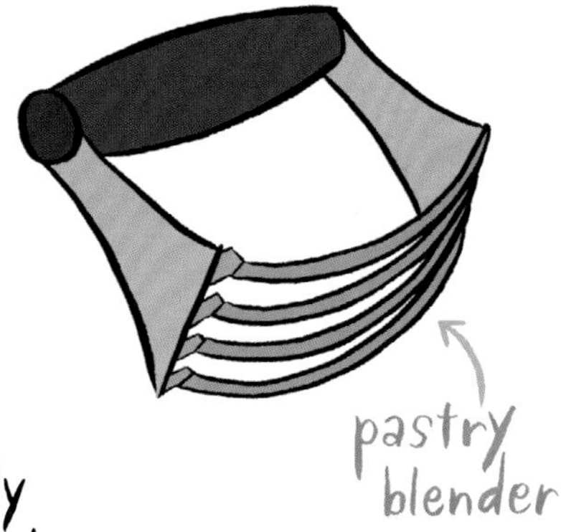

pastry blender

7. Once the crust is cool, spread the raspberry preserves evenly over the crust, leaving a 1/4 inch edge all around. (Any of the preserves that are touching the side of the pan will dry out when baking.)

8. Pour the topping evenly over the preserves.

9. Bake for 20-25 minutes until lightly browned.

10. Allow to cool before cutting into squares.

Brownies! (From page 52)

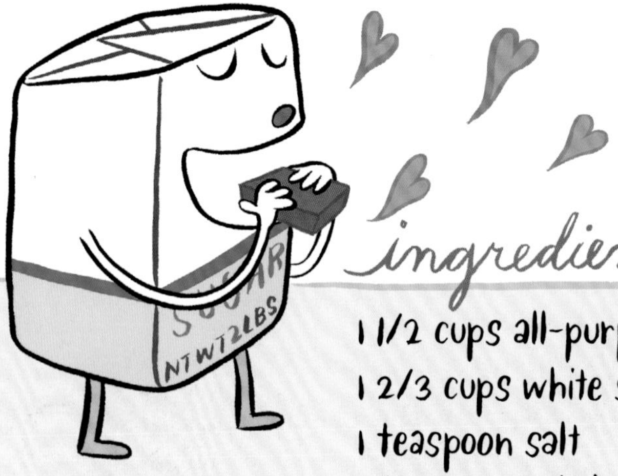
NT WT 2 LBS

ingredients:

1 1/2 cups all-purpose flour
1 2/3 cups white sugar
1 teaspoon salt
6 large eggs, lightly beaten
1 teaspoon vanilla extract
1 2/3 cups (3 3/8 sticks) butter at room temperature
13 ounces high-quality bittersweet chocolate

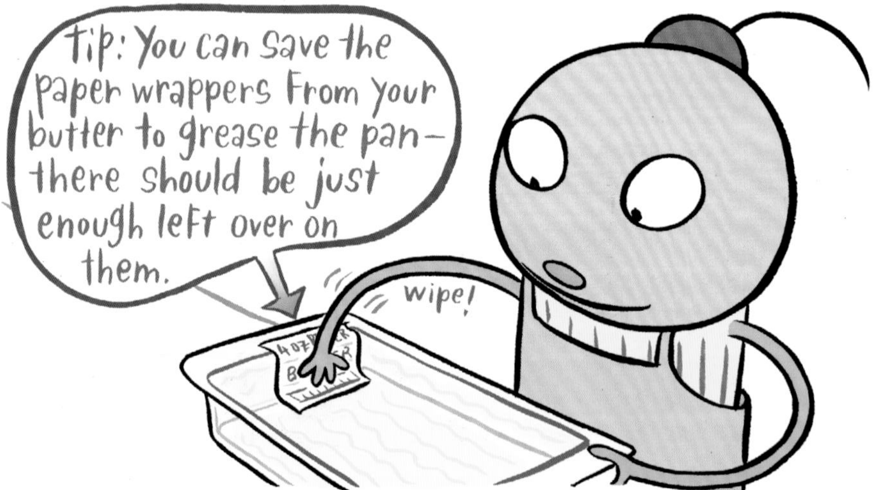
Tip: You can save the paper wrappers from your butter to grease the pan— there should be just enough left over on them.
wipe!

1. Preheat oven to 350° F and grease a 9 by 13 inch glass pan with butter.
2. In a double boiler, small pan, or microwave, melt the chocolate and butter.
3. Whisk melted chocolate and butter until well blended and let cool.
4. While chocolate and butter mixture is cooling, whisk together eggs, sugar, and vanilla. They should become frothy and slightly lighter in color.

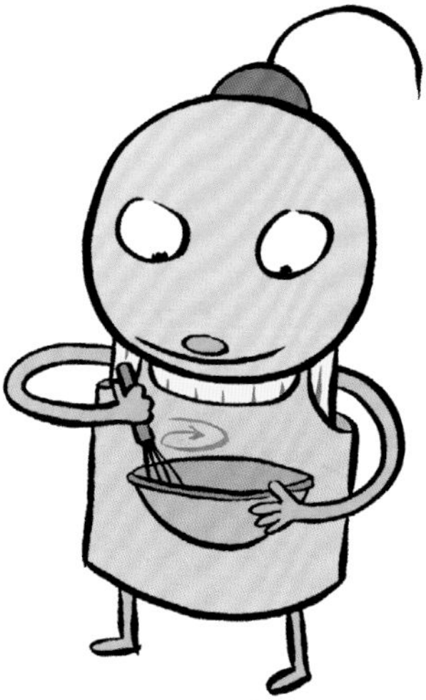

5. Carefully fold the cooled chocolate and butter mixture into the eggs. Whisk until everything is well mixed.
6. Fold in flour and salt. Mix thoroughly.

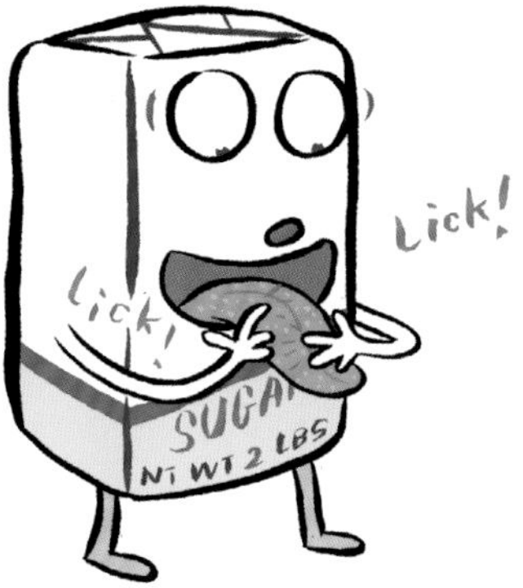
Lick!
Lick!
SUGA
NT WT 2 LBS

7. Pour mixture into pan. Bake 32-37 minutes. Note: when they are done, the center of the brownies should still be a little gooey when you remove them from the oven.
8. Slice when cool.

Vanilla Cupcakes with Vanilla Frosting (From page 62)

The Cupcakes

ingredients:

2 sticks unsalted butter at room temperature
2 cups white sugar
4 large eggs at room temperature
1 1/2 cups self-rising flour
1 1/4 cups all-purpose flour
1 cup milk
1 teaspoon vanilla extract

1. Preheat oven to 350° F.

2. Line two 12-cup muffin tins or one 24-cup muffin tin with muffin papers. (If you make mini-cupcakes, this recipe will make 96! So you may want to cut the recipe in half for 48 mini-cupcakes. Also reduce the baking time by 1/3.)

3. In a large bowl, cream the butter until smooth, using an electric mixer on medium speed.

4. Add sugar gradually and beat until fluffy, around 3 minutes.

5. Add eggs one by one, beating well after adding each egg.

6. Combine flours in a bowl and whisk together.

7. Add flour mixture in three parts, alternating with milk and vanilla, and beating well (still using your electric mixer) after each addition.

8. Spoon the batter into the muffin papers so they are about 3/4 full.

9. Bake 20-22 minutes, until tops spring back when lightly touched.

10. Remove cupcakes from pan and cool completely before frosting.

the Frosting

ingredients:

2 sticks unsalted butter at room temperature
8 cups powdered sugar
1/2 cup milk
2 teaspoons vanilla extract

1. Place butter in a large mixing bowl.
2. Add 4 cups of sugar and all the milk and vanilla.
3. Beat like crazy with electric mixer, until smooth and creamy. (Note: Although you should mix on medium to high speed, start on the slowest setting or the powdered sugar will fly everywhere.)
4. Gradually add remaining sugar, 1 cup at a time, until frosting is the desired consistency. You most likely will not use all the sugar.
5. Store in a covered container at room temperature for up to three days.

PURE CANE POWDERED SUGAR
CONFECTIONERS SUGAR
NET WT 1 LB.
4 OZ. BUTTER
Pure
Vanilla Extract
ORGANIC
WHOLE MILK
half gallon
keep refrigerated
ORGANIC WHOLE MILK

Some Frosting Advice

to color your Frosting, add a Few drops of Food coloring and mix thoroughly. Gel Food colors work very nicely and come in a large selection of colors. You can Find them at a baking supply shop or online. Use them sparingly – just a drop at a time – as they are very concentrated.

Tools

to Frost regular-sized cupcakes, use a small rubber spatula, an oFFset spatula, or a butter kniFe. For mini-cupcakes, you can use a small spatula or piping tips.

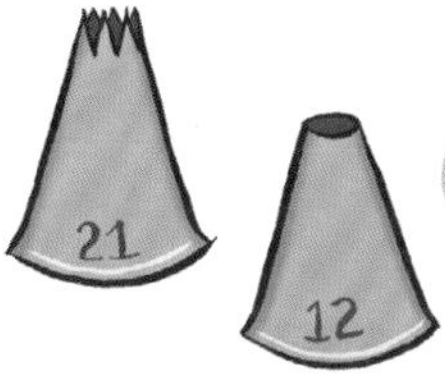
21
12

tips on using Piping Tips

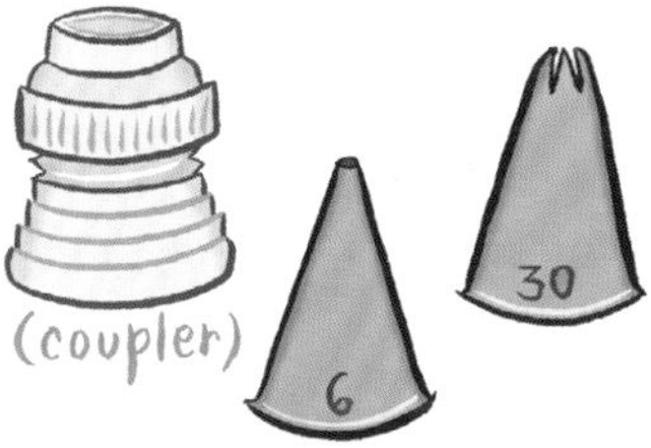
(coupler)
6
30

You can use a pastry bag or a Ziploc bag Fitted with a metal piping tip. (IF using a Ziploc, snip oFF one corner and, From inside the bag, place the tip into the opening.) Using a rubber spatula, Fill the bag with Frosting. Starting at the outer edge, careFully pipe a circle around the cupcake, coiling it until you reach the center. Once you reach the center, stop squeezing the bag and pull upwards.

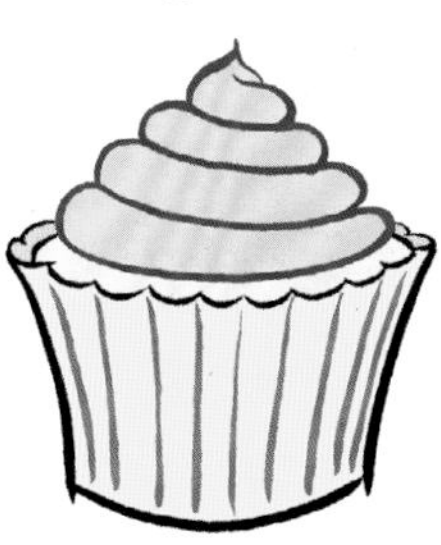

marzipan (From page 75)

ingredients:

> 1 pound (16 ounces) almond paste
> 1 pound (16 ounces) powdered sugar
> 3 ounces (by volume, not weight) light corn syrup
> 1 teaspoon vanilla extract

Almond paste comes in a can...

and almond paste comes in a roll, like a sausage.

almond paste

1. Cut up the almond paste into smallish pieces and place into bowl. Use electric mixer on low speed until oil begins to separate from the paste, about 30 seconds.

(IF you have a stand mixer like this, mix using the paddle attachment.)

2. Add half of the sugar and keep mixing while slowly pouring in corn syrup and vanilla. Continue to mix until the dough comes together and sticks to paddle or beaters. Unstick the dough.

3. Sift remaining sugar onto counter top.

4. Knead the sugar into the dough. If the dough is still sticky, you can knead in additional sugar. Keep kneading until the texture of the dough is fine and smooth. It should be soft but firm.

5. Thoroughly wrap the marzipan in plastic wrap. Then place in a sealed plastic bag, like a Ziploc, and store in refrigerator until ready to use. It can be kept in the refrigerator in a covered container for several weeks and kept in the freezer for up to 5 months.

Dog Treats (From page 85)

Sniff!
Sniff!
Sniff!
Sniff!
Sniff!

ingredients:

1 egg
2 teaspoons dry yeast
1/2 cup lukewarm water
2 tablespoons dried parsley
1 1/2 cups chicken broth
3 tablespoons honey
5 cups whole wheat flour, more if necessary

1. Preheat oven to 350° F.

2. In a large bowl, combine yeast and warm water.

3. When the yeast has dissolved in the water, whisk in egg, parsley, broth, and honey.

4. Gradually blend in flour, until dough becomes stiff. You may need to add a little extra flour.

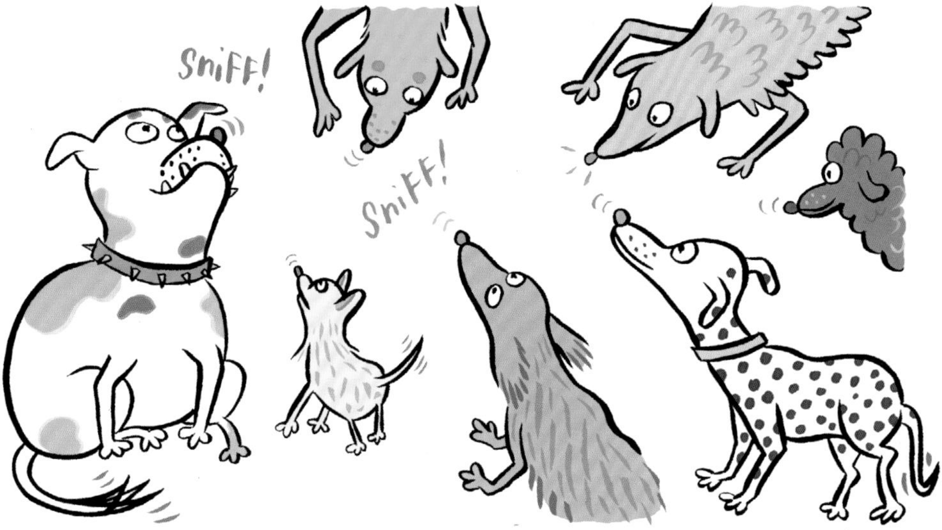
SniFF!
SniFF!

5. TransFer dough to a Floured surFace. Knead until smooth, about 3-5 minutes.
6. Shape dough into a ball, then use a rolling pin to roll to about 1/4 inch thick. Use a bone-shaped cookie cutter (or whatever shape you have handy) to cut out biscuits.
7. TransFer biscuits to ungreased baking sheets.
8. Consolidate scraps oF dough, roll out again, and cut more biscuits.
9. Bake For 30 minutes. Remove From oven, Flip biscuits over, and bake For 15 more minutes or until lightly browned on both sides.
10. Cool overnight and serve!

Peppermint Brownies (from page 90)

ingredients:

Brownies:
1 1/2 sticks unsalted butter
8 ounces bittersweet or semisweet chocolate
3 large eggs
1 1/2 cups sugar
3/4 cup all-purpose Flour
1/2 teaspoon peppermint extract
1 teaspoon vanilla extract
1/4 teaspoon salt

Frosting:
2 cups sifted powdered sugar
1/2 stick unsalted butter at room temperature
2 tablespoons whole milk
3/4 teaspoon peppermint extract

1. Preheat oven to 350° F.

2. Grease a 9 by 13 inch glass baking pan.

3. Stir butter and chocolate in small saucepan over low heat until smooth. You can also melt them using a microwave. Set aside when melted.

4. Using electric mixer on medium speed, beat eggs and sugar in a large bowl until light and fluffy, about 5 minutes.

5. Add the chocolate and butter mixture, flour, salt, vanilla, and peppermint extract, and stir until just blended.

6. Pour batter into glass pan. Smooth out with a spoon or spatula. Bake for 25 minutes, or until a toothpick inserted into center comes out with moist crumbs attached. Cool before frosting.

7. For frosting, beat (using electric mixer) powdered sugar, butter, milk, and peppermint extract in bowl until creamy. You may need to add either more butter or powdered sugar to achieve desired texture. Also, you can add a little pink or green food color to make the frosting look mintier.

8. Spread frosting over brownies.

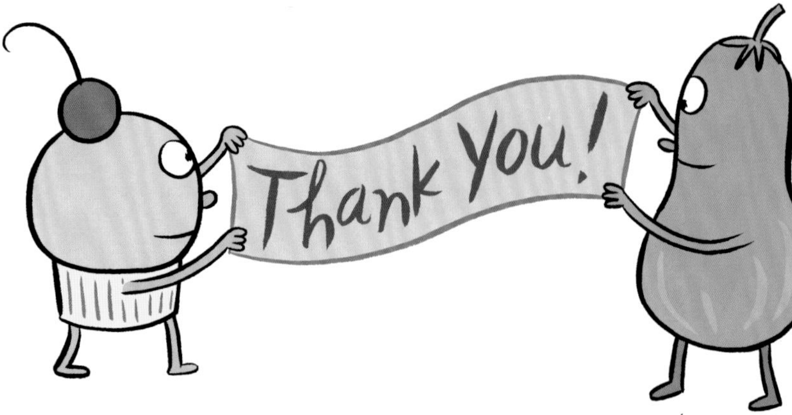
Thank you!

Special thanks to Melanie Schrimpe, who was kind enough to show me around her bakery "Cheeks" in Williamsburg, Brooklyn; to let me take reference photos; and to explain the daily routine of running a bakeshop.

Extra big thanks also to Tanya McKinnon and, as always, my mom.

Thank you, John Douglas and Eddie Hemingway.

To my new friend Miles: May your days be sweet.

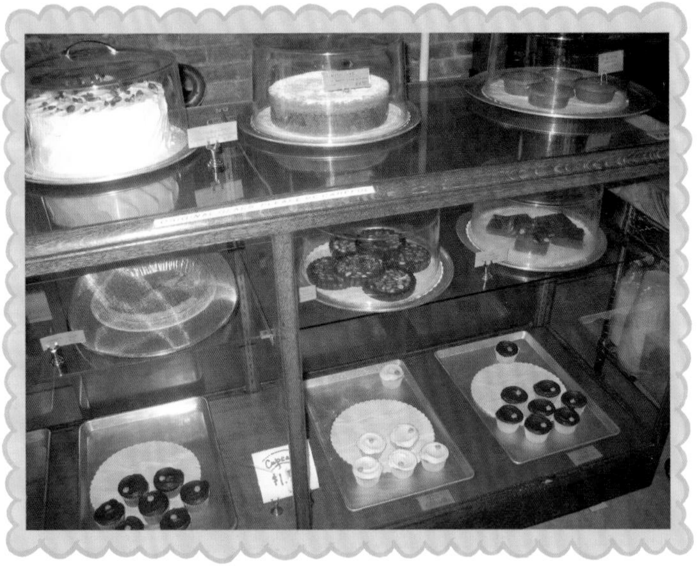

Cheeks Bakery, Brooklyn, 2005-2009